At the sight of her trembling lips, Sebastian said in alarm, "Olivia? Are you all right?"

She feigned a shiver. "C . . . cold."

He wrapped his arms around her. "Let me warm you."

She felt triumphant, yet no smile passed her lips. "Mmmm. You're so strong, sir." She snuggled closer, her breasts touching his firm chest, teasing her nipples.

"You're lips are blue," he murmured. And pressed his to warm hers.

She arched her back to meet his kiss. All thought flew out of Olivia's head. Need drove her . . .

BOOK YOUR PLACE ON OUR WEBSITE AND MAKE THE READING CONNECTION!

We've created a customized website just for our very special readers, where you can get the inside scoop on everything that's going on with Zebra, Pinnacle and Kensington books.

When you come online, you'll have the exciting opportunity to:

- View covers of upcoming books

- Read sample chapters

- Learn about our future publishing schedule (listed by publication month *and author*)

- Find out when your favorite authors will be visiting a city near you

- Search for and order backlist books from our online catalog

- Check out author bios and background information

- Send e-mail to your favorite authors

- Meet the Kensington staff online

- Join us in weekly chats with authors, readers and other guests

- Get writing guidelines

- AND MUCH MORE!

Visit our website at
http://www.kensingtonbooks.com

Too HOT For A SPY

PEARL WOLF

ZEBRA BOOKS
Kensington Publishing Corp.

http://www.kensingtonbooks.com

ISBN-13: 978-1-4201-0480-6
ISBN-10: 1-4201-0480-2

First Printing: March 2009
10 9 8 7 6 5 4 3 2 1

Printed in the United States of America

To Shelley Freydont
Friend, Mentor, Critique Partner, Wine Lover

Acknowledgments

I am fortunate in my choice of friends and colleagues, for they have been of immense help to me in the writing of this book. In particular I wish to thank first reader Sally Metzger for her comments, and Shelley Freydont, whose guidance and humor I cannot live without.

In addition, surgeon Dr. Rick Nedelman continues to amaze me with his knowledge of medical history. I owe him many thanks for his intelligent input.

My thanks also to all the authors who have written books on the Regency period. Their scholarly works have been an invaluable research tool for me.

Lovers of historical romance are notorious in their diligence when it comes to informing an author of errors in their work. I invite you to let me know when you find mine. I promise to take full responsibility and apologize to you for them.

Chapter One

London, 1816—Saturday, The Twenty-second of June

His Grace, the Sixth Duke of Heatham, and his family were trapped in the crush of carriages that lined the road in Berkley Square. Shouts of drivers and ostlers, snorts of horses, the clatter of hooves and the oohs and aahs springing from the mouths of curious onlookers, greeted their ears with a bizarre street symphony. The duke, however, paid it no mind, for he was engaged in a battle of wits with his eldest daughter, Lady Olivia.

"I'm merely asking you to give young Smythe-Jones serious thought. Why won't you at least consider his marriage offer, Livy? He has all the qualities I deem appropriate to make you a fine husband."

"Then you marry him, Father!"

"You aren't getting any younger, you know."

"Thank you for that reminder, Father," she said with asperity. "I hadn't been aware that my four and twenty years make me such an ancient crone."

The duke prepared to retaliate with an equally tart retort, but the duchess put a restraining hand on his arm which caused him to swallow his reply. The ongoing war of words between father and daughter had begun almost as soon as the crested brougham had started out for the Hobbleton Ball, one of the last entertainments of the London season.

The battle with her father ran a crease across Lady Olivia's brow, marring an otherwise lovely face. Emerald green eyes, hair the color of wheat, a pointed chin and seductive lips were an irresistible magnet for many a young man. Tonight she had a special reason for looking her very best. She had chosen a shimmering green gown of silk moiré and Belgian lace cut low to enhance her well-shaped figure. Green ribbons the color of her eyes entwined her long curls, artfully arranged by her clever French abigail Nancy. Matching green slippers sparkled with tiny crystals as they peeked out from under her gown.

When the duke and his family were presented to Lord and Lady Hobbleton, Lady Helena, the more diplomatic of the two Fairchild sisters, turned to her parents and said, "Would you mind if Livy and I take ourselves off to the withdrawing room to freshen up?" With an approving nod from her mother, Helena took Olivia's hand and spirited her away.

The two sisters were close confidantes, yet they were not at all alike in appearance. Where Olivia was a fair-skinned beauty, Helena, four years her junior, was a dark exotic whose olive skin, slightly slanted brown eyes and high cheekbones held a hint of the Orient. Her hair was brown, lightly bronzed by streaks from the sun. She wore a gown of ivory silk that became her. She was taller than her sister, yet had an equally well-formed figure.

When they entered the withdrawing room, it was already crowded with young ladies gossiping, fixing stray strands of hair, or simply envying one another's attire. Helena dragged her sister into a quiet corner. "Sit," she ordered. "It's clear you need some time to compose yourself. You've allowed Father to crawl under your skin once again, you foolish girl. When will you learn? He likes nothing more than to draw you into battle, thinking to wear you down until you bend to his will."

"A hopeless cause, for I won't bend, I promise you that. You know as well as I do that he tries to control all of us, though it's worse for me because I'm the oldest." A wicked grin crept across her face. "If he only knew my real purpose, he'd have a fit."

Her sister laughed. "I agree. If you succeed, father won't be able to stand the shock, not to mention the humiliation."

"Humiliation? No, I don't think it would come to that. Not if I were successful. You know perfectly well he can't stand for any of his children to fail. Good thing for me he doesn't know what it is I actually do in the home office. It's menial clerical work to be sure, but it's merely a first step to what I really want. Tonight's the night for me, Helena. I'm determined to confront the home secretary and persuade him to give me the opportunity to move up the ladder, so to speak. See if I don't."

Helena smiled at her determination. "You'll do it, too, if I know you. No one is more tenacious than you, dearest. If the home secretary survives your planned onslaught, I've no doubt you will prevail. But what will you do when you succeed and Father discovers your plan? He will surely forbid it, especially if it involves leaving home without benefit of marriage."

"He can try to forbid me, but I'm of age and I fully intend to follow my own course."

"What if he threatens to disown you?"

"He knows better. I have my own competence, thanks to dear departed Aunt Gwen, bless her soul."

Helena sighed.

"What?"

"I wish I had your courage, Livy. I'm not capable of standing up to Father, for I've no spine. I'm not even determined enough to convince Chris to elope with me to Gretna Green.

He agrees with Father. Why do they both think I'm too young for marriage?"

Olivia hugged her sister in sympathy. "I know how much you love Chris Darlington, but bide your time, dearest." She paused in thought. "Why not consider a new tack? Agree with Father that you're too young. Then confess that you're willing to wait to marry Chris, if only he will consent to a betrothal. That at least would be a first step for you."

Helena brightened. "Do you think such a tactic will answer?"

"It won't hurt to try, will it?"

The two left the withdrawing room in much better spirits, only to face a daunting ballroom crush.

"How shall I ever find Chris in this throng?"

She laughed. "I wouldn't worry, if I were you, love. Try to stand in place and allow him to find you." For her sister's sake, she tried to sound full of cheer, but her own quest to locate the home secretary appeared to be just as difficult as finding Helena's beau. A tap on her shoulder caused her to turn her head.

"Oh, it's you, Percy. I must thank you for the flowers, but you needn't send a new bouquet every day." Though the young man was tall and handsome, in her mind Olivia dismissed him as too bland looking. Besides, he was a dead bore. She had no intention of encouraging his suit for her hand, yet she didn't object to flirting. The sport was second nature to her.

"They are meant to be a daily reminder of my suit for your hand, Lady Olivia. It is but a poor tribute, for no flower is as exquisite as you, my dear. May I have the honor of this dance?" Sir Percival Smythe-Jones offered his arm.

"I'm sorry, Percy. I'd rather not leave my sister in the lurch."

"Go ahead and dance with him, Livy. I'll be fine."

* * *

Sir Sebastian Brooks suffered more than a twinge of regret. A stray lock of dark hair fell over his thick eyebrows. His gray-blue eyes stood sentinel above sculpted cheekbones and a square chin. At thirty years of age, the chief spymaster was a large man whose good looks never failed to please eligible ladies. He had no wish to marry, however, and learned to be adept at avoiding any such attachment, both from the young ladies and their marriage-minded mothers. No easy task during the London season.

"I envy you, Darlington. You're a lucky dog to be posted to the Continent on such an exciting mission," he said to his good friend and colleague. The two lounged near the open terrace doors to catch a breath of air, for the night was hot and humid.

Chris squinted at him. He reached into his waistcoat pocket and fiddled with his spectacles, an unconscious habit, yet vanity prevented him from wearing them in public. The twenty-five-year-old aide to the home secretary was tall and slim with flaxen-hair, eyes of pale blue and an aristocratic nose.

"If I didn't know you any better, I'd say you were filled with envy, Sebastian. You needn't be, you know. You've already accomplished extraordinary work at Wilson Academy. It's all the talk at the home office, I'll have you know. Everyone who has seen them thinks your renovations to the building and the grounds are excellent for the purpose. I think the plans are so good, you might well have taken up architecture instead of spying when you sold out." Chris paused, his eyes searching his friend's face. "What's eating you, Sebastian?"

"You're very perceptive, my friend. All right. I'll tell you what's eating me. I thought Wilson Academy was just the challenge I needed after the devastation I witnessed at Waterloo. I was sick of the stink of death and the awful sight of the mindless destruction of war. I believed that this assignment was a challenge, so I jumped at the chance when it was offered to me."

"It *is* a challenge. It's time our country develops an organized spy system. What's keeping you from enjoying your new position? What changed your mind? Why are you so troubled? It's clear from the look on your face."

As if Chris had wrung the words from him, Sebastian blurted out, "Chief spymaster is nothing more than a glorified clerk's position! Day in and day out all I do is shuffle papers and sign them. It's a dead bore, Chris. Maybe I should take up architecture after all. Designing Wilson Academy was the only part of this project that gave me any joy." Sebastian paused, breathing hard. When he was calmer, he said, "Perhaps when I begin to train the next generation of spies, the post will take on a more stimulating aspect, but for now, I miss the challenge and the fellowship of army life."

Chris sighed. "It is I who envy you, Sebastian. I wish I had been in the war. My brother even offered to buy me a commission, but the army rejected me as unfit because of my poor eyesight."

"That you are standing here still alive tells me the army was right to reject you. You would not have survived Napoleon. Sorry if it troubles you, but they made the correct decision."

Chris acknowledged this truth with a nod. "Why waste your time pining for the past? Has it occurred to you that, if you hadn't sold out, you might have been just as bored in peacetime?"

Before Sebastian could answer, they were interrupted by a voice familiar to Chris. "Here you are, my dear. I'm glad I found you. Poor Helena has been looking all over for her beau. I left her pining away near the main stairwell." Olivia pecked him on the cheek.

"Hallo, Livy." He turned to his companion. "Allow me to introduce Lady Olivia Fairchild to you, Sebastian. I've lived next door to the Fairchilds all my life. I don't mind admitting to you that I'm dangling after her lovely sister Helena. Livy, this is my good friend Sir Sebastian Brooks."

"Pleasure," said Olivia with the slightest of curtseys, yet her eyes held indifference.

"Will you both excuse me?" asked Chris. "I must go and find my lovely lady." Without bothering to wait for a response, he hurried away with the eagerness of a man in love.

Sebastian was irritated as he watched Olivia's eyes wander all over the ballroom. He was stirred by her extraordinary beauty. At the same time, he was annoyed by her indifference to him. It was not a response he was accustomed to from a lady of marriageable age. He wondered why she was not paying her attentions to him.

"It appears we've been abandoned, ma'am," he said. "Will you join me in the next waltz?"

She looked up at him in surprise, as if noticing him for the first time. "My pleasure, sir." She took the arm he offered and allowed him to lead her onto the floor. When the music began he placed his hand on her waist, she placed hers on his shoulder, and he guided her around the perimeter of the dance floor. She entered into the spirit of the waltz, enjoying its rhythm of movement, for she loved to dance. Yet her eyes wandered as she continued to search.

Bloody hell. I've chosen a dimwit for a partner even though she dances well. Why does her head keep twisting every which way? Why the devil is the chit so distracted?

"Are you feeling well, ma'am?" he asked in exasperation.

Olivia looked startled. "What a silly question. Of course I'm feeling well. Why do you ask?"

"If that is the case, ma'am, I can only conclude you must think me a dead bore, since your full attention seems well out of my reach. It's clear to me you are not enjoying our dance. Would you prefer to take a stroll on the terrace?"

"Oh, but I am enj—" She paused, much in favor of his suggestion, for it would afford her another place to search for the home secretary. "Yes. A stroll on the terrace would be lovely." She allowed him to lead her out the terrace doors where her eyes resumed their wanderings.

Sebastian's irritation was rapidly turning into anger. He wasn't accustomed to receiving such a blatant rebuff. He determined to direct the lady's attention his way, at which point he would turn the tables and snub her. It was only what she deserved. He brightened, intrigued by the challenge. He had never lost a battle in his life. With this in mind, he began to plan his campaign. *Does the lady seek her pleasure elsewhere? When I get through with her, she'll rue the day she ignored me.*

"Lovely evening for a stroll, is it not?"

Olivia took little notice of the edge in his voice. Her head continued to turn, her eyes searching this way and that. "What? Oh yes. Lovely. Lovely indeed."

He led her down a less-crowded path until he spied a small secluded bench. "Sit here and rest, ma'am, until you feel better."

"Feel better? Why do you persist in thinking I feel ill?"

His lips quirked. "Well, ma'am," he drawled, "your pretty head must be quite sore by now, it seems to me. You've been turning it every which way at such an alarmingly swift pace, I began to fear it was in danger of falling off your shoulders."

Olivia stared at him, uncomprehending for a moment. Then she laughed. "You're teasing me, sir."

Sebastian smiled at her, a most agreeable smile. His eyes turned seductive. "Perhaps I am." Without warning, he drew her to him and kissed her. She was stiff with resistance at first, but he persisted, one hand holding her chin so he could invade her luscious mouth, the other holding her firm until she ceased struggling. It didn't take too long. To his astonishment, she pressed closer and returned his kiss with a passion of her own. Satisfied, he removed his lips and nibbled her ear.

"You smell like roses, ma'am. I like it."

She forced herself to pull away, adopting anger as a weapon. "How dare you kiss me, sir! Why, we've only just met."

"How else was I to engage your attention, ma'am? Can you not locate your lover? Is that who you have been searching for? Won't I do in his stead? You gave me cause, you know, to believe that you enjoyed our kiss as much as I did." His eyes held wicked amusement. "At the very least, my lady, I had the satisfaction of at last gaining your full attention. You're far too lovely for me to resist, you know, in spite of those wandering eyes of yours."

There was a sharp edge in his voice which maddened her enough to issue a tart rebuke. "I most certainly did not enjoy being mauled by you, sir!"

"Yes, you did."

"No, I didn't, Mr. . . . What did you say your name was?"

"Sebastian," he said in a husky, sex-filled voice. "Call me Sebastian, dearest Livy."

"I've not given you leave to address me thus, have I?"

"No, Livy." He planted a kiss on her neck.

"You, sir, are impertinent." But she didn't stop him when his fingers traced the edge of her gown, causing goose bumps to raise her flesh.

In one swift motion, he pulled her to her feet and kissed her hard, his tongue bruising the inside of her mouth.

Shivers and thrills slithered through her body when he held her close enough to feel his erection. In a mindless haze, she ground into him, pressing closer, wanting more. One of his thumbs rubbed her breast through her gown and she moaned. He edged her bodice down and freed one nipple, teasing the nub between two fingers.

"Good God! What do you think you are you doing, sir?" She gasped when he bent to take the rigid nub into his mouth.

He backed her into a nearby tree, out of sight of curious onlookers. His lips returned to her nipple while one hand gathered her gown all the way up to her waist so his hand could gain access to the searing heat between her thighs.

"Don't! Stop!" she breathed in an anguished moan.

He removed his mouth and looked into her glazed eyes, but his hand had already found what he was looking for. His fingers began to work their magic, an easy task, for she did not struggle. Amused, he said, "Which do you mean, my lady? Do you mean me to stop? Or do you mean don't stop?"

But he already knew the answer, for she was wet with desire. His mouth crushed hers to muffle her screams when she climaxed. He waited for her spasms to end before he smoothed down the skirt of her gown and tucked her nipple back into her bodice. All the while, his lips rained little kisses on her ear, on her neck, on her eyes.

"Thank you for a lovely diversion, my lady. I can't wait for our next encounter. What did you say your name was?"

Her voice shook with rage. "Who gave you leave to assault me thus? You're an unspeakable cad! It may interest you to know that I don't know your name either, Mr.—whatever your name is!" Without waiting for his answer, she wheeled away and stalked off.

She missed the sight of his lips curling with satisfaction. *Bloody hell. She's a temptress. The chit enjoyed our little tryst as much as I did. Hope she doesn't have a designing mother waiting in the wings.*

In a whisper, he said, "My name is Sir Sebastian Brooks, milady. You won't forget me." He watched her disappear in the direction of the ballroom, content in the knowledge that he had won the match. He hadn't lost his touch after all. She'd paid attention to him in the end, hadn't she?

Olivia reentered the ballroom through the terrace doors only to find herself facing her father, who waited with a man she had never met before.

"There you are, Livy. I've been searching all over for you. I want you to meet Lord Wentworth, a good friend of mine," said her father. He turned to a middle-aged, portly gentleman, one who had already lost most of his hair. "This is my daughter, Lady Olivia Fairchild."

Olivia bit back a groan. "Happy to meet any friend of my father's, sir." Her eyes darted right and left, contemplating escape.

"Your father sings your praises, ma'am. I can see with my own eyes he speaks the truth, for you are beautiful. May I engage you for this next waltz?"

Her father glared at her, his eyes pointing to the gentleman in an unmistakable gesture. "Um, I'd be delighted." She took his arm and allowed him to lead her to the floor, but kept scanning the crowd.

At the end of their waltz, Olivia curtseyed to her partner and hurried away. She vowed to burn her father's ears for entertaining the idea that she would welcome an offer from such a ridiculous excuse for a man. Wentworth was as old as Father was, for heaven's sake!

Olivia had almost given up hope of finding the object of her search when she saw him chatting with two matrons not ten steps away. She cleared her throat and waited for him to turn in her direction. "Viscount Sidmouth? What a pleasant surprise. I never thought to meet you here in this mad press of people."

"Good evening, my dear. Having a good time?" The elderly gentleman's words were courteous, but the look in his eyes told Olivia he had no idea who she was.

She tilted her head and offered a flirtatious smile. "Meeting you, sir, has made my evening wonderfully complete."

Flattered, the viscount eyed her with approval. "Really? How so?"

"We met last summer at Lord and Lady Marshall's garden party, but I'm not at all sure you recall it."

"Of course I remember you. How could I forget such a beautiful young woman who flatters me?" The viscount was a slight gentleman with only a few strands left of his hair, yet his keen brown eyes hadn't lost their sharp intelligence.

Olivia checked her grin. The poor man hadn't a clue. "That day last summer, my lord, when you revealed to me your secret, was the best day of my life. It changed me forever. Believe me when I say that your brilliant plan has never once left my thoughts."

The viscount tried to hide his puzzlement, but she gave him no time for reflection. She lowered her voice. "Trust me, my lord. My lips were sealed from that day to this. I revealed to no one your innovative plans. Of course, I was deeply honored to have you share your secret with me then. I only hope . . ."

She bent her head and examined her slippers, annoyed because they were beyond repair now that Lord Wentworth, unable to see beyond his protruding stomach, had ruined them with his clumsy feet.

Her eyes returned to the home secretary's face. Should she shed a tear to advance her purpose, or would that be too theatrical? she wondered. She decided she shouldn't. It might be overdoing it.

To her advantage, the home secretary was not too old to enjoy a harmless flirtation. "What is it you hope, my dear?"

Olivia looked around her. "Might we continue our conversation out on the terrace? The issue you spoke of to me is so sensitive, I'm sure you wouldn't wish it to become common knowledge, my lord." She took his arm and led him out, well aware that his eyes had glazed over. *He still doesn't know what I'm talking about.*

She found an unoccupied marble bench out of earshot from inquisitive guests, took his hand and said, "First, let me thank you for arranging for me to be employed in your office sir. Of course, I'm very happy to be of service to you in any way I can. Indeed, my position is quite gratifying, but . . ."

"I gave you a position? What is it that you do in the home office, my dear?"

"I have been charged with handling secret documents, sir, but I yearn to give so much more of myself to my country. So much more."

"You've placed me in a state of utter bewilderment, my dear. What on earth are you talking about?"

Her words rushed out like an avalanche. "I'm talking about your plan to train women as spies, of course. In truth, I have followed the progress of those plans, from the rebuilding of the property to the training program. I know it is already in place."

The viscount eyed her with suspicion. "How do you know such a plan exists?"

"I came across the papers in the course of my work."

His gray eyes smiled as an indulgent grandfather might to a child. "I'm not sure I understand you. What is it you're really after, my dear?"

Olivia laughed, showering him with the musical sound of bells. "Ah. You have me there, my lord. I won't lie to you, of all people. Like everyone else who petitions you, I want something from you."

It was his turn to laugh. "No, no. I didn't mean to imply that you are too forward."

"Of course you didn't." She took a deep breath, looked both ways to make sure no one overheard her, and said, "Last summer at the Marshall garden party, you shared with me your desire to establish a program for women to be trained for clandestine work. A woman spy is a brilliant idea, if I may say so, sir. Will you honor your promise and assign me as one of the candidates, my lord?"

The viscount scratched his head. "Well, I . . ."

As if she hadn't heard him, she continued, "To be in the forefront of such a bold program has become my life's dream. You did promise you would consider me as a candidate for training, you know. May I hold your feet to the fire? Will you keep your word to me?"

"You wish to be a spy? An odd request, my dear. You can't imagine how dangerous such an occupation can be. What put the idea into your pretty little head? You are much more suited to marriage and a family."

Olivia now produced her single tear. To add weight to it, she sniffed. "My duty to my country comes before marriage and raising a family, my lord."

"Now, now. No need to weep," the home secretary said, squirming in his seat.

"Sorry, sir. It's just that I feel so passionate about this. The first training class is about to begin . . ."

He paused in thought. "You will have to allow me time to give your request some serious consideration."

"Then you'll entertain it? Oh, thank you, sir. To me, that is clearly tantamount to a yes. I knew you would honor your word to me. A man who has been prime minister and now heads the even more important position of England's home secretary, has earned his place in history, to be sure."

Viscount Sidmouth had the look of a helpless bear whose foot was caught in a trap, but Olivia gave him no chance to wriggle out of it. "Be assured I shall reveal our conversation to no one, my lord. My lips are sealed." She kissed him lightly on the cheek. "Forgive me for taking such a liberty, my lord, but you do remind me of my beloved father, the Duke of Heatham. Do you know him?"

"Tony Fairchild? We went to Oxford together."

"You see? I knew there was a positive connection between us!" She stood up without letting go of his hand. "I shall make you proud of your decision when you allow me to be the first woman to enter your training program. It's getting late, my lord. I must leave you, for my dear father is waiting to take me home."

When she reached the terrace door, Olivia turned to wave to the viscount. She wasn't surprised to find him looking confused, his brow lined with worry.

When Sebastian found the home secretary seated on the terrace bench where Olivia had left him, the old man was in a thoughtful pose.

"Are you all right, my lord? I've come to escort you home."

"Oh, it's you, Brooks. Yes. I'm fine."

"It's growing late, sir. Are you ready to leave? Shall I call for your carriage?"

"In a moment." He raised his eyes to the spymaster and patted the seat next to him. "Tell me about your new training program, Brooks. Has it begun yet?"

Sebastian wondered why the viscount showed such a sudden interest when he never had before. "We hope to begin next week, sir, but . . ."

"Is there a problem?"

"Nothing we can't resolve, sir. We're one man short of our quota."

The two sat side by side, the viscount lost in thought, Sebastian unable to decide whether the old gentleman was growing forgetful or whether he had something pressing on his mind.

"Let me ask you something, spymaster."

"My lord?"

"No. Not now. See me Monday, Brooks."

"Of course, sir."

"You may escort me to my carriage."

When he had handed the home secretary in, Sebastian folded the steps, closed the door, nodded to the driver, and stepped out of the way, all the while wondering what was on the old man's mind.

Chapter Two

"Afternoon, sir."

"Sit," Viscount Sidmouth said. The home secretary, a short man, was conscious of his lack of height. Both the enormous desk and the high-back leather chair in which he sat were raised on a platform. The elevation was a reminder to visitors of who was in charge.

Sidmouth templed his fingers. "Tell me all about your new recruits."

The old man's up to something. Better tread carefully. But what? "Well sir, at twenty-two, the oldest is John Carter, a battle-smart soldier. We can expect good things from him. The next is Harold Perkins, aged twenty-one. A brilliant mind and a whiz at codes and deciphers. He's one of Aaron Foster's protégés. The youngest man—a likeable lad—is eighteen. Rufus Riggs was under my command. He acquitted himself well during the war. In fact, he was awarded a medal for bravery. And finally, we have a matched set." Sebastian grinned.

"Matched set? What do you mean?"

"Identical twins, sir. Robert and William Reed are twenty-year-old country boys. None of us can tell them apart."

Sidmouth allowed himself a small chuckle. "Twins, eh? That's good. They'll confound the enemy wherever we send them."

"Exactly what we had in mind."

"Have you found anyone to fill the last spot?"

"Not yet, but we have several promising applicants in mind, sir. My staff and I will decide this week."

"Don't bother. I've already selected the final candidate."

"Indeed?" *Why, the old bastard is meddling in my affairs.* "I'm sorry, sir. That has always been my privilege. I respectfully request that you leave it that way."

Sidmouth swiveled his chair and stared out the window of his office for a time. When he turned back, he said, "I do not usually interfere, nor do I make important decisions lightly, spymaster, but I am convinced this is the right one. A groundbreaking one, if I may. I've had it in mind for at least a year."

"He must have very unique credentials to have attracted your notice, sir. Who is he, may I ask?"

"No. Not 'he.'"

"A woman?" Sebastian's voice raised a full octave. "You can't be serious, sir. No woman is capable of mastering our rigorous training program. It's just not possible."

"Lower your voice, Brooks. The walls have ears and I don't want this spread about. It is my firm belief that a woman would be a distinct asset in the business of intelligence gathering."

"But sir! Think of the demands of our program. Calisthenics. Boxing. Martial arts. Fencing. Riding. Swimming. Codes and deciphers. You can't expect a mere woman to succeed in such difficult tasks. It would be beyond her physical and intellectual capacity."

"I don't agree, spymaster. There are precedents, you know. Other countries have used women as spies for years." He frowned at the spymaster.

Sebastian's eyes narrowed. "No, sir! Absolutely not. I will not accept a woman in my program!"

"Perhaps you've misunderstood me. I am not giving you a choice, spymaster. I've already sent the young lady a letter of acceptance."

Sebastian stood abruptly, knocking over his chair in the process. "You've done what?"

"You're shouting again, Brooks."

"With all due respect, your interference in the affairs of my program is damnably unconscionable! I won't have it, sir. I. Won't. Have. A. Woman. In. My. Program!"

The home secretary did not raise his voice, yet his words were menacing. "Pick up that chair and sit down. Who do you think you are talking to me that way, you hothead! *I* am your superior!"

Sebastian had never heard that threatening tone from Sidmouth before. It surprised him into obeying the order, though his eyes continued to smolder.

When he was seated again, Sidmouth added in a conciliatory tone, "There is no doubt in my mind that you will accept my decision, Brooks. You are a veteran of the war, well accustomed to accepting orders from your superiors. Where would England be if you hadn't obeyed Wellington? Try to remember that you have an excellent record in the army and now you are under my command. Don't besmirch that outstanding record by resisting me in this."

Sebastian refused to be soothed. "What if I refuse to accept your . . . decision, home secretary?"

Sidmouth shook his head in regret. "I would never have thought it of you, but if you cannot obey my orders, you leave me no choice but to thank you for your faithful service to the Crown"—he paused for effect—"and accept your resignation."

Sebastian was stunned. "Resignation? You would force me out?"

"No one is indispensable," said the man who had once been prime minister.

Both men were silent for what seemed an eternity.

At last, Sebastian said, "Am I meant to pamper this woman spy, sir? What if this woman you've chosen fails our program?"

Sidmouth shrugged. "If she fails, she fails, but I expect you to give her every opportunity to succeed. Do I make myself clear?"

"Yes, sir." Defeat colored his words as if they were in mourning.

"Good. The location of Wilson Academy is secret, is it not? Send word to my office as to when the young lady will be escorted there. That will be all, spymaster. Good day."

"Good day, sir."

By the time Olivia had finished collating the papers in her files, it was half past five, nearly the end of her workday. She stacked the folders in a neat pile. *I'll wager no one bothers to look at these once I've tucked them away in their proper file drawers.*

She had read through each and every one when she put the pages in proper order, but in her view they didn't amount to much. At the very least, most of them contained nothing even a spy would take the trouble to read. With titles such as, "Committee to Facilitate the Quartermaster's Supply System" and "Agenda for the Meeting of the Home Secretary's Task Force on Office Reorganization," there was hardly anything earth shaking in any of them. No intelligent person would consider these reports worth the paper they had been written on.

Her supervisor had warned her to collate all the folders and store them in the filing room before she left her desk at the end of the day. The man had the gall to insult her intelligence as well. "You *do* know how to alphabetize, don't you, Fairchild?" How petty.

There were at least forty folders to be filed in alphabetical drawers and less than half an hour left in her workday to accomplish this odious task. She took a deep breath, picked up the pile, and staggered down the hall to the filing room. She was forced to sidle along the wall since she could not see very well above her heavy burden. As she neared the end of the hallway, she let out a sigh of relief. The filing room was just around the corner, a mere dozen steps away.

Sebastian strode down the hall from the opposite direction, his brows knit together as if sewn fast by an invisible weaver. His thoughts were filled with disgust over his disastrous meeting with the home secretary. Sidmouth was a stubborn man who was afflicted, like so many men in power, with an inability to entertain any opposing point of view.

Caught in the web of his anger, he turned the corner and collided with a clerk whose arms were full of folders. The woman went sprawling and the folders flew all over the floor in hopeless disorder.

"Oof!"

"Why don't you look where you're going?" Sebastian spat out, taking his fury out on the poor clerk.

"Why don't you look where you're going yourself, you miserable . . . excuse for a man?" Olivia challenged without so much as a glance. She scrambled to her knees and gathered the file folders. Drat! She would have to stay late to put them all back in proper order. She'd also be late for dinner, and what a state *that* would put her father in. Her cap had flown off, releasing a riot of blond curls.

"I'll send for help if you need some."

"No! And don't you dare tell anyone about this."

"As you wish." He held his hands up in surrender, but she was too absorbed in gathering papers to notice. He couldn't see her face, since her hair covered most of it. Indeed, he wondered how she could see anything at all with that unruly mop. He began to walk away, but glanced back in time to see her hitch her gown up as she bent to the task.

The sight of her enticing derriere, outlined through her thin chemise, was the only bright spot of his wretched afternoon. If she weren't a mere clerk afraid of being sacked, he might just be able to relieve both his gloom and his growing hardness in some nearby broom closet, but it was not to be. He suppressed the bitter laugh that threatened to escape his lips. Without another backward glance, the spymaster continued on his way.

"A letter for you, milady," said Dunston. "Hand-delivered early this afternoon along with instructions to deliver it to no one else but you."

"Thank you, Dunston. I haven't any time to read it now. As you see, I'm already late for dinner. Please leave it on my desk." She rushed into the dining room.

"Forgive me everyone. I was unavoidably detained at the home office."

"Father is very angry with you, Livy," said eight-year-old Jane, understating the duke's sentiments by several degrees. The chubby child had a round, cherubic face. Freckles danced up to her green eyes, her red hair plaited with ribbons. She reached for another sweetmeat.

"Be silent, Jane, before you find yourself banished to the schoolroom when the family dines alone." Though he made every effort, the duke could not bring himself to love his youngest daughter.

At fifty-six years of age, he retained his good looks but

for the hair graying at his temples and his faded blue eyes. Even so, the family resemblance between him and his eldest daughter was remarkable. He turned his attention back to her. "You're late again, Livy."

"I beg your pardon, Father. Forgive me, but it was vital that I finish my work before I left the office."

"Saved the empire from invasion this day, did you?"

She ignored his sarcasm. Instead, she looked around at her mother and her sisters, and realized all eyes were upon her. She allowed the footman to fill her plate with beef and vegetables, and summoned another to fill her wineglass.

"My apologies for being late, Mother. I should have been home in time, but for a foolish accident. You see . . ."

"Run over by a mail cart, were you?" The duke's snide remark stung his intended target.

Olivia glared at him and emptied her wineglass in one swallow. "No, Father. I was putting away important papers, my last task of the day, when this strange man came barreling round the corner of the hall and knocked me down. I went sprawling and so did my day's work. I was forced to stay late to sort them all out again, you see."

"Serves you right," he grumbled, but that brought a warning look from his wife.

The duchess, a celebrated beauty in her youth, could still turn heads. Only fifty, she looked far younger than her years. Her eyes were slightly slanted, almost black, like two obsidians. Helena resembled her mother most closely, having the same hair color, the same eyes and the same height.

"Were you hurt, dear?" asked the duchess in a soothing tone.

"Thank you for inquiring, Mother. No. Not at all."

"Did the fellow at least help you up, Livy?" asked Georgiana, fast becoming the loveliest of the Fairchild sisters. Already the young bucks in Hyde Park stopped to stare at the sixteen-year-old beauty with the raven hair, sparkling blue eyes and a charming dimple on her chin.

"He did ask, Georgie, but I'm convinced he didn't mean it. He just kept walking when he spoke. The man was an utter boor."

"Who was he?" asked Mary. At fourteen, she was a tall, gangly girl who had her father's coloring without his harshness. Mary's blue eyes were softened as it were by having inherited her mother's warm eyes. The shy child spent her days engrossed in her music, for she dearly loved to play the pianoforte.

"I haven't the faintest notion, Mary. I never even saw his face."

"Livy," interrupted her father in a familiar tone, the one that usually preceded a lecture. Rather than argue, she tilted her head and gave him a warm smile. "Your forbidding tone hints at more disapproval, dearest. What else have I done to displease you?"

"Work." He spat the word out as if it were a curse. "How many times must I tell you that a well-born lady does not work. Why must you persist in this charade? I'd hoped that, after these first few weeks, you would have gotten it out of your system. It won't do, I tell you. It won't do." He peered at her over the rim of his wine goblet. "Well? Have you no answer?"

Her sisters sat quietly, their heads swinging from father to daughter as if they were watching a tennis match.

Before she could respond, the duchess came to Olivia's aid. "Livy has every right to pursue her own interests, my lord. If she's happy, that's all that matters."

Olivia curbed a gurgle of laughter and fixed her eyes on her plate, knowing full well that her mother would win the day for her.

But the duke refused to give an inch. He glared at his daughter. "You're wasting your time in an office full of common clerks and scribes. You can't fool me, Olivia. I know the sort of work done in that office."

"Have you been spying on me, Father?"

He ignored her question. "The fact is, your mother and I are concerned for your future. We want you to marry and raise a family of your own. Find a respectable purpose to your life. It isn't as if you don't have suitors, you know."

"Your choices, Father. Not mine. Percy is sweet, but he's a dead bore. And where, pray, did you dig up dear old Lord Wentworth? A contemporary of yours, is he? He ruined my shoes because he couldn't see his feet over his enormous stomach. No, Father. Neither of your choices is acceptable to me. I may marry some day, but for now, I prefer to distinguish myself in my chosen career."

"You are fit for nothing better than clerking. Do you call that a career?"

A mysterious smile stole across Olivia's face. "You'd be surprised, Father. You'd be surprised."

"Enough, you two," said her mother as she rose from the table. "Come, girls. We'll leave your father to his brandy and cigar and await him in the drawing room." She glared at her husband and added, "Where I trust civility will reign. There will be no more of this distressful conversation."

As was customary, Mary played the pianoforte while Georgiana turned the pages for her. Helena held a skein of silk spread taut between two hands while Olivia separated the colors for their mother. Her Grace occupied herself with her needlepoint, at the same time keeping a sharp eye on Jane. The child had an overactive sweet tooth and was much in need of supervision if she were not to grow from chubby to obese.

By the time His Grace joined the family in the drawing room, calm had been restored, just as the duchess had ordered. It stayed that way, for the duke knew enough to surrender to his wife's rare, but ominous warnings. He settled into his favorite chair by the fire and engaged in a child's card game of casino with Jane.

At eight, the children's governess, Mrs. Trumball, came to escort Georgiana, Mary and Jane to bed. When the clock struck ten, Her Grace rose and said, "Time we were all in bed. Goodnight, children."

Olivia's abigail prepared her for bed, but Olivia had no thought of sleep. She dismissed Nancy as soon as she was able and hurried to her desk to read the letter Dunston had placed there. She broke the seal and read the official heading: OFFICE OF THE HOME SECRETARY. The letter itself was brief.

"You have been accepted into our new program.
Be prepared to leave for training in one week.
You will be notified as to time and date."

It was signed by Viscount Sidmouth.

Olivia clutched the letter in both hands, her heart beating fast. Had she really succeeded in her quest? Yes! She tiptoed down the hall to her sister Helena's chamber.

"Are you awake?"

"Of course I am, Livy. Do come in." Helena's abigail Amy was busy brushing her hair. When she waved her hand, the young woman put down the brush and disappeared.

"I was expecting you. You had that troubled frown all evening. It quite gives you away, you know. Not seemly for a would-be spy." Her sister rose from her dressing table, moved to the divan and patted it. "Anything the matter?"

Olivia settled next to Helena and thrust the letter into her hand. "Read this."

Helena took the letter from her. She looked up when she finished, and said, "Livy! You've been accepted! I'm so proud of you."

"I wish I knew where the training academy was. I've never been able to find out, no matter how much I poked through the files." Tiny rivers of tears rolled down Olivia's cheeks.

"What's wrong? Spies aren't supposed to weep, Livy. Here. Wipe your tears."

Olivia took her sister's handkerchief and did as she was told. "I want so much to succeed, Helena."

"You can't mean you are afraid you might fail?"

"I'd be a fool not to face that possibility. But I'm determined to succeed. I don't want to live a life of boredom, merely attending balls and routs and picnics and raising children and . . ."

Helena smiled. "You've made your point, my dear."

"I want to travel the world. I want *adventures.*"

Helena clasped her sister's hands in hers. "Then by all means, follow your dream, Livy."

"Easier said than done."

"You've been accepted. That's an excellent start and you should be jumping for joy instead of wallowing in tears. What's troubling you?"

"How am I to be ready in a week? And how shall I keep it from Mother and Father?"

Helena considered this. "You can't keep it from them, Livy. I'd advise you to go and tell them at once."

Olivia's spirits sank. "Must I?"

"It would be too shabby of you if you didn't tell them. Be brave and don't allow Father to bully you."

"You're right, of course. I'll go to them at once." She kissed her sister on the cheek and padded down the stairs to her parents' suite of rooms.

When she knocked on the door and entered, she glanced around the comfortable room. "Where's Father? I had hoped to talk to you together."

"He's in the library, dear."

"I need to speak to you both. It's important, Mother."

"Shall I send for him?"

"Yes, do please. You may read this while we wait for him."

It didn't take long for the duke to respond to the unusual summons. He took in the scene—his wife looking bleak, holding a letter, his daughter's head bowed.

"What's wrong?"

Without a word, the duchess handed him the letter. He read it quickly and looked up. "No need to get yourself into a pet, my dear. Livy will of course refuse the invitation and that will be the end of that."

"I have no intention of refusing, Father." Olivia spoke in a sober voice. She rose and took the letter from his hand. "You know perfectly well that I want this too much to give it up. I've made no secret of the fact that I wish to become an intelligence agent. Know this. If I didn't have your consent, it would make me unhappy, for I love you very much, but I shall proceed nevertheless. Can you not see your way clear to giving me your blessings in this endeavor?" Olivia directed this question to her father.

"Damned if I will, you disobedient child!" the duke said bitterly.

"Leave us, Livy dearest," said her mother. "I wish to discuss this news in private with your father."

"Of course, Mother." She hugged her mother, but when she tried to hug her father, he turned away, his face twisted in anger.

Olivia spent a sleepless night in misery for having caused her parents such pain. She knew in her heart she would not give up her right to realize her ambition. In time, they would accept her decision, for deep down, she knew her parents loved their firstborn child.

When her abigail woke her, she said, "His Grace wants to speak to you before you leave, milady."

Now what, she thought, weary of quarreling. She dressed, took two sips of chocolate and went in search of him. She found him in the breakfast room reading the paper and drinking his coffee, his eggs untouched. She went to the head of the table and kissed him on the cheek.

Olivia took a seat by his side and said, "You asked to see me, Father? I'm not going to work today. I never do on Sunday."

Her heart thudded when he put the paper down and looked at her, for his face was drawn. It was as if he had grown ten years overnight.

"This dream of yours? I have only myself to thank," he confessed, his voice laced with bitterness. "I'll never forgive myself for treating you like the son I wanted when you were born. It was I who taught you how to ride like a man. It was I who taught you how to hunt and to shoot. It was I who taught you how to swim. It was I who . . ."

"Oh, Father," she cried, and fell on her knees before him. "Don't you know how proud I am to be your daughter? Only let me do this with your blessing and I'll make you proud in return. I must seize this opportunity. Can't you see that?"

She heard him blow his nose. At the same time, his hand patted her head and she felt a glimmer of hope.

"I haven't much choice, have I, puss? We don't want to lose you, Livy. It would break your mother's heart and I won't have her hurt. We have agreed that you may go with our blessings, but I can't bear to be here to see you off. Your mother and I have decided to leave for Brighton tomorrow with Georgie, Mary and Jane. Your brother Edward is coming home today from Oxford and he will chaperone you and Helena. They'll join us at Heatham after you leave."

"You can't know how much this means to me, Father," she said in a humble voice.

* * *

"Edward our chaperone? Imagine that," said Helena in wry good humor when she heard the news. She rolled her eyes and that made Olivia laugh. "Brother Edward won't care a fig for what we do. He's bringing his friend Madison with him so they can practice their skills in curricle racing in Hyde Park."

"Father's approval is such good news for me, Helena, don't you think?"

"I couldn't agree more. Do you have a plan yet? If not, I think that, after our parents leave, we'll have a week left to get you ready."

"Oh, yes. That would be perfect. First off, you must help me shop for the proper attire. Do you think our modistes can have everything ready in one week? No matter. What they can't finish might be sent to me." She hesitated, a quizzical look on her face. "What do spies wear, do you suppose?"

Helena giggled. "Certainly not ball gowns, you ninny. I would guess you'll need riding clothes, sturdy shoes, warm sweaters and coats, walking skirts . . ."

Olivia made a face. "Sounds a little dull."

"Keep focused on the goal, Livy. Not on a fancy wardrobe."

Olivia sighed and laid her head on her sister's shoulder.

"What is it, dear?"

"I'll miss you, Helena."

"You can always write."

Chapter Three

Wilson Academy—Sunday, The Thirtieth of June

When Sir Abercrombie Wilson died without an heir, his will deeded his property to the Crown. This patriotic gift was never used during England's Napoleonic Wars. But afterwards, when the deed came to his attention, the home secretary maneuvered Parliament into handing it over to the home office and providing funds for the renovation of the property.

Sir Sebastian Brooks, a war hero, sold out to accept the post of chief spymaster, and at once set about converting the mansion into a training center, named Wilson Academy. To the uninitiated, the property appeared to have undergone little change, causing locals no undue alarm. Indeed, none but those in the highest echelons of government knew the real purpose of the academy.

Located near enough to London for ease of communication with the home office, the academy lay hidden within some sixteen hundred acres of land. Havelshire, a small parish surrounded by rolling hills and well-tended tracts of farmland was the village nearest to the academy. And though the townsfolk did not know what took place behind the small forest of trees and high hedges that surrounded it, they were happy to supply its inhabitants with ample mutton and fresh produce. What the farmers were left with was transported to London for sale in the open markets.

St. Michaels Church stood in the center of the modest village, next to the town hall. This building held the constabulary, a rarely used jail and a large assembly hall. Various small commercial enterprises included a tobacconist, a library and The Gray Swan, an inn next to the public stables. The mail coach stopped on its way west to other destinations every day. Havelshire, at its furthest point, ended with a lovely park and a pond, well-used in summer by the local populace.

Sebastian stood peering out of the tall windows, a deep frown on his face. His office, on the first floor to the right of the entryway, faced front. When he heard the sound of horse's hooves approaching, he removed his watch from his vest pocket to check the time.

The new trainees were returning from their first afternoon riding session punctual. He smiled to himself, knowing how rigorous his stable master, Tom Deff, a former circus rider, taught the lads his tricks. He tried to imagine his newest recruit doing circus tricks on a horse and smiled, yet his eyes remained grim.

Bloody hell. She'll fall on her arse. Maybe that will force the chit to resign in disgust. With a sigh, he put the delightful thought out of his head and seated himself at his desk to study the reports demanding his attention. Yet thoughts of the new recruit persisted.

Why did Sidmouth humiliate him and force the woman on his operation? Why couldn't she remain a mere clerk in the home office? What made the home secretary think she could succeed in such a rigorous training program? What reason would a sensible woman have to choose to train as a spy anyway? Heaven only knew.

* * *

Olivia was right behind her sister Helena as they proceeded out the side door of Fairchild House. She wished her brat of a brother had had the courtesy to remain at home to witness her triumphant departure. Instead, Edward had elected to ride his curricle in Hyde Park and show off his skill to the young ladies who dangled after him. Almost eighteen, the heir apparent was a handsome lad who favored his dark-skinned mother. Aside from the fortune and the title he stood to inherit, his bold black eyes, his dark hair streaked with the light of the sun and his lively disposition enhanced his popularity.

Olivia was dressed in her new blue silk morning gown, matching pelisse, blue silk shoes and a fetching bonnet that framed her face and allowed her curls to fall just so. She was alive with anticipation as she glanced to the right and noted with approval her two waiting coaches. They were full to the brim with numerous trunks packed with the new wardrobe she'd purchased in a frantic whirl through every fine London shop preferred by the Fairchild women. She and Helena had had a wonderful time shopping, but it had taken every bit of their time after she'd learned of her acceptance into the spy training academy.

"I'm more than ready, Helena. According to my last letter, a messenger will deliver directions to the secret location. He should be here at any moment." She squeezed her sister's hand as they watched the footmen secure the last of her trunks on top of the second carriage holding all her new belongings.

The clatter of horses' hooves caught her attention. Startled, she glanced quizzically at Helena.

"A carriage appears to be approaching, Livy."

Olivia's stomach lurched. "Are you expecting someone, perhaps?"

"No, dear. It must be your messenger."

The coach drew abreast of them and the driver swung down from his perch. He removed his hat and said, "Beggin' pardon, miladys. Which one of you is Lady Olivia Fairchild, if you please?"

"What business have you with her ladyship, my good man?" demanded Helena.

"I've been sent to fetch her, milady."

"How thoughtful, Helena. They've sent an escort for me," said Olivia, pleased.

The driver blushed. His hands twisted the brim of his tri-corner hat. "As to that, milady, I'm to bring you." He glanced at the other woman. "Alone."

"No need, my good man. My abigail and I shall follow you in my carriage. The other one holds my personal effects, you see."

The blush deepened to scarlet. "Sorry, milady. I've strict orders to fetch you in this here coach. You are to bring only one portmanteau. You won't be needin' more."

Olivia's eyes widened in astonishment. "Only one port-manteau? Impossible." She waved toward her coaches. "I cannot travel with less than . . ."

"Livy," Helena said, and shook her head as if to say, "not in front of the driver." She took her sister's hand and led her out of earshot.

"I cannot fit everything I need into one trunk. Impossible! There must be some mistake. I'm going to find out who issued such a ridiculous order and let him have a piece of my mind. It cannot be the home secretary, can it? No, not him. He's too much of a gentleman."

When Olivia took a breath, her sister found the oppor-tunity to reply. In a firm tone, she warned, "Now, Livy. Think for a moment. You are not on your way to visit friends in the country in order to dance at balls and have picnics. You are going to be trained for clandestine service. If that is what you've always wanted, why fuss over your wardrobe?"

"It is what I want. You know very well it is. But all my new gowns and my riding habits and my shoes and my bonnets and my pelisses and my reticules and my abigail . . ."

Helena clasped both Olivia's hands in hers. "If this opportunity is indeed what you want, you must do your duty and obey orders without question. Unless, of course, you wish to change your mind and stay here?"

Olivia thought a moment, as if struggling with her conscience. "No. I won't give up, Helena. I've dreamed of this for too long. You can be sure I'm equal to whatever awaits me." She tried to sound brave, yet the fall of her shoulders betrayed her. "All right. One portmanteau it is." She beckoned to her abigail, who hurried to her side.

"Have the footmen remove the largest portmanteau from the second coach, and fit as many of my things into it as you can."

"There's my brave girl," her sister said as they returned to the driver sent to fetch her.

But his eyes were on the two footmen removing the large trunk. He shook his head. "Too big, yer la'ship. Ye're allowed only a small portmanteau. It's me orders, you see."

"A small . . . ?" She glared at him.

He raised both hands in a helpless gesture and whined, "It's me orders."

"Livy," her sister warned in a low voice.

"Oh, for heaven's sake! All right! Put the large sac back and bring me my travel portmanteau," she called to the footmen. To her abigail she added, "Have the men return the rest of my trunks to my chambers, but don't unpack just yet. I'm sure there must be some mistake. I'll send for you and for the rest of my baggage just as soon as I clear up this misunderstanding."

The sisters watched in silence as the two footmen removed her portmanteau from the first carriage and handed it to the driver, who secured it to the back of his cab.

While they waited, Helena said, "Now that you've decided to accept the challenge of this new position, you must promise me two things, Livy."

"What is it you wish me to promise, dearest?"

"For one, promise me you will obey orders without question."

Her eyes flew open in surprise. "Why wouldn't I obey orders?"

Helena laughed. "You do have a tendency to see things differently, dear sister. Don't try to substitute your interpretation of an order to suit yourself."

"Don't be ridiculous, Helena. I would never do such a thing. And what is the other promise, may I ask?"

"Don't be angry with me, Livy. The other is that you never give up, no matter how hard the task set before you."

Olivia hugged her sister. "I promise I won't let you down, you goose. How can I when you know I mean to be the first successful woman spy in the world?" She turned to observe the waiting driver who had already let down the steps. "Goodbye, Helena. I'll miss you. Wish me well." She kissed her sister on both cheeks and entered the carriage, but before the driver shut the door, she added, "I've left two notes, dear. One for father and one for mother. Will you see to their delivery?"

Upon hearing this, the driver shook his head. "No correspondence allowed yer la'ship. I'll have them, if you please."

"You exceed your authority, sir! I'll not give them up."

"Me orders are to leave you here, then."

Her sister glanced from one to the other and turned to a footman. "Bring me the letters Lady Olivia left on the mail table."

"Helena!"

"Remember your promise, Livy. Besides, it's such an insignificant detail."

Olivia sat back in her seat, folded her arms and fumed.

As soon as the letters were handed to the driver, he shut the coach door, nodded a curt farewell to the other woman and climbed up to his seat.

Olivia sat back in the luxurious coach, trying to calm her nerves. It didn't take her long. In spite of her annoyance at the driver's orders, she was on her way to becoming the first woman spy in the history of England. Perhaps in the entire world.

Two lamps within the carriage glowed well enough for her to take in her surroundings. She noted with approval the elegant black velvet curtains covering all the windows, yet she was eager to discover where he was taking her. She pushed the curtain nearest her aside, only to find that she could not see out the window, though it was still daylight. She removed one glove and scratched the glass with a long, well-cared-for fingernail, but nothing happened. The panes had been painted black on the outside.

Indignation stirred her sense of injustice and she banged on the ceiling of the carriage with her parasol. She banged. And she banged. And she banged. There was no response from her driver, though she felt the carriage speeding along at a brisk pace. She tried the door handle. It was locked from the outside. The truth dawned on her at last. She was not meant to know where she was being transported.

A delicious shiver ran through her. How thrilling. She recalled her solemn promise to her sister and closed her eyes. *My rendezvous with destiny.* Olivia laughed out loud. She had no doubt that she would learn to be a fantastic woman spy. She fell asleep with dreams of glory dancing in her head.

Olivia woke with a start when the carriage jolted to a halt. She rubbed her eyes, eager for a glimpse of her new home, at least for the next twelve weeks. There was no mirror inside the carriage. Unfortunate. She patted her hair as best she could and placed her fashionable bonnet, its colorful ribbons streaming down, on her head.

Would there be a large welcoming committee? Perhaps Viscount Sidmouth himself would be in attendance. She conjured up a vision of the staff lining the driveway very like the duke's servants did when the family went to Heatham for the summer. Would the eager onlookers cheer resoundingly and applaud her courage at this truly historic moment? Perhaps an orchestra would play "God Save the King" as soon as she stepped down. Olivia smoothed her wrinkled blue gown and straightened her matching pelisse. She pinched her cheeks for color as she waited on the edge of her seat for the carriage door to open.

Sebastian could not focus on the words in reports sent by operatives in the field. He had to read them again and again before he managed to grasp their meaning. He went over the list of requested supplies from the quartermaster. He read the detailed reports on each of the new recruits. He reread the note Mrs. Hunnicut, the housekeeper, had left for him. She respectfully requested additional staff as well as more funds for household supplies. He initialed each report, wrote notes on some, approved the quartermaster's requests, as well as Mrs. Hunnicut's plea.

After the war, when Sebastian had sold out and agreed to take the post of spymaster—his official title was under secretary of security—it seemed to him to be a prestigious position full of promise. He could sink his teeth into such a grand assignment, he thought at the time. Too late he learned that his new post amounted to nothing more than being a mere drudge who trained spies for government service.

He was chained to his desk most days, doing the work any competent clerk might accomplish just as easily. It made him feel useless in spite of the fact that he was required to confer with numerous under secretaries whenever the whim took the home secretary. He still smarted over being told by that gentleman that no one was indispensable.

Why hadn't he had the good sense to refuse the position when it was offered? He should have remained in the army where he'd been content. His poor decision cost him sleepless nights, not to mention endless hours of boredom.

Today he could not focus on anything but this latest humiliation. How on earth was he to tolerate a woman in the program? He knew only too well that she was likely to be a silly slip of a girl who valued nothing more than her own good looks. The very thought of an empty-headed, frivolous woman made his stomach turn. Bitterly, he recalled his futile conversation with Sidmouth. Nothing moved the stubborn old man. Nothing.

At the sound of Denville's voice, he raised his eyes.

"Sir?"

"What is it, Hugh?"

"The coach has arrived. Would you like to greet the new trainee?"

"No. Send for Mrs. Hunnicut. She knows what she must do." He rose from his desk and watched from behind the drape at his window. *Welcome to Wilson Academy, Fairchild. Life as you know it is over. You are in for a big surprise.*

Martha Hunnicut, a woman in her fiftieth year, hurried to greet the new trainee. She stopped a moment to examine her starched white cap under which wisps of gray hair escaped, her gray eyes scrutinizing her appearance. Satisfied that all was in order, the tall, thin woman stepped through the front door held open for her by a footman.

She clasped her hands in front of her and said in a kind voice, "Welcome to Wilson Academy, Fairchild."

Olivia looked around at the empty driveway, disappointment etched on her face. "Where is everybody?"

The housekeeper chose to ignore the question. "I'm Mrs. Hunnicut, the housekeeper. Follow me, please. I'll show you to your room." She nodded to the footman who untied Olivia's portmanteau. "Take your portmanteau along with you."

Olivia swallowed her disappointment. *Greeted only by the housekeeper? How boorish. At the very least, the chief spymaster should have been here to welcome his new female spy.*

"To your right is the formal dining room," Mrs. Hunnicut pointed out as they proceeded. "To your left is the library. You will learn your way soon enough, I'm sure."

The newest trainee followed Mrs. Hunnicut up the grand staircase directly ahead of them to the second floor. But there the wide staircase ended. "Is this the floor where my chambers are located?"

"No, my dear." She offered no further explanation and proceeded to the end of the hall where a narrow staircase led up to the next floor. Olivia trailed behind.

At the top of yet another floor, Olivia paused, breathing hard. "Here?"

"Not yet, Fairchild." The housekeeper led her all the way to the farthest end of the hall, through an opening and up a final narrow staircase, easily maintaining her brisk pace.

"Here is your room." She opened the door to a room smaller than Olivia's closet in London.

Olivia's heart sank into her toes. "Is this not the attic?"

"It is."

"There must be some mistake. Or perhaps this is a jest, meant to test my mettle?"

The housekeeper said, "No, Fairchild. This will be your room during your entire stay."

"I am meant to live in this tiny room with no mirror? There is nothing but a cot, a washstand, a writing desk and a chair. Impossible! Where are my bathing quarters? Where is my clothing closet?"

"Use the hooks on the wall behind the door for the clothing you brought with you. You won't need them while you're here, since the academy provides appropriate attire for all the trainees."

"But . . ."

"You shall have an opportunity to take up all your questions with the spymaster this evening. He has invited you to dine with him at six." The older woman spoke in an awed tone, implying that such an honor was an extraordinary event.

"I'll leave you to unpack your things and rest a bit. An under maid will call for you five minutes before six to show you the way to his private dining room. Please be prompt, Fairchild. The spymaster does not like to be kept waiting."

"There's no hot water in this washbowl. Will a maid bring me some?"

"That's not our way at the academy. If you want hot water, you will have to fetch it yourself from the well outside the kitchen, which is in the basement. You may heat it if it doesn't interfere with the chef."

Olivia's eyes opened wide as she pleaded, "Wait, Mrs. Hunnicut."

"Yes?"

"What is this roll of . . . *things* on my cot?"

"The roll contains your bedding and your training clothes. Forgive me, but I have pressing duties to attend to. All will be made clear to you in due time. For now, make up your cot and have a bit of a rest before your dinner this evening."

When the door shut behind the housekeeper, Olivia bit back tears of frustration. *Bloody hell! What have I gotten myself into? Our under maids at Fairchild Manor live in quarters far better than this! Fetch my own wash water? I'd as soon go unwashed.*

But she thought better of this and grabbed the pitcher. She trudged down four flights to the kitchen. No one paid any attention to her as she found the door to the outside at the far end of the galley. She placed the pitcher on the uneven ground under the pump. Exerting all her strength, she began to pump, but this produced no results at first. After several tries and without any warning, the water gushed out with such force, it tipped the pitcher over and soaked the hem of her gown. It took several attempts to fill the pitcher before she got the hang of it. By the time she reentered the kitchen, the staff was busy preparing dinner and all the fireplace hooks were too full for her to heat the water.

Back in her room, she took off her sodden gown and hung it on a hook, unrolled the thin mattress, lay down, curled up in a ball and sobbed her heart out.

"You!" Olivia blurted when she entered the dining room on the dot of six. She found herself facing the man who had tried to seduce her—and had very nearly succeeded—at the Hobbleton Ball.

Sebastian looked grim. "*Sir*, Fairchild. The trainees are instructed to address me as 'Sir.' You will do the same."

"*Lady* Fairchild to you, *sir.*"

"Here you shall be known as Fairchild. All trainees are addressed thus and we make no distinctions." He took his seat at the head of the table and nodded toward a seat at the opposite end.

He seats himself before he seats a lady in his presence? Man has no manners. She marched to her seat, took it and folded her arms in a gesture of defiance.

"We'll dine first, after which you may speak." They ate in silence, though Olivia was bursting with a myriad of questions.

At the end of the meal, Sebastian waited for the servants to withdraw. He raised an eyebrow and said, "Well?"

"Well what, sir?"

"This shall be your only opportunity to voice your complaints. You will not be given another."

"Which complaint, sir, would you like me to address first, sir? How do I like my quarters, sir? How did I enjoy the warm welcome I received, sir? How did I feel about leaving my wardrobe and my abigail at home, sir? How did I like lugging my own icy cold wash water up four flights of stairs to my tiny cell, sir? How did I like my cot, which I was forced to make up on my own, sir?" She sat back, her eyes blazing.

Sebastian sipped his wine, put the goblet down, wiped his mouth and asked, "What did you do to come to the attention of the home secretary? He was most impressed with your credentials. Kindly furnish me with them."

"I was employed in the home office, sir."

"And what work did you do there, may I ask?"

"I handled sensitive materials."

A light dawned in Sebastian's mind. Of course! This was the clerk he knocked down when he left Sidmouth's office in a blind temper that day. Does she know it? He thought not. His lips twitched when he recalled his glimpse of her derriere. But he didn't let on.

"You were a file clerk, then. You may not find the rigors of Wilson Academy to your liking, Fairchild. If that proves to be the case, inform me and I will arrange to have you escorted home at once."

Don't celebrate my departure too soon, spymaster. I'm not a quitter. And you, sir, are far too eager to be rid of me! Defiance bubbled up within her. She raised her chin and said,

"I am up to the challenge, *sir*. Have you no more answers to my questions, sir?"

Sebastian shrugged, thinking it a great pity he couldn't take this sassy bit of skirt in his arms and make love to her once more. Too bad. She had such delicious breasts. The thought roused an involuntary response. He hoped he could rise from his chair without embarrassing himself. "You insult me with your foolish questions, and since they amount to nothing more than mere petty grievances, I have no intention of responding."

"Then why have you invited me to dine? Sir?" The word took on the color of an insult.

"I did so in order to outline our rules. For one, there is no favoritism shown here. For another, the high standards our instructors set for you will be no different from the ones they set for all trainees. We run a tight, efficient operation here, Fairchild. If you cannot keep up, you will be dismissed. Is that clear?"

"Perfectly."

"Perfectly, *sir.*" Sebastian said. "Forgetting to address me or your instructors as '*sir*' is a serious offense and will earn you a penalty." He could not fail to see the fire in her eyes. "Though you may find it difficult, Fairchild, your most pressing task is to learn to obey orders. Do you understand me?"

"Yes, *sir.*"

"Good. Breakfast is served at half past four, calisthenics begin promptly at five. Wear the regulation training clothes we have provided."

"Do you mean half past four in the morning, *sir*?" That last word constricted her throat.

He had already risen from his seat. Pleased that his erection had subsided, he allowed himself a smirk. "Pleasure to meet you once again, Fairchild." He reached the door, and added, "Don't oversleep. If you miss breakfast, you won't be fed again until lunch is served at half past noon."

Olivia remained at the dining room table after the spymaster left, lost in the misery of her thoughts. This was not turning out as well as she had hoped. She hadn't touched any of her wine during dinner. Now she reached for it, removed the stopper and guzzled it directly from the decanter. She rose unsteadily and trudged up to her room, disheartened, dispirited, disillusioned.

Her eye caught an unfamiliar sheet of paper on her desk that hadn't been there before dinner. She picked it up. Tomorrow's schedule. It read:

4:30– 5:00	AM	Breakfast
5:00– 6:00	AM	Calisthenics
6:00– 8:00	AM	Codes and Ciphers
8:00–10:00	AM	Fencing
10:00–12:00	AM	Intelligence
12:00– 1:00	PM	Luncheon
1:00– 3:00	PM	Housekeeping
3:00– 5:00	PM	Horseback Riding
5:00– 6:00	PM	Dinner
6:00– 8:00	PM	Study Hall
8:00	PM	Lights Out

She shivered. Could she do all these things? All in one day? She had to. She couldn't fail. She wouldn't fail.

She sat on the chair at her desk and slowly pulled the pins from her hair, allowing her lengthy tresses to fall in confusion. She'd never combed her own hair before when she'd gotten ready for bed, but she took up the brush and gamely tried to untangle the knots, wincing at each pull.

Bloody hell! I'll brush it in the morning. She put the brush down and began to rise when a vision of her sister Helena floated before her eyes.

Don't fail me, Livy. Pick up that brush and finish the task or you will have the devil of a time untangling the jumble in the morning. She heard the words in her mind, as clear as if her sister had spoken them aloud. Olivia picked up the brush once again and counted the strokes. *One. Two. Three . . .*

When she reached twenty-five, the strength in her arms failed her. She braided it as best she could to prevent morning tangles, tied it with a ribbon plucked from her bonnet, rose from her chair and turned to the cot. Her body yearned to drop down without another thought. Again, Helena clouded her vision and shook her head from side to side.

An exhausted Olivia sighed, unfolded the sheet and tucked it around the thin, lumpy mattress as best as she could manage. She stuffed the pillow into its case, wrapped the thin blanket around her shoulders and lay down on the cot. Seconds later, she fell into an exhausted sleep.

Chapter Four

The jarring noise of a bell woke Olivia at four. In the fog between sleep and wakefulness, she fancied she was home in London and wondered who could possibly be calling at this unearthly hour. And why didn't they use the knocker instead of the bell? She'd have to complain to the butler. She turned over, only to fall out of her cot and clunk onto the bare floor. At once her eyes flew awake, though it took several seconds to recall her whereabouts.

Shivering from the cold, for there was no fireplace in her room. She rose and groped her way to the candle on the desk. Her fingers shook as she lit it and surveyed the room. It took her two steps to reach the washbasin, for her room was so small, she could almost touch it from wall to wall.

Olivia turned the latch to her door and pulled it open as an under maid hurried by. "Excuse me? If I paid you, would you fetch me some hot water?"

"You one o'them trainees, an't you?"

"Yes. I'll pay you a crown if you bring me some hot water. Please?"

The under maid called out from the stairwell, trying to be

helpful. "I'd lose me job if'n y'paid me a guinea. Y 'ave to fetch yer own water, miss. The pump's just outside the kitchen door. Kitchen's in the basement. Follow this staircase till you reach bottom."

"I know bloody well where the kitchen is," she grumbled as the young woman hurried off to her duties. Olivia shut the door and reached for her silk chemise and knickers. She cast a disgusted eye on the outer clothing left for her. With considerable distaste, she stepped into the pantaloons, but they slid down to the floor. She removed another of her new bonnet's ribbons to tie round her waist. The coarse shirt was far too large for her small frame, but when she buttoned the thick warm vest over it, it kept the shirt from slipping off her shoulders. She rooted around in her portmanteau until she found stockings and undergarments to stuff her boots with until they fit well enough for her to walk and not wobble.

She grasped her pitcher and hurried down the stairwell until she reached the kitchen. A kitchen maid coming out of the pantry nodded her head in the direction of the door at the end of the kitchen without stopping her work.

Olivia hurried outside, a blast of cold morning air causing her breath to release smoke. She filled the pitcher and trudged back upstairs to her room, for she didn't have time to heat it. By the time she'd washed with the icy water, it was almost five.

Another under maid, more accommodating than the first, showed her the way to the trainees' dining room, two flights down the back stairs. Her stomach growled as she flew down the stairwell.

But breakfast for her was not to be, for as soon as she reached the large room on the first floor, a stream of young men, dressed as she was, were making their way down the steps.

"Where are we bound?"

The last man crooked his finger. "Riggs here. Calisthenics. Follow me."

Olivia had to run to keep up with his long strides. By the time she reached the training grounds, her breath was short.

The trainees lined up to face Hugh Denville, a young man—not more than thirty, Olivia guessed—who wore his black hair tied back with a ribbon. His weathered face held high cheekbones, a straight nose, brown eyes and a dimple in his cheek that deepened when he smiled. Denville, the spymaster's aide during the war, also served as Sebastian's secretary. It was well known that little could be said in his hearing that would not be repeated to Sir.

"Morning, lads." He acknowledged Olivia with a nod. "Fairchild."

"Morning, sir," the men answered as one.

"Morning, sir," Olivia's voice followed in a high squeak.

"Warm-ups. Run in place. Five minutes." Denville consulted his timepiece. "Begin."

Olivia noted the posture and began to pump her legs like the others, raising them as high as she could.

"Chin up. Knees higher, Fairchild. You're not at a picnic."

"Y . . . yes, sir."

To the casual eye, Wilson Academy appeared to be the country estate of a peer of the realm. A fine example of Renaissance architecture, the imposing facade was built of brick early in the seventeenth century. Inside, it boasted the most modern facilities in the world, perhaps.

The ground floor was designed for offices, the staff dining room, a separate dining room for trainees, a reception room and a grand ballroom whose design was meant to accommodate large groups of government officials as a meeting place rather than as a space for the frivolous balls it once held.

The spymaster's quarters, consisting of three large rooms, were also on this level. The first was a dining room with two doors, one at the back stairwell for kitchen access and another leading into his bedchamber, which also had two doors, one leading out to the hall and the other leading into his office, the third room. A second office door admitted visitors.

Below ground, the basement housed a full kitchen galley and below that, a storage cellar.

The first floor held instructors' chambers, a lounge for their leisure use, and additional chambers to accommodate visiting guests. As well, the trainees' study hall was below the male trainees' rooms. Servants and trainees alike used the narrow back staircase to reach all their activities.

The second floor was designed for classrooms, the largest space outfitted for fencing on one end and boxing on the other. The spymaster designed two hidden walkways on either side of this floor, their entrances rendered invisible by the same wood panels adorning all the hallways. Slivers of rectangular windows, placed at eye level, enabled him to observe indoor and outdoor training activities without being seen.

From this vantage point, he watched Olivia's pathetic attempt to keep up with the other trainees at calisthenics and wondered how long it would take for her to give up and go home where she belonged.

"Fifty push-ups. Hit the ground, lads," Denville said when they had finished running in place. When he noticed Olivia still standing, he added, "You, too, Fairchild."

"Yes, sir." She observed what the others were doing and lay down on her stomach. She put her hands on the ground and pushed hard, but when she raised her head, her stubborn body refused to follow. On the third try, she caught sight of a pair of boots close to her face and turned her head up to face Denville. "I've never done push-ups before, sir. I don't know how."

One of the men snickered.

"There's no call for that!" Denville said sharply. He turned back to Olivia. "Lie back down, Fairchild. Elbows bent, but stiff, hands flat, in line with your brea—er, chest. Not too near your shoulders, mind. Keep your body stiff as a board, toes pointed down. Now push as hard as you're able."

To her astonishment, Olivia succeeded in lifting her upper body a few inches off the ground. But not her torso. Perhaps women were not meant to do push-ups, she thought with despair.

"Right, then." He coughed to smother a chuckle and walked back to his place.

By the time the other trainees had completed fifty push-ups, Olivia had wobbled through five. Triumphant at her small victory, she darted a glance at Denville, but he paid no heed.

"Jumping jacks. Begin."

I can do this! Yet when she jumped apart, her arms would not follow, and when she raised her arms over her head, her feet turned to lead.

Denville chose to ignore this, at the same time admiring her determination. "Time," he announced, and strode away in the direction of the spymaster's office.

She trudged after the other trainees, relying on them to lead her to the next activity. She tapped the young man in front of her on the shoulder. "Where are we going?"

He threw her a lopsided grin, his face covered with freckles. His light brown hair was stringy, but his eyes were lively. Rufus Riggs was the youngest of the trainees.

"Codes and ciphers. On the second floor," the young man

whispered. And shot a gap-toothed grin at her. He added, "Name's Riggs. Rufus."

The kindness in his voice nearly undid her. "Fairchild," she whispered back.

Sir Aaron Foster, a short, balding man with gentle blue eyes had been knighted by the Regent for code work that defied Napoleon's staff. He'd meant to retire from government service after the war he helped win, but Viscount Sidmouth had other plans for him. The home secretary persuaded him to take his current post as instructor for future undercover agents.

Once seated in the two-hour class, Olivia relaxed, though every bone in her body screamed in protest after her unaccustomed physical exertion. She enjoyed the mental challenge, thinking it very like solving intricate puzzles. Although she did not grasp everything the master teacher said, she was pleased with herself. Codes and ciphers class was far easier than calisthenics.

When Foster dismissed them, the trainees moved across the hall to the fencing room on the same floor.

Riggs appointed himself her guide. He helped her find a suitable vest, a glove and a wire mask. They were too large for her, yet not as ill-fitting as the clothing she wore.

Olivia had been tutored in fencing when she was still in the schoolroom. The duke wished to share his favorite activity with her, for she threatened to be his only child at the time. She suppressed a giggle at the thought of her father. Little did he know to what use she would put it.

Andre Fourier, a Frenchman with a thin mustache, black hair and a slight frame, swept into the room wearing his fencing vest. He carried his glove and his mask, and eyed his students as if he were inspecting sides of beef, a familiar task for him, for he was also chef for the academy.

"I am Fourier, *messieurs.*" His Gallic eyes fell on Olivia and he bowed to her. "*Mademoiselle.*"

"*Bien!* We begin." He launched into an explanation of the art of dueling and paired the trainees off for practice, replacing one or another to illustrate his point when he thought it necessary. Which was often.

"We commence wiz ze lunge and ze parry—*Prime, seconde, tierce, quarte, quinte, sixte, septime, octave.*"

Olivia was partnered with Riggs, whose clumsy handling of his foil, rendered safe by the button at its tip, forced Fourier to stop him. He took Riggs' foil, placed one hand behind his back and faced Olivia.

"*En Garde, sil vous plait. Prime.*" The others stopped and turned to watch. Surprise registered on more than one face when Olivia acquitted herself well in her first parry. But when she dropped her foil in the second, silence rang in the air. Until Fourier laughed heartily.

"I am saved from shame. Well done, Fairchild."

At the end of class, Fourier turned to Olivia. "Your fencing glove ees too large, as is ze vest and ze mask, eh? I shall order better equipment for you." He waved his hand in the direction of the other trainees and turned to leave. "Dismissed."

The trainees replaced their fencing equipment and proceeded to the library on the ground floor. They were seated around a long table, when the other young men introduced themselves to Olivia.

The trainee next to her offered his hand. He was small-boned—mid-twenties, Olivia thought—his high forehead exaggerated by sparse hair. "Name's Harold Perkins. Well done in fencing, Fairchild. Fourier's an exacting taskmaster. Praise from him is praise indeed."

"Good show, Fairchild. We're the Reeds. He's Billy and I'm Bobby. No one can tell us apart so they call us BillyBob."

Tweedledee and Tweedledum, Olivia thought, swallowing

a giggle. She could look them in the eye, for they were not much taller than she was. They had mischievous eyes as blue as the sky on a cloudless day.

"Carter here," said the last man. Well-groomed in spite of the unflattering uniform, Olivia sensed there was something arrogant about him. He seemed to have a smirk on his thin lips when he spoke, as if to underline his superiority. His abundant head of hair was always in place, as was a thin mustache. How old was he? she wondered. She couldn't tell his age, though he acted as though he was far wiser than the other lads. "You've fenced before, haven't you, Fairchild?"

Startled by the hostility in his voice, she said, "Yes, it's true. Do you find fencing difficult, Carter? I find push-ups far more difficult. Tell you what. I'll fence for you if you do push-ups for me." The other trainees laughed in appreciation at what they took for a set-down.

The door to the library opened and the spymaster entered, putting an abrupt end to the laughter and the cameraderie, but not to the loud grumble emanating from Olivia's stomach.

"What's that sound? Did you miss breakfast, Fairchild? Ah, you overslept in spite of my warning, didn't you? No matter. Have the goodness to silence your rebellious stomach for the next two hours."

No one laughed as he'd intended. "That was a jest," Sebastian said in exasperation.

Carter laughed, but the others did not join him.

Olivia's face burned with shame at what, in her mind at least, clearly amounted to an insult. In a voice full of scorn, she said, "Kind of you to take such an interest in my welfare, sir."

If the spymaster felt chastised by the bitterness of her response, he did not show it. He cleared his throat and began. "The gathering of intelligence is an important key to the success of a spy. Another term for this process is espionage, the accumulation of secret information designed to help you forge a suitable plan of action against the enemy."

At the spymaster's dry explanation, Olivia swallowed the laugh threatening to bubble up from within. *Hmmph! He has the gall to call "the accumulation of information" intelligence gathering? What nonsense. It's nothing more than just plain gossip. If he expects me to fail this class, he'll be terribly disappointed. Intelligence gathering, indeed! I've been gossiping ever since I learned to speak the King's English.*

At noon, when class was dismissed, Olivia followed her classmates to the trainees' dining room for a hearty meal of mutton stew, bread and cheese, warm apple pie and tea. They served themselves from the sideboard against the far wall and took their seats at a long table in the middle of the room, one or the other rising occasionally to refill their plates.

Not only did Olivia clean her plate, she rose for a second helping, suffering teasing comments for her pains.

"Jolly good appetite, Fairchild."

"Easy does it, Fairchild. Leave some for us."

"That'll teach you not to miss breakfast, lass."

She grinned, pleased, for their good-natured jests signaled acceptance. But what was eating Carter, she wondered when he hadn't joined in.

Their first class after the noonday meal was housekeeping, taught by Mrs. Hunnicut. She took the entire group on a tour of the building, from the storage cellar to the attic and above that to the chimneys on the roof. She explained in detail the workings of a large country house, something she knew well, for she had been housekeeper at an earl's estate in Leeds before she married.

Heatham was much larger than Wilson Academy, Olivia noted. The procedures were familiar to her, but not to the other men.

"You will be expected not only to learn the function of every servant in this house, but also to practice their roles. Male trainees will be assigned to spend time as footmen dressed in proper livery, performing tasks such as carrying coal to the chambers, cleaning out the ashes, trimming the lamps, serving meals and the like. It will stand you in good stead should you be required to infiltrate a household for the purpose of espionage.

"As for you, Fairchild, you will learn to perform the various duties of maids. Their task is to keep the house clean, supply the chambers with water for washing and bathing, and keep the fires going. As a kitchen maid, you will be required to help the cook and as a scullery maid, you will wash dishes, pots and pans, and scrub the floor at the housekeeper's request. All outdoor tasks will be described to you by the stable master. You may proceed to his class now. Good afternoon."

As they filed out, she put a restraining hand on Olivia's arm. "Fairchild? A moment please."

"Yes, ma'am? What is it you wish?"

"The spymaster has requested that I arrange for you to be clothed properly. Come to my sitting room before you retire this evening, and I'll take your measurements for the seamstress. She's one of our under maids and she's very handy with a needle. Our tanner will measure your feet as well. Those boots are far too large for you."

"Yes, Mrs. Hunnicut. Thank you, ma'am." As she hurried off, she couldn't help but wonder. Could this order mean something more than merely to provide her with suitably fitted clothing and boots? Could the spymaster be softening toward her? Could he have relented and accepted her role? If that were so, she'd have to work hard—harder than the others, perhaps—to reinforce that view.

The day turned warm and sunny by the time Olivia reported

to the stables. The lads were already busy brushing the horses down, feeding them and cleaning their stalls.

Stable master Tom Deff, a gray-haired, Irish gentleman with a brogue to match, had been an accomplished circus rider in his youth. His innocent blue eyes belied the fact that he could be stern when necessary. "Afternoon, Fairchild. What kept ye?"

"Mrs. Hunnicut detained me, sir."

He looked her up and down as if she were a filly he planned to purchase. "Any experience w'horses?"

"Yes, sir. My father believed that a rider could not be considered accomplished unless said rider knew how to care for a horse properly. I know how to brush my horse down, feed him, apply a hock when necessary, and clean his stall. My father says I have a good seat—for a woman, that is."

Deff laughed heartily. "Yer da's a man's man, fer all that he's a duke. You won't embarrass him here, I expect. I have a horse for you in mind, lass. He's young and frisky. Think you can handle him?"

"What do you think, sir?" she challenged with a smile.

"I think I'll wait and see, but if you can bring this fidgety colt to heel, I'll take me hat off to you."

After dinner, the trainees repaired to study hall. There they concentrated on studying the day's work they were expected to master. The twins put their heads together, but Carter and Perkins sat by themselves.

Riggs asked, "Shall we study together, Fairchild? Learning's easier that way. At least for me."

"I'd be honored, Riggs. Let's take that corner so we don't disturb the others."

The two opened their manuals and set to work, turning to one another for explanation over one puzzling point or another. Most questions involved decoding, the most difficult of topics.

At half past the hour, Olivia said. "I have to leave you now, for I promised to report to Mrs. Hunnicut." Olivia paused. "A question, Riggs. It's about fetching wash water in the morning. It took me too long today. That's why I missed breakfast."

"Yes, I know," he said kindly. "Here's the trick to it, lass. Fetch the water from the well just before bedtime and heat it to a boil in a kettle in the kitchen—no one's working there at that hour. When you return to your room, cover it well with a washing cloth. It may not be as hot as you would like by morning, but it will still be comfortably warm."

"Good advice. I'll try it tonight." She gathered her manuals and began to rise, but Riggs stayed her hand. "What is it?"

He half rose to whisper in her ear. "Carter's a toadeater. He reports everything to the spymaster. Be careful what you say in his hearing."

"You saw Livy off all right? Where's she gone to?" the duke demanded of his daughter Helena when she and Edward arrived at Heatham.

"I don't know her exact location, Father. A coach came to fetch her away."

"So she's got her wish. In training to be a spy, is she?" he asked bitterly, without expecting any answer. "Much against my wishes."

"Don't raise your voice dear," said the duchess calmly.

His Grace bit back a sharp retort. "I'm sorry, Helena, my love. Not your fault. Tell us all you know."

"It was all very hush-hush, I fear." Her eyes lit with amusement.

"What do you find so funny, child?"

"My dear parents, if you only knew the half of it. Her

new wardrobe filled two coaches, but when a driver came for her, he wouldn't allow her to take more than one small portmanteau." She and her mother burst out laughing, for Livy's fondness for new clothes was well known.

"Extraordinary," grumbled her father. "Did she send for them?"

"They won't allow it. You can't see her bed for all the clothing and the trunks she was forced to leave behind. Her chamber resembles an elite shop in Bond Street. She tried to leave you each a letter saying good-bye, but the driver took them. She's not to be allowed to communicate with the outside world during the twelve weeks of her training."

His Grace held his head in his hands. "That long?"

"It's the path she's chosen, Father."

"Chosen? Chosen? What gave her the right to make such a dangerous choice? She forced me to approve, but in truth I never wanted this for her and well she knows it. Am I not her father?"

"Stop it, Tony!" Her Grace warned in a sharp voice. She turned to her daughter and added kindly, "Leave us, dear. Your father and I need to talk."

"Of course, Mother." She rose and kissed first her mother's forehead, and then her father, crossed the room and closed the door quietly behind her.

"Livy must be allowed to follow the path she's chosen. You must accept that, Tony," said Her Grace.

"Why should I, Ellen? Tell me that, will you?"

"Because if you don't, we'll lose her." She went to him and held his head in her hands. "I won't lose my firstborn, Tony. It is you who must give in. Put your mind at ease, dearest. It's a government program, which means she is in capable hands and no harm will come to her. If she fails, you will see her home soon enough. Besides, you did agree to let her go, didn't you?"

The duke ignored this reminder of a weak moment. "What if she succeeds? We lose her to her success. Did you ever think of that?"

"Oh my foolish, foolish darling. If Livy succeeds we shall rejoice for her, for that will be our daughter's finest achievement."

Chapter Five

"There we are, miss," the young girl said, as she finished tying the apron in a neat bow. The plump, round-faced scullery maid adjusted the starched white cap over Olivia's curls and added, "Me cleanin' gown fits you right well."

Olivia nodded and with some hesitation asked, "Thank you for helping me. What's your name, lass?"

"Jenny, miss." She curtseyed, reached to the floor, and handed Olivia an empty pail, a hard-bristled scrubbing brush and a large soft cloth. "Here you are, miss. You'll need these."

Olivia frowned, but took the offering. "What must I do with these?"

Jenny's eyes opened wide. "Don't you know how to scrub a floor?"

"I'm sorry, no. I've never done it before. Can you tell me how?"

Jenny cast her eyes down. "It's a lowly task fer a fine lady like yourself, miss, but on Fridays, I scrub the kitchen floor tiles. You're to do it 'stead o' me today. Mayhap Mrs. Hunnicut told you how it's done?"

Olivia's eyes pleaded as if she were begging for alms. "Please. Tell me how you do it, Jenny."

"Why, on me hands and knees, o'course. I do one small piece o' floor at a time, see? First, you fetch the water from the scullery sink, see? Then heat it. Not too hot, mind, or you'll burn y'self. Dip your rinsin' cloth in and wring it out afore you add a bit 'o soap—it's in that bin next to the sink. Scrub hard with the brush and use the cloth to mop up the suds. You start in the hall from the back stairwell landing, see, and work your way all the way to the galley. Take special care in the galley, miss. Chef Fourier carries on somethin' fierce if there's dirt on the floor where he does his work."

Olivia tried to look cheerful. "Is there anything else I should know?"

Jenny tapped her finger to her cheek. "No need to scrub any of the rooms down here that has a door. Them that's in charge of 'em do that theyselves. Change the water often, mind. Once you empty the final pail outside in the yard, you're done."

Olivia bit her bottom lip. "How long should it take me?"

"I'm allus finished by noon, in time for me lunch." She noted the look of terror in Olivia's eyes. "Don't fret so, miss. It's not hard. You'll get the hang of it in no time. 'Sides, you're better off scrubbin'. T'other lads do much dirtier work. They're made to clean the muck from the chimneys or the ashes from the fireplaces or the horse droppins in the stables. I'm off now. Got to help Mrs. Hunnicut mend the linens."

When Jenny was gone, Olivia filled the pail, heated the water, dipped the rinsing cloth in and wrung it dry, then added some soap. At the stairwell entrance, she lifted the hem of Jenny's uniform, fell to her knees, dipped the brush and began to scrub the tiles. It was tedious work, but she managed to make a game of it. She scrubbed hardest when she pictured the spymaster's face on the floor.

By the time she reached the wider kitchen galley where all meals were prepared, her eyes burned from the strong soap. She had no notion it was laced with lye. Her back was sore, her arms were heavy, her hands were red and raw, Jenny's gown was soaked, and worst of all she'd torn three fingernails.

At last, she scrubbed up to the kitchen door that led to the yard. She opened the door and emptied her final pail. She wrinkled her nose and sneezed from the smell of lye when she returned the pail, the brush and the rinsing cloth to the scullery room and dragged herself up the back stairs to the attic to change for lunch. But when she glanced at the clock on her wall, she heaved a sigh of defeat. She needn't hurry. She'd already missed lunch.

The spymaster presided over staff meetings in the library every Friday afternoon. His instructors arranged themselves on either side of the library table in the middle of the room, seated in comfortable chairs designed for reading and study as well as for staff discussions. Sebastian sat at its head, his secretary Hugh Denville opposite him, quill in hand, ready to record the proceedings. The only one missing was Harry Green, archery and rifle instructor, for he was out on the archery range supervising the trainees.

Sebastian surveyed his staff with a great deal of pride. He'd selected well—the best he could find in each field. Except for long holidays at the end of each training session, the men lived in comfortable quarters at the academy, took their meals together and developed an easy camaraderie among themselves.

Mrs. Hunnicut lived in a well-appointed suite of rooms on the attic floor where Olivia and all the maids had their quarters.

"Good afternoon, gentlemen," he began with little ceremony. He glanced at Mrs. Hunnicut and added, "Ma'am. Reports, please." On his right sat Aaron Foster, codes and ciphers instructor. Sebastian nodded for him to start.

"Not much out of the ordinary to report, except for Carter. He seems to rub the others raw with his superior pose, but as a group, they've acquitted themselves well during this first week. Fairchild shows promise, sir." He chuckled.

Sebastian looked startled. "What?"

"Fairchild doesn't like your class, Spymaster. She told me she thinks intelligence gathering is nothing more than gossip."

It was clear the spymaster didn't appreciate the jest for, when everyone else laughed, he did not. "It is no secret that I was dead set against a woman in our program. How does she fare in martial arts, Sensei?"

Sensei Yukio Nori, the Japanese martial arts expert, whose grasp of the English language was limited, sucked air through one side of his mouth. "Faihchil' velly good in tai chi. Bettah than othahs."

"Fairchild eez my star fencing pupil. Ze others? Pooh! Zey cannot compare, but zey do try to learn," said Fourier.

Sebastian grinned at him. "I understand Fairchild also speaks fluent French. Might that influence your glowing report, Andre?"

"*Oui!*" Given to Gallic exaggeration, Fourier kissed his fingertips and threw them into the air, which caused his colleagues to chortle. He was well-liked, not only for his fencing skills, but also for the excellent cuisine he arranged day in and day out.

Stable master Tom Deff said, "I've no complaint with Fairchild, either, sir. She's become accustomed to riding astride like the others, rather than sidesaddle, the way she was taught. She's fearless. Takes hedges and fences like a gazelle."

"Take care she isn't also reckless. I don't want her to break her foolish neck, Tom. That advice goes for the rest of you as well." He shook his head. "I cannot impress upon all of you more forcefully than this. She must not come to harm under any circumstance. We shall all have to answer for it if she does. Do I make myself clear?"

Tom Deff grinned. "I'll take care she doesn't fall off her horse, sir."

"She's a right one, she is. For a woman, that is. She determined to master push-ups on her first day and refused to give up, though she appeared ready to sink from the effort," Hugh Denville added.

Sebastian frowned.

"Fairchild may need a great deal more practice in the art of self-defense, I fear," said Evelyn Hawes. "I shudder to think what will happen to her when she begins boxing lessons next week."

Sebastian barked a laugh. "Shall we invite Gentleman Jackson to train her, do you think, Evelyn?"

"If Jackson were daft enough to agree, he'd be no gentleman, would he? Who would dare strike a lady? I'd like to recommend we allow her to forgo boxing and work an extra session with Sensei Nori since she does so well with him."

Sebastian's eyes gleamed. "Afraid to climb into the ring with her?"

"No, sir. Not afraid. Terrified, more like."

This brought an amiable laugh from the table.

"You wrong her, my friends. She won't cry off. She isn't missish in the least," objected Mrs. Hunnicut dryly.

"Give us your report, Martha," said Sebastian. "How does she in domesticity?"

With a twinkle in her eye, she said, "This morning she

scrubbed the kitchen floor from the stairwell to the kitchen door leading outside. That's the full length of Wilson Academy. She was so intent on performing her duty, she missed her lunch."

Sebastian struggled to quell the urge to laugh. "Fairchild scrubbed the floor? Astonishing. And she registered no complaint?"

"No. Well, only one small one that doesn't signify." The housekeeper blushed.

"And what was that, if I may ask?"

"It distressed her that she broke her last three nails."

Saturdays were set aside for the trainees to perform personal tasks. They were expected to wash their own clothing, clean their chamber, change their linens and perform all necessary personal grooming activities.

The men set up their bathtub in the study hall on the first floor and took turns bathing. Riggs had thought to tack an amusing note on the door that read, KEEP OUT! THIS MEANS YOU, FAIRCHILD!

But he needn't have bothered with the sign, for Olivia was luxuriating in her own hot bath in front of the warming fireplace in Mrs. Hunnicut's sitting room. Pure heaven. How had she taken such a luxury so for granted all these years, she wondered.

Mrs. Hunnicut peered into the room. "The lads are waiting for me to trim their hair and pare their nails. I'll do the same for you when I return."

"Thank you, Mrs. Hunnicut. My nails are sorely in need of paring now that they've all been shortened by the week's er . . . activities. As to my hair, will you do it up for me?"

"I'm not handy that way, but I'll send Jenny to do it for you, dear. She's much better at it than I am. I'll attend to your nails when I return. Our Saturday luncheons are the only time instructors and trainees have an opportunity to become better acquainted. We find the relaxation of the rules invigorating and you will too, I imagine."

"I look forward to it, then."

Olivia rested her head on the edge of the tub and let her thoughts wander.

What an extraordinary week this has been! It's as if I've never known any life other than this one. An odd sensation. Do I miss my family? Yes and no. I find being here much to my liking, except for the dour spymaster who clearly wishes me as far away as Scotland. Or Hades, perhaps. Yet when he made love to me at the Hobbleton Ball in London, it was as if he were a different man. I liked his touch then. I'd like it now if he weren't such a grumpy bear.

When the bathwater cooled, she rose and dressed for teatime. Mrs. Hunnicut had suggested she wear her own clothing for the occasion, the gown she'd worn when she arrived at Wilson Academy. When Jenny appeared and fixed her hair for her, she couldn't have been more pleased. The young scullery maid had talent far beyond scrubbing floors. While she waited for Mrs. Hunnicut to repair her ragged nails, Olivia occupied herself with the many ladies magazines the housekeeper was so fond of reading. It was a most relaxing morning.

A luncheon buffet was served in the drawing room on the ground floor. The terrace doors had been thrown open, for it was a warm summer day.

"Riggs! How well you look," said Olivia. "And you, Perkins. You too, Carter. Why, we all look almost human. I feel as though we're at a party in London." She stopped to look around her. "But where are the twins?"

Rufus Riggs laughed. "They'll be here shortly, Fairchild. They're planning a bit of mischief, I think."

The door opened to their instructors, all dressed in the pink of fashion. Olivia should not have been surprised to find the spymaster outshining his instructors in dress. He wore well-made buckskin trousers tucked into gleaming Hessians and a blue coat obviously made by the finest of London tailors. A handsome light blue vest was buttoned over an excellent white shirt, his neatly tied neckpiece completing the costume.

He lost no time in mingling with the trainees. In a warm voice, he said, "Congratulations to you all. I received nothing but glowing reports on your progress at our staff meeting yesterday. You do us proud. I trust your second week will be just as rewarding." He looked around him. "But where are the twins?"

"Here, sir," they answered in unison. They were dressed in matching apparel down to their boots.

"Who, may I ask, is whom, gentlemen?"

"Ah, that's for you to guess, sir. *We* know who we are, but do you? We challenge all of you. Can anyone tell us apart?"

Much delight was taken in trying to guess, a sport in which the trainees and their instructors ventured varied opinions. But Olivia did not participate. Instead, she hung back and observed the merriment, her hand stroking her chin.

"What is your guess, my dear?" Mrs. Hunnicut asked her at last.

She looked around the room. "I needn't guess. I've always been able to tell these two rascals apart, no matter how hard they try to swindle me."

"How clever you are, Fairchild. Do tell. I can't wait to hear," challenged John Carter, his voice dripping with sarcasm.

Olivia tilted her head at him and smiled. "I warn you, Carter. You'll owe me an apology for your challenge." She walked up to the twins, took each by a hand and searched their grinning faces. "You devils! Your dimple is much deeper when you smile, William. And you, Robert, curl your lip when you frown."

"Right you are. Good show, Fairchild!" said Robert. "Apologize, Carter. You owe it to her."

Carter turned his attention to the sideboard and filled his plate. He looked up at the others and said, "Apologize? For what? Fairchild merely ventured a wild guess and happened to hit the mark. I knew the difference between you two all the time."

Olivia's self-appointed champion, a very red-faced Riggs, confronted him. "That's unkind in you, Carter. Apologize to the lady, or I'll land you a . . ."

The room went silent until Hawes spoke up. "No challenges here, Riggs. Save it for the boxing ring."

"With pleasure, sir!" said Riggs, uncurling his balled fists.

"As you wish, but I'm handy with the gloves," added Carter in a bored tone.

Hawes narrowed his eyes. "Which do you prefer, then? Boxing or wrestling?"

"Boxing," said Carter.

"Wrestling," said Riggs at the same time.

"A coin toss, then. In class on Monday, gentlemen."

When the two combatants continued to glare at one another, Sebastian intervened. "That's enough, you two. On Saturdays we behave like ladies and gentlemen. This is meant as an essential part of your training."

The instructors rose to the occasion by attaching themselves to one or the other of the trainees and engaging them in animated conversation.

Mrs. Hunnicut was left to engage Carter in conversation, for no one else approached him to sooth his arrogant feathers. She drew him to a quiet corner of the drawing room. "Tell me, Carter. Where were you raised? Have you family? How do you take your tea?"

Sebastian offered Olivia his arm. "I fancy a stroll in our garden, Fairchild. Care to join me?"

Shocked at this pleasantry, she placed her hand on his arm. When he covered it with one of his hands, his touch sent a quiver of excitement through her. She drew in her breath and said, "Yes, sir. I would like that." He led her outdoors and down the two steps into the garden where summer flower buds were already a riot of color lining the pathway.

"Don't look so down in the mouth, Fairchild. I don't consider you at fault for the unpardonable behavior shown by Carter and Riggs."

"Kind of you to say so, sir. I was afraid you'd think otherwise."

"Shall we sit here?" He pointed to a bench and led her to it. "I owe you an apology."

She looked up at him in surprise. "An apology, sir? For what?"

"For *my* unpardonable behavior on your first day."

"Thank you for that, sir. May I ask what made you change your mind?"

"I received glowing reports about your progress from my staff. I only hope . . ."

His final words made her wary. What was he getting at? "What is it you hope, sir?"

"Let me be frank, Fairchild. I hope that my instructors aren't easier with you than with the other trainees because you are a mere woman."

His remark took her warm feelings away and replaced them with indignation. When she could trust herself to speak, she asked, "Have you reason to think they have been too easy with me?"

"You complained of breaking some of your fingernails, didn't you?"

She forced a laugh, but her eyes betrayed her anger. "To

shreds. Not some. All ten of them. My remark was directed to Mrs. Hunnicut when she asked if I needed her to pare them."

Bloody hell! I've put my foot in my mouth. He threw his hands up in surrender. "I'm sorry. No need to chastise me."

"It appears you have little faith in your instructors' opinions. Or in me."

"I've made you angry, I see. I beg your pardon. Can you forgive me?"

"Of course, *sir.*" She rose and curtseyed. "How kind of you to favor me with your attentions this afternoon. Will you excuse me?" She turned toward the terrace and hurried away.

Sebastian watched her depart. *Damn! I made a mess of it. Just when I was making progress with her, too.* He shifted uncomfortably on the bench. He was hard and it showed. He didn't know whether he wanted to kill her for the way she made him feel, or kiss her senseless for the very same reason.

After chapel on Sunday morning, the trainees were free to rest and to study. It rained all day, destroying all thought of outdoor pursuits. Having had enough of the company of her fellow trainees, Olivia took advantage of Mrs. Hunnicut's offer to make use of her sitting room. She brought her study manuals from her room down the hall, and settled into one of the comfortable chairs in front of the fireplace. She was seated opposite her hostess, who was busy with her needlepoint.

"How peaceful it is here, ma'am. You are very kind to allow me to intrude on you in this way."

"Nonsense, Fairchild. I enjoy your company." A knock on the door interrupted her. " There's our tea, dear." She began to rise.

But Olivia objected. In a soft voice, she said, "I'll get it, ma'am." She waited at the door while the maid placed the tea tray on the table, bobbed a curtsey and left the room.

Olivia shut the door and asked, "How do you take your tea, ma'am? Let me prepare it for you."

"Cream, no sugar, thank you."

Olivia served her the tea, offered her the pastry tray, and served herself before sitting back down. "Have you always been the housekeeper at Wilson Academy, ma'am?"

"I was an earl's housekeeper in Leeds before I married. In fact, I met the spymaster when he visited there before the war. When Wilson Academy was completed to his satisfaction, he wrote to me and offered me this position. I jumped at the chance, for the challenge of being an instructor as well as housekeeper intrigued me. My employer did not stand in my way. And here I am.

"I feel as though the trainees have become my children and the instructors my family. We all live on the grounds, you see. We meet for cocktails in the drawing room before dinner, so we've grown to know one another quite well. I'm a widow and it's less lonely for me here among such congenial company."

"Are none of the instructors married?"

"Aaron Foster is a widower. He came out of retirement at Viscount Sidmouth's urging. He's well-known in his field. He has a son in the army, I believe. The others are unmarried, except for Tom Deff. He has a wife, three grown sons and two daughters in Ireland. They rely on his financial support. There's not much honest work to be had there. He owns a horse breeding farm that his sons tend in his absence. He returns to see them all when we take our holiday in the fall, after your training is done."

"Do you enjoy your role here?"

"Oh yes. It's important work and I take it seriously. Most gratifying, my dear. And not in the least bit difficult. I've managed to earn enough to see me in comfort when I retire. And having no family I can call my own, I dearly love to mother all you young ones."

Olivia smiled. "You are like a mother to all of us, ma'am."

"Do you have a mother?"

"Oh, yes. And a father. And four sisters and one brother. I miss them all."

"I expect you do." She glanced at the clock on the mantel. "Oh dear. Just look at the hour. Time to make ready for dinner, my dear."

Chapter Six

A coin was tossed and the news that the grudge between Carter and Riggs was to be settled in the boxing ring swept through the academy like rain on a windswept day. Indeed, secrets of any kind weren't easy to keep, for the staff was large and their ears larger.

The boxing ring, raised less than a foot off the floor, occupied space on the second floor where all the classrooms were situated. The ring's heavy ropes were tied securely on posts, to form a square. The floor of the ring was covered with canvas over a layer of straw meant to cushion falls.

The match between Riggs and Carter caused great interest. For the Reed twins, having booked bets at local county fair competitions, this was an unexpected opportunity. Thus, betting fever gripped the entire household, infecting staff and servants alike. News spread that the twins were giving odds on the sly, charging every bettor a mere ha'pence for their services. A copper would gain you even money if Carter, the odds-on favorite for his extra weight, won. If Riggs chanced to win the match, the odds were ten to one. Perkins bet his copper on Riggs, more out of loyalty than of any hope

Riggs would be able to defeat Carter, but Olivia chose not to bet at all, though her heart was with Riggs, her defender.

The instructors, older, wiser and less loyal, put their money on Carter. The servants also bet heavily on Carter, while a few favored the underdog in the hope of making a killing. Besides, the odds were favorable.

When the trainees and the teaching staff filed into the room at the appointed time, they discovered an unusual number of servants already there. Armed with buckets, mops and brooms, cleaning cloths and polishes, those present— footmen and under maids—appeared to take an unusual interest in exercising their diligence in cleaning tasks. Grooms, stablemen, gardeners and kitchen workers found reason to help their burdened brethren.

"Quite a crowd today, Hugh," Sebastian remarked, referring to the mob crammed into his supposedly secret observation walkway, their noses pressed to the small windows within.

Denville grinned. "Windows need cleaning, sir. Haven't been washed in years. Shouldn't we let them have their bit of fun today?"

"Far be it from me to spoil it," Sebastian answered, his speech tinged with amusement. His eyes swept the room and lit on Olivia, her brows knit with worry as she watched the combatants climb into the ring.

Rufus Riggs and John Carter faced one another stripped to the waist. Boxing master Evelyn Hawes entered and planted himself in the middle of the ring, at once beckoning them to come forward.

"Right, lads. Three rounds, three minutes each. Perkins, Denville and Foster have agreed to judge. Their decision is final and will settle your grievances once and for all. If either of you carry your grudge any further, you'll be subject to severe penalties. And no hitting below the waist, mind. If you do, you forfeit at once."

Hawes nodded to Tom Deff, who held the stopwatch. "When I say 'begin,' go at it, lads. And when I say 'time,' stop. Is that clear?" Both men nodded in agreement.

"Begin."

The two circled one another like tigers. When Carter jabbed, Riggs danced back. Carter stalked and connected with a right cross. Riggs responded with a jab of his own, followed by an uppercut. Their moves drew shouts from the spectators, but neither fighter paid attention to them. Carter was aggressive in his pursuit, and Riggs used clever foot-work to avoid the worst of Carter's hits.

Just as Hawes shouted " Time," ending the first round, Carter connected with a right cross to Riggs' eye. Shouts of "foul" were heard from some who thought Carter landed his vicious punch *after* Hawes ended the round. Hawes ignored the protests and waved the two men to diagonally opposite corners where waiting footmen wiped their sweating faces and offered them water.

The second round passed with Carter besting Riggs in the sheer number of punches thrown. Alarmed that Riggs' eye had begun to swell, Olivia hurried to the spymaster's side and pleaded, "You must stop the match now, sir. Riggs can barely see."

He frowned at her yet his eyes were kind. "Sorry, Fairchild. Much as I'd like to bow to your wishes, to stop it now would be a mistake. There's nothing to be gained from it except an indignant uproar from the servants and the staff. The men must be allowed to finish."

"I might have known you'd be enjoying this *barbaric* slaughter. *Sir!*"

"You'll have to accept my judgment in this, Fairchild. It's too far gone."

"Time," said Hawes, but he had to step in and separate them, for neither man stopped jabbing at the other. He took each man by the ear and shouted angrily, "I said time!"

Olivia ran to Riggs' corner and pleaded with him. "Give up, Rufus, and end it! Carter outweighs you by at least a stone and you're tiring. You've already acquitted yourself well. There's no shame attached to you if you concede."

"Never! Don't ask it of me, Fairchild, please." He turned his head to the footman who offered him water. As he drank, the servant wiped the sweat from his glistening body. He grasped the cloth from him and mopped his face.

"Begin, gentlemen," said Hawes and both men surged toward one another for the final round, Carter again having the advantage of weight and speed. Riggs heaved forward and stumbled. It was obvious that he was tiring. His right eye was swollen shut, yet he fought on, landing occasional blows to Carter's ribs while Carter pummeled him with bruising jabs and uppercuts and right crosses.

The match ended halfway through the final round, an ending that stunned every spectator and brought a hush to the room. Riggs had managed to summon some hidden strength within him and, with perfect coordination and timing, blocked Carter's final left hook, swept his right fist up and connected it to Carter's chin. The uppercut snapped his opponent's head back, his legs buckled and he fell to the canvas.

The spectators held their collective breath while Hawes counted to ten. When Carter did not rise, the boxing master took Riggs' hand and held it high in the air. "Winner!" he shouted.

Pandemonium broke loose. Winning bettors cheered and losers grumbled as Hawes waved the winner to his corner and bent to the floor on one leg to examine the fallen man.

Carter rose on one elbow and whispered, "Will you help me up, sir?"

Hawes held him so he wouldn't fall, for his knees failed him. The loser held up a hand and waited for the room to quiet.

He turned to the victor and saluted him. "Good show, Riggs. My apologies to you, sir." His eyes searched the room for Olivia. "Fairchild? I offer you my apologies as well."

London—Helena sat on the bench in Darlington's garden. She fidgeted with her handkerchief while she waited for her love to return from the home office. When he arrived at last, she said in a rush of words, "Oh my darling. We haven't much time. I promised my father I would be ready to return to Brighton with him tonight. Heaven only knows it was hard enough to get him to allow me to accompany him to London. I had to lie and tell him I must see my modiste for a fitting. What kept you so long?"

Without a word, Darlington took both her hands and pulled her up into his arms. She received his kiss with passionate eagerness, as though she hadn't seen him in years. He stopped and searched her eyes when he felt her tears on his face.

"Is something wrong, my love? Why all the tears?"

"Oh, Chris. I dread being separated from you just when I need your strength most. If we were already married I could bear it better."

"What's the matter?"

"Father is still in such a pet about Livy, I haven't the heart to broach him about our betrothal."

Chris hugged her to him. It soothed her to be held thus by the man she had loved since they were children. At last she said, "Livy suggested we settle for a long betrothal. Do you think he would agree?"

Chris laughed. "Yes. If you threaten to elope with me to Gretna Green."

She giggled. "She thought I might hint at that."

"If you really want such a result, you may have to bludgeon your father with a sledgehammer."

"Heaven forbid!" Helena paced back and forth. When she stopped, she said, "What then? I want to be your wife, Chris. And I don't want to wait for years and years. As it is, we won't see one another until the fall. By then, you may be assigned to a foreign post, and we'll be separated even longer. Perhaps we ought to run off to Gretna Green and end the misery of being apart."

He took her hand and searched her face. "No, Helena. No Gretna Green for us. You are my goddess. I worship you too much to subject you to such a sorry affair."

"Anything is better than nothing! This interminable waiting for married life to begin is maddening! Chris? Why don't you seduce me? If I'm with child, my father will have no choice."

He looked affronted by the idea. "Never, my darling. That way leads to misery and censure as well. Besides, I won't have our child born out of wedlock." He paused a moment. "There may be a way, after all."

"Do tell, my irresistible lover." She nuzzled him.

"Don't distract me with your kisses, you minx. The time is right for me to pay another visit to Heatham to see the duke. I'm sure I can arrange for a brief leave from the home office."

"Father has already turned you down twice. What will you say this time that will make him change his mind?"

"He turned me down before because I'm a second son and my prospects were bleak. Now if you had fallen in love with my brother Aubrey who is a marquis . . ."

She laughed. "Pooh! He's the stuffiest man alive. Not at all like you."

"I intend to inform your father that my prospects have greatly improved since the last time I begged for your hand. The house next to yours is mine, generously deeded to me by my brother on my birthday this year, and I have my eye on a parcel of land not far from Bath. The owner has accepted my offer and we've drawn up a contract, with the provision that he be allowed to remain there for the rest of his days. And though I wish him no ill, he *is* old and frail. He has no family, either. The money I shall pay him will go to his faithful servants."

Helena's eyes sparkled in triumph. "Chris! That means you'll become landed gentry! That would make such a difference. Let's hope Father sees it that way."

"I'll stop to see Olivia on the way to Heatham as well." He grinned at the look of surprise on her face. "Did you think I didn't know where she is, you goose? Why shouldn't I know? After all, I work for the home secretary."

"How stupid of me. What a good idea, my darling. And you'll inform Father that Livy is well?"

"That's the ticket, my love." He removed his watch from his vest pocket and examined the time. "We have only one hour left, wife-to-be. Barely enough time to say our final farewells properly."

"When will I see you?"

"Give me time to clear things with Viscount Sidmouth. I'll spend a day or two visiting your sister and leave for Brighton from there. We'll see one another soon, I promise you, my dearest goddess." He took her in his arms and kissed her long and hard.

The duke finished the meeting with his three financial advisors in time to lunch at White's where he was expected by two old friends, both colleagues in parliament as well. Lord Gilliam Davis and Marquis Jarvis Henshaw arrived there before him, he was pleased to see. The three had much to talk about, for they were Tories—leaders of their party—and though Parliament was adjourned, preparations for the next session were necessary.

"You're late, Tony. What kept you so long?"

"How are you, Gilly? Jarvis? Sorry I'm late. Financial advisors talked far too long." The duke took his seat and gave his order to the waiter. He was about to say something to his companions when they were interrupted.

"Hello there, Fairchild. Fancy meeting you here. I thought you were at Heatham," said Viscount Sidmouth standing at the table.

His familiarity irked the duke, who had more than one reason to dislike the trespasser. "Hello, Sidmouth. You know my associates, I'm sure."

"Of course I do. Good afternoon, gentlemen." He appeared to hesitate, as if waiting for an invitation to join them. Sidmouth was nothing if not politically astute. It was a point with him to curry favor with members of Parliament. One never knew when one might need their votes.

"Nice to see you again, home secretary," the duke said affably, hiding his true feelings. He turned to his friends, sending an unmistakable message of dismissal to the viscount.

But the gentleman was undeterred. "I hear your daughter is doing quite well, Fairchild."

The duke considered murder. It would not be out of place for such a social blunder. His colleagues knew nothing about the whereabouts of Olivia and he preferred to keep them in ignorance. "Yes. Now if you'll excuse us?"

"I understand. You're busy." Sidmouth bowed, an obsequious smile on his face, and withdrew.

"Can you believe the nerve of the man?" asked Lord Davis. "He wants something, but what?"

"Can't be he wants to be prime minister again, can it?"

said Marquis Henshaw. His sly wit met with laughter, for Sidmouth had proved such a disaster as prime minister, William Pitt the Younger was requested to return to the position.

"Sidmouth is a bloody fool," exploded the duke. "He mucked up that sorry Treaty of Amiens with France, didn't he? What's he planning now, I wonder?"

"Rumor has it he's trying to crush the opposition. He's even created a spy school to support his plans. Have you heard anything about this secret operation?"

"No, nothing," said the duke. He beckoned to the waiter and said, "I'll have another brandy. Make it a double this time."

Chapter Seven

The outdoor archery range was within walking distance of the main building. The space that had been cleared resembled a long rectangle facing several round white paper targets. These were attached to round straw mats attached to easels. The paper targets contained clearly marked concentric circles, each painted a different color, each narrower in circumference than the next, beginning with the largest at the outer edge, and ending in the smallest circle in the center, which was painted black.

Olivia rummaged through the pile, searching for an archery glove small enough for her hand. Weaponry instructor Harry Green, an expert marksman in archery, rifle and pistols, observed her and offered, "I'll have one made to fit you, Fairchild. Find one that you can make do with for today." He was a short, block of a man, powerfully built, with a ruddy complexion. He turned to the other trainees and began his lecture.

"Right, then. Pay attention, for archery will help you sharpen your skills in marksmanship. Any of you had training?"

Carter's hand shot up. "I have, sir."

" Toadeater," Riggs whispered to Olivia.

Green said, "Let's see what you can do, lad. Step up to the line. Two tries."

John chose a bow and two arrows and took his stance. When the instructor nodded, he let loose the first arrow. It fell into the grass, several feet short of the target. Derisive laughter erupted, but it was short-lived.

"I'll have none of that, you lot!" the instructor warned in a firm tone. Carter's second shot hit the target on the gold circle, the outermost ring. "Nice try, Carter."

As he was about to speak, Olivia interrupted in a small voice, "Excuse me, sir. I've had a bit of training."

"All right, Fairchild. Show us what you can do."

Olivia chose a bow and two arrows, put her left foot on the line and assumed the proper stance. She leaned forward and squinted at the target, then placed her arrow in the bow, pulled it back and let go. It soared in an arc and hit the circle just above the bull's eye. Her second shot was a direct bull's eye.

Her face flushed with pleasure when she heard murmurs of approval, but Instructor Green scotched the sounds with a stern look. "That will do, lads. Good work, Fairchild. You have a keen eye." He turned to the others and added, "We'll begin with proper stance."

Carter turned to Olivia. "Nice work, Fairchild."

Surprised at the sincerity in his tone, she said, "Why thank you, Carter. Appreciate it."

"Darlington," said Sebastian in surprise. "Welcome to the academy. A rare pleasure indeed. I hadn't expected you. Thought you'd be long gone on your special assignment by now."

Chris shook the hand Sebastian offered. "I'm anxious to

be off, but Sidmouth finds one task after another to detain me. How are you, Sebastian? How is your new class faring?"

"No complaints. Come. Join me for lunch and tell me what brings you here."

Sebastian led him into his private dining room. He signaled to the footman to set another place while a second footman filled their goblets with wine. He dismissed them both by saying, "Thank you. We'll help ourselves from the sideboard." They bowed and retreated at once.

The two filled their plates and returned to the table. "We're private now, but I must caution you. Speak in a low voice, Chris. The servants are like bees bent on pollination. Secrets flit from flower to flower until the whole of the academy blossoms with gossip."

Chris grinned. "Just like the home office, if I may say so."

When they had finished their lunch, Chris sat back in his chair. "I've come for two reasons. The first is official business. Prince Joachim of Zarkovia has been invited to visit London by the Regent. He's to sign a treaty allowing favorable trade between our two countries. It gives us our first port on the Baltic Sea for trade purposes."

Sebastian refilled Darlington's goblet. "Go on."

"It's a small country. Our spies report that the king is a despot and there is some unrest in the state. We must protect the prince from assassination."

"From Zarkovian anarchists?"

"No. We don't think they are the problem. While they would rejoice if the young prince were assassinated on English soil, we have more to worry about from the Russians. The czar does not like this treaty by half. It threatens his domination of the Baltic, you see. Russian assassins may already be hiding here in England. We'll need every man available to see no harm comes to the young prince. He's a mere seventeen, but his father is dying. It won't be long before he takes the reins. Needless to say, England wants his friendship."

"When is the prince due to arrive?"

"Barring foul weather, he and his delegation will disembark at the East India docks in six weeks. The Regent is planning a grand celebration to herald his arrival. You mustn't share this news with anyone, Sebastian. We don't want the information to fall into the wrong hands."

"Who's in charge of the prince's protection when he steps on English soil?"

Chris smiled. "Who do you think? The responsibility falls on your head and mine. I'm assigned to direct operations from the home office and you're in charge of your people. As usual, we'll communicate through our customary channels. I brought preliminary plans with me."

Sebastian's spirits rose. Here was a challenge worthy of his talents. "Excellent. We'll go over them in my office."

Chris grinned. "And when we're finished, I'll tell you my other reason for today's visit."

Riding instructor Tom Deff sat astride his horse in the stable yard and faced the trainees. "You'll be jumpin' fences this afternoon," he said. "Some fences higher than others. We've had so much rain, I don't have to remind you to beware the soggy ground beneath each fence. And mind you don't over-tax your horse. They're all prime goers, well used to taking jumps, but they'll balk if you push 'em too hard. You've all been over the course, so you know your direction. Be back in one hour. Questions?"

"Can we make it a race, sir?" asked one of the twins.

Deff thought a moment. "What say you all? Shall it be a race?"

Eager heads nodded as one for the sheer sport of it.

Deff glared at the twins. "But there'll be no betting, BillyBob."

Disappointed, Billy answered for them both. "Yes, sir,"

"Sir?"

"Yes, Fairchild?"

Olivia had mischief in her eyes. "Begging pardon, sir, but a race should have a prize."

Tom Deff checked the urge to laugh. "What do you suggest, lass?"

The taciturn Perkins made the winning suggestion. "Last one back forfeits tonight's dessert to the winner!" There were so few pleasures during their harsh training program, this seemed to everyone an excellent notion. Especially since they had learned at breakfast that the prize was to be plum pudding and a dollop of crème fraîche.

Deff consulted his watch and announced, "Ready? Go!"

The trainees tore across the open field with reckless abandon. Olivia surged forward, head down, reins held high, but the others were not far behind. She took the first fence easily. But Carter overtook her on the open field. She spurred her horse on and took the next fence first. He was right behind her.

Her advantage was her skill. An accomplished horsewoman, she'd been riding beside her father at Heatham as well as in London since she was five years old. When Her Grace seemed unlikely to bear more children, the duke had despaired and had devoted himself to teaching his willing daughter.

His Grace was overjoyed when his wife managed to birth three more healthy children in rapid succession—Helena, Edward his heir and Georgiana. Mary was born two years later, but Jane, his youngest at eight years of age, was born at a time when the duke and his duchess had supposed themselves to have been past having more children.

Olivia was determined to win the race. She pressed forward, neck and neck with Carter. They rode that way up to the final fence, when disaster struck. Carter, whose horse hesitated at the height of the fence, managed to rein in, but Olivia was unable to do the same. Her horse reared back on his hind legs and stopped so abruptly, she flew over the fence and landed in the muddy ditch on the other side.

Carter dismounted and hurried to her, concern on his face. "Are you all right, Fairchild?" He lifted her out of the way and set her on her feet just as the others thundered by.

"Thank you, Carter. But for you, I'd still be in the mud. We've both lost the race, I fear, but I'll forfeit my dessert to you anyway."

He grinned. "I'll take it as my reward for my unaccustomed chivalry, lass. Here. Hold my reins and I'll get your horse."

"Keep it up, Carter. Your new . . . humility is a good thing." Her laugh caused a stitch in her side. Once back at the stables, when she finished brushing and watering her horse, Olivia made her way slowly back to her room, surprised to find Mrs. Hunnicut waiting for her.

"You're limping, Fairchild. Are you hurt? Heavens, you're covered with mud! And today of all days. Well, there's no help for it. Come to my room and I'll send for a tub. We must hurry."

Puzzled, Olivia asked, "Why must we hurry, ma'am?"

"The spymaster has ordered you to join him for dinner. He has a visitor from London. You know how annoyed he gets when anyone is late."

"Who is his guest, ma'am?"

"I don't know, lass. I do know we have less than an hour to make you presentable. I've already had your dinner gown brushed. Jenny will come up to do your hair."

Olivia was grateful for the bath, but she did not have the

luxury of relaxing in the hot water for too long. Her thoughts were occupied with the mysterious dinner guest. Could it be her father? Had he come to plead with her to come home with him? How did he find out her secret location?

The second week of training was coming to an end. There were only ten weeks remaining and she was determined to complete the course. The questions plagued her so, she had little time to dwell on her aches and pains.

When she was fully dressed, Mrs. Hunnicut had to tie her sash tighter, for she had lost weight and her gown had grown too large. The housekeeper sat Olivia down at the dressing table where Jenny proceeded to curl her hair.

"Have a look, milady," said Jenny when she had finished. "Is it to your liking?"

The image staring back at Olivia startled her. *Is this me? How can I have changed in so short a time? I don't recognize this lady in the ball gown, hair curled over ribbons in such a delightful manner. This can't be the same woman who began just two weeks ago at Wilson Academy, can it?*

She turned to the maid and said, "You're a genius, Jenny. With your skill, I'd recommend you as abigail to any one of the finest ladies in England."

The young scullery maid beamed with satisfaction. When Mrs. Hunnicut entered the room, she drew in her breath.

"Oh my dear. How lovely you look. I barely recognize the proper London lass I see before me. I've become far too ac-customed to seeing you in your training clothes, Fairchild. Thank you, Jenny. You've done a fine job. That will be all." When the scullery maid curtseyed and departed, Mrs. Hun-nicut examined Olivia with a critical eye. "You look a bit pale, dear. Are you feeling quite the thing?"

"I'm well enough, ma'am. The thing is, I'm suffering the

effects of a tumble from my horse this afternoon. I dearly hope I'll be able to sit through dinner."

Mrs. Hunnicut smiled. "I see it in your face. Of all places to feel sore. I'll send word ahead to cushion your chair with a soft pillow."

"Thank you, ma'am."

"Pinch your cheeks for color, Fairchild. Oh, dear. Look at the time. You mustn't keep the spymaster and his guest waiting. Do hurry, won't you?"

She took the stairs as quickly as she could, given her injury. When she reached the drawing room, the footman held the door for her. An unfamiliar gentleman with his back to her stood at the terrace door looking out. When he turned around to face her, he gasped in delight.

"Chris!" she shouted. She flew across the floor and flung her arms around him. Her words came out in a rush. "You can't know how happy I am to see you. How is Helena? My other sisters? What news of Edward? My parents?"

"All well, Fairchild. They're at Heatham except for Edward, who's visiting friends." He held her at arms-length. "Let me look at you, Livy. Only Helena knows I'm here and she's bound to press me for a full report. You've lost weight. And you're pale. Are you all right?"

"It's nothing, Chris dearest. My horse bolted at the last fence and I flew over it right into the mud." She leaned forward to whisper in his ear. "Truth be known, my seat hurts a great deal more than my pride."

"Evening, Fairchild. What would you like to drink?" asked Sebastian upon entering the drawing room.

"Thank you, sir. Nothing, sir."

He eyed her, the corners of his lips trying to suppress a quiver. "How are you this evening, Fairchild. Everything all right?"

He knows! "Yes, sir. Thank you for your kind invitation this evening, sir. Mr. Darlington is an old family friend, sir."

He poured Madeira for Chris and himself. "Nothing to do with me. Thank Darlington. He requested your presence. I'll leave you to discuss family matters. You may join us for dinner." He turned and left the room, his Madeira in hand.

She sighed. "Oh dear, Chris. He's always so angry with me."

"No, Livy. It's just his way."

"No it isn't. He wishes me to hell." She had a brief vision of that other Sebastian. The rude man who tried to ravish her at the Hobbleton Ball. The man she had half hoped would succeed.

Chris laughed. "Nothing of the kind, you ninny. I will admit that the spymaster may be irritated because he wasn't given a choice in your selection for his program. I've known Sebastian since our school days at Oxford. He rather likes having his own way. Unfortunately, so does the home secretary. Rumor has it that there was an explosion that day, what with the spymaster threatening to resign and the home secretary threatening to accept his resignation."

Another vision brought her back to the hallway on her last day of work in the home office. Of course! The man who knocked her down was none other than the spymaster storming out of the home secretary's office!

Olivia changed the subject. "Why have you come, Chris? Am I the reason? Has my father ordered you to escort me home in disgrace?"

He barked a laugh. "Whatever put that notion in your head, you silly child? It's no such thing, but you have to own you've caused quite a bit of a stir. Your father ran into Viscount Sidmouth at White's when he was in London on business, according to Helena. My good fortune that she accompanied him, for it gave us some time together."

"They met? I was afraid of that."

"They are acquainted, you know."

"So the viscount informed me when I pressed him for this opportunity. Well? What's the verdict? Am I to stay or am I to go?"

"You lead a charmed life, Livy. Sidmouth told me he took a tough stance and wouldn't back down. He convinced your father that, should you succeed, you would be a major asset to our program."

Olivia laughed at that. "Are you telling me that Sidmouth won the day? I know my father, Chris. He doesn't take kindly to opposition." She paused. "However, if Sidmouth so much as hinted that I might fail, it would get father's back up. In our family, we aren't allowed to fail, you see."

"So Helena tells me. She's as stubborn as you are, Livy. She refuses to fail in her quest to marry me." He fell silent for a moment, a frown on his face.

"What's troubling you, dear friend?"

"It's your father, Livy. He behaves as though Helena is sinking beneath her for wanting to be my wife."

"I know he's rejected your suit twice, but you must keep after him. He'll give in eventually. In spite of his bluster, he loves us all too much to cause a permanent rift."

"To tell the truth, Helena and I have come up with a new plan. I'm on my way to Heatham, to try to convince him to change his mind."

Her eyes lit with laughter. "And you stopped here so you'd have news of me to report? He'll be happy to hear it, but don't you dare tell him I fell off a horse. I'd never hear the end of it. My father's bark is much worse than his bite. He'll rant and he'll rave, but eventually, he'll give in."

"I'd almost given up hope, but my fortune has taken a turn for the better. If my new plea falls on deaf ears, your sister and I may well have to elope to Gretna Green."

"No. Don't do that. Not the thing at all, Chris. With my

father, all his children know that to get what we want, we need only to threaten him with defiance. We learned that lesson early on. Trust Helena to find a way to succeed should you fail this time. She loves you too much to give in to Father. And she'll have help."

"Help?"

She grinned. "From my mother. When we cannot convince the duke of the justice of our cause, we turn to the duchess. Should you fail, remind Helena to confide her plans for Gretna Green to Mother and leave her to do the rest."

"Dinner is served," interrupted the butler.

They entered the dining room in high spirits. The spymaster was already there. He was holding her chair out for her, the one with the added pillow. As she took her seat, he murmured into her ear, "Having trouble sitting, Fairchild?"

"What do you mean, sir?"

He took his own seat and said, "How was your ride this afternoon? Manage to take all the fences, did you?"

Oh how she wished she could wipe that detestable smirk off his face. "Why no, sir. How kind of you to inquire. Matter of fact, my horse bolted at the final fence and sent me flying. Fortunately, the soft mud cushioned my fall."

Chris couldn't fail to notice the hostility between them. He chuckled. "She's usually a bruising rider, Brooks. I ought to know. She's beaten me in races many times over."

Sebastian's smile was strained but he did not respond.

Even with the pillow, the seat was uncomfortable. Olivia squirmed as she nodded to the footman to refill her goblet with wine.

"Enjoying the wine, Fairchild?"

"My first opportunity to sample it, sir. You have an excellent cellar, sir." She emptied her glass and waved it at the footman for another refill.

Chris tried to warn her to behave. He whispered, "Go easy, Livy. You're not accustomed to wine."

"Nonsense.. I'm well able to judge for myself when enough is enough." She drained her third goblet and signaled the footman for more. He did not so much as favor her with a glance, for he had received a discreet signal from the spymaster.

"You may retire to the drawing room, Fairchild," Sebastian said at the end of dinner.

"Of course, sir. I'll leave you gentlemen to your brandy." She rose and added, "Do join me for tea afterwards." Though she was unsteady on her feet, she managed to reach the door without stumbling. She tilted her head and smiled a flirtatious smile. "Don't be long, you two."

When the door shut behind her, Chris collapsed in a burst of laughter.

"I fail to see any humor in this, Darlington. She's as drunk as a tavern wench," Sebastian said, his lips pressed together as if he were a disapproving schoolmaster.

"Where's your sense of humor, old chap?"

Sebastian frowned. "I seem to lose it when I am forced to deal with Fairchild."

"Be warned, my friend. She feels the same way about you. You've got her back up. I've known her most of my life. She'll cross you every chance she gets. She's the oldest of a large family and is much indulged. If I were you, I'd ignore her attempts to get the better of you."

Not until Hell freezes over. I'll pluck this thorn from my side if it's the last thing I do. He finished his brandy and rose from his seat. "Perhaps we should join Fairchild. I'd like to make sure she hasn't fallen and hit her head on the marble floor."

Chris laughed at his intended jest, at the same time aware of the resentment behind this remark. "Good idea. I'll say my good-byes to her, for I leave for Heatham early in the morning."

As it turned out, there was no need for them to rush. Olivia was sprawled on the sofa, snoring loud enough to wake the dead. Sebastian lost his reserve and collapsed in a chair, his laughter at the sight of his inebriated trainee infecting Darlington as well.

Chapter Eight

Wilson Academy—Monday, The Fifteenth of July

Sebastian made notes on a separate pad as he read Darlington's proposal for safeguarding Prince Joachim and his entourage. The time was drawing near, for the Zarkovian prince was due shortly. So intent was he, he never heard someone enter his office until the clearing of a throat caught his attention.

He turned the report face down and rose to greet his visitor. "Sorry, Evelyn. I didn't hear your knock. Have a seat." His visit was unusual, to say the least, thought Sebastian. He leaned back in his chair opposite the instructor. "What's on your mind, my friend?"

The man, who had been in his unit during the war and proved himself trustworthy on the battlefield, held a look of despair as he searched for the right words. "I've come on a most delicate matter, sir."

"Go on."

"It's to do with Fairchild."

Sebastian frowned. "I might have known. What has she done this time?"

"It isn't so much her, sir. Well, not exactly. It's to do with the other trainees. To a man they refuse to spar in the ring with her."

"Then you do it. Why bother me with such a trivial matter?"

"Sorry, sir. I can't. Don't ask it of me, I beg you," Hawes said in desperation.

Sebastian placed the quill he was fiddling with on top of his report. "Can't? I beg your pardon." he said, his eyes tightening. "I gather you mean that you won't. Why?"

Hawes leaned forward and said, "I've never hit a woman in my life, spymaster, and I don't intend to start now. If you want my resignation, so be it. You shall have it on your desk within the hour."

Sebastian's laughter was genuine. "You needn't bite my head off, Evelyn. Do you mean to tell me that boxing a woman terrifies you?"

"To death, sir!"

"I see. If you are entertaining any hope that *I* will offer to take your place, put it out of your mind at once, for I won't."

Hawes choked back a chortle. "It never entered my mind, but you have to admit that it makes a comical picture. With BillyBob making book, it would set all the Wilson Academy servants to washing windows again."

"I'm tempted. But no. A boxing match between her and me or any other fool willing to climb in the ring with her won't do at all, though she deserves a good wallop or two in the right places." Sebastian sighed. "I suppose I'll have to leave that chore to her father. I hear he's furious with her for insisting on being part of our program. All right, Evelyn. I know you well enough to know you didn't come in here without a plan in mind. What do you suggest we do with the baggage?"

Relieved at having confessed a burden that had cost him a night's sleep, he said, "What if we train Fairchild to defend herself in other ways in place of boxing?"

Sebastian templed his fingers. "Go on."

"As we all discussed earlier, Sensei Nori might be persuaded to provide additional training for her in martial arts while the lads are in boxing class. Makes more sense, if you ask me."

"Interesting idea. All right. Seek him out. I'm sure he'll be agreeable. In the meantime, tell Fairchild she must confine herself to using the punching bag to increase her strength. And if she insists on practicing her boxing skills, order her to practice them on the dummy." Sebastian picked up the report on his desk and turned it over, signaling the end of their conversation.

Hawes rose and studied his boots, but did not make a move.

"Is there something else on your mind, Evelyn?"

Hawes' chin rose in defiance. "You're the spymaster, sir. Not me. You tell Fairchild of the er—change in her training schedule."

Sebastian's eyes came alive with mischief. He understood that the boxing master quaked at the idea of facing Fairchild's anticipated outburst of anger when she heard the news. "Courage, my friend. Make it your task."

Hawes folded his arms and raised his chin in defiance. "Well, I won't do it!"

The spymaster's lips twitched. "Coward!"

Heatham—His Grace, Lord Anthony Fairchild, the sixth Duke of Heatham, valued above all, not his title, not his estates, not his vast wealth, but his family. He loved his wife and was a devoted father to his children. Although he adopted the air of a curmudgeon, he wished only for their happiness. It was his good fortune to marry a woman he adored and respected. He wished the same for his children.

It saddened him that his daughter Olivia, the one child

who clutched his heart, had spurned countless offers of marriage in order to pursue an unusual course.

As for his daughter Helena, next in age and a beauty in her own right, he knew her heart's desire was fixed on the young man who grew up next door to them in London. He thought it an entirely unsuitable match, though he liked the lad well enough.

"Beg your pardon, Your Grace," said the butler.

"What is it, Dunston?"

"Mr. Darlington begs an audience, Your Grace."

"He's here at Heatham?"

"Yes, Your Grace."

"Send him in at once, then."

The butler bowed out and returned a moment later with the visitor.

"Good afternoon, Your Grace." Chris bowed.

The duke rose from his desk and came round to greet him. "Young Darlington, is it? How is your mother? And your brother?" He led his visitor to a seat and took one opposite him.

"She's in good health, Your Grace. My brother Aubrey will stand for Parliament the next session."

"Happy to hear it. You are also doing well, I hear. I met with Viscount Sidmouth. He tells me you are a distinct asset to him in the home office. Your father would have been proud of you."

"Kind of you to say so, Your Grace. In fact, I come here partly at the home secretary's request." Chris hesitated, then added, "By the way, I stopped on my way here to visit your daughter, Lady Olivia."

The duke's eyes bore into him. "How did you find her? Is she well?"

"Quite well, Your Grace. She's thriving, considering the rigors of the program."

The duke chuckled in spite of his opposition. "She'll not

fail, that one. Ought to have been a lad, what with her determination to blaze new paths. Don't look so astonished, Darlington. I know my children well. She's made no secret of the fact that she desires to be a spy. Sidmouth warned me that the physical rigors of the program may well be beyond her capacity to endure, but I know my daughter."

Chris grinned. "I couldn't agree more, my lord duke. Her determination to succeed astonishes everyone involved in her training."

The duke sat silent for a time, absorbing this news. "Thank you, Darlington, for assuring me she is safe."

"I'm glad to have been able to ease your mind about her, but there is a further reason I am here, Your Grace, if you can spare me a few more moments of your time?" Chris spoke without a quaver in his voice, though in his heart he was shaking.

"Yes? What is it?"

"It's about another of your daughters, Your Grace. Lady Helena."

The duke barked a laugh. "Don't tell me she wants to be a spy as well?"

"No, Your Grace. I ask your permission to pay my addresses to Lady Helena."

The duke glared at him. "I've turned you down twice, haven't I? You're persistent. I'll say that for you. But you must know I cannot give you my consent. Such a match is unsuited to her station as the daughter of a duke."

"She wants to be my wife, a state I desire as much, Your Grace. We've been devoted to one another since our schoolroom days."

"Nonsense. You mistake proximity for love. You were merely thrown together as children. Helena put you up to this, didn't she?"

"Not at all, sir. She tried hard to dissuade me, in fact.

She has even gone so far as to be willing to defy you and elope with me to Gretna Green, but that's not the way to our happiness and so I warned your daughter. It is I who want your blessings, Your Grace, for without that, neither of us can be truly content."

"Well said, but you are only a second son, Darlington. You have no title, nor do you have any prospects. How can my daughter continue to live in the manner to which she has been brought up?"

"My financial position has altered, Your Grace. I am well able to support your daughter now. My brother deeded our London town house to me on my birthday, and I have signed an agreement to purchase a country seat near Bath.

"I am well aware, Your Grace, that the woman I love is a duke's daughter. But I can now provide a comfortable life for my future wife. And though I cannot offer her a title, your daughter shall want for nothing, as I am sure we both would wish for her. For most of the year we'll live right next door to Your Grace, for I intend to continue my work in the home office. In time, I shall own an estate near Bath, which includes park-like grounds and a large pond which will suit us and the children we hope to have quite well."

Their conversation lasted for more than two hours, for the duke questioned his daughter's suitor with an intensity born of financial wisdom, but Darlington would not waver. He countered every objection with firmness. At last, the weary duke rang for his butler, who entered almost at once, causing His Grace to suspect that he had been listening just outside the door.

"Didn't take you too long, Dunston, did it? Find Lady Helena and ask her to come to the library."

When the door closed, the duke rose and said to Chris, "I wish to speak to my daughter alone, young man."

"I understand, Your Grace. Thank you for giving me the opportunity to speak from my heart."

"How long are you staying in Brighton, may I ask?"

"I'm on holiday, sir. I shall be in the vicinity for a fortnight. I'm planning to stay at an inn nearby."

"Nonsense. I insist you be our guest. Dunston will escort you to one of our chambers."

Chris bowed himself out and turned, only to face Helena when she came to the library door. He put one finger to his lips to silence the question in her eyes, yet there was a decided twinkle in his. He mouthed the word "garden," bowed, and retreated.

Helena went to her father's chair and planted a kiss on his cheek. "You sent for me, Father?"

"Sit down, Helena. It's time we talked."

Wilson Academy—"I've met every challenge, done everything every other trainee has done, borne every indignity . . ."

"Indignity, Fairchild? The only indignity you have voiced to us is that you've broken all your precious fingernails."

Olivia planted her hands on her hips and said, "I demand the opportunity to box, sir. How can I learn to defend myself otherwise?"

Sebastian rounded on her. "You are not in a position to demand anything at all, my girl! Nothing would please me more than to see the back of you. And the sooner the better. You cannot obey orders and you cause no end of trouble. Besides, it's nothing to do with me. None of your mates will climb into the ring with you."

"And why is that, may I ask? *Sir*?"

"Isn't it obvious? Boxing is a gentleman's art. Don't you know that no gentleman will strike a lady?"

Her eyes were on fire. "Since you are no gentleman, sir, why don't you undertake the task?"

"Don't tempt me, Fairchild!" Sebastian said, seething at the provocation. "I've arranged alternate training to replace boxing. Sensei Nori has agreed to design private martial arts training for you in place of boxing. He will see that you learn to defend yourself should the need arise."

"Have I no say in this matter?"

"None at all. Dismissed."

Olivia returned to boxing class, furious at what she considered shabby treatment. She put on her padded gloves and proceeded to pummel the punching bag that hung from a chain as if it were the spymaster's head. *Take that, you beast! And that. Here's one on the chin, you miserable cur!*

"Fairchild!" Hawes said in alarm. "Stop beating that bag so hard. You'll knock it off its chain."

She turned her head in surprise at this unexpected interruption. "Right, sir," she said, but when she turned back to the punching bag, the wildly swinging missile struck her in the eye and knocked her flat.

Hawes rushed to her aid. Alarmed, for her eyes were closed, he said, "Wake up, Fairchild." Much relieved when she opened one eye, he added, "Are you all right?"

"Knocked the wind out of me, is all, sir. If you'll just help me up . . ."

But when he tried to set her on her feet, her knees buckled.

"It's lunchtime, sir," said Riggs, rushing to hold her other side. "We'll take her there and look after her."

"No. She should be taken to her room to rest. I'll see she's dismissed for the day."

"No! Please, sir. I'm all right," Olivia pleaded.

"We'll be responsible for her, sir, I promise you. No need to worry," added Carter.

When Hawes gave his reluctant consent, the trainees

trooped downstairs to their dining hall, Riggs holding one arm and Carter the other. Once seated, the twins took it upon themselves to fetch her lunch, while Perkins poured her tea.

"Drink it, Fairchild," he said. "It will help revive you."

Olivia let out a weak laugh. "I've finally turned you all into my slaves. If you think that pleases me, you're wrong. I wouldn't need any of you to help me, if you hadn't all been such traitors."

Riggs looked puzzled. "What are you talking about?"

"I've been excused from boxing and consigned to work with the sensei while you lot pummel one another. And that's because none of you are brave enough to face me in the ring."

"No, Fairchild. Not lack of bravery," said Perkins. "Sheer terror of your skills. I won't box you for fear you'll knock my head off my shoulders. By the way. What made you hit that bag with such ferocity?"

A wicked gleam lit up her good eye. "I was imagining the punching bag was the spymaster's thick head."

The others laughed just as the door opened to admit Sebastian, who pretended he hadn't heard her last remark. "Let me have a look at that eye, Fairchild."

"It's nothing, sir," she protested, while the other trainees cast their eyes down and concentrated on eating their lunch.

"Finish your lunch and report to my office." He nodded to the others and withdrew.

"Buck up, lass. He can't dismiss you for something so trivial as a blackened eye," said Perkins.

"Nor would we let him," said Carter.

Riggs patted him on his back. "Right on. We'll all resign if he does."

"Thanks, lads," she said, too choked up by their loyalty to say more.

With words of encouragement ringing in her ears, Olivia

went downstairs and knocked on the spymaster's door. She was not only battle-ready, but spoiling for a fight.

"Come in."

"You wanted to see me, sir?"

"Yes. I want to examine your eye more closely. Come over to the window. The light is better there."

"Why, sir?"

"Don't be impertinent, Fairchild. I mean to send for a physician if I find it necessary."

"Is it to be a physician of your choice, one who will then find an excuse to dismiss me from the program? You'll do no such thing!"

His face reddened, for that thought had crossed his mind. "Oh, do be quiet, you odious creature!" He put his hands on her shoulders, propelled her roughly to the window and lifted her chin to the light. "Your eye is closed shut. On second thought, a physician won't do. We'll have to send for an oculist."

"But, you . . ."

"You'll do as I say, or I'll . . . !"

"Or you'll what?" Olivia's good eye blazed as she added, "Sir!"

Sebastian, having not yet let go of her chin, tried to restrain himself, but wild visions of permanent damage to her eye tortured him. He bent as if to examine her injured eye more closely. Without thinking, his lips found hers. He parted them and probed the inside of her mouth with his tongue.

Every conflicted feeling stirred within her as he kissed her. The right thing to do was to stop this invasion, but she had lost the will to protest. Instead, she savored the sensations that coursed through her body. She'd allow him his way a few moments longer, perhaps.

When she broke away she said, "You've just kissed me, sir."

He brushed her hair from her face and smiled. "So I have."

"Why?"

He grinned at her. "How else am I to quiet your foolish chatter?"

"Well," she protested a bit lamely, "don't you dare try that again, sir."

His eyes danced. "Why not? You enjoyed it, didn't you?" He pulled her to him and pressed his lips to hers once again. *Good God! Why is this temptress lurking in my spy school when she was made for love?*

His hands caressed her back as the kiss deepened. He could feel her response, a slight shiver that sent a message, one that threatened to embarrass him. But it disappeared at once when her knees buckled.

He caught her in his arms, carried her to the sofa and put her down gently, oddly pleased at the flush on her face. "Are you all right?" he asked.

"Just a bit . . . dizzy, sir."

He rang for a servant. "Send for Denville and Mrs. Hunnicut and find footmen to carry Fairchild to her room."

When Denville entered the room, the spymaster said, "Do you know of an oculist residing in Havelshire or must we send for a London practitioner?"

"I believe there is one nearby, sir."

"Summon him at once, Hugh. I need him to examine Fairchild's eye for damage."

The news spread throughout the academy like an avalanche of pebbles rolling downhill. It took no time at all for an army of servants, trainees and instructors to gather outside the spymaster's open door. In truth, it wanted only the stable boys and the gardeners to complete the roster. Rumors ran the gamut from poor Fairchild suffering a mere fainting spell to her untimely death, the last horror quickly to be scotched.

But the mob cheered when Olivia appeared very much alive in the arms of a strong footman. She waved to them as he carried her up the grand staircase. Instead of placing Olivia in her tiny cell, Mrs. Hunnicut directed the footman to carry the patient to her own more comfortable sitting room, where he placed her on a cot that had been assembled for the purpose. The housekeeper directed an under maid to request from Fourier a slab of raw beef.

In the days to come, traffic on the back staircase, from the basement kitchen to the attic, where Olivia lay recuperating in the housekeeper's sitting room, threatened to disrupt the entire spy program.

This reaction astounded Sebastian, who had to fight his way from his ground floor office to the attic to visit the patient. "How are you feeling today?"

"Better, sir. Thank you for sending for the oculist. I own it was a relief to hear from his lips that there will be no permanent damage to my eye."

"He relieved my mind as well." Sebastian's eyes fell on a table laden with an inordinate amount of fresh fruit, cheeses, pies and tarts. "What's all this?"

She shrugged. "Gifts from some of my . . . friends."

"You appear to have many ah . . . admirers," he said, wondering how, in so short a time, Fairchild had managed to win the hearts of so many at Wilson Academy.

A startling thought intruded. He wondered how it was that this hoydenish creature threatened to win his heart as well.

Chapter Nine

Olivia hurried down the path to the swim class at the lake, her first. She had been forced to wait for her eye to heal and had missed the first two classes. Olivia felt the sun warming her face, or was it the flush of anticipation upon her cheeks? She was all eagerness to swim, something she hadn't done since the previous summer at Heatham.

When she rushed upstairs to change into her bathing costume, she'd missed the cart taking the other trainees there for swimming. Her modiste in London had assured her that it was all the rage. The costume was made of the finest wool, its dark blue color enhanced by white stripes on the flared hem and again on the long sleeves. She wore the knee-length dress over bloomers. The daring outfit had been named after Amelia Bloomer, who urged women to adopt the new, more practical, far less cumbersome costume. Such a garment would eliminate the need for a bathing machine, that horse-drawn room on wheels with a back door out of which a woman could be assisted into the water by attendants.

Olivia found the walk invigorating on such a fine day. She drew in her breath when she sighted the ripples of water on the lake. When she spied movement ahead, she called out, "I'm coming, mates!" A few steps more brought her in sight of the other trainees. Her mouth fell open, for the other trainees had not a stitch of clothing on.

"It's Fairchild," someone shouted. Hoots of laughter greeted her as the trainees dove into the water while swimming instructor Ned Mason shouted encouragement. "That's the ticket. Dive in and cover up, lads."

"No one said anything about swimming in the buff," Olivia grumbled, taking a few timid steps closer.

Mason cleared his throat. "The lads have been used to swimming this way, you see. We didn't expect you today, Fairchild."

"I missed the other classes because of my eye, sir."

Mason, whose grizzled beard and sharp blue eyes reminded everyone of St. Nicholas, answered in an apologetic tone, "I know that, lass. The lads began training while you was ill and all. Best for you to go back the way you came. You can't very well join them in the water. It wouldn't be proper-like."

A wicked gleam lit her face. *Just you try and stop me!* "Oh yes, I certainly can join them, sir. I've a brother, you know. It isn't as if I'm shocked, or anything. Well, just at first." She began to disrobe.

Aghast, Mason covered his eyes. "No, no, Fairchild. Keep your clothing on. I beg you!"

The trainees took in every word as they treaded water.

"I dare you, Fairchild," egged Carter.

"Five to one odds, she don't do it," offered one of the twins.

"A shilling says she does," Riggs shot back. "Come on, Fairchild. Join us!"

Sebastian, on his customary morning ride, heard a loud commotion coming from the lake. Curious, he steered his horse round the bend to investigate. When he dismounted, though he was well able to witness Fairchild's shocking behavior, he hid behind a convenient oak tree to shield him from sight. *Why, that shameless hussy! Are there no limits to the depths of her depravity?*

"Turn your eyes away, lads," Olivia said as she walked out to the end of the log from which the others had launched themselves.

Sebastian bit his lip to keep from laughing. *What demon possesses her?*

She dove in, cutting the water without a ripple, but the cold water brought forth a gasp as well as a most unladylike choice of words.

"Good show, Fairchild. You're a right one!" said Perkins in admiration.

"Race you lads to the far end of the lake—where that weeping willow tree is—and back," she challenged. "Be warned. I mean to show you no mercy! Ready? Go!"

BillyBob had no time to offer odds as the trainees paddled furiously toward the other end. Sebastian stepped out from behind the tree and beckoned to the swim instructor.

He spoke in a calm tone of voice, as if nothing were amiss, "Had you planned to teach something today, Ned? Whatever it may have been, I'm sure this isn't it."

"Diving, sir. Thought the lads could use more practice." His voice was filled not only with chagrin but with admiration. "Did you see Fairchild's dive? Doesn't need any instruction from me, let me tell you."

"You've lost control of your class, Ned. You'll not be able to teach anything at all this day, I assure you," *Not with that hoyden mucking up the works.* "Go on back to the academy. I'll finish this for you. And no more dipping in the buff. All right?"

"Don't have to say it twice, sir. Me heart stopped beating

when that saucy little puss shed every stitch." Mason hurried off. He raised his hand and waved without looking back.

Sebastian planted his feet and crossed his arms, his eyes on Olivia, who won the race with ease. When the others swam up behind her, he said in an unmistakable tone of authority, "Out, you lot! Find your clothes and return to the academy at once. Not you, Fairchild. Be so good as to remain in the water. And turn your eyes away. Give the lads some privacy."

Olivia turned her back and tread water while the others followed orders. *Bloody hell! Now I'm in for it.*

She listened to the crackling of twigs underfoot as the men dressed until, at last, the sound of footsteps receded and there was silence. She asked through chattering teeth, "I'm cold, sir. May I come out now?"

"At once, if it pleases you." His tone was anything but friendly.

She began to climb out in full sight of the spymaster, his back turned to her. He was holding her bathing costume with one finger while the rest of it flowed down his back.

"You'll pay dearly for this outrageous bit of business, Fairchild."

"You don't mean to . . . to send me packing, sir?"

"That thought has definite appeal. It would serve you right."

A wicked gleam lit her eyes. *Oh, no you don't! Not without a fight.* In one swift motion, she turned and dove back in.

The splash startled him into turning around. "I thought I told you to come out of the water!"

"If you wish to send me packing, you'll have to catch me first, sir." She was halfway across the lake when she heard him splash into the water. She pictured him without his clothes and swallowed what seemed like half the lake in her next breath. When she reached the other side of the lake, she pulled herself out of the water and collapsed under the willow tree, her breath coming in little gasps. She closed her eyes and waited for the stitch of pain in her side to subside.

Sebastian pulled himself up beside her. "What the devil did you think to accomplish, my girl?"

Olivia made no answer.

At the sight of her trembling lips, Sebastian said in alarm, "Olivia? Are you all right?"

He called me by my name! She feigned a shiver. "C . . . cold."

He wrapped his arms around her. "Let me warm you."

She felt triumphant, yet no smile passed her lips. "Mmmm. You're so strong, sir." She snuggled closer, her breasts touching his firm chest, teasing her nipples.

"Your lips are blue," he murmured. And pressed his to warm hers.

She arched her back to meet his kiss, and felt his manhood grow against her.

Sebastian lost himself in her softness. Heedless of where he was, his body strained closer. His breath quickened. His hands caressed her breasts. He let out a strangled sigh when she groaned with pleasure.

All thought flew out of Olivia's head. Need drove her. She felt wetness and warmth engulfing her. She strained closer to him. She wanted all of him. Her hands caressed his firm buttocks. So warm, yet like sculptured marble, she thought, savoring the sensation. She returned his kisses with a fire of her own, igniting him, burning him.

He stopped. Raised himself on one elbow. Propped his head on one hand and searched her face. "Surrounded by water and I'm dying of thirst, you little shrew."

Her eyes laughed. Her husky voice teased. "I'm still cold. Sir."

"Do you know my name?"

"Yes." Her fingers touched his face. She traced his lips with one finger.

"I want to hear you say it."

"Sebastian," she breathed. "Your name is Sebastian."

The sound of her sex-filled voice drove him wild. He drew both her hands together in one of his and pressed them over her head. When she opened her mouth to speak, he murmured, "Shhh. Be still, my little one." He began to kiss, first her breasts, then lower, below her waist. His hand slid down to the mound of hair between her legs. He parted them and found her sex.

When he stroked her there, she screamed, for he had begun to take her to another country. A strange place she never dreamed existed. She was not under a willow tree. Not on the lake. Not at the academy. She was someplace else. A new land she'd never explored before. Her hands crushed his hair as she writhed and moaned beneath his assault. Her groans reached her ears. *Are they mine,* she wondered. *Did they really escape from my lips? Can that be?*

Her body convulsed when she reached a climax. And then another. And yet another. At last, her breath calmed and she lay still.

Sebastian rolled to her side, moaning as if in pain.

"What is it?" she asked in alarm.

"It should be obvious. You have only to look."

Olivia raised her head. "Oh," she said in awe. "I've never seen anyone else but my young brother when he was twelve. His wasn't anywhere near that large. Is something wrong with your . . . that?"

Sebastian howled a laugh between gasps. "There are remedies, you know. Have you never made love to a man before?"

"I thought we just did."

"No. That was merely, er—a prelude."

"A prelude? To what? I want to know the rest."

Every fiber within him strained to teach her, but he resisted the temptation. "Not on your life, siren. With my luck, you would grow with child within the first month."

The idea pleased her. "And?"

"And I'd be forced to marry you."

Her eyes danced. "Oh no, really? Would you go that far just to thwart my career as a spy? That wouldn't suit me at all. Not at all, sir." She ran her hands over his firm stomach, coming dangerously close to his engorged sex. "But I want to help your . . . what do you call it? Your affliction. Most sincerely, I do."

"There are ways, you know."

"Then I beg you to teach me."

He took her hand and placed it over his throbbing member. "Stroke, Fairchild. Faster. Don't. Stop."

All that week, Olivia strained for a glimpse of Sebastian, but he was nowhere to be found. Instead, Hugh Denville presented the trainee schedule every evening, a task the spymaster usually performed. She wondered if he had gone to London, or perhaps someplace else. She prevailed upon Riggs to ask only to learn that the spymaster was closeted in his office, otherwise engaged.

Saturdays, set aside for individual tasks, was dubbed "sweetening day" by the trainees, a bit of wit that recalled Shakespearian times, when bathing took place once, in the spring of each year when the weather warmed.

As usual, the day was devoted to personal grooming, at least until teatime. A barber from the village of Havelshire visited and trimmed hair while Mrs. Hunnicut was kept busy clipping and trimming nails. As usual it was Jenny the scullery maid who earned her gratitude, for she had a talent for fashioning Olivia's wild tresses atop her head in a most becoming fashion.

Saturday evenings after dinner and study hall afforded the trainees what little entertainment for the week there was to be had. Instructors were careful to avoid putting in an appearance on that night, for the trainees loved nothing more than their bit of fun. This included country dances to the tunes Billy played on his harmonica as well as making sport of the foibles of the entire staff.

On Sundays, the morning bell rang to wake the trainees one hour later. Services in the chapel followed breakfast, but after lunch, the trainees were free to do as they wished.

Olivia was in the habit of spending her Sunday afternoons with Mrs. Hunnicut in her sitting room, where she took tea with the housekeeper. She looked forward to this time, for it served as a reminder that she was, after all, not just a trainee, but also a woman.

After a week of physical exertion and gruff male camaraderie, she found it a welcome change to share the latest fashions in the women's magazines, discuss the news in the London papers and talk about things not at all related to the business of learning to be a spy.

On one particular Sunday, when an under maid answered her knock, Olivia glanced around the sitting room, and asked, "Where's Mrs. Hunnicut?"

"She'll be back soon, miss. She begs you to make yourself comfortable till she returns. Would you like your tea?"

"No. You can go. I'll wait to have it with Mrs. Hunnicut." The young under maid bowed herself out.

Olivia spied the London papers on a small table near the sofa. They were a week old, but she hadn't as yet seen them. She thumbed through the paper until she reached the society page, the news that interested her most. She settled in her favorite chair by the fire and began to read all the latest London gossip.

It took but a moment for her sister Helena's name to leap out at her. It was an announcement of the betrothal of Lady Helena Fairchild to Mr. Christopher Darlington. *Good for you, Helena! You've persuaded Father to give in at last.*

She read the item once more to make sure her eyes did not deceive her. One detail that skipped her notice the first time now imprinted itself in her brain. Under news of her sister's betrothal, was the announcement of a country ball to be held at Heatham in Brighton, given in the couple's honor by the Duke and Duchess of Heatham. The ball would take place on Saturday evening, the tenth of August.

An overwhelming wave of homesickness assaulted her. She yearned once again to watch Georgie flirt with eager young suitors, to listen to Mary play the pianoforte, to scold dear Jane to watch her diet, to tease her brother Edward about his latest racing exploits. To congratulate Helena, her closest confidante. To hear her mother's soothing voice. To listen to her father scold them all, with his customary blend of loving sternness and pretended irritation at their silly foibles.

A betrothal ball for Helena and Chris! This Saturday evening! I must go to wish them happiness. But the spymaster will never allow me off the grounds. Never mind. I'll find a way, no matter what! But how?

The door opened to admit Mrs. Hunnicut. "Sorry to be late for tea, dear. I had to settle a tiresome dispute between two of our staff." She sat opposite Olivia and poured two cups.

"What happened to vex you so, ma'am?"

"Let's have our tea first, child. I've the need for something to soothe me after such an ugly scene."

Olivia knew from her own experience that friction invariably arose within a large staff. She sipped her tea and asked, "Who were the warriors?"

The housekeeper sighed. "Mrs. Haskin, our linen-keeper, accused Mrs. Berkle, in charge of the scullery, of not only demanding too many cloths for her work, but also of allowing the scullery maids to wear them out too quickly. Such a to-do over nothing."

"And on Sunday, too, you poor dear. Were you able to settle it, ma'am?" Olivia took a cookie from the tray.

"Dear me, no. It's a battle that's fought over and over between those two, I'm afraid. I merely postponed the outcome by requesting a list of their grievances in writing. Only then would I render my decision."

Olivia laughed, but her heart wasn't in it. "Clever, Mrs. Hunnicut."

They drank their tea in companionable silence for a time.

At last Mrs. Hunnicut said, "Why are you frowning, Fairchild? Is there something troubling you?"

"Was I? No, there's nothing troubling me, ma'am. I suppose I'm just weary after a long and arduous week." She smiled, her eyes wide. To mask her pain, she changed the subject. "Where have you hidden those new fashion magazines you sent for, ma'am? Let's look at the designs together, shall we?"

London—"Everything in place for the arrival of the prince?"

"I have the preliminary plans with me, sir. Have a look at them and let me know if you have any suggestions for their improvement," responded Chris.

Viscount Sidmouth set them aside on his desk. "Yes, of course. I'll read them at my leisure. Any obstacles in your way?"

"No, sir. Preliminary plans are moving along well. I met with the spymaster when I stopped at Wilson Academy and we're in agreement on all points. We'll use every available man in protecting the prince."

"Does the spymaster plan to include all the new trainees in this operation?"

"Yes, sir, with your approval, of course."

Sidmouth swiveled his chair to face the window, a well-known signal to his subordinates. It meant the home secretary was weighing a delicate issue in his mind.

When he turned back to Darlington, he said, "Inform the spymaster he's to find a way to keep Fairchild out of this operation."

"You wish him to bar her participation?"

Sidmouth eyed him thoughtfully. "Do you disagree?"

"No, sir. Not in the least." Chris smiled. "Especially since she's to become my sister-in-law."

"Much more to the point, Darlington. The Duke of Heatham is to become your father-in-law, is he not? I wish both you and your betrothed happiness. But if you desire contentment in your marriage to his daughter Lady Helena, you would do well to do everything in your power to make sure his eldest daughter is kept out of harm's way."

Chapter Ten

Wilson Academy—Saturday, The Tenth of August

Olivia could hear the stirring of activity from Mrs. Hunnicut's sitting room window, for these were three flights above the stables. The sound of stable boys calling to one another as they rubbed neighing horses down, or fed them, or watered them reached her ears through the open window as she lingered in her bath. Mrs. Hunnicut was in the study hall occupied with the other trainees.

She listened for the sound of the spymaster's voice, the only one that interested her at the moment. When she heard him, she rose from her bath, wrapped a towel round her and ran to the window in time to see him ride off.

She didn't give a thought to his direction. She only wanted him well away from the academy so she could carry out her own plans. "Come in, Jenny," she said at the knock on the door.

Olivia had taken special pains to befriend Jenny who loved to do up her hair. Together they had chosen to do Olivia's hair in a coif they had discovered in one of Mrs. Hunnicut's fashion magazines.

Jenny had ambitions. She yearned to be more than a mere scullery maid, Olivia knew. She encouraged her in this dream, for the young maid was gifted enough to become an abigail to a fine lady. As a result, there was nothing Jenny would not do for Miss.

"Perfect, Jenny," Olivia said when the maid held up the mirror for her inspection. "You're so clever."

"Much obliged, Miss." Jenny performed an awkward bow. The red-haired maid's green eyes, freckles marching across her turned-up nose, as well as the lilt in her speech clearly marked her Irish ancestry.

"Can you keep a secret, Jenny?"

The young woman's eyes opened wide. "I'd never tell anything about you to anyone, Miss. I swear it."

"I'm going to sneak away this very day, but you're the only one who knows it. All right?"

"Cross me heart and hope to die, Miss."

Olivia rose and hugged the young girl. "The only thing is, I need your help."

"Yes, Miss, but . . ."

"What is it?"

"I shan't be sacked, shall I?"

"Oh no. I'll see to it, I promise." Olivia put one finger to her lips and held her elbow in a studied pose. "But if by some chance you are, I shall find you employment in a grand house somewhere. As an abigail. Would you like that?"

Jenny blushed to the roots of her red hair. "More than anything, Miss."

"Then you have my word. Here's what I want you to do."

London—"Good afternoon, sir."

"Come in, spymaster. I've been expecting you," said Viscount Sidmouth. "Brandy?"

"Thank you, sir. Allow me." Sebastian picked up the

decanter and poured two goblets. He handed one to the home secretary. "Thank you for seeing me in your home today, sir."

Sidmouth sat back and sipped his brandy. "Of course. You're on your way to Brighton to attend Darlington's betrothal ball, I gather. Unfortunately, I found it necessary to decline the invitation, for I had already committed to a prior engagement. I assume Darlington informed you of my wishes concerning Fairchild?"

"Yes, sir. He sent me a copy of your letter. The duke's daughter will not be at the pier on the day the prince disembarks. I'll see to it."

"Don't fail me in this."

"I won't, sir," Sebastian said, wondering why the old man had found it necessary to saddle him with the chit in the first place. So she was to be a privileged spy, was she? Whoever heard of such a thing? A mischievous thought struck him and he nearly laughed out loud. *Perhaps I ought to marry her after all. That would be one way to get her out of my hair!*

"Hi there, Teddy," said Jenny to the stable boy. "Busy?"

Teddy winked at her. "Never too busy for you, lass." He tried to grab her, but she backed away.

"Keep yer hands to yerself, lummox," she said, yet her voice welcomed his touch.

"What's on your mind, Jenny, me love? Can I hope it's the same as is on mine?"

Jenny laughed in a teasing way. "Keep your knickers on, Teddy boy. I just wanted to ask you a question is all."

"And what might that be, lass?"

"Stay right where you are, Teddy, while I ask. How might I get to Brighton if I'd a mind to go there?"

"Why are you talkin' so loud, lass? There's no one here but you and me."

She ignored the question. "Well? Do y'know the direction or not?"

"'Course I know the direction. D'ye think me a fool?"

She beamed at him. "I didn't ask anyone else, did I?"

"Want me t'take you there? I could saddle up the cart and . . ."

"Don't be daft. I'm just curious." She let him take her hand. "Well?"

"It's easy. At the end of the drive, you turn left. Then when you reach the end of the road, turn right. That road takes you right onto the main road to Brighton."

Jenny stroked his cheek. "Is it dangerous?"

"Not that I ever heard." He tried for a kiss.

"Not here where everyone can see us, you ninny. If you promise to behave, we can take a walk. And maybe then . . ."

"And maybe then wot?"

Jenny winked at the lad she'd set her cap for. " That's fer me to say and you to find out."

Olivia hid in the stable until she could no longer hear Jenny and Ted's footsteps. She prepared her horse with a man's saddle, mounted and rode off in the direction the stable boy had described.

Brighton—Lady Helena was resting in an attempt to still her rapid heartbeat. She could not believe her good fortune. Her darling Chris had bearded her father in his den and had won him over. She was betrothed to the man she loved. And tonight at Heatham, they would celebrate and accept the good wishes of all of Brighton society.

"Is that you, Amy?" she called out to her abigail when the door opened to her darkened chamber. The door closed, but there was no answer.

"Who's there? Speak up or I'll ring for help," she said, fear in her voice.

"Don't ring, you goose. It's Livy." She pounced on the bed and hugged her sister hard.

"Livy? You frightened me half to death! How did you get here?"

Olivia reached to turn up the lamp. She gazed at her sister. "I wouldn't be much of a sister if I missed your betrothal ball, now would I? I'd rather be drawn and quartered."

Helena sat up. "Have you permission? Chris said . . ."

"No one knows I'm here, but what does that matter?"

"You'll be dismissed if you're discovered."

Olivia shrugged. "Perhaps. But I do have a problem."

"What is it, dearest?"

"I've nothing to wear. All my gowns are in London."

"You haven't changed in the least, you vain, selfish girl." Helena's laugh infected her sister, at which point the door opened once again.

"What's all that noise?" Georgiana stopped in her tracks and screamed, "Livy!"

"Georgie, dearest," Olivia squealed. She hugged her close, tears of joy streaming down her face.

"I heard some noise . . . is that you, Livy?" Mary rushed to her side and hugged her. "Why you're nothing but skin and bones! Don't those beasts feed you?"

"Oh Mary. How I've missed you. I dream about hearing you play the pianoforte every night."

Mary's face lit up. "Do you really? I've missed you, too, big sister."

"Ouch!" Olivia protested when Jane entered the room. Her chubby eight-year-old sister pounced on her, shrieking, "Livy. Livy. Livy."

"What's all this commotion? The servants said . . . Livy!" her mother shrieked. And promptly began to weep.

Olivia's tears mingled with her mother's. Her heart felt

full to bursting as her sisters added their shouts and their laughter to the symphony of a happy family reunion.

Her mother dried her tears at last and said, "Stop all this nonsense my dear gaggle of geese. The Darlingtons are joining us for a family dinner before the ball. We must all get ready. What shall you wear, Livy?"

"We're the same size, Mother," said Helena. "I'll find an appropriate gown for her and Amy can shorten it." She rang for her abigail.

"I must go and tell your father, Livy. Come to our chambers just as soon as you're dressed. I'll lend you my pearls. Oh, and one of you tell your brother Edward, please." After one last kiss planted on her daughter's cheek, she flew out of the room.

"How is Edward?" Olivia asked as Helena's abigail helped her choose a gown.

"Still racing curricles to an inch. He's all puffed up since he's won a few races. He's so fearless, we all worry for his neck. He's grown handsome, too, though he doesn't seem to have discovered the charm we women offer. In a few years he'll be the despair of scheming mothers all over England. They'll be dying to land the next Duke of Heatham for one of their eligible daughters."

Olivia laughed at that. She proceeded to search through her sister's wardrobe until she found something suitable. "I'll wear this one. Do you mind, Helena?" She had chosen a pale blue silk under gown, with matching chiffon over it.

"If you want the gown I planned to wear tonight, I would gladly give it up to you. I'm that happy you're here, dearest."

The bustle of activity caused a spate of girlish giggles while Olivia was helped into her gown. She stood very still while Amy shortened the hem and another young maid stood on a chair to fix her hair. Afterwards, she ran down the wide hall to her parents' suite, but before she could reach it, another pair of hands pulled her into the shadows.

"Did you think to avoid my clutches, my pretty?" her brother asked, twirling an imaginary mustache. He wrapped his arms around her.

"Let go of me, you incorrigible brat. You'll crush my gown. Go chase the girls. I hear they're all over you like flies on honey."

"I'd rather ravish my beautiful sister instead." He nuzzled her neck and she giggled.

"I've missed you so, Edward. But you have to let me go. Father's waiting."

"In that case, I have no choice." He let her go, but as she passed him, he swatted her in the rear.

"Beast!" she muttered, but she was all smiles when she entered her parents' drawing room.

The duke had steel in his voice when he spoke, yet his eyes were welcoming. "I take it you have given up and resigned your post."

Olivia paid no heed to his harsh words. "Father!" She ran to him and threw her arms around his neck.

"It would be the worse for you if you disobeyed orders to be here," he grumbled, trying hard to hide his pleasure.

"Whatever can you be thinking, Father? I am not allowed to fail. All your children well know that we cannot disgrace you in such a way. Have I got that right?" She batted her lashes at him and he laughed in spite of himself.

The duke rose and offered one arm to his wife and the other to Olivia. "Come along, you two. It's time to greet Helena's prospective in-laws."

Dinner was a small, but lively affair that included only the immediate family and their guests, Darlington's mother, the dowager marchioness, as well as the Marquis and Marchioness of Thorpe, Darlington's brother Aubrey and his wife Cecelia. Since the family lived next door to one another in London, there were no awkward moments.

After dinner, Olivia entered the glittering ballroom on her brother's arm. She couldn't recall there having been such an event at Heatham. Their country estate was designed for intimate family pleasures in warm weather, when the London heat was oppressive. The duke and duchess much preferred to entertain in London during the season.

"See what you're missing, Livy?"

"Indeed I do, Edward. But there will be other opportunities. After I complete my training, of course."

"You're determined to go back, then. That won't please our dear father."

"I haven't come this far merely to give up." Out of the corner of her eye, she saw Sir Percival Smythe-Jones bearing down on them. "Oh, oh. Trouble. Dance with me again, Edward. That awful Smythe-Jones is here. I couldn't bear another of his unwanted marriage proposals."

"With pleasure, beautiful sister of mine." He swept her into his arms as the band struck up a waltz and they whirled off. Olivia couldn't help but notice the attention focused on her brother.

"Edward, there are daggers being thrown at me from the eyes of some very beautiful young ladies. Are those your flirts?"

Her brother laughed. "Can I help it if I'm irresistible? I'll have you know that every woman here is my flirt, dear sister. The young ones for themselves, the old ones for their eligible daughters."

"Is it because you're so rich or because you're so fabulously good looking, my love?"

"More like it's because I'm the heir to a wealthy duchy. Will you rescue me if I lose my head to some beautiful damsel with a witch of a mother?"

"Of course, I will. I'm learning all the martial arts, so I'll be well able to rescue you from a designing damsel's clutches."

"Martial arts? You? I don't believe it."

"You'd be surprised, Edward. After six weeks of training, I'm as strong as an ox."

When the waltz ended, a group of eager young men surrounded Olivia. She looked helplessly at her brother, but he winked before leaving her to her fate and disappearing into the crowd. For the next hour, she danced with six handsome young bucks, the waiting line at the end of each set never appearing to diminish.

"Thank you, my lord," she said to her seventh partner when the music ended. To the next young buck in line, she added, "Forgive me, but my poor feet need a rest."

A hard rap on her shoulder made her turn in surprise.

"No strength for another dance? Do you dare to disappoint me, my lady? I so looked forward to a turn with the most sought-after woman here tonight." Sebastian's lips were tight. He clutched her waist, gripped her hand and glared at her. When the band struck up the next waltz, he guided her none too gently across the floor.

"You're hurting me," she gasped.

"Serves you bloody well right!" He squeezed her hand harder.

"Stop it this minute, sir! If you're bent on giving me a scold, do so in private."

"Where may I find a paddle to punish you with?" he answered loud enough to turn heads. His face was twisted into a wrathful glare. He pulled her along, as if she were a limp rag doll, in full view of astonished guests.

He nodded left and right and said in a voice raised by several decibels, "Excuse me, but I must escort Lady Olivia outside for a bit of fresh air." His lips held an unpleasant semblance of a smile.

Sebastian held her arm in a painful vise-like grip and propelled her toward the open terrace doors.

Olivia's heart pounded in tune to the beat of the music. *I'm in for it now, but what's he doing here?*

As if he could read her thoughts, he said, "Did you think I would not attend tonight? Darlington is one of my closest friends." His nostrils flared as he spoke. "What am I going to do with you, Fairchild?"

She stuck her chin out. "I haven't the faintest notion. What are your thoughts on the matter, sir?"

"Why, you unscrupulous vixen!" His temper heated, he ticked off each accusation by counting on his fingers. "You disobey me. You redesign my program to suit your whim. You're disrespectful. You deliberately challenge every one of my orders. You flirt so outrageously, all the trainees have fallen in love with you!"

She ignored his wounding words, put her hands on her hips and fought back. "As well as some of the instructors, sir. Not to mention the footmen and the stable boys."

"You deliberately challenge every one of my orders, you hoyden. You . . ."

She put her hand up to stop him. "Excuse me, sir. You already said that one, sir."

Sebastian's eyes widened. "I said . . . *what one*?"

"The one about challenging your orders, sir? You said that twice. Sir. I don't really mean to vex you, sir." Rather than look him straight in the eye, she examined what was left of her fingernails.

He glared at her through narrowed eyes. "Then what, pray tell, is it you do that irritates me enough to want to strangle you?"

"Well," she began, in a thoughtful voice. "I don't deliberately set out to irritate you, sir. I merely try to simplify your orders, sir. You do have a tendency to be terribly long-winded, you know. Sir."

"I'm terribly long-winded?" He drew in an audible breath and snorted it out through his nose. "Never in all my life have I encountered such a willful, obstinate, destructive, irritating piece of work . . ."

His harsh tone, not to mention his loud voice, was again attracting a curious audience. When she observed this phenomenon, Olivia took his arm. "Allow me to show off our lovely rose garden, sir. The flowers are in full bloom this time of year." She dragged him away from the terrace.

When they were out of earshot, he groused, "Damn you, Fairchild! I can't bear it any longer. Have the goodness to crawl out from under my skin, will you!" He pulled her into the shadows and crushed his mouth on hers.

Olivia closed her eyes and inhaled his scent as she pressed closer, wanting more. Wanting to feel every inch of him. *Mmmm. Delicious. I'm under his skin? That may have some advantages after all.*

Chapter Eleven

London—Monday, The Twelfth of August

Instead of returning directly to Wilson Academy from Brighton, Sebastian detoured to London to confront the home secretary. And since he had not thought to make an appointment, he cooled his heels for an hour before Sidmouth summoned him.

"Sorry, spymaster. I was tied up in an unavoidable meeting with some very important committee members of Parliament." He smiled at the look of surprise on Sebastian's face. "Did you think I had no one I need answer to for my actions? There is a pecking order everywhere in government, my friend."

Sebastian's mouth performed a smile, but not his eyes. "I never thought otherwise, sir."

"What brings you here today, Brooks?"

"Since you have taken a personal interest in trainee Fairchild, I thought it my duty to report that she disobeyed orders and left the academy grounds."

The home secretary's eyes flew open in surprise. "You don't mean to tell me she's disappeared?"

"No, sir. She had the audacity to steal a horse and ride off without my permission."

Sidmouth stroked his chin, yet his eyes never left Sebastian's face. "There must have been a reason. Have you discovered her intentions?"

"A family matter, sir. Fairchild was determined to attend her sister's betrothal ball at Heatham."

"Her sister is betrothed to Darlington, is she not?"

Sebastian drew in a breath, for he knew he was treading on tenuous ground. "That's correct, sir. Lady Helena Fairchild is your aide's affianced."

"Tell me, spymaster. Would you have given her your permission had she petitioned you first?"

The question caused his face to color. "That isn't the point, sir. She didn't ask, which is typical of her behavior. She never asks. She just does what she pleases, sir. I suspect that, being the daughter of a duke, she is accustomed to having her own way in all things. She doesn't think rules apply to her. That's a dangerous notion for a spy in government service, you'll have to agree." Sebastian was startled by the odd sound of his own words. Was he actually whining?

"What do you suggest we do to remedy this fault in her?"

"Let me be frank, sir. If it were up to me, I'd send her packing. She's not good spy material."

The viscount clasped his hands and spoke in the patient voice of a father to his son. "But it isn't up to you, spymaster. From what you have just told me, Fairchild is guilty of nothing more than a foolish omission. Had she asked, I'm sure your sense of compassion would have allowed her to attend such a joyous family celebration. If one of your other trainees came to you with a request to attend a family funeral or a joyous event such as Fairchild broke your rules for, you wouldn't think twice in giving your permission, now would you?"

The truth of this struck Sebastian with the force of a thunderbolt. He hung his head and said, "No, sir. I suppose I would allow it."

"I advise you to think of some suitable reprimand for Fairchild and get on with your training program. But under no circumstance will I allow you to send her packing. Good day, spymaster."

Heatham—Olivia stayed the night in spite of the spymaster's threats. Indeed, they did little to mar the afterglow of the family reunion. She knew she would have to face his wrath when she returned to the academy, but she was determined to prevail no matter what punishment he had in store for her.

What she had not anticipated was this new tactic. He dogged her every step when she returned. He witnessed Olivia sail through calisthenics. Inspired by his frown, she performed twenty-five push-ups, her highest number thus far.

The feat prompted Denville to say, "Good show, Fairchild! Congratulate her lads." This brought a lusty cheer from the others.

"Thank you, gentlemen," she said, pulling her pantaloons wide, and performing a mock curtsey. She never once glanced in Sebastian's direction.

At the same time, Sebastian took Denville aside and said, "Why praise her performance? Fairchild didn't once raise her knees off the floor like the others."

Denville slanted his eyes toward the spymaster. "Ease off, spymaster. She's not built the way we are. She's a woman, or haven't you noticed?"

In answer, he made no comment, yet the look on his face was not kind. He followed her into codes and ciphers class, where Foster handed the trainees a message in an unfamiliar code and requested them to solve it.

As though it were merely a simple puzzle, Olivia was the first to do so and was rewarded with Foster's praise.

Sebastian sat silent in the back of the classroom, his hands folded across his chest.

Their next class was fencing. "Why is the spymaster on our tails this morning?" Riggs asked Olivia in a whisper as they entered the changing room.

"Don't let it bother you. It's me he's after. As usual."

Riggs nodded in understanding. "By the way. Where were you? I haven't seen you since breakfast on Saturday morning. You didn't show up for lunch or for dinner and on Sunday you missed chapel as well as all your meals."

It didn't take her long to invent an answer. "I took a large midday meal with Mrs. Hunnicut on Saturday, and by dinner-time, I wasn't hungry. On Sunday, I did not at all feel the thing—something I ate, no doubt—so I stayed in bed all day. Jenny brought me some broth."

Riggs cast her a suspicious glance, but he said no more.

The trainees donned their chest protectors, fencing gloves and wire net masks. They each chose a foil and took their place along the wall in the fencing room, awaiting Fourier's orders. But their instructor was deep in conversation with the spymaster, who also wore a fencing vest, held his sword glove in one hand and his fencing mask in the other.

At last, Fourier nodded, turned to the trainees and said, *"Bien!* You are to fence Monsieur Brooks this morning. When he calls your name, step forward and assume the po-sition. Be alert, I warn you. He is—" Fourier kissed his fin-gers and threw them in the air, a familiar gesture to the trainees—*"formidable!"*

The spymaster put on his glove and his mask, tested several foils by flexing them, and chose one with a curved

French grip handle and a pommel on the hilt of the sword. He crouched, knees flexed, his bent rear arm pointed upward, his sword arm extended in position.

"You first, Carter. *En garde.*"

After disposing of Carter quickly by scoring a hit, he called out, "*En garde,* Riggs."

Much to the surprise of the others, Riggs acquitted himself better, forcing Sebastian to work harder for a hit. "Good show, lad. With enough practice you will turn out to be a first-rate swordsman."

The spymaster removed his mask and wiped his forehead with the towel Fourier offered him. His mask back in place, he studied the remaining trainees, as if trying to decide on his next opponent.

"*En garde,* Fairchild."

"Yes, sir." Mask and glove in place, she took her stance, her steady eyes boring into her opponent. Olivia thrust forward with such agility, she took him by surprise. "A hit," she said, when her sword touched him.

Sebastian bowed. "I wasn't ready. We begin again. *En garde, mademoiselle.*"

There wasn't a sound to be heard in the fencing room. It was as if the spectators were holding their collective breath. They watched the combatants parry, each thrust designed to protect different parts of the body—*prime, seconde, tierce, quarte, quinte, sixte, septime, octave.*

To mislead him, Olivia feinted and made running attacks, returning each of his thrusts for one of her own. They dueled with ferocity, neither scoring a hit. Each time Sebastian appeared to have the advantage, Olivia managed to force him to retreat. They continued to thrust and to parry as though in a battle to the death. When she tripped in retreat and fell down, she expected him to hit. And win the match.

Instead, he took several steps back and said in a voice

dipped in poison, "I never take advantage of an opponent who is already down. I give you leave to rise, Fairchild." She did as she was told, but her strength was ebbing fast. She didn't think she could go on much longer. Nor was she aware that the protective ball on the tip of her foil had disappeared when she fell. It had flown off, exposing the sharp point of her foil.

Gathering what strength she had left, she feinted and lunged in a running attack—a *fleche*—catching her opponent by surprise. Unaware of it, the unprotected point of her foil met with his upper arm.

"A hit," she cried in triumph, letting go of her foil. Olivia removed her mask and waved it at the other trainees. "I've scored a hit. I win."

"What the—?" Sebastian dropped his foil as if it were on fire and clutched the arm that had held it. His knees sank to the floor and he fainted, blood gushing onto the canvas from the wound in his arm.

"Stand away, Fairchild," Fourier shouted. "Someone hand me that cloth! And ring the alarm bell for help. Find Mrs. Hunnicut and bring her here at once."

The trainees disappeared to sound the alarm while Fairchild and Fourier were on their knees on either side of the wounded spymaster. Fourier wrapped the cloth around the spymaster's arm and twisted it to stop the bleeding. Olivia slapped the victim's face lightly to revive him.

"I'm so sorry, sir. I didn't mean to . . . I didn't see that ball fly off the tip of my foil. Wake up, sir. Open your eyes." Unbidden tears clouded her vision. When she turned away to hide them, Sebastian opened his eyes and winked at the fencing master before closing them again.

"Hold zee tourniquet tight, Fairchild, while I fetch some brandy."

"Yes, sir." She turned back to Sebastian and held the

tourniquet, tears beginning to stream down her face. She bit her lip hard to keep from fainting at the sight of the copious amounts of blood Sebastian had already lost. She wiped his sweaty brow with her other hand, and looked around her. Satisfied that they were alone, she bent to kiss his lips. *Don't die, my love. Please don't die!*

Sebastian lay as still as a corpse, though his heartbeat quickened when he heard her whisper aloud, "I love you."

Tears ran down her cheeks. "What have I done? Forgive me, dearest. I never meant to harm you. Open your eyes, my darling. Show me you still live."

The room filled with a stream of staff. With trainees. With servants.

"Move, Fairchild. You're in the way," said Mrs. Hunnicut. She beckoned to two footmen.

"Wh—where are you taking him?"

"To his chamber, of course. The men will make him comfortable until the doctor arrives." She was quick to see that Olivia was about to faint. "Take Fairchild up to her room, Jenny. See she lies down to rest."

"Yes, ma'am," said the maid. She took one of Olivia's listless arms and wrapped it around her own neck. Holding her waist in a firm grip, she led her away.

When Sebastian woke from a laudanum-induced sleep, it took him a few moments to recall the duel.

"Evening, sir. How are you feeling?"

"Groggy, Hugh. What's the time?"

"It's eight in the evening, sir. Wednesday. You've lost a day, I'm afraid. Shall I ring for some supper for you?"

"Yes. I haven't eaten since Monday. Have Fourier prepare something substantial. Plenty of rare beef and potatoes. And

Hugh, be so good as to fetch me a decent bottle of wine from the cellar."

"Sorry, sir. You're allowed only light broth tonight. Doctor's orders."

"Doctor's orders be damned! I want something substantial."

"You can damn him yourself when he returns in the morning. Better mind his advice tonight, sir. You've lost a good deal of blood."

Sebastian swallowed a sharp retort. He eyed Denville, one eyebrow higher than the other. "What's the damage, Hugh?"

"Fairchild's last thrust nearly cost you the use of your arm. It came dangerously close to severing your median nerve which, according to the doctor, is your main nerve, the one that makes most of the muscles in your arm do their work. You're in luck, sir. Doctor says you'll have full use again in due time, but only if you're willing to allow it to heal. The real danger is infection. I urge you to cooperate and follow the doctor's orders, sir. Can't have a spymaster with the use of only one arm, now, can we?"

Sebastian smiled at the grim jest. He glanced down at the dressing, which snaked its way around his chest. He couldn't move his arm at all. He let out a sigh of relief and said, "Good God, Hugh! To have this happen after all you and I have been through at Waterloo." He sighed. "You win. Send for some of Fourier's healing broth instead of the steak I pine for."

Jenny brought Olivia some dinner, but she made her take it away. She couldn't swallow a morsel, for nausea filled her stomach, dejection clouded her vision and misery parched her throat. Why hadn't she noticed that tiny little ball flying off her foil? How stupid she was, wanting only to win the match, not caring how. She had wanted to humiliate him in front of the others, just as she supposed he was trying to do to her. Instead she nearly killed him. The thought iced her bones. She shivered, feeling as if it were the middle of a harsh wintry day and she wore no clothing. She tossed and turned for hours, unable to sleep.

Jenny had reported that he was alive, but she had to see for herself. She glanced at her clock. It was three in the morning. Everyone in the academy should be asleep at this hour. She lifted the latch and pushed open her door a crack. She looked up and down the hall. No one was in sight.

A stair creaked halfway down to the first landing and she froze. When her heart stopped its loud beating, she removed her shoes and continued on, stopping to listen at each landing. She reached the ground floor and pushed the entrance door an inch at a time. Nothing stirred. She slipped into the first door on her left and waited for her eyes to become accustomed to the dark. She'd been in this room before, she realized, for it was the spymaster's private dining room. She spied another door on the far right wall and made for it. She edged it open. The book-lined walls and a large desk in front of the window marked it as Sebastian's office. She noted still another door on the far wall, just past his desk. His chamber? Of course. It had to be.

She peered through the keyhole and saw nothing but the dim light of a candle. She waited for her heartbeat to calm before turning the knob. The door squeaked. She ignored the sound and crept into the chamber. She shut the door as quietly as she could manage.

Sebastian's large four-poster bed rested against the wall opposite the windows. A lone candle glowed on the table nearest her. She heard snoring coming from the other side of the bed. Denville was fast asleep in a chair next to the door to the main hallway.

Sebastian turned his head to the left when he heard a noise. At the sight of her, the grin across his face accompanied the gleam in his eyes. He had had many hours to reflect and he was ready for her.

"Morning, Fairchild. What took you so long?"

Chapter Twelve

Denville woke with a start at the sound of the spymaster's voice. "What are you doing here, Fairchild? Go back to bed. Haven't you done enough damage?"

"Leave off, Hugh," Sebastian said. "I want to talk to her."

"But, sir, you're not well enough . . ."

"I said, leave off. And go away, for heaven's sake. Give us some privacy. What I have to say to Fairchild is for her ears alone." Sebastian voiced a command whose meaning was clear to Denville.

"Five minutes, then," he said, "but no more than that."

"I'll ring for you when I'm bloody well ready. Take yourself off, Hugh. Now!" He turned back to Olivia, but not before he was sure his aide had caught his wink.

"Denville was only trying to protect you, sir," she said when the door closed.

"From you? Why? You wounded me enough. Are you planning to finish the job?" To hide the joy in his heart at the sight of her, he glared at her with a stern eye. "Don't think you can order me about now that you've rendered me a helpless invalid."

Her eyes opened wide in consternation. "I—I just came to see how you were, sir. And—and to plead with you to forgive me. It was an accident." Her breath hitched, she clutched the corner of his quilt, fell on her knees and began to sob.

His good hand reached to cover hers. "Stop your caterwauling, my foolish darling, and sit up."

She raised herself up to meet his eyes. "What did you just call me, sir?"

"I believe I called you foolish."

"No. That other. . . . Heaven knows I'm foolish, but did you call me darling?"

A look of innocence widened his eyes. "Did I? I can't recall. I'm under the influence of large amounts of laudanum. For the pain, you see. Can't be held responsible for anything I say in the circumstances, now can I?"

She laughed, a blissful sound to his ears. "You did, sir. You just called me darling."

He shrugged his good left shoulder. "All right, I did. Come here then, my darling." He tried to tug her onto the bed with his good hand.

"On your bed? But I can't do that. I'm liable to hurt your arm."

He sighed in exasperation. "Can you not follow a simple order just this once? I command you to climb up here on my bed, Fairchild."

"Yes, sir." She scrambled her knees onto the bed and placed one hand on each of them as though she were a child.

"Good God, no woman has a right to look so intoxicating. You take my breath away. Do you realize how incredibly beautiful you are?"

Olivia reddened in embarrassment and ignored his question. "What can I do to ease your suffering? Shall I plump up your pillow or straighten the sheets or . . . or something? Do you really think I'm incredibly beautiful, sir?"

"Of course I do. I always say what I mean. Let go of my pillow you foolish girl. I'd much rather have you kiss me."

"Now that kind of order is one I'll be happy to follow, sir." She planted her lips on his for a brief moment and he groaned. "Better, sir?"

"A bit better, but it doesn't quite ease my pain." He wet his lips. "Continue the treatment, if you please." As she bent to him, he grabbed a fistful of her hair and brought her lips down hard. His tongue probed her mouth. A shiver of contentment escaped from her lips. "Lie down next to me, Fairchild."

"Are you sure you're well enough, sir?"

Enjoying the game, he managed nevertheless to suppress a chuckle. "For heaven's sake! I'm not *asking*. I'm *ordering*."

"Well, if that's an order, I suppose I must obey it, mustn't I, sir?"

"It's permissible to call me Sebastian when I'm making love to you."

She locked her eyes to his. "No, sir. If I call you Sebastian, you see, I'll not have to obey your orders. I've only been trained to obey when the spymaster gives me an order."

He snorted. "As if you've ever obeyed any order of mine, Fairchild!"

"Livy."

"What's that you say?"

She rubbed his nose with hers. "I permit the people who are fond of me to call me Livy. You're welcome to join them." She nuzzled his neck.

"Do that again, my darling Livy. You drive me wild every time you come near me. Take a look." His eyes lowered.

She raised the quilt to inspect his erection. "I see what you mean. The last time you er . . . rose to the occasion so to speak, you were in pain. Is it so now?"

"Don't be impertinent." What the bloody hell was he

doing? Where was his iron control when he needed it? Why couldn't he stop?

He made an effort to put an end to this episode. "You'd better go, Fairchild. Send Denville back in."

"Sorry Sebastian. I only obey the spymaster. You said so yourself. I can't leave just yet. Not until I take your pain away down there. It's the least I can do, after wounding you so badly."

"I forgive you for that, my foolish darling. Besides, it was my fault for challenging you. Now go in peace and allow me to recuperate."

Her hand encircled his member. "Is that an order, spymaster? Or shall I continue my ministrations, Sebastian dearest?"

"Sebastian dearest? You little witch. Have I given your arsenal yet another weapon with which to destroy me?"

"What if I . . . ?" She began to remove her nightshirt.

His eyes opened wide. "What do you think you're doing?"

She put a finger to his lips. "Shh, Sebastian. I can't obey you unless the spymaster gives me an order." She straddled him.

His breath came heavy. "This is unseemly. You have no idea of the consequences, my girl. Besides, you wouldn't even know what to do."

"Oh, wouldn't I?" She rolled back on her knees, held an elbow with one hand and put the finger of the other to her lips. "Let's see now. Can't be that hard. I grew up in the country, you know. Animals do this without any instruction at all and they never even learned to read or to write." She wiggled her bottom against him and he mewled like a helpless kitten, his voice an octave higher than usual.

"I have to . . . to make room for you, don't I?" She spread herself wide with one hand. "Now, if I lower myself . . ."

He let out a long, low whistle. "Don't do this to me. I'm a sick man."

"Don't worry, Sebastian dearest. I'm of age and I promise you won't have to marry me. Besides, this time *I'm* in charge." She pressed herself down over him. "I'll try not to hurt you."

A sound halfway between a groan and a laugh choked his throat. In spite of it, he managed one last protest. "It only hurts a woman her first time."

She guided him into her and pressed down. "Mmmm. Big."

"Dear God, Livy!" All thought was lost to him. He grasped her buttock and raised his own, plunging himself into her further.

She met him thrust for thrust, taking care not to touch his injured arm.

She cried out when a stab of pain sliced her in half.

"You mustn't stop, my darling. Your pain will ease more quickly if we continue, I promise."

She bit her lip and obeyed, yet her breath quickened as she moved her hips up and down. A flush of pleasure replaced the pain she felt a moment before. He met her hips and thrust faster, driven by his own need.

"Yes," she breathed in short gasps. "More. Yes. Yes."

He reached between her legs and found her nub. She whimpered when his touch drove her wild. When she climbed the peak of passion, her screams mingled with his shouts of release.

She collapsed at his side, her breath escaping in short gasps. They lay still for a time, eye to eye, until a stab of pain assaulted him and he grunted.

"You're hurting, my darling. What must I do to help?"

"More . . . laudanum," he gasped. "Get Denville."

She began to rise. To her embarrassment, the sheets were covered with blood. Her blood. "Oh, dear."

"What's wrong?"

" The sheets. They're bloody and so am I." She grabbed a fistful of soiled sheet and used it to clean herself.

Could it be? Was he her first lover? The notion made him giddy. "Don't give it another thought. Denville will know what to do about the sheets. It won't be the first time, you know. He was my aide-de-camp in the war."

Olivia stopped pulling down her nightshirt. "Won't be the first time? You beast!"

"What made you think I've had no experience? I am thirty after all."

"I wanted to be your first. Your last. Your only," she pouted.

"In that case, you shall be my last, my love. We can wipe the slate clean and forget those other women ever came my way. Besides, no one has ever given me half as much pleasure as you, my foolish darling."

"But . . ."

He narrowed his eyes and used the voice of command. "Don't argue with me, Fairchild. You forget I'm a sick man."

She drew in her breath. "I'm sorry, sir. I didn't mean . . ."

"Come here and show me how sorry."

With a sly grin, she found his lips and kissed him. And kissed him. And kissed him.

"Enough! My body is rising to the occasion again, but I haven't the strength for another tumble. Come back tomorrow night after I've had a day to rest."

Olivia picked up the corner of the quilt, glanced at his new erection and laughed in delight. "My oh my. Who would have thought I could have this much power over you? If I knew that sooner, I'd have exercised it more often."

He tried to frown, but grinned instead. "Try for a bit of sobriety, you ridiculous creature."

"But I don't feel sober at all. I feel like celebrating."

"In that case, let us make this a real celebration. Give me your hand."

"What for?"

"Good God! Do not, I beg of you, question everything I say.

I'm not in a position to offer for you on bended knee, you odious girl. My hand in yours will have to do in the circumstances. Will you do me the honor of becoming my wife?"

"Your wife? You can't be serious."

"Never more so, my love. Well? What say you?"

"Oh, Sebastian! Yes. A thousand times yes!" She began to sob.

"Stop blubbering, dearest. You're soaking my bandages. Now be a good girl. Summon Denville and go back to your own bed. I must have another dose of laudanum to ease the pain."

She blew him a kiss as she opened the door to the main hall and whispered over her shoulder, "I love you, Sebastian. I love you spymaster. Whichever."

Denville was about to administer a dose of laudanum, when he observed the condition of the bedsheets.

Sebastian let out a shout of laughter. "Yes, that's it. Wish me happiness, Hugh. Fairchild has agreed to marry me. I have made the little hoyden mine. I wish you could have seen her duel! She's magnificent!"

"That 'magnificent' hoyden nearly killed you," Denville answered dryly.

Sebastian's joy would not be dampened. "Nothing more than an accident caused by my own stupidity. The lady has accepted my hand. Heaven grant me strength. I shall need it to marry her, for I cannot live without her."

Denville's lips twitched. "Are you under the influence of too much laudanum, sir? Perhaps I should lower the dosage."

"It's not the laudanum, Hugh. Don't try to dampen my happiness. I'm mad for her, but it's wiser to keep the news to ourselves for the time being. All right?"

"As you wish, sir. In that case, let me be the first to congratulate you."

* * *

Heatham—Lady Helena hurried across the lawn toward the garden. When she entered, she paced up and down, waiting for Chris to appear. Half an hour later, he arrived through the terrace door, a grim expression on his face.

"What's wrong, dearest?"

"Trouble at the spy academy. I must go there to see what I can do."

"Livy! Is my sister hurt?"

"No, my love. She stabbed the spymaster in a fencing duel."

Helena paled. "She . . . what?"

"No need to be alarmed. It was an accident. Livy and the spymaster were fencing as part of a training exercise. I gather the protective ball on the tip of her foil fell off, but no one took any notice. The point of the foil lodged in his shoulder."

"Oh, dear. How serious is it?"

"I don't know. Sidmouth orders me to return to London at once. Say nothing of this accident to your father, dearest." He took her in his arms to soothe her.

"No, of course I won't." She raised her lips for his kiss, disappointed in its brevity.

"My horse is waiting outside. Be brave, my darling. No, don't see me off." He took her arms from his neck, placed them by her side, turned and strode away.

Wilson Academy—It was rumored that the spymaster's wound was not healing as it should. The news seemed to have subdued the academy. Only Riggs stood by Olivia now that she needed a friend. The other trainees ate their meals without saying a word to her. Study hall, boisterous in the past, was reduced to silence. And no one commented about the cancellation of the popular fencing program. At least not in Olivia's hearing.

She took this as censure. Did the instructors also stare at her a moment longer than necessary during calisthenics, during archery, during martial arts? Olivia couldn't be sure, for the slights were subtle. But she couldn't rid herself of that sinking feeling in the pit of her stomach. She followed each day's training program to the letter, yet her mind counted the hours until she could visit Sebastian.

When she was observed sneaking down to the spymaster's chambers in the middle of the night, gossip buzzed like a swarm of bees denied entrance to their hive. Indeed, every one of her movements caused a hiccup among the staff.

"You have dark circles under your eyes, my love," said Sebastian one evening. He traced them with his finger. "You aren't getting enough sleep. I'm supposed to be the invalid. Not you."

His face was flushed, which alarmed her. She ignored it and said, "Hurry up and get well and you'll see how rapidly I improve, sir."

He raised one eyebrow. "Sir?"

She smiled and said in a soft, seductive voice. "Sebastian, dearest."

"That's better. Care to tell me what's troubling you, my foolish darling?"

It was her turn to raise an eyebrow. "What makes you think I'm troubled?"

"Those circles, for one. And for another, you have frown lines on your forehead. Letting the rumormongers get to you?"

She laughed. "Of course not. Did the doctor examine you today? What did he say?"

"Don't change the subject, my girl. What can I do to ease your worries?"

She played with the fingers of his good hand as she spoke. "If you were to be seen fully recovered, I might be able to hold my head up again."

"I'm at the mercy of the doctor, my darling. I must remain in bed, and therefore immobile, for another week, he says."

A single tear ran down her cheek. He wiped it away with his thumb. "Through no fault of yours, the point of the foil came dangerously close to severing the most important muscle in my arm. The doctor calls it the median nerve. If you had intended to render my arm useless, you missed the mark. No, no, I'm only teasing. Don't cry, my foolish darling. I assure you I shall be right as rain in no time at all."

She was relieved when Chris Darlington arrived at Wilson Academy, but he was not alone. He brought with him a London physician, Sir Clive Davis, to examine Sebastian. When Chris had suggested the famous doctor to Sidmouth, the home secretary urged Darlington to escort him to Sebastian's bedside as soon as possible.

Sidmouth made this decision as he did so many others, not so much for humanitarian purposes, but for political purposes. There were delicate ramifications for a man who owed his current position by appointment of the Regent. His record as prime minister had not been sterling. Simply put, he feared damage to his career should the news spread that the daughter of the Duke of Heatham, an influential member of Parliament, had seriously wounded a war hero. That Sidmouth had personally approved her admission as a spy trainee, added to his anxiety.

"How are you feeling, Sebastian?" asked Chris. "Allow me to present Sir Clive Davis, a much respected London physician. I've brought him to examine you."

Sebastian was polite, but indifferent. "How do you do, sir? I wasn't aware that I had requested yet another physician."

Sir Clive Davis, a short round man with a jolly disposition, laughed. "That tells me you're not too fond of doctors, my boy, eh? Can't say I blame you. We are a bloody nuisance to all our patients. Be that as it may, will you allow me to take a look-see at your wound? I've come such a long way to examine you."

Sebastian warmed to him at that remark. "Of course, sir. Wouldn't want to waste your valuable time."

"Good lad." He turned to Chris. "Have someone bring my bags in from the coach. And be so kind as to see to it that I have several pitchers of well-boiled water, and a copious amount of clean dressings." The doctor put his nose near the dressing on the wound. He wrinkled it in disgust when he smelled the foul odor. "Phew!"

When Chris returned, he took him aside and said, "I don't like the smell of that wound. It's festering. Not a good sign. You'll need to have a cot set up for me in this room. I shan't leave until I'm convinced he's well on the way to recovery."

As if it had been asleep since the accident, Wilson Academy came alive under the doctor's brisk orders. A table was brought in for the physician to lay out his tools. And when he sent back the first batch of water, proclaiming that it had not been boiled thoroughly enough to suit him, the footmen hurried away to obey.

Davis ordered everyone out of the room as soon as he was satisfied that all preparations suited his exacting standards. When Denville lingered, he raised an eyebrow at him, put his hands on his hips and waited until the aide scurried out of the room like a schoolboy caught with his hand in the cookie jar.

The sight made Sebastian laugh. "Since you can terrorize a martinet like my aide, you shall have my full cooperation, sir."

Davis smiled as he removed his jacket and rolled up his sleeves. He took one of the water pitchers, sprinkled powder from a large jar he'd brought with him and proceeded to scrub his hands.

Sebastian observed this ritual with awed respect. It took the doctor five minutes to scrub. He rinsed them thoroughly in the cooled water that had been boiled, wiped them dry and discarded the used linens in a sack on the floor.

The doctor approached Sebastian with the largest pair of shears he had ever seen and proceeded to cut away the bandages wrapped around his patient's waist. "These country doctors use too many bandages," the London physician grumbled as he worked. "Such unnecessary waste."

Sebastian yelped when the last bit of bandage sticking to his open wound was removed. "Bloody hell! That hurt!"

The physician paid him no heed while he took up his magnifying glass from the table and examined the fissure with intensity. "Just as I thought."

"What is just as you thought, sir?"

"When Darlington said your wounds had not healed, I suspected infection and I was right. Country doctors pay little heed to the value of cleanliness around a wound. Unfortunately, when it festers, the patient becomes feverish, the result of a serious infection."

"Comforting thought," muttered Sebastian. "And after that?"

"What do you think? The patient dies, of course. I shall have to open the wound and clean it out if you are to live. The point of that foil may well have been rusted and therefore full of harmful germs." He looked around him.

"Bell pull is by the door, sir."

Denville nearly fell into the room at the first ring.

"Make yourself useful and bring me an unopened bottle of brandy, more boiled water and more clean sheets torn in strips," the doctor barked. When Denville disappeared, he turned to Sebastian and said, "I'm going to render you unconscious with a combination of brandy and laudanum. You won't feel a thing after that, believe me."

Sebastian tried for a bit of humor, but he was alarmed nevertheless. "Take care not to cut off my arm, sir. I've grown fond of it."

"I doubt I'll have to, but I can't guarantee it. You may become feverish. I've seen such a result linger for days, in fact. Let us hope I can remove enough of what's causing the infection to render its effects harmless and leave your arm right where it was always meant to be."

When Denville knocked, the doctor took the brandy bottle from him and shut the door in his face. Again Sebastian watched, fascinated, as the doctor washed the outside of the bottle with his special powder and rinsed it off. He removed the cork and wiped the neck thoroughly. Davis poured it into a goblet, filling it to the top and added laudanum from a tiny vial. He raised Sebastian and held him up, putting the goblet in his good hand.

"Take your time, but you must drink it all, son."

While his patient drank, the doctor chatted in a conversational tone, as if they were enjoying a pint in a cozy tavern. "Among my colleagues, I am a laughingstock. They ridicule me, you know. They mock my methods. I am known as the cleanliness maniac, but I don't mind."

"Why is that, sir?"

"Sheer stupidity on their part, if you ask me. However, I always have the last laugh, you see, for I rarely lose a patient to infection." He poured more of the brandy mixture into Sebastian's goblet.

"We've known for near on fifty years that infection, caused by lack of cleanliness in my view, can be deadly, but do doctors pay attention to this information?" He poured more brandy. "Not at all. Far too many of them do not even bother to wash their hands."

Sebastian's eyeballs fluttered in an involuntary fight to keep awake. Davis kept on chatting and pouring until his patient's head drooped to one side. The doctor removed the empty goblet from Sebastian's limp hand and said softly, "Pleasant dreams, son."

Davis kept his tools steeped in the boiled water until he was ready to use them. He sprinkled more of his powder on all of them, rinsed them off and began to clean out the poison festering in Sebastian's wound.

Chapter Thirteen

Doctor Davis was a demanding taskmaster. Olivia was no longer able to sneak in at night to visit Sebastian. Even Denville was kept at bay. The only person allowed into Sebastian's chamber by the good doctor was Mrs. Hunnicut, who acted as Sebastian's nurse whenever Davis felt the need to sleep.

As Davis had predicted, Sebastian began to run a high fever. He ranted and raved in delirium, shouting orders to his men, for he believed himself to be back with Wellington's army, in the thick of the battle of Waterloo. Davis applied cool wet dressings. In this task, he had the efficient help of the housekeeper. He was delighted to find that her zeal for cleanliness in a sickroom matched his own.

By the end of the week, Davis shook his head and said to Mrs. Hunnicut, "I had hoped to see some extrusion from the wound by now. Such leakage would be a good sign, but this infection's a stubborn one. Not good for a man to run such a high fever for so long a time. I'm afraid I can't guarantee his survival."

"Will it help if we sponge him more often, sir?"

"I don't know, to be frank. We can only try."

Gossip ran riot in the academy. The most optimistic rumor was that the spymaster was healing. But when it was rumored that the spymaster had taken a turn for the worse. Many believed that the spymaster was at death's door.

Why hadn't the spymaster recovered, everyone wondered? The customary boisterousness of a lively staff was reduced to hearsay, often groundless. Talk of the spymaster's persistent illness filled the air. Everyone from the lowliest under maid to the haughty butler had a surefire cure to offer.

"I hear tell there's a woman in the village who swears that hot wax poured on the wound will cure it of the disease in his system," an under maid declared.

"Mayhap she knows better than that uppity London doctor," snorted a footman in reply.

"Starve a fever. That's what I always say."

"You're wrong. Feed a fever does the trick better."

"My uncle was saved once by a man who lives alone in the woods hereabouts. He makes his own special miracle potion. Swears it will cure any ill."

Yet beneath all the rumors lay fear. The service staff feared they would lose their positions if the spymaster were to die. What if the academy were to shut down, as a result?

Olivia was faced with so many accusing stares wherever she went, she kept her eyes downcast. Backs were turned when she approached and sullen silence greeted her questions.

The worst of it was that she was not allowed to visit Sebastian. The first time she tried to sneak down the back staircase, she faced two angry footmen who blocked her way and sent her scurrying back to her room.

She pleaded with Riggs, her only friend in this terrible crisis, to discover news of the spymaster. To no avail, for the doctor had insisted upon a veil of secrecy to counteract the rumors. In his experience, sickroom news frequently became distorted in such a large establishment. He believed it made his task more complicated than necessary. To his relief, he found a staunch ally in Mrs. Hunnicut. That wise woman knew how to keep her own counsel even though she could not scotch the exaggerated rumors.

"Good evening, Mrs. Hunnicut," said Olivia. She rose from a chair in the housekeeper's sitting room, the one she had been resting in for hours.

"Shouldn't you be in bed, Fairchild? You need your sleep, you know."

"You know why I'm here, don't you? Is the spymaster going to live? I'm mad with worry. You must give me reason to hope, for I am to blame for all this."

Mrs. Hunnicut sighed. "It was an accident, Fairchild. Everyone knows that."

Olivia frowned. "They may know it, but they don't believe it was an accident. Behind my back, people whisper that I deliberately stabbed the spymaster. Oh, don't shake your head in disagreement, Mrs. Hunnicut. You know how deadly hearsay can be."

"You must forgive those foolish enough to repeat such ridiculous lies. You know very well that they do this out of ignorance. Most of our service staff were raised with little education. As for the spymaster's condition, I can tell you nothing, my child. The doctor has sworn me to secrecy and I must respect his wishes. Rest assured that Doctor Davis, a most admirable man in my estimation, is doing everything he can to save the spymaster's life."

"Save the spymaster's life? Do you mean to tell me he's near death?"

"I tell you this in the strictest confidence, my dear. Have I your word you won't repeat what I say?"

"Yes, of course, ma'am. Go on."

"The spymaster has developed a serious infection as a result of his wound. It has caused a high fever."

Olivia turned ashen. "I see. Thank you for the confidence. I'll leave you to rest now."

Mrs. Hunnicut's brutally frank news stunned her. She paced her attic room most of the night, but found no release from the fear engulfing her. With little sleep, she woke at four the next morning when the morning bell sounded. She washed and dressed and hurried down to breakfast in the trainee dining hall. She could hear the chatter even before she entered, but when she did, all conversation died.

"What's wrong?" she said in alarm. "Have you had . . . bad news?"

"It's just a rumor, Fairchild," said Riggs. "Can't place much faith in rumors."

"All right," she said evenly. "What is the rumor?"

Perkins answered in a sympathetic voice. "You have a right to know. Spymaster's taken a turn for the worse."

"Open those windows as wide as you can, Mrs. Hunnicut. Our patient is burning with fever. The cool night air may help."

"Yes, doctor." She hurried to the window to do as he bid, while the doctor removed all of Sebastian's clothes and proceeded to wrap him with cold wet linens in an effort to reduce the fever. The housekeeper helped him to finish the task.

Doctor Davis looked at his nurse with keen eyes. "If the fever doesn't subside soon, we'll lose him. It's going to be a long night. Get some sleep, Mrs. Hunnicut."

"I won't leave you here alone, doctor."

"All right, my dear. I'll take the first watch, then. Take the easy chair by the fire and close your eyes. I promise to wake you in an hour."

Several hours passed in this way, each resting in the fire-side chair for an hour. Four hours later, the doctor felt Sebastian's head again. Relief spread across his face. He shook Mrs. Hunnicut awake. "The fever's broken, ma'am. We shan't lose the spymaster after all. Our patient lives to see another day."

"Thank the Good Lord. If he lives, sir, it is only through your excellent care. You've performed a miracle."

Olivia spent a good part of that same night pacing back and forth in her room. It was three in the morning when, her skin crawling as if invaded by insects, she crept downstairs and out the kitchen door, taking care to avoid being seen. She tiptoed around to the front of the academy and stopped under Sebastian's window to try to glimpse the man she loved. She moved up to it as stealthily as a cat, searching for a way to reach the sill, but it was too high. Instead, she sat below the window, her back against the wall and closed her eyes. To be this near the man she loved was small solace but it was enough. Her eyes flew open at the sound of a male voice coming from Sebastian's room, for the window was open. No, not Sebastian's voice. The doctor most likely, for it was the voice of an older man.

"It's all over, Mrs. Hunnicut. Our patient rests in peace now, poor soul. It's clear I'm no longer needed here. I shall return to London first thing in the morning. I know I may rely on you to make whatever arrangements you deem necessary."

Olivia next heard Mrs. Hunnicut speak. "Poor lad. He suffered so much. I never thought his illness would lead to this. I'll have to inform Denville."

Over? No longer needed? That can only mean one thing.

Sebastian's dead. I've murdered the man I love! She stumbled to her feet and ran away, blinded by tears. She never heard Mrs. Hunnicut's final comment.

"I'll tell his aide to inform the local doctor he's to take your place now that the spymaster is on the road to recovery."

Olivia stumbled back to her room she knew not how. She threw some of her things into her portmanteau and crept down the back stairs through the kitchen galley again. She snatched a fresh baked loaf of bread, some cheese and an apple and stuffed them into the bag, opened the door and fled into the night.

When Doctor Davis awoke in the morning, he strode over to his patient's bed, pleased to find Sebastian's eyes open.

"Morning, sir. Looks as though I slept off that drunken stupor you caused when you forced me to drink all that brandy laced with laudanum."

A wide grin covered the doctor's face. "Indeed you have, son. Indeed you have. I hope you noticed that you still have your arm."

"I did indeed. Thank you for sparing it. May I have a bit of breakfast, sir? I'm as hungry as a bear."

"Of course, lad." He rang the bell.

A sleepy-eyed Denville opened the door a crack. "Sir?"

"You can come in now, Denville. The fever's broken. Our patient is going to heal just fine."

The aide's eyes lit up. He turned and repeated in a shout, "Fever's broken. Spymaster's going to live. Pass the word!" He shut the door and hurried to Sebastian's side. "Morning, sir."

"Order up a large breakfast for me, Hugh. Eggs, a rasher of bacon, lots of bread and butter, coffee and tons of drinking water. I appear to have a huge thirst."

"Yes, sir! At once, sir." Denville hurried out of the room.

Sebastian eyed the doctor. "What's gotten into my aide? He's as frisky as a puppy. Acts as though he hasn't seen me in ages."

"He hasn't. You've been asleep all week, lad. You've also been delirious, a result of high fever. Fortunately for you, the fever broke and the crisis has passed. I'll spare you the gruesome details, son, but I don't mind owning that I'd almost given up hope for your recovery."

Sebastian grinned. " Then you, sir, are the first doctor who has ever admitted his doubts in my hearing. So many in your profession are happy to boast that, if it were not for their skills, their patient would be dead."

The doctor's round belly shook with laughter. "We're a disgraceful bunch of charlatans, aren't we? Medicine is the only profession I know of in which the practitioner gets to bury his mistakes, no questions asked." He examined Sebastian's wound for the last time. Satisfied that the wound was extruding its poison, the doctor redressed it with a less cumbersome bandage. "You're on the mend, lad. The wound's healing well." When Denville returned, he added, "Send for Mrs. Hunnicut, will you?"

The housekeeper entered while Sebastian was busy attacking the first meal he'd had in a week. "Morning, sir. How pleased I am to see you in such good form."

"You owe Mrs. Hunnicut a great deal of thanks for your recovery, lad. She helped me nurse you during your ordeal."

" Then you have it, ma'am." Sebastian wiped his mouth and signaled to Denville to remove the tray. "When may I rise from this bed, sir? I'm anxious to resume my duties."

"Not so fast, spymaster. You must follow my prescription for your full recovery to the letter. Your housekeeper and your aide have promised to help. Now your only task, you young scamp, is to obey their orders. Understood?"

"Understood, sir," Sebastian answered with unaccustomed meekness.

Wilson Academy came to life again as news of the spymaster's recovery made its way in and out of the building. Clive Davis, the London doctor who saved their leader's life, became a hero to them. And all talk of magic potions and odd remedies were forgotten.

Hugh Denville escorted Doctor Davis to the carriage that would take him home to London. To the doctor's surprise, the driveway was lined with servants and staff. He acknowledged their cheers with a wave of his hand and a flush of pleasure on his cheeks, stepped into the carriage and rode off.

"Doctor Davis is on his way home to London, sir," Denville said when he returned to the spymaster's chamber, pleased to see Sebastian sitting in a chair wearing his robe and his slippers. His wounded arm was resting in a sling, just as the doctor had prescribed.

Two chambermaids were busy changing the linens on his bed, while two more removed all evidence of the sickroom the doctor had left behind—the table, the water pitchers, the linens—all but the necessary bandages and powders meant to aid Sebastian's recovery.

"I heard the cheers, Hugh. Wish I might have joined the staff in their rousing send-off. Davis is a good man, though God knows I hope never to need his services again." Sebastian sat back in his chair, and rested his head. "I feel so weak, Hugh. I had thought to allow the staff and the trainees to visit, but . . ."

"That must wait till after you've had your morning's rest, sir. Let me help you back into bed."

The last thing in Sebastian's thoughts before he drifted off to sleep was the good doctor's parting words; "Don't let that bloody country doctor bleed you, son. You've lost enough blood to fill a cow." He slept for two hours, a smile never leaving his face.

London—"Sorry for the interruption, sir."

Viscount Sidmouth looked up from the paper he was reading. "Oh, it's you, Darlington. What news of the spymaster?"

"The very best, sir. The crisis is over. The spymaster's fever broke yesterday morning. He's on the mend."

"What of Davis? Still at Wilson Academy?"

"No, sir. He's on his way home to London. He left instructions for the spymaster's care in the hands of the local doctor."

Sidmouth sat back, a look of smug satisfaction on his face. "I knew Davis would save the day. Glad I thought of sending him."

"Yes, sir," said Chris with a straight face.

"What is it Hugh?" asked Foster, the decoding instructor. "Why have you called us together so hurriedly? Is it more bad news about the spymaster?"

"Don't tell me that Brooks has taken another turn for the worse," said Hawes.

Mrs. Hunnicut said, weariness in her voice, "Allow me to explain, gentlemen. I asked Hugh to summon you here this morning. The news I have is bad enough, but it has nothing to do with the spymaster's health. It's Fairchild."

"What has that little troublemaker gone and done now?" asked Ned Mason, the humiliating scene of her nudity at the lake still fresh in his mind.

"Fairchid not come to martiar arts today," said Sensei Nori, as yet unable to master the letter 'L' within a word. "She sick?"

"No, Sensei. Not sick. She's run away. I've searched

everywhere for her. What's more, I've ordered every servant from the stable boys to the scullery maids to help me search for her. She's nowhere to be found."

"If she's gone missing, she hasn't done it on horseback," added stable master Tom Deff. "All our horses are in their stalls."

"Maybe she's resigned from the training program and returned home. Has she left a note to that effect?" asked Hawes, a barely discernible note of hope in his voice.

"No, she hasn't. Nor has she returned to her home. Her family lives in Brighton for the summer. I even sent a groom to Havelshire to check the passengers on the mail coach to Brighton. There's only one a day and she was not a passenger. Frankly, I'm worried for her safety, gentlemen."

"If our security was breached and she was abducted by enemy agents, we'll all have a lot to answer for," said Foster.

"We have no reason to suspect any such thing, Aaron. I've a bigger worry to share with you all. It's the spymaster. Let me assure you all that he will ask after her soon. If Fairchild isn't found, what shall he be told?"

The instructors froze at this startling thought. Each man waited in uncomfortable silence for one of the others to speak. It was Denville who was forced to shatter the silence. "Bloody hell, you lot! Speak up! Any suggestions?"

Chapter Fourteen

Wilson Academy—Thursday, The Twenty-second of August

News of Fairchild's disappearance spread through Wilson Academy like a spark of tinder on dry hay. Mrs. Hunnicut had cautioned the servants to keep the distressing news from reaching the spymaster's ears. She swore them to secrecy, but for how long they would do so, she knew not.

Hugh Denville, an experienced campaigner, took charge of the search. He set up one of the classrooms—for there was no thought given to training during this crisis—as his headquarters, spread maps of the areas surrounding the academy as well as Havelshire on a large table. He marked off small sections and assigned search parties. He also made sure to leave enough staff behind to gull the spymaster into believing that the business of the academy was running smoothly.

Trainees, instructors and every able-bodied servant volunteered to help in the search for Fairchild.

Olivia had no thought of any particular direction when she ran away. She no longer cared what happened to her.

Even her quest to become a spy no longer mattered. What point in going on when she'd murdered the man she loved? But she was too much of a coward to take her own life. What good would it do anyway? Yet death would be a welcome relief from her torment.

Perhaps she should find her way home to Heatham and beg her father to allow her to enter a nunnery where she could spend the rest of her days repenting her grievous sin. She imagined herself on her knees before the altar, dressed in a novice's habit, taking vows of poverty, facing a suitably harsh life as a penance for the unpardonable act of murder. Might the authorities hang her for it? Well, she would welcome the gallows.

She knew little of the woods surrounding Wilson Academy, yet she was clever enough to avoid the route to the lake and the equally familiar route she'd taken when she hiked with the other trainees. Instead, she chose to lose herself in the dense forest, cutting her way through thick branches and climbing over tangles of rotted underbrush. She paid no heed to the deep scratches unruly twigs etched on her arms. She only yelped in pain when sharp branches snarled her long hair in their web. To free herself, she was forced to hack off her curls, glancing with disdain at the fallen ringlets. What did it matter? There was no one to care how she looked any longer.

Her legs buckled when a wave of exhaustion forced her to a halt. She spied a small glade hidden by surrounding woods ahead of her, managed to make her way to the clearing and fell asleep, her head resting on her portmanteau.

After Sebastian's bath, rather than leaving his care to a footman, Denville changed the bandages. He shaved him and helped him to dress. He tied a cloth around the spymaster's neck to form a sling, one of the orders left by Doctor Davis.

"Not half bad, Hugh, for someone lately at death's door," said the spymaster examining himself in the mirror. "Alert all the instructors, will you. I'd like them to join me for lunch."

"Yes, sir. Except . . . I've granted Hawes and Mason a free day today. They'd some pressing personal business to attend to. That all right with you?" Denville held his breath, for the men were out leading two of the day's search parties.

"Of course. You're in charge until I'm fully healed. I'll see them when they return."

Denville grinned, but warned, "You're not to tire yourself, sir. You promised."

"I know. I know. I'll nap after lunch, you tyrant. While you're at it, be a good chap and inform the trainees to report to my private dining room at five for dinner."

Denville's heart dropped into his boots. "That's a bit much all in one day, sir. Put that off till tomorrow."

Sebastian turned to him, the silly grin of a schoolboy pasted on his face. "You know which trainee I can't wait to see. In fact, I'm a little surprised Fairchild hasn't fought her way past you and burst in here already. Has she taken the news of my recovery well?"

He stopped, for his aide stood frozen, his face turned pale. "Where's Fairchild? There's something wrong, isn't there? Why hasn't she been to see me? You'd better tell me at once."

She woke to the faint sound again. At first, it seemed part of her dream, but within moments, she knew it was real. She rose to her feet, trying to determine the direction of the sound. The rush of running water was nearby somewhere. She listened for the sound again. It came from the same direction. She took her knife out of the bag, hefted the heavy load on her back and followed the noise of the rushing water.

She cut more brush out of her way as she advanced toward the sound. It grew louder with each step. When she cut away a final tree limb, she faced a small rock formation shaped like stepping stones, one on top of the other, perhaps five feet taller than she was. The water came rushing down from the top, creating a waterfall. To her astonishment, a mewling kitten clung to a branch on the third rock.

Olivia put her portmanteau down on a dry patch, removed her boots and rolled up her trousers. She stepped carefully onto the first rock, for it was covered with slippery moss. For purchase, she held onto the thin branches sprouting from between the rocks. When she reached the bedraggled kitten, she tucked it into her jacket and climbed down.

Her eyes searched the terrain as she drew on her boots. It was obvious that the kitten was new-born. Where was its mother? The half-drowned puss had to come from somewhere nearby. Her eyes focused on the gully filled with water at the bottom of the rock formation. She spied the kitten's dead mother and three tiny offspring drowned in that shallow pool. The gruesome sight made her feel sick.

The trainees had been warned that poachers plied their trade in the forests surrounding the academy. They must have drowned the lot. She hurried away from the grave site.

"How long has she been gone?" demanded Sebastian. "She took none of our horses you say? Have you checked the mail coach rosters in Havelshire? Have my horse brought round, Hugh. I'm going out to search for her."

Denville protested in a loud voice. "No! You're not going anywhere in your condition. Let me remind you that I am in charge. You said so yourself not five minutes ago. With all due respect, you're far too weak to ride a horse. Let me assure you if I have to tie you to your bed, I will. I'll handle this. I promise you we're all doing everything we can to find her."

Sebastian rose from his chair and said in a heated voice, "I don't take orders from you. I'm still the spymaster."

"You will take orders from me," Denville shouted back. "You're simply not well enough. I'm directing the search and that's the end of it. Sir."

Sebastian sat back down and held his head in his good hand, a tacit acknowledgment of the truth of Denville's words. When he looked up at his aide, pain was etched on his face. He said in a pleading voice, "Allow me to do *something*, Hugh, I beg of you. Give me some role in this or I'll go mad."

How odd, Olivia thought, when she noted a lift of her spirits. Hope began to replace the despair she had lived with throughout Sebastian's illness. Perhaps she was meant to save the kitten's life. Perhaps the poor thing would save hers as well.

"You're a game little thing," she crooned aloud, holding the soft ball of fur to her face. "You're full of spunk, puss. How brave you were to climb out of danger. I must give you a name, my little man. What shall I call you? I'll have to think of something suitable."

She rummaged through her bag and found the cape she'd worn when first she came to Wilson Academy and put it to practical use. She secured the top of the cape on an overhanging branch of a shade tree and spread it into a makeshift tent to shelter her and her small kitten. By the time she'd finished, it was almost dark. She crawled inside with the kitten and made a quick meal of some of the bread, cheese and a bit of apple. For each bite she allowed herself, she prepared a tiny nibble for her kitten, softening his food with water from her bottle.

The open side of the tent let in the light of the moon for a time, but a sudden squall forced her to pin it shut when the rain swept down. When she curled up beside him, the kitten fell asleep. She closed her eyes and tried to sleep, without success.

Where is the Duke of Heatham's daughter, Lady Olivia? she wondered. Where is the easy life she once knew? Where is that vain, frivolous lass who loved to primp before a mirror, who fretted over broken nails, who spent days searching for the right fancy ball gown, who flirted so charmingly with every eligible male? Had she vanished into thin air, never to return? Well, good riddance to her and to her old life.

She had survived, just like the kitten asleep beside her. Would Sebastian have been proud of her had she not murdered him? No. He never wanted her to be a spy. He'd made that clear, hadn't he? Yet she had heard admiration in his voice just the same. Perhaps she was meant to perform brave deeds to protect her country after all, if only as a monument to his memory. Much soothed by these thoughts, she fell into a peaceful sleep untroubled by haunting dreams.

Sebastian studied the map of the academy acreage which had been divided into sections. He said, "Good work, Hugh."

Denville beamed, for the spymaster's tone was filled with admiration. "During the war, it was you who taught me how to plan a campaign."

"So I did. Let us concentrate on planning a similar campaign to find Fairchild before any harm comes to her. Send word to Darlington in London to be on the alert for her, should she by some miracle find her way there." He paused in thought. "No. I rather think she'll try to find her way to Brighton where her family remains for the summer." He took up a pen in his good hand and began to examine the map, marking off several segments as his eyes searched.

"Sound the alarm, Hugh. I want every available man to assemble in the ballroom. At once."

It took very little time to fill the large room with the entire male staff of Wilson House. When Sebastian strode to the musician's platform where he could be seen and heard, he said, "We must find Fairchild as soon as we can, for there is always the possibility she may encounter unforeseen danger. She took no horse, which means she can't have gone too far. Mr. Denville and I have divided our land into small sections of approximately one square mile each. With the exception of Mrs. Hunnicut and the under maids who will remain here with me to care for Fairchild when she is brought home to us, each instructor and each trainee has been assigned to a team. The leader has been given one section where we think she may have wandered. When your name is called, please join your leader and follow his directions. Get a good night's sleep. It may be your last until she is found. We begin the search at first light. Thank you."

Mrs. Hunnicut followed him out of the ballroom and into his chamber. "Will you pour me a brandy, ma'am?" He rubbed his eyes.

"Of course, sir. Sit down and rest while I fetch it for you."

"Why did she run away, Mrs. Hunnicut? What possessed her? Did anyone chastise her for the accident? I did not blame her, I assure you." Sebastian took the goblet from her hand and drained it in one swallow.

"I wish I knew, sir. I do know that she suffered much remorse for having been the cause of all your difficulties. But she kept to herself. I suspect she thought everyone blamed her."

"She'd run away for such a flimsy excuse? No. That can't be why she ran away. She never cared a fig for what others thought of her." *Not my Livy.* " There has to be a better reason than that."

"We can't always understand the depths of another's secret thoughts, sir."

"Yes, that's true. But it wasn't her fault, ma'am. You know that. You heard the doctor explain the cause of the infection. The culprits were the unseen germs on the end of that exposed foil. Fairchild had nothing to do with it, and so I shall inform her. When we find her." *If we find her alive.* The thought terrified him.

Olivia's day dawned clear and crisp. She spread the cape out to dry while she fed herself and her stalwart companion the last of her provisions. But her mind turned in turmoil. Where should she go? What should she do? What would dear Sebastian want her to do? The thought startled her at first, but the answer became clear.

"No help for it, puss. We'll have to return to Wilson Academy and face the consequences, be it dismissal or whatever else they may have in store for me, no matter how drastic." She spoke the words aloud to the furry little creature in her hand.

"Meow."

She laughed for the first time in ages. "Well said, puss. All right, little one. I've made my choice. Give me the courage to face their wrath."

The need to refill her empty water bottle drew her back to the waterfall where another thought struck her. "Let's see what's on the top of that waterfall, puss. Maybe there's a path we can follow." She tucked her companion into her shirt and removed her boots, this time stuffing them into her bag along with her dried cape. Taking great care not to slip on the moss-covered rocks, she reached the top of the waterfall and found herself standing on the final rock, a long boulder embedded in the middle of a small creek, its cool waters bathing her feet as it rushed past her and flowed down to the gully.

She shielded her eyes from the sun and explored the landscape. At the far end of the creek, she made out a white steeple rising over the top of the trees. "Why that must be the church steeple in Havelshire, puss! I've found the way back to the academy."

She waded through the shallow creek to dry land. There she sat to dry her feet and put her boots back on before hurrying off in the direction of the steeple. She reached a rutted dirt road and paused to catch her breath. "We'll rest here for a moment, puss." When she peeked at him, she grinned, for he was fast asleep. *I've thought of a wonderful name for you, my brave one. When you wake, I shall bestow it upon you.*

The rumble of wheels on the road reached her ears. She jumped up and hid behind a tree at the sound of horse hooves. Her heart pumped frantically. Could this be friend or foe? When an open cart filled with hay rounded the curve in the road, she breathed a sigh of relief. It was a farmer on his way to market in the village most likely.

Olivia ran to the middle of the road and waved him down. "Excuse me, sir. Are you going to Havelshire?"

"Mayhap," the farmer said, suspicion in his voice. "Who wants to know, lad?"

Olivia had forgotten she'd cut off all her curls. She affected an accent and said. "Please, sir. I've lost me way. Me mum will thrash me if'n I don't hurry home."

"How old are you, lad?"

"Twelve, sir."

"Big fer yer age, an't you? All right, I'll take ye home. Hop up next to me."

"Meow."

"What's that noise, lad?"

"It's only a poor kitty I found in the woods, sir. Somebody drownded its mum and t'other newborns."

"Poachers, likely."

"I 'spect so, sir."

The two rode in silence for a time, Olivia wondering how hard it would be to find her way back to the academy with her kitten. This cheerless thought stayed with her until the farmer's raspy voice intruded.

"Where d'ye live lad? If y'tell me the direction, I'll take you to the door."

"Much obliged sir, but if'n you just leave me front o' the church, I c'n walk home from there."

"We're almost there, lad. Mind yer mum and don't go gettin' lost in the woods again. All right?"

"Yes, sir," she said. "Much obliged, sir. I thank you for yer kindness."

"There's the church up yonder. Have a look, lad. They's lots of people about. Mayhap a weddin' today. Mayhap a funeral."

Olivia shuddered at the suggestion of a funeral. Was it Sebastian's funeral? She stiffened her resolve to confront her fate, whatever the cost. She wondered if the farmer could hear the loud beating of her heart as they drew nearer the church.

The shouts that assaulted her ears made no sense at first. She watched in astonishment as an unruly mob ran toward the farmer's cart.

"It's Fairchild!"

"We've found her, thank the Good Lord."

"Is she all right?"

"Why's her hair look so funny?"

"Looks like summat the cat dragged in."

The first man to reach her was Denville. He lifted her

down before she had time to thank the farmer and was surrounded by footmen and stable boys.

"Don't crush me, sir. I've something precious in my jacket." She pushed him away with one hand and removed the kitten. Olivia stared at the grinning group of men and boys surrounding her. She turned back to Sebastian's secretary, sank to her knees and bowed her head.

"Stand up, Fairchild." He helped her to her feet.

Her answer came in a rush. "I'm so sorry, sir. I hadn't meant to be the cause of the spymaster's death. Are you all here for the funeral service? Will you take me to his coffin so I may say a final good-bye?" Stunned silence greeted her words. She took the silence as condemnation and began to sob.

"Calm yourself. He's alive, lass, but if we don't bring you back at once, he'll have my head on a plate."

He turned to one of the stable lads. "Ride home like the wind and inform the spymaster we're bringing Fairchild home."

"Yes, sir. At once, sir." The young boy took off at a run, in the direction of the village stables where the group had left their horses.

"Is the spymaster really alive, sir? You're not just saying that so I'll come back with you? For I had already made up my mind to return to the academy, whatever the consequences."

Denville bent to her ear. "Fact is, lass, he can't wait to get his hands on his betrothed. Told me so himself."

Olivia blushed from ear to ear. "Then I'm ready, sir."

Denville heard the kitten mewl. "What's that noise?"

"It's just a kitten, sir." She took it out of her jacket. "He's hungry. Truth be known he was near dead like his mum and his brothers and sisters who were drowned. I saved his life." *And he saved mine.*

He eyed the kitten with distaste. "We don't need any

more cats, Fairchild. The academy's overrun with 'em. We'll have to drown him as well."

"Don't you dare touch him!" she thundered, her eyes ablaze. "You'll have to drown me first before I let you drown my helpless little puss."

Denville's lips quirked at her determination. "All right, all right. Does that thing have a name?"

"He's not a thing. He's a he. Of course he has a name."

"Well? What have you named him, lass?"

"Sebastian."

Chapter Fifteen

Wilson Academy—One Hour Later

On the journey back from Havelshire to the academy, Olivia wondered what condition she would find the spymaster in. He was alive she knew, but she had been afraid to ask the extent of the damage she had caused him. Instead, she invented tragedy.

She pictured him with only one arm, an invalid for the rest of his life. In her mind's eye, she became a heroine like Joan of Arc. She vowed she would sacrifice everything to care for him, give up her dream of becoming a spy, throw away the gay life she once knew in London, though that wasn't much of a penance. They would retire to a quiet life in the country. She would read to him as he sat before the fire. She would take him for long walks through the countryside. She would walk barefoot through hot coals for him. There was nothing she would not do for his sake.

When he rode up beside her horse, Denville asked in exasperation, "Why are you crying, Fairchild? What's wrong? Didn't you believe me when I told you the spymaster is in fine form?"

She wiped her eyes with a knuckle, but the tears continued to flow.

Denville rarely had had to confront a crying woman. He could lead a charge in battle without a hint of fear, but the tears of a woman terrified him. "Pull yourself together, lass. The academy is just ahead."

On the driveway at the entrance, cheers from the instructors, the trainees and the servants rang out when the horses drew up, Denville and Olivia leading the way. Her eyes searched for Sebastian, but he was not out front.

She turned to Fourier. "I've found a little kitten, *monsieur*. Will you take care of him for me? He's very hungry."

The fencing master grinned. "But of course, Fairchild. He shall have a good home in my kitchen and you may visit him there whenever you wish. Give your *petit prince* to me. Does he have a name?"

"His name is Sebastian, sir." She dismounted to the sound of the fencing master's laughter. The staff pressed in close, eager to pump her hand, pat her shoulder, wish her well.

"Welcome back, Fairchild," said Mrs. Hunnicut, all smiles. She was standing at the door. "Spymaster's in his office waiting for you."

"I'm such a mess, Mrs. Hunnicut. Shouldn't I clean up first?"

The housekeeper chuckled. "Best not keep him waiting, dear. I'll have a bath ready for you after your interview."

A smiling footman bowed to her. "Welcome home, Miss."

When he attempted to lead her to Sebastian's office, she said, "I know my way, thank you," and flew past the astonished servant.

Sebastian turned away from the window overlooking the driveway. At her knock, he said, "Come," in a forbidding voice.

"Fairchild reporting, sir."

"Come closer. Let me have a look at you."

"I'm covered with filth, sir." *He has both of his arms!*

"I shouldn't wonder. What happened to your hair?"

"I cut it off."

"May I inquire as to what caused you to do such an outrageous thing?"

Her words came in a rush. "Well, you see, I had to hack my way through all this brush to make a path, you see, and my curls got tangled in a low-hanging branch, you see, with a lot of thorny brambles, you see, and . . ."

"Enough! Cease all your foolish chatter, hoyden." Sebastian walked slowly round to the front of his desk and opened his good arm to her. "What took you so long, my most precious, most irritating, most stubborn, most disobedient, most adorable, most foolish, most beautiful, most impatient thorn in my flesh?"

She hiccupped a strangled sob and flew at him, his good arm grasping her as she buried her head on his chest. "I thought you were dead!" she sobbed, soaking his sling with her tears.

He lifted her chin. "Stop your blubbering, darling girl. You're soaking my bandages with your muddy tears. How any woman can still look magnificent in spite of all the dirt, in spite of missing half her beautiful golden locks, in spite of looking very much like a chimney sweep, I'll never understand. Do stop your bawling, my love. I have another occupation in mind." Without waiting for an answer, he crushed his lips to hers and kissed her without mercy.

London—"Three Zarkovian ships have been sighted at Dover, sir. They're about to enter the channel. The prince should be ready to disembark in three days if the weather holds," said Darlington. "But I must warn you that we've received some disturbing reports from our agents. Russian spies are already on our soil to try to prevent the signing of this treaty."

"I'm not surprised to hear it. The Russians are in an uproar over it."

"Why would the czar want to prevent such an insignificant country from increasing their livelihood, I wonder. Zarkovia is no bigger than Cornwall."

"That may well be so, but its port faces St. Petersburg, my boy. It is just below Russian-controlled Estonia, you see. With this treaty, the Russians will be unable to bar Great Britain from expanding trade along the Baltic Sea. We'll protect Zarkovia from Russian invasion in exchange for opening a trade route to the Scandinavian countries."

"We stand ready to put a stop to any assassination attempt. I'll inform the spymaster, sir."

"Be sure to remind him that Fairchild is to be kept away from taking any part in this operation. His Grace would not approve, I'm sure. We must keep his daughter safe from danger at all costs."

"I'll make that quite clear to the spymaster, sir." Had his future father-in-law made such a request? he wondered. He doubted it. Sidmouth meant for the duke to be beholden to him, more like.

"Get on with your work, Darlington," Sidmouth said, dismissing his aide. The home secretary turned his attention to the unfinished report he was preparing for the Regent.

Sebastian read the home office directive Darlington sent him and rang for his aide. "Where's Fairchild, Hugh?"

"She's in martial arts class with the rest of the trainees, sir. Doing quite well, I hear."

"I didn't ask you for an evaluation of her skills, did I?" Sebastian snapped.

"Sorry, sir. Are you wanting to see her?"

"At once!" His anger evaporated at the stricken look on the man's face, especially since Hugh had become more of a friend and a confidante than merely an aide. "Sorry for lashing out, Hugh. I'm not angry with you, my friend.

"Fact is, I've received a letter from the home office. It's our marching orders to protect Prince Joachim of Zarkovia. He arrives at the East India docks in London tomorrow afternoon."

Denville looked surprised. "You knew the prince was expected. Why are you so snappish? Is there a problem?"

"Yes, a big one. I've been directed to exclude Fairchild from this operation." He thrust the letter at Denville to read. "For her own safety," it says here. Her father may have had a hand in this, I suspect. The Duke of Heatham has enough power in government to force his will on Sidmouth."

"We both know Fairchild won't take the news very well, sir. Do you wish me to break it to her?"

Sebastian considered the offer, but rejected it out of hand. "No, Hugh. Thank you for the offer, but I'm not such a coward as all that."

Olivia knew at once from the look on his face that something was wrong when she entered his office. "What's troubling you, my darling? I can see it in your eyes." Olivia tried to circle his desk to embrace him, but he shook his head to hold her off.

"Sit, Fairchild." He pointed to the chair opposite and leaned back.

Something's terribly wrong. Else why would he call me Fairchild? "Sir? What is it you wish to see me about?"

"The staff has been given an assignment in London,

which I am to lead. I have appointed you spymaster in my absence. You will be fully in charge of all activities here."

"In charge of what activities? The scullery maids? What on earth are you talking about, my love?"

He half rose from his seat and pounded his fist on his desk. "This is vital government business! For heaven's sake Fairchild, do your duty and for once obey my bloody order!"

Was there a pleading note in his harsh voice? she wondered. "Are the other trainees part of your team, sir?" she asked in an even tone.

Sebastian shuffled the papers on his desk. "Dismissed, Fairchild." He did not raise his eyes to her when he heard her push back her chair, but he winced when she slammed the door hard. He sat frozen for what seemed to him like hours, elbows on his desk, holding his head between his hands.

At dawn the following morning, the stable boy held the reins of Sebastian's horse while he mounted. All the instructors, all the trainees, as well as every able-bodied footman, groom and stable hand were mounted on horseback awaiting the spymaster's signal to depart for London.

Mrs. Hunnicut, Olivia at her side, witnessed the departure from the open front door. The two women watched in silence as Sebastian raised one hand in signal, and rode off at the head of the contingent, like a general leading his army into battle.

"Why not take the rest of the day to rest, Fairchild?" the housekeeper said when the last of the group were out of sight.

"I think I will, ma'am, but first I must complete a task the spymaster left for me in his office."

"Of course, dear. I'm off to inspect supplies. Will you take lunch with me?"

"Yes, I'd like that." Olivia strolled away at an unhurried pace toward the spymaster's office. An under footman stood guard in front of his door, but she couldn't recall his name.

"I'm in charge of operations today, lad," she said with her most ingratiating smile. "Allow me to enter please, to do my work."

"Of course, ma'am," he said, and held open the door to the spymaster's office for her.

She sat at Sebastian's desk and began to read through the neatly stacked files he had left for her. She read them through, but she didn't find what she was looking for. She tried the desk drawers. They opened easily to her touch—all but one. She crawled under the desk in search of some sort of spring mechanism that would release the locked drawer, but she found none. Nothing for it but to force it open, she knew, convinced that there she would find the information she desired.

Olivia sat back in her seat, smoothed back her hair, and contemplated how best to accomplish this. She tried the letter opener on the desk, but it wasn't strong enough. Her eyes scanned the office for some sort of implement that might serve in its place. When her eyes settled on the fireplace andiron, she knew she had found the appropriate tool.

The locked drawer was no match for the heavy iron, though the wooden desk drawer splintered in the process. Ignoring the damage, Olivia searched through the contents of the drawer until she found the detailed plans to protect visiting Prince Joachim when his ships were secured at the East India docks. She kicked the splinters under the desk and covered the mess she'd made as best she could.

She spread Sebastian's files out all over the desk to make it look as though she were working, and rose to leave.

"Thank you," she said to the footman outside the door. "I haven't finished my work as yet. Make sure no one enters the office until I return."

"Of course, ma'am," he said, hoping his diligence in

following her orders would earn him a promotion. With the extra pay he would be able to marry at last.

Olivia kept a calm pose during lunch with Mrs. Hunnicut. She returned to Sebastian's office and pretended to be busy until dinnertime. It was easy to disguise her intentions when she and the housekeeper dined. All she had to do was to ask Mrs. Hunnicut questions about her past. The lady was flattered enough to respond throughout the entire meal.

When she retired for the night, Olivia lay on her cot fully dressed. She managed a light sleep, but she rose at first light and crept down the back stairs. She stopped in the kitchen to see her kitten, who purred contentedly when she tickled his belly. "Be a good lad, little Sebastian. I'm off to save the prince," she whispered, pouring extra milk into his dish.

London—Darlington was waiting for him when Sebastian led his small army into the yard of the home office. Waiting stable boys gathered all the reins and led the animals off to be watered, fed and brushed down until such time as the Wilson Academy men were ready to leave for home.

Darlington escorted them all into a large dining room where lunch awaited the men. "The ships haven't docked as yet," he said to Sebastian in a low voice as the hungry men fell to their task.

"Disguises? Weapons?"

"Ready and waiting for all your people. My clerks have been instructed to escort your men to the changing room when they finish their lunch."

Sebastian grinned. "I needn't have asked. You are the most efficient soldier in our small army."

Darlington smiled. In jest, he said, "What else have I to do today, spymaster, but your bidding? Let's leave these hungry warriors to their feast. We're invited to lunch with the home secretary." He led the way to Sidmouth's office.

"Welcome to London, spymaster. Plans all in place, Darlington?"

"Yes, sir," Chris replied. "The academy men are downstairs having their lunch."

"I trust my special order was followed?" The home secretary nodded to the footman to begin serving them.

Sebastian said, "Of course, sir. Fairchild remains in safety at the academy. I assigned her to take my place as spymaster in my absence."

"Clever of you. I have to admit that I am relieved to hear she's safe. Her father has been breathing down my neck for days."

Chris bent to the task of eating his soup, trying hard not to chuckle at what he suspected was a blatant lie.

"Where are you off to so early in the morning, Fairchild?" asked Mrs. Hunnicut when she entered the kitchen.

"It's such a fine day, I fancy a brisk walk, ma'am. Just a quick one before I join you for breakfast."

"Be sure to take someone with you, dear."

Olivia grinned. "No need to worry, Mrs. Hunnicut. I have no intention of getting lost again. I'll not be long, I promise."

"Have a good walk, then."

"I'll join you in the dining room soon. I promise, ma'am."

As soon as she was out of Mrs. Hunnicut's sight, Olivia rushed to the stables where Jenny was waiting. She entered an empty stall to change into the tattered clothing Jenny supplied. She smeared some ash to dirty her face and pulled the wool cap over her hair to cover it completely. "How do I look, Jenny?"

"Like any other London chimney sweep. Try not to show your hands, though. They're a dead giveaway."

"Hand me those filthy work gloves, then. They should do the trick. Where's Teddy?"

"Outside, holding the reins."

"Then let's get on with it."

When she was mounted, Jenny said, "Teddy will lead you to my brother Bill. He's waiting just outside the village. Here's a lunch I prepared for you and my brother. London's a long way off."

"I can't thank you enough, Jenny. You too, Teddy. Let's be off, then. I want you back at the academy with these horses stabled before anyone has a chance to notice you're gone."

"Right, then." Teddy blew Jenny a kiss and spurred his horse, Olivia following behind.

They found Bill just where his sister said he would be waiting. Olivia climbed up beside him, took the food basket Teddy handed her and waved good-bye.

Conversation was limited on the journey to London, for Bill was a man of few words. But he did have a hearty appetite and Jenny's basket was empty by the time they reached London. His destination was the open market near Covent Garden where he sold hens' eggs as well as vegetables he and his wife grew on their farm. The East India docks weren't far out of his way.

When Bill stopped his cart to let Olivia climb down, he tipped his hat and pointed. "Docks are ten minutes' walk down that lane yonder, lad." Jenny hadn't told her brother that Olivia was not a boy.

"Thank you kindly, Bill," Olivia answered in a voice lowered by two octaves. She waved to him and watched his wagon disappear before consulting her map, the one she'd copied from Sebastian's plans. From these, she knew the exact location of each man involved in the operation.

She heard the militia band playing, "God Save the King" before she actually came upon the colorful scene. When she turned the corner, her eyes widened at the sight of the three magnificent sailing ships festooned with colorful banners, the Zarkovian flags proudly flying on all three. She made her way through the crowd, where she spied Carter near the bandstand below the visitors' platform.

Sidmouth and Chris were on the welcoming platform seated on either side of the lord mayor of London. There were many other men as well, prominent members of Parliament, she guessed.

Olivia eyed Riggs at the bottom of the gangplank on the left side and Perkins on the right side. She checked her map and followed its path with one of her fingers. Riggs was posted nearest Denville, positioned ten feet away. Her heart skipped a beat when she spied Sebastian a few steps behind Perkins, his eyes glued to the top of the gangplank. By then, it was well past three in the afternoon.

When the band struck up what she supposed was the Zarkovian national anthem, Olivia stood stock still and drew in her breath. From the report in Sebastian's office—the one she had committed to memory—she knew it was the signal for the prince to disembark.

Chapter Sixteen

London—Same Day

When the Prince of Zarkovia made his appearance at the top of the gangplank, he waved to the cheering crowd below. Olivia noted that he was a handsome young man, tall, dark-skinned, with high Slavic cheekbones, an aquiline nose, shining black hair and a thin mustache. Prince Joachim took a step down when a shot rang out, the noise barely discernible above the music.

But Olivia heard the shot and whipped her head toward Sebastian who had also heard it. She watched him take off at a run in the direction of the rifle blast. She sprinted after him through the crowd, ignoring the shouts and the disorder nearest the ship carrying the prince. She left the task of safeguarding the prince to the others. Her concern was for Sebastian. She was forced to bounce up often to keep him in sight, no easy task in the crush of people on the docks. He turned into a dark, narrow lane where she lost sight of him, but only for a moment.

She was perhaps twenty steps behind him when she got to that lane, just in time to see an unconscious Sebastian being dragged along by two of four men into a nearby building. She pressed herself against the wall, her eyes glued to Sebastian, whose head was hanging limp, his eyes shut. A third man ran up the steps of the ramshackle building and held open the door. When she caught a glint of steel, part of a pistol held by the last man turning into the building, she let out a tense whoosh of breath. *Four men. Sebastian unconscious. Think up a plan to rescue him from the assassins.*

Olivia stood frozen in her tracks, trying to decide on what action she could take, when two strong hands gripped her shoulders and held tight. "Let go of me," she growled, struggling to free herself.

"Don't make another sound, Fairchild," a familiar voice whispered in her ear.

"That you, Riggs? Thank heaven you're here. How did you find me?"

"I knew something was up when I saw you running away from the docks after the shot was fired—the prince wasn't hit, by the way—I figured you saw something and decided to follow." He grinned at her. "I knew you couldn't have been running away because you've never run from a fight in your life."

She smothered a laugh. "I was never more happy to see you, Riggs. The spymaster's in trouble. He was knocked unconscious and dragged into that building over there. You go get help. I'm going in."

"You're not going anywhere, my girl. Not without me."

"There are four of them. The two of us can't fight them alone."

"All the more reason you're not going in alone. We have to make a plan."

"You're right. We need to come up with a strategy."

"Do you have a gun?"

"No. Where's yours? I thought everyone was issued a gun before you left the home office for this mission."

Riggs blushed. "I lost mine when I ran after you."

"I have only my knife. We'll have to make do with that. You stay here and I'll saunter past the building, to see what I can see. Then I'll come back. Okay?"

Riggs scratched his head. "I don't know, Fair—"

But she slipped out from under his arm and walked the few steps toward the building just as one of the assassins came outside, apparently for a breath of air, for it was a stifling hot day. Riggs heard her ask him in a deepened voice, "Got a copper, guv? I'm that 'ungry, I am."

The man mumbled something in an unfamiliar tongue. He waved one hand at her in a dismissive gesture, a glint of steel visible in his other hand.

"Keep yer knickers on, guvnor. Didn't mean no 'arm."

Riggs ran up and grabbed her by the collar. "Don't be beggin' fer yersel', lad, when ye're workin' f' me," he yelled. "I paid fer yer to do an honest day's work pickin' pockets, not beggin'." He turned to the man on the steps. "Beg pardon, guv. Brat's allus runnin' away."

The man waved his hand in dismissal once again and disappeared inside the building.

Riggs pulled Fairchild around the corner out of sight should the man return. "I'll give you a boost up to the window sill, lass. Tell me what you see."

She stepped onto Riggs' clasped fingers and boosted herself up to the sill. "Nothing," she whispered. "Let's try the next one."

Riggs repeated the boost at the next window. "He's in there, Riggs! Trussed up like a pig, poor sod." She jumped to the ground just as the noise of footsteps caused them to flatten against the wall. Two of the assassins passed right by them as they hurried down the street. They did not so much as glance down the lane where Olivia and Riggs were hiding.

"Phew! That was a close one," said Riggs, wiping his brow.

"Stay on your guard. They may be back all too soon." She crept back to the front of the building and looked both ways. "See here, Riggs. Just look at all the people on the street. That's to our advantage."

Riggs peeked over her shoulder and said, "Prostitutes and drunks. Unsavory bunch, if you ask me. What good can they do us?"

"This is our chance, don't you see? The spymaster's in there with only two men. We're trained to take advantage of unusual situations. I have an idea, but we'll need some money. How much do you have with you?"

He reached into his trouser pocket and came up with a few coins totaling just under a pound. Olivia grabbed them all. "That all you have? Well, it will have to do." She tucked the coins into her trousers.

"You're not alone in this, Fairchild. Tell me what you plan to do," he said.

"Look out, Riggs. The first two are coming back. They're munching on a paper full of fish and chips, for heaven's sake! We'll have to take his kidnappers one at a time. That's the only way we can save the spymaster's life. Be right back."

She sauntered away from the puzzled trainee as if she hadn't a care in the world. At last she saw what she was looking for. A woman covered with garish face paint slouched in a doorway, her hands on her hips. She was dressed in a gaudy costume meant to attract male customers.

Olivia swaggered up to her and said in a gruff voice, "Ow much, then?"

The woman looked her up and down and said, "Off w'you, lad. I don't do little boys. I 'ave me pride, y'know."

Olivia checked her grin and flashed the coins she held in her hand. In her natural voice, she said, "Good for you, lass. I don't want your trade. I just want to pay you to borrow your clothes for ten minutes."

"What'll I wear, then? I'll catch me death."

"Change into mine. It's only for ten minutes. And you can rest your feet and have a pint while you wait. I'm sure that inn across the way has a tavern."

The woman eyed Olivia and thought a moment. "Only ten minutes? You won't be stealin' any o'my customers, then? Guess you could pass for a woman, lad. Follow me." The two changed clothing under the staircase in the hallway. Olivia tried to hold her breath against the rank smell, a mixture of urine and alcohol and God knew what all else.

"'Ere. Let me fix yer face a bit." Without waiting for an answer, she opened her purse and found her color pots, just like the ones actresses at Covent Garden used, most likely. She used her fingertips and applied various shades to Olivia's face. "There. Yer own mum wouldn't reckonize you now."

"Where shall I find you when I'm finished, ma'am?"

"Like you said, I'll be awaitin' 'cross the way in that there tavern." She walked off, whistling and jingling the coins in her pocket.

"Fancy a tumble, sir?" Olivia asked Riggs when she returned to him.

He barely looked at her. "Go away. Can't you see I'm busy?"

She laughed softly. "It's me, Riggs. If I fooled you, I'll fool those men. Wait here and when I lure one of them into the alley, bash his head in. Pick up that heavy board over there and keep your fingers crossed. Give me time to make them think I'm what you thought I was. Here's my knife. Keep it handy."

With hope in his voice, Riggs said, "It might work, but it's dangerous."

Olivia shrugged. "We're spies, aren't we? Now's the time to put it to the test. I'm off, then. Wish me luck, lad."

* * *

"The prince and his followers are safe at Carlton House, sir."

"Thank heavens for that, Darlington. It would have been our heads if anything happened to the prince. Have the assassins been caught yet?"

"No, sir. Denville, the spymaster's aide, is conducting an intensive search for them."

Sidmouth looked puzzled. "Denville? Where's the spymaster?"

"I'm afraid he's disappeared, sir. We can't find him anywhere."

Sidmouth glared at his aide as though the messenger were to blame. "Intensify the search, then. Enlist the Bow Street Runners. Alert the militia. Do everything in your power to find him, for if the assassins have him, they'll torture him to try to get him to reveal Prince Joachim's whereabouts."

"Yes, sir. At once, sir." Darlington knew it was useless to point out that he'd already notified Bow Street and the local garrison. Far more diplomatic to allow the home secretary to believe it was his own idea.

As Chris turned to leave, Sidmouth added, "Thank heaven I've managed to keep Heatham's daughter out of this botched operation. One of my best strategies, eh?"

"I couldn't agree more, sir." Chris hurried out of the office, anxious to find a secure place where he could not be heard. He let loose a crack of laughter at the home secretary's insistence on taking credit where none was actually due.

Olivia put one hand on her hip and one foot on the bottom step and began to whistle. When he heard it, a man came out of the door to the right of the rickety steps to investigate. Olivia gave him what she hoped was a lascivious come hither look and crooked her finger. He understood her meaning at once and followed her to the corner. She allowed him to grab her, giving her the chance to turn his back to Riggs, who promptly rendered the unsuspecting man unconscious with the aid of the heavy board. He removed the man's belt and tied his hands securely behind his back.

"One down, three to go," Olivia whispered, and hurried back to the steps. It didn't take long for a second man to peer out, searching both ways for his colleague. She repeated the come-hither look and the man swaggered down the steps toward her. He was heavier than the first, but when Riggs hit him, he fell like a ton of coal.

"That leaves two," she said when she had helped haul him out of sight. "Do you think we ought to storm the building and try to take them?"

"Good idea, lass. Why don't you sashay up those stairs and knock on the door? When one of them opens it, we'll force our way in."

But no one answered her knock. She tried the door handle. It was locked. Without a word, Riggs pointed to her shoulder then to the door. She nodded in understanding and the two put their shoulders forward as one and rammed into it. The door gave way at once.

The spymaster was lying on his side, securely tied hands to feet. His mouth was gagged, but his eyes were in motion. He used them to point to the direction of the assassin's gun. To no avail, for Fairchild and Riggs were too busy to notice.

"You take the one near the spymaster. I'll take the other one."

The man she chose was a burly six-foot monster more than three times her weight. She bowed to him as Sensei Nori had taught her. And swept his leg out from under him. When his head connected to the floor, he was knocked unconscious.

She turned to Riggs, locked in a struggle he appeared to be losing. "Sensei, Riggs," Olivia shouted. They both knew how to overcome superior strength with martial arts tactics.

With a mighty heave, Riggs rolled out from under his opponent and rose to his feet. He bowed to his opponent, in the ancient Japanese style, startling his enemy into confusion. He then proceeded to outwit his opponent by employing holds, chokes, throws, trips, joint-locks and well-placed kicks and strikes with the side of his hand. But the remaining assassin fought back with ferocity. And appeared to be winning when Riggs began to lose steam.

Sebastian's eyes caught hers and again they directed her to the gun on the floor. She reached for it at the same time the assassin attempted to kick it away with one foot, but his hands were kept busy throttling his opponent. Riggs' face was as red as a ripe tomato.

Olivia released the catch on the assassin's pistol, took aim and pulled the trigger. The bullet went through the man's head, splattering unlucky Riggs with his blood as the assassin fell to the ground.

"Ugh!" cried Riggs in disgust, wiping what was left of the man's brains off his face.

"The other one's still alive. Tie him up while I free the spymaster."

Olivia removed Sebastian's gag and cut the ropes away with her knife when Riggs threw it to her. "Are you all right, sir?" she asked.

"Bloody hell! Who are you?" He turned to Riggs. "Where'd you find this bit of baggage?"

Olivia shook her head at Riggs, to silence him. In a cockney accent, she bent to whisper in Sebastian's ear. "Oi came from the gutter, sir. Fancy a tuppin'? Send yer friend away from 'ere, an' fer a shillin', oi'll give yer a gran' tumble, oi will. Such as ye've never 'ad in yer life."

She sat back on her heels, put her hands on her thighs, tilted her head and licked her lips in a lewd gesture.

A slow smile found its way across Sebastian's face. "Fairchild? That you?"

Riggs could hold his laughter no longer as he took the knife from Olivia's hand. He cut away the final rope and helped the spymaster to his feet.

Sebastian rubbed his chafed wrists together to ease the pain of the rope burns, but could not take his eyes off her. "I fail to see much humor in this, Riggs."

Olivia stood stock-still, her hands on her hips, her coquettish eyes meeting his.

It took a moment, but when the truth dawned, he barked a laugh. "Where did you find those outrageous clothes, Fairchild?" He reached over and wiped a smudge from her cheek with his thumb.

"Oh, dear. I forgot. I promised to return to the tavern and change back with the lady." She walked toward the door.

"No, don't go." Sebastian reached for a pound note, turned to Riggs and handed it to him. "Go to the tavern and give the lady this. Tell her to buy herself a new costume."

"But why?" asked Olivia in a mystified tone.

Sebastian grinned. "We'll keep this one, if you don't mind. I think we need just such a costume at the home office, you see. It's a perfect disguise for undercover operations." He turned to Riggs and added, "No need to rush back. Take your time. Here's another pound note. You must be thirsty after fighting so hard. Have a tankard and don't hurry back."

Riggs looked dubious, but an order was an order. He brightened when the reason for the spymaster's request dawned on him. There were no secrets at Wilson Academy. Everyone knew they were betrothed. "Right, sir. Anything you say, sir." He turned to Olivia and asked, "How shall I know the woman whose clothes you borrowed?"

"She's wearing the boy's clothing I wore earlier. Tell her she can keep them."

"Right, then." Riggs took his leave, a sly grin etched on his face.

When he tapped her on the shoulder, Olivia turned to Sebastian with a question in her eyes. "What?"

He reached into his pocket and came up with a coin. "Here's a shilling for a tup, ma'am."

"In these smelly rags? You're daft."

"Can I help it if those 'rags' inspire me? Take a look."

Her eyes traveled downward.

"As you see, my irresistible lightskirt, I cannot control myself when you present such an inviting picture." He drew her to him in a crushing embrace that spoke volumes.

"With a dead man in the room?" she protested when he allowed her to come up for air.

Sebastian's hands brushed across her breasts and she gasped. "He's beyond caring."

"The other spy might wake up," she said in a hoarse whisper.

His hand crept between her legs and she groaned. "If he does, I won't share you with him. I promise you that."

"What if Riggs comes back too soon?"

He nuzzled her ear and lay her down on the floor. "In that case, we must be quick about it, mustn't we? But not too quick, my love. Why spoil all our pleasure?"

Her eyes lit with mischief. "Slow will cost you extra. I have me business t' think of, you know."

He removed all his clothes and let them fall to the floor. "You drive a hard bargain, ma'am. All right. I'll take four shillings worth."

Olivia gurgled a laugh. "Bragging again? Bet you can't do it twice."

In answer, he took off every stitch she wore and added them to his pile. She shivered. "Cold, my love? Let me warm you." He lay her down on top of the heap on the floor and fell to his knees beside her, his eyes feasting on her body. "Good God, Livy! You're bloody beautiful."

"Hurry, Sebastian. Riggs . . ."

"Never mind him." The back of his hand made a slow journey from her tousled hair to her toes. When she gasped, he settled between her legs.

"Remember, it's my shilling. Give me your best, ma'am." His voice turned hoarse.

Olivia felt herself to be at peace. She had her Sebastian back. Safe. Sound. In her arms where he belonged.

Her eyes flew open when he rose to his feet.

"Why have you stopped? What are you doing?"

He put a finger to his lips to silence her, reached for a discarded piece of rope, took her hands, tied them together, pulled them over her head and secured the rope to the leg of a chair.

"Sebastian! What . . . ?"

"You'll see," he said, his breath labored.

She licked her lips in anticipation. "What are you doing?"

His crooked grin was answer enough as all thought fled before her primal need.

"Mmmm. Delicious feast," he murmured when his tongue found her nub.

"Untie me, you wretch," she gasped when she thought she could bear the pain of his exquisite torture no longer.

"Not on your life."

She screamed his name as wave after wave of heat pulsed through her.

"Ready for me? Tell me you want me," he demanded.

"Yes! Oh yes! Please," she pleaded, and met him thrust for thrust. She felt as if she were drowning in a pool of lust.

When he reached his climax, his shouts of joy ripped through her like lightning.

Sebastian lay down by her side, turned her face to his and met her eyes with a smirk of satisfaction.

"Good God, Livy. I'll never let you go. Not after this. Never."

"Bloody well enjoyed it, did you? All right. Wipe that idiotic grin off your face and hand over another two shillings. A girl has to earn a living, you know."

"Thanks, but no thanks. I'm bloody well done in, minx."

"So soon? I don't believe it." Her eyes glanced down at his flaccid sex. "Untie me, seeing as how you'll need a little help to tup me again like you promised."

He reached over her head and pulled the rope to free her hands, but caught them in his before she could do what she threatened.

"Stop it! What are you trying to do to me, you insatiable lightskirt? Kill me?"

Chapter Seventeen

London—Same Day

By the time Riggs returned, they had adjusted their clothing as if nothing of any import had taken place in his absence.

"What shall we do with the assassins, sir? There are two more outside," he asked.

"Best we leave them where they are. We'll check to make sure the two outside are tied securely before we leave here."

"Where are you taking us, sir?" Olivia's voice held a hint of suspicion.

"Are you questioning yet another one of my orders, Fairchild? Can't you do as I say just this once?" Although he growled, his eyes did a jig at the flush of sex still coloring her face.

Riggs and Olivia followed the spymaster back toward the docks where they came upon Denville and a good many others, all academy men.

"Spymaster! Thank God you're alive. I have half of London out searching for you," said Denville, relief on his face. "The Bow Street Runners were called in to help in the search. And all the militia stationed in London."

"What of the prince, Hugh?"

"That shot went wide of the mark. He's safe. He and his envoys were taken to Carlton House. They're with the Regent as we speak while some of our people are out searching for the assassins."

"The assassins have been found, thanks to Fairchild and Riggs. They're tied up in a building nearby. Send some of our people for them. Riggs will show you the way. When you have the lot, hand them over to the militia for the time being. A decision will be made as to what to do with the three that are still alive. Fairchild shot one of them when she and Riggs rescued me."

"Good lad, Riggs! But, where's Fairchild?"

Sebastian kept a straight face. "She's right behind you, my good man."

Olivia put her hand on her hip and ogled Denville when he turned to her. In a cockney accent, she said, "You 'is boss? 'E din't pay me fer me services. Ow'm I sposed to make a livin' wifout pay? I gave 'im a good one too, I did."

His eyes bulged at the sight of this painted, scantily dressed creature. He reached into his britches, pulled out a pound note and thrust it at her.

"Be on your way, then."

Olivia stuck it in her cleavage. "Thankee kindly, sir. Mayhap you fancy one, too? No extra charge."

Sebastian let out a shout of laughter at the look of horror on Denville's face. "You've been snookered, my friend. Don't you know who this lightskirt is? Take a better look."

Denville licked his lips as if he were dying of thirst. He wondered what was so humorous as he examined the cheeky lass before him, carefully inspecting her from head to toe. His eyes bulged when the truth dawned on him. "Fairchild?"

Olivia curtseyed. "What do you think of my disguise, sir? It certainly fooled the assassins, let me tell you."

Embarrassed, Denville removed his coat and put it round her shoulders. "You fooled me as well, Fairchild. Where did you get that outrageous outfit? No, better not tell me, for it's sure to shock me. I won't even ask you why you're in London instead of minding the academy as you were ordered to do." He turned to Sebastian and added, "By the way, the home secretary wants you to report to his office as soon as possible."

"I'll do so at once, then." Sebastian turned to Olivia. "Come along, Fairchild."

"No, sir. I can't greet Viscount Sidmouth looking like this. Can you arrange to take me to Fairchild House? My family is in Brighton, but there are always a few servants left behind to care for the property. I'll bathe and find something more appropriate to wear and meet you at the home office. It won't take me long."

He let out a sigh. "Try for some new conduct and obey my orders, Fairchild."

"I won't face the home secretary in these rags and you can't make me, sir."

He raised an eyebrow.

Olivia gave in. She lowered her eyes and said, "As you wish, sir."

Sebastian handed her into the hack Denville had hailed for them and climbed in beside her. When they were under way, he took out a clean cloth and wiped the dirt and the makeup off her face.

"What are you doing?"

He kissed her forehead. "I'm trying to clean you up so you'll feel more presentable, my lusty wench."

But she wasn't amused. "I rather think, you're trying to make me look ridiculous in the home secretary's eyes, so he'll be persuaded to dismiss me."

He lifted her chin and looked into her eyes. "Good God!

You're even more beautiful when you pout. How many times must I tell you? You were made for me."

She shoved his hand away and crossed her arms. "I take that to mean you are still determined to get rid of me, spymaster."

"No, my love." He managed to take her in his arms in spite of her struggles. "I have merely decided to assign you a different role. Haven't you agreed to be my wife?"

She eyed him with suspicion. "That was before you left me in the lurch at the academy while you went gallivanting off to save the prince. I have no doubt, sir, that your proposal was meant only to turn me away from my determination to become a spy."

"The spymaster has been found, sir. He's on his way here to report to you."

"Good news. What about the assassins? Have they been located?"

"Yes, sir. Two of the spymaster's trainees rescued him. One of the spies was shot dead in the struggle to save the spymaster. The three remaining have been turned over to the local militia for safekeeping until a decision is made as to their final destination."

"Clever move. The prince will surely wish to take them back to Zarkovia to face punishment. I'm told that their system of justice is far more Draconian than our own, but we shan't meddle in their internal affairs. Has the Regent and the prince been notified?"

"Yes, sir."

"Good work, Darlington." The viscount placed his hands on his desk and sat back. "All's well that ends well, as they say. The prince is safe, our spymaster is safe, and Heatham's daughter is safe. He'll be pleased, I'm sure."

Chris took a deep breath. "I think I ought to prepare you, sir."

"Prepare me? For what?"

"Fairchild is the trainee who saved the spymaster's life. I'm told it was she who shot the assassin."

"Wha—at?" the viscount said, as if the word had two syllables. "Who disobeyed my orders? Tell me who is responsible for allowing her to participate!"

"Fairchild is to blame for disobeying your orders, sir. She came to London in time to see the assassins overpower the spymaster. She followed and saw four of them drag the spymaster into one of those seedy buildings near the docks. With the help of trainee Riggs, they overpowered the four men and freed the spymaster."

"His Grace will surely rake me over the coals for this." Yet Sidmouth chuckled in spite of himself. "She has pluck, the stubborn puss. I'll give her that."

A knock on the door interrupted them. Chris opened it to Sebastian and Olivia.

"Afternoon, sir," said Sebastian.

Sidmouth's eyes opened wide at the sight of Olivia in the costume of a lady of ill repute. "And who's this, spymaster? One of your people in disguise?"

"This, sir, is Fairchild. She saved my life."

"Tell that to her father, sir. Perhaps, coming from you, it will ease his wrath at me for not keeping her out of this operation."

"If you please, sir," interrupted Olivia. "Allow me to tell my father. It will be better for all of us."

The viscount rubbed his chin for what seemed an eternity. But then his mood lightened. "Perhaps you're right, my dear. Be sure to offer my apologies, for being unable to restrain your, er . . . enthusiasm for your work. By the way, that's a fine disguise. You certainly fooled me."

"Might I accompany Fairchild home, sir? As your

representative, I could offer His Grace our apologies. In fact, I would welcome the opportunity to do so."

Olivia betrayed no emotion, but she wondered what he meant. *He's up to something. Whatever it is, I'm sure it doesn't bode well for me."*

Sidmouth rose and came around his desk. He took both their hands. "Congratulations on a job well done, both of you. Feel free to tell your father that you saved England today, young lady." He kissed her on both cheeks.

"Thank you, sir."

"On your way, then."

"Excuse me, sir," said Darlington. "As you know, the duke and his family are in Brighton. Allow me to arrange transportation for Fairchild and the spymaster, if I may."

When the door shut behind them, Sebastian said, "I need some time to make myself presentable to His Grace. I brought a change of clothing with me from the academy. My things are in the changing room."

"You know I can't go to Heatham looking like this, Chris. I'll have to stop at Fairchild House so I can change as well."

Darlington laughed. "What a stir you'd cause if you did appear before your father in that outrageous costume, Livy. Suppose I take you home while the spymaster gets ready. The home office carriage can bring him to Fairchild House when he's finished and you can both begin the journey to Brighton from there."

Olivia followed Chris out, stopping only to allow him to give the necessary orders.

Once underway in his curricle, Chris asked, "Why are you sulking, Livy? Are you angry with me?"

"Oh, no, Chris. I could never be angry with you. It's the spymaster. I don't trust him. He's been trying to get rid of me ever since I began the program. He's even gone so far as to ask me to marry him, as if that would serve his purpose. I suspect he's planning to tell my father something underhanded."

"His proposal sounds genuine. Do you love him?"

"No. I can't love a man who orders me to stay behind like a good little girl."

"Obviously, you didn't obey. I think you're being too hard on him. Leaving you behind wasn't the spymaster's idea. It was Sidmouth's. He told me your father pressured him into it to keep you out of danger."

Olivia frowned. "Did he? Just like Father."

"Perhaps."

Olivia didn't notice the doubt in her friend's voice. "Poor Father. Thank heaven he gave in to you and Helena. Which reminds me. Have you set a wedding date?"

"No, not yet."

"If Father is putting more obstacles in your way, my sister Helena will be furious."

"She's furious all right, but not at your father. I'm the one she's angry with. Now that the Zarkovian treaty's been signed, I leave on special assignment. Helena wishes to marry before I leave, but your father won't have it. I must say I agree with him in this instance. Neither one of us wants to deprive her of what every girl should have—a proper church wedding and a grand breakfast to follow."

Olivia thought for a moment. "Is your assignment dangerous, Chris? Is that why you're siding with Father?"

"Every assignment for the home office has the potential for danger. I know you've learned as much in your training. I might have been long gone and back again, but Sidmouth kept me here to oversee the Prince of Zarkovia's safety. I expect to leave for the Continent as soon as the prince sails home."

"Poor Helena. She's loved you ever since the three of us were children cooking up mischief together."

Chris looked pleased. "That long? Has she really? She never gave a hint of it."

"It's true just the same. When she was a mere twelve years old, she declared she was planning to marry you just as soon as you both were old enough."

Chris laughed in delight. "And all this time, she's had me convinced that *I* was in pursuit of *her.*"

When the carriage drew up to Fairchild House, Olivia said, "Take care, Chris. Come home safely to Helena." She ran up the steps and pulled the bell.

"Milady! How good it is to see you. We'll have your chamber ready in no time," said the under butler when he opened the door. Forrester paid no attention to her garish apparel. The skeleton staff when the duke and his family were in Brighton consisted of the under butler, his wife who acted as housekeeper, two footmen and two under maids.

"Hello, Forrester. I'm not staying long. I'm on my way to Heatham. All I need is a hot bath and a change of clothing."

"Mrs. Forrester and the maids will see to all your needs, milady. Go on up to your chamber. Shall I send up something for you to drink or to eat?"

"Tea, please, but not too much fuss. My escort and I will have dinner in Brighton with the family."

The hot bath was a blessing, but Olivia didn't linger. She was anxious to be underway. Mrs. Forrester helped her dress. And an under maid fixed her short hair.

She kept Sebastian cooling his heels in the drawing room for the better part of an hour. There was no place for him to sit, since all the furniture was well hidden under Holland covers for the summer.

"I'm ready, sir," she said.

He turned to the doorway to face an angel. She wore a white muslin gown dotted with tiny bluebells, a blue ribbon tied under her breasts. Her short hair was held off her face with a matching bonnet tied under her chin with ribbons.

"You want only a halo, love. May I have my breath back, if you please?"

Olivia smiled. "I'd forgotten how pleasant it is to be dressed as a lady for a change. Shall we go?"

Sebastian pulled on his gloves. He was dressed in the finest fashion—Hessian boots, form-fitting buckskins, a pale yellow silk vest, a superfine blue coat and a starched neckcloth expertly tied.

She wondered why he was turned out in such elegance. Did he have yet another scheme in mind she might not like? She took his arm as he led the way to the waiting carriage.

Chapter Eighteen

Brighton—That Evening

Sebastian handed her into the carriage and stepped in to sit beside her.

"Sit opposite," she ordered. "Or I will, if you prefer it. *Sir*."

"As you wish, ma'am." He shut the door and took his seat. As the carriage began to move, he asked, "It's clear that you're angry, my love. What have I done to upset you?"

She kept her voice low, yet she could not hide her fury. "Saving your bloody hide from the assassins didn't change anything, did it? My deeds in the course of my work mean nothing to you. The only time I please you is when you make love to me. Women are good for nothing but bedding. Isn't that what you believe?"

"You're wrong, my darling."

"I'm not your 'darling.'"

"What's wrong with wanting to marry you? I can't keep my hands to myself because I love you. Do you doubt my sincerity?"

"I'd much rather you thank me for a job well done, spymaster."

"That, too, of course. Good God. You tie my tongue in

knots when you're angry. And when you look so luscious, all I can think of is to take you in my arms and . . ."

"I don't want to hear that either. You're two people, Sir Sebastian Brooks. I can't seem to please the spymaster in you no matter what I do, yet I can always please the lusty Sebastian in you, can't I?"

He grinned. "What else is there?"

She glared at him with fire in her eyes. "It's no use talking. You'll never understand me. What hurts me the most is that you don't even bother to try."

No further attempt at conversation was offered by either, but when the carriage drew up to Heatham, Olivia's joy at being home overcame her rage. Without waiting for Sebastian to hand her down, she leaped out of the coach and ran up the front steps. The huge front door opened at the first ring and the haughty butler's habitual look of disdain turned to one of delight, for Dunston considered her as one of his own beloved children, just as he did her sisters and her brother, having known them all since birth.

"Miss Livy! Do come in. How I have missed you! May I say it for the staff as well?"

"Thank you, Dunston." She patted his gloved hand. "What time is dinner? Are there guests?"

"You'll have ample time to freshen up, milady. The family is getting ready as we speak. Shall I announce you?"

"No, Dunston. I'd rather surprise everyone."

"As you wish, milady. I'll send an under maid to help you freshen up."

"Have my abigail do it."

"Sorry to say that Nancy took other employment right after you left London."

A cough interrupted, reminding her that Sebastian stood waiting.

"I almost forgot, Dunston. This is Sir Sebastian Brooks. He has requested an audience with His Grace."

The butler examined the visitor as if he were an unwanted insect, for he had detected a disapproving note in his mistress' voice. "Very good, milady. Follow me, sir. You may wait in the library while I see if His Grace is prepared to receive you."

Olivia grinned, enjoying the butler's haughty tone very much indeed as she ran upstairs to her room. No one could equal Dunston in making a guest feel like an odious insect. As proper a set-down as she had ever heard him give. Serves Sebastian right, she thought.

She hadn't long to wait before news of her arrival swept through Heatham like a sudden squall. The first to burst into her chamber was her mother.

"Livy, darling!"

"Oh, Mother! I haven't the words to tell you how glad I am to see you." She turned to the under maid. "Thank you, Milly. You can go, dear."

Her Grace waited until the maid left to ask, "What have you done to your hair, child?"

"It's such a long story. Suffice it to say I was just doing my duty."

"And what duty was that, my sweet, adorable Livy?" asked Helena, rushing into the room. She gave her sister a hug.

"Stop, stop, you silly girl. You're crushing my gown."

Helena snapped her fingers. "I don't care one whit for your gown. I'm just that happy to see you."

"Where are the other brats?" asked Olivia.

"Miss Trumball took them out for a walk. They'll be back soon enough," replied Helena.

Olivia noted that her mother looked thoughtful. "Something on your mind? What is it, Mother?"

"How long shall you be staying with us, dear? Your father . . ."

"Truth is, I don't really know. The spymaster is here seeing father as we speak."

"About what, dear?"

"If I had to guess, I'd say it's about enlisting Father's aid in forcing me to resign, most likely. He consistently tries to sack me, but I have no intention of resigning without a fight. Training ends in a few weeks. I've come too far to allow that odious man to deny me the privilege of completing the course now."

"Then you shan't have to, dear, if I have anything to say to the matter," said her mother with a forcefulness that surprised both sisters. "I'll talk to your father."

"The spymaster tried to prevent me from participating in protecting Prince Joachim of Zarkovia, but I found a way. I even saved the spymaster's bloody life," she added.

"Don't use such vulgarities, Livy. If you saved his life, he should be grateful to you."

"Hmmph! A lot he cares! The only thing he cares about is that I disobeyed his orders."

"Why did you do such a thing?" Helena asked.

Olivia looked at her mother. "It was Father's doing."

"What do you mean, dear?"

"Father made Viscount Sidmouth promise to keep me out of danger. As if I needed his interference and so I shall tell him!"

"Go easy on him, Livy. You know what a temper he has," warned Helena as she pulled the brush through Olivia's short hair and rearranged the ribbons. There wasn't much to style, as her short curls appeared to have a mind of their own. Even so, they surrounded her face in becoming fashion.

Just as Helena lay the brush down, the door burst open and three young girls shrieked, almost in unison, "Livy!"

"Hello, brats!" said Olivia to her youngest sisters Georgiana, Jane and Mary. She opened her arms to them. "Come here, you little terrors. Give your big sister a hug."

The three ran to her, all talking at once. "Stand away and let me look at you," Olivia demanded, disentangling herself at last. "Hmm, Georgie. You're fair to becoming the most beautiful of all the Fairchild women. And you, Jane. How you've er . . . grown." She didn't have the heart to say what she thought, which was "how much wider you have grown." "You too, Mary! You're at least a foot taller." Olivia stood up and smoothed her gown, rumpled by her sisters in their eagerness to greet her.

"It's time I bearded our dear father in his lair," she said with a twinkle in her eyes. "I wonder if he's finished his interview with . . ."

"Do you mean that handsome man I saw in the library with Father?"

"Jane! Were you spying again?" said Georgiana.

"I wasn't spying! I just happened to pass the terrace door and I just happened to notice this handsome . . ." She stopped and looked from one sister to another, and the disapproval she saw made her burst into tears. "You're all against me! Mother, make them stop."

"There, there, Jane. No one's against you, my child," soothed her mother. "It's just that it isn't ladylike to tell tales, you see. Why don't you go to your room and rest until dinner?"

"All right, Mother," she sniffled. "Welcome home, Livy." At the door Jane threw her other sisters a look of scorn. In defiance, she added, "Anyway, Father and that handsome man were laughing their heads off!"

Her Grace changed the subject as soon as Jane shut the door. "You look lovely, Livy my dear. A bit thinner, but as beautiful as an angel. Go on down to see your father straight away. And try not to vex him."

"I'll try, Mother." The sympathetic eyes of her sisters were on her as Olivia left the room. She walked slowly, all the while wondering what on earth Sebastian and her father found to laugh about.

"My butler informs me that you accompanied my daughter. Who are you?" asked the duke when Sebastian was ushered into the library. His tone was anything but welcoming. "What is it you wish to see me about?"

"I am Sir Sebastian Brooks. Forgive me for the intrusion, but I am here as a representative of Viscount Sidmouth, Your Grace."

"Why didn't you say so at once? What's that old rascal up to now?"

"He wishes to offer you his apologies for being unable to er . . . restrain your daughter as promised, sir."

The duke's eyes narrowed. "I never asked him to promise me any such thing. Explain what you mean, young man."

"Your daughter deliberately disobeyed orders. She came to London to help protect Prince Joachim of Zarkovia this morning. Fortunately, no harm came to her."

"Who gave these orders?"

"I did, Your Grace, at the direction of Viscount Sidmouth. I am employed as the home office chief spymaster."

The news did nothing to soften the duke's ire, directed pell mell at anyone who had anything remotely to do with his willful child. "Where is my daughter now?"

"She's here, Your Grace. In her chamber."

"Tell Sidmouth his apology is accepted. You may go young man. What did you say your name was?"

"My name is Sir Sebastian Brooks, Your Grace. May I beg a bit more of your time? It's a matter of utmost importance. At least to me."

"Well? What is it?"

"I beg leave to ask your permission to marry your daughter."

"Which one? I have five daughters."

"Lady Olivia, Your Grace."

"Why should I give such permission to the very man who has been training her to become a spy? Are you not aware of the fact that she does not have my blessing in this foolish venture of hers?"

"The home secretary so informed me, Your Grace. I couldn't agree with you more. A woman has no place in such a dangerous field. Your daughter will confirm that I have done everything possible to discourage her from this pursuit."

His Grace barked a laugh and rang for a servant. "I wonder you want to marry her, for she's as stubborn a lass as they come. Do sit down, Brooks. We'll discuss this business over brandy."

"Bring us brandy, Dunston. And see to it we're not disturbed," the duke said when the butler answered his ring.

"Yes, Your Grace," said Dunston. Sebastian noted his disappointment with hidden amusement. The rascal was itching to show him the door.

"Why haven't you succeeded in discouraging my daughter?"

"Fairchild . . ." Sebastian noted the scowl on the duke's face and quickly apologized. "Beg pardon, Your Grace. We are accustomed to addressing all of our trainees by their surname."

His Grace nodded his acceptance. "Go on, then. Fairchild what?"

"She had to meet the rigorous standards we set for all our trainees, Your Grace."

"Did she do so?"

"Yes, Your Grace, but . . ."

"But?"

"May I speak frankly, sir?"

"By all means."

At this encouragement, Sebastian, no longer able to hide his frustration, proceeded to pour his heart out to the duke. "Your daughter has caused me no end of trouble in pursuit of her foolish goal. She rides like the wind, she swims like a fish, she shoots an arrow with greater precision than any other man at the academy, she fences better than I do . . ."

"Why do you stop, Brooks?"

Sebastian's face turned beet red. "I nearly died because she bested me in a duel. The ball at the end of her foil flew off, you see, and when she lunged, the point pierced my shoulder, causing an infection. It really wasn't her fault since no one else noticed either."

"You make my daughter sound a perfect spy. Does she do nothing to displease you? Nothing to give you cause to send her home in disgrace?"

Sebastian exploded at this. "I would like nothing more than to send her packing and she knows it. Your daughter plagues me day in and day out, Your Grace. Not only does she disobey orders, she questions my authority at every turn." He used his fingers to tick off all his grievances. "Like all the trainees, Fairchild knew she was forbidden to leave the premises during training, but did she listen? She did not. The worst was when she ran off thinking she had murdered me. I had to send the entire staff of Wil—the spy academy out searching for her. And what did she do when she was found? She brought back a kitten and had the effrontery to name him after me!" He sat back, exhausted by his outburst. To his astonishment, His Grace engaged in a hearty laugh.

"I fail to see the humor in this, Your Grace."

The duke said, "It's a wonder you want to wed my daughter after everything she's done to upset you and your program."

This brought Sebastian back to his purpose. With a sheepish grin, he said, "The truth is I am in love with your mulish daughter, Your Grace. And the devil of it is that I wish I knew why. She haunts my days and causes me no end of sleepless nights."

"Well and good. Well and good, but I cannot give my consent to a man who hasn't the pluck to stand up to my defiant daughter."

"Let me assure you, Your Grace, that I have no intention of allowing any wife of mine to become a spy."

The duke's eyes flew open at this. "Given that my willful daughter refuses to obey your orders, how do you plan to stop her?"

"When we marry, the first thing we shall do is start a family. I plan to give you an army of grandchildren, sir. Your daughter will be too busy raising our children. She will have little time to think about becoming a spy." He hesitated, then added, "Even with the knowledge that she may indeed make my life miserable, I confess I cannot live without her, Your Grace. Isn't that odd?"

The duke rubbed his chin. "I trust you have ample means to provide for my daughter?"

"More than ample, Your Grace. I can arrange for my man of business to meet with yours to confirm this."

"Then I suppose there's no cure for your malady except to marry the wench."

"Do I take that to mean I have your consent, Your Grace?"

"You do, with one caveat."

"And that is, Your Grace?"

"I shall not force her to marry you. You will have to win her consent first."

Chapter Nineteen

Heatham—Same Night

"Where is Sir Sebastian Brooks, Dunston? The gentleman who accompanied me here?"

"He has already had his audience with His Grace. He is waiting for you in the morning room, milady."

When she entered, Sebastian came toward her at once. He took her hands and searched her face. "Have you been crying, my love? Your eyes are all red. But for all that you look lovely."

Olivia disentangled her hands from his and said, "They are nothing but tears of joy at seeing my family again." She paused and added. "Why do you call me 'my love,' sir, when I'm no such thing?"

He took both her hands and obliged her to face him. At once, he dropped to one knee.

"What are you doing, sir? Get up this instant!"

"Will you keep your promise and marry me, Olivia? I love you beyond reason. Will you restore my sanity and allow me to make you my wife?"

She pulled her hands from his and folded her arms. "Are you mad? You can't abide me. You treat me shabbily and you thwart my every wish. You believe yourself to be fair, but that isn't so. You only *think* you treat me as you would treat any other trainee. Hah! You really believe that lie, don't you? A worse fish tale I have never heard!"

"I do treat you as I would any of the other trainees, my sweet!" His lips quirked as he added, "Though I must admit, I have no desire to bed any of the others."

"That's a bigger whopper. Not your jest, of course. Let me ask you this, *sir!* If you treat me like the others, why didn't you fight for my right to be a party to the protection of Prince Joachim? Do you know how humiliated I felt at being left behind like a 'good little girl'?"

Sebastian was stung by the accuracy of her words. In a meek voice, he said, "It wasn't my idea. It was your father who pressured the home secretary . . ."

"How brave of you to hide behind my father!" Her words dripped with sarcasm even as her heart shredded into tiny little pieces. They flew away like a shower of shattered stars.

"You cannot know how sorry I am for it, my darling. I should have defended your right to accompany the group to London. Can you not find it in your heart to forgive me?" Sebastian attempted to kiss her.

"Don't. Touch. Me!"

His hands fell to his side. "My darling. Your father has already given his permission for us to marry."

Her eyes blazed. "Has he indeed? How kind of you to request his permission before you thought to receive my consent. I give you permission to marry him, then!"

To her astonishment, a single tear rolled down Sebastian's cheek. "It's you I want to wed, my love. Not your father."

"Don't call me your love, for I am not now, nor will I ever be." Her words grew a shade softer, for the look on his face was one of sheer misery.

"I promise to spend the rest of my life making you happy, Olivia. You have my word on that."

"Your words are empty, sir." She paused, breathing hard. "I loved you once, you know. When I thought you were dead, I was in such despair, I was ready to enter a nunnery. But when you began to treat me like the lowest of scullery maids, fit only for scrubbing floors, that feeling was lost in the dirty water."

He grimaced as though she had struck him. Sebastian felt as though the sun-filled morning room had been filled with ice. "I beg your forgiveness my dearest Olivia. Won't you consider giving me another chance? I'm determined to change to win your love now that you have shown me the error of my ways."

"When I decide to marry, it will be to a man who encourages me in all my aspirations as indeed I shall encourage him in all of his. In short, sir, what I want in a husband is a dear friend as well as a lover. No, Sebastian. I cannot marry a man such as you."

"You loved me once."

"Oh, I'll admit to that vice, but like a bad headache, it has passed, let me assure you. Come to think of it, how foolish of me even to have entertained such a brainless idea. You, sir, are a snake. A worthless excuse for a man. What did you and my father find to talk about? No, don't tell me. Permit me to guess. I know my father well, you see. He would not have given his consent unless you assured him you would join him in his quest to prevent me from becoming a spy, isn't that so?"

Sebastian was stunned into silence, yet his eyes gave him away. Clearly, she had hit the mark.

"You wormed your way into receiving his approval by promising to force me to give my dream up, didn't you? Didn't you? You don't love me, you arrogant, double-dealing, underhanded, treacherous excuse for a man!" She turned toward the door. "I'm ready to return to Wilson Academy. Shall we go?"

His face turned dark with fury. "Stop ripping me apart, you shrew! I may be all those things you accuse me of, but never of not loving you. What's more, in spite of every bit of evidence in my head that warns me to stay away from you, I cannot help loving you. You've infected my heart like an incurable disease. Only God knows why, you detestable creature." He backed her into the wall and crushed her into his arms. His lips bore down on hers and didn't let up in spite of her fierce struggle.

One hand found her breast. The other pulled her gown up. He forced her legs apart with his knee, for he was hard and he wanted her to feel it. His hand soon found what he was seeking. He teased it with his thumb and he didn't let go until he felt her rigid body relent and surge toward his.

Sebastian eased her to the floor none too gently. He unbuttoned his trousers and released his engorged member. His hand guided him into her with ease, for she was wet with desire. He lay still, penetrating only part of him within her, and listened to her hard breathing.

His voice was hoarse with need. "Open your eyes, my love."

She did so, arching her back at the same time, in an attempt to receive more of him, but he wouldn't allow it.

"Look into my eyes. What do you see there, dear heart of my heart?"

"Lust," she said as she fought for more of him.

He held back. "What else?"

"Heat." She tried to pull him further into her, but he caught her hands and held them still.

"What else?"

"Desire," she groaned. "Isn't that enough? Stop torturing me and get on with it."

His lips brushed hers before searing her with eyes full of pleading. "I'll give you what you want when you give me what I want. Tell me you feel what I feel. Say you love me. Admit you know that I love you."

"Bloody hell. Yes," she groaned, as if in agony.

He inched further into her. "What's that you say?"

"Yes. I know you love me," she gasped, lifting herself off the floor.

He stopped and put his mouth on one breast, her nipple hardening as his tongue played its silent tune. "What else do you know, my darling?"

"I . . . I know that I . . . love you, too!"

"Yes!" he shouted and drove her into the floor again and again. He did not relent until he felt her spasms, until her shouts reached their peak. It was only then he let go and allowed himself to soar to the heights along with her.

When he was spent, he rolled on his back and pulled her on top of him. "Do you want to know a secret, my love?" He reached over and tousled her wild hair.

"I want to know all your secrets."

"As a young man, I used to daydream I would find an obedient, compliant woman to be my wife."

Olivia laughed. "Then you don't want me."

"Be serious, you odious wretch." His eyes burned into hers as if to fathom her very soul. "Without realizing the truth of it, I lied to your father this morning to win his approval. Now I wonder how I ever could have entertained such foolishness. How could I possibly know that only a hellcat would suffice for me? How could I possibly realize, even when it hurts most, how much I love the sting of your nettles?"

"Then I shall be sure to sting you often." Her brows creased, yet her eyes performed a country dance.

He brushed his lips across her brow, as if to erase their

lines. "Once we're married, my heart, if we should battle from sunup to sundown, I give you leave to remind me that this is the very thing that I bargained for. I shall savor your stings for the rest of my life, I promise you. Heaven help me for wanting you along with the sheer bliss of battle. What a fool I was for not knowing that this is what it feels like to be alive. This is what it feels like to be in love." He took her face in his hands and showered kisses over every part of it.

"Stop for a moment, Sebastian."

"What is it?"

"You must make me one promise, and let me warn you, I shall hold your feet to the fire for the next fifty or so years."

"Do you want all of England? It's yours. The world? The universe? The stars? The . . ."

"No. I'll settle for three things. First, I want to graduate with my class."

"Done."

"Second, I want to become a spy."

"Done. And the third?"

"Third, promise me you will never betray me again. Not with my father. Not with Sidmouth. Not with anyone."

"Done." Sebastian helped her to her feet and straightened her gown as best he could before setting his own clothing to rights. "Your father has invited us to stay for dinner. We can leave for the academy afterwards."

The thought made her ill. How could she face the people she loved most in the world? If she remained for dinner, her family would surely know she had accepted his proposal of marriage. She wasn't sure she was ready for that announcement just yet. "I would prefer to wait to announce our betrothal after I complete my training."

"Oh no you don't, you little minx. Do you think I'll give you the chance to worm your way out of this? We must announce it to your family tonight."

She shocked him when she said in unaccustomed compliance, "If that is what you wish, dear."

"That's my girl." When they had adjusted their clothing, Sebastian opened the door for her, and Dunston nearly fell into the room.

Without missing a beat, the butler announced, "Your family is on the terrace, milady. Dinner shall be served at five, a bit earlier than usual, in order to allow you and your escort ample time to return to your destination."

Olivia checked her grin. News of her behavior with the stranger, which in all likelihood must lead to their marriage, would be the spicy topic of discussion below stairs tonight, thanks to the butler's eavesdropping. "Thank you, Dunston. We'll join them there at once. No need to announce us."

Disappointed at not being allowed to witness the family reunion, Dunston's long face fell to the floor. "Cook has been preparing all your favorite dishes."

"Offer her my thanks, then." She took Sebastian's arm and they proceeded to the terrace.

Their jubilant reception was reinforced by Olivia's father. "Well, you two? Have we reason to celebrate tonight?"

Olivia's red face, giggles and a violent nod gave the answer, which was greeted by whoops of joy.

"I wish you as much happiness as your mother and I have had all these years," said the duke, his voice cracking. He embraced Sebastian and added, "Welcome to the Fairchild family, son."

Olivia was nearly knocked off her feet by her sisters.

"What good news, Livy," said Helena.

"That's two down everyone. I'm next," said Georgiana, her eyes alive with mischief.

"I shall compose a special piece in honor of your betrothal," whispered Mary in Olivia's ear.

"I'd be honored, sweet Mary," Olivia whispered back, unwilling to embarrass the shy child by hugging her.

"Why is your gown so wrinkled, Livy?" asked Jane, her mouth betraying evidence of the sweet she had just gulped down.

"It isn't polite to ask such rude questions, Jane," said her mother. She turned to Olivia, her eyes brimming with tears. "I cannot tell you how happy you have made me, Livy." She hugged her daughter and took her hand. "Come along, dear, and make your mother known to your fiancé."

Olivia led her mother to Sebastian, who was surrounded by her sisters, all atwitter like birds in a bush. "Make room for Mother, girls. Sebastian, this is my mother." She added in a whisper loud enough for everyone to hear, "The *real* head of our household."

No one laughed louder than the duke at the jest, for all that it was true.

When Dunston announced dinner, the duke led the procession into the dining room, followed by Olivia on Sebastian's arm.

"I wish Chris were here for this occasion," said Helena to Georgiana in a wistful tone as they followed the betrothed couple.

Mary and Jane followed. Rather than consigning them to the schoolroom with Mrs. Trumball, the special occasion allowed for their presence at dinner.

"Raise your glasses, children," said the duke. He turned to Olivia on his left, and to Sebastian on his right. "Your health and your happiness."

"Thank you, Father," said Olivia. "It only wants dear Edward's presence to complete our celebration."

"No, it doesn't, Livy," said Edward as he entered the dining room. He pecked his mother on the cheek and added. "Knew something was up when Father sent for me." He turned to

Sebastian, "This my new brother-in-law? Welcome, sir. About time we added more men to our roster. Father and I are tired of being knocked about by all these women."

The heir's gaiety infected them all throughout dinner, and as the end neared, Sebastian rose, his glass in hand. "You may not know it, but I have no family of my own. Therefore, I count myself most fortunate this evening, for not only have I won my future bride's consent, I also have gained the very best of in-laws. A mother, a father, four charming sisters and a brother. I am the luckiest of men."

When the women retired to the drawing room, Helena took Olivia aside. "Jane was right, you know. Your gown is shockingly wrinkled."

Without missing a beat, Olivia said, "Spy practice, if you must know. We were wrestling." The sisters burst out laughing, inspiring Georgiana to demand that they share the jest with her.

"I heard," said Jane in triumph. "Livy said her gown got wrinkled because she and Sebastian were doing spy practice. They were wrestling on the floor."

Her innocent words were met with scandalized silence, but only for a moment. The women's laughter ushered the men of the family into the drawing room. Her Grace could not be prevailed upon to divulge the source of their humor.

"Play for us, Mary," said the duchess, changing the subject. To Sebastian she added, "Mary is accomplished on the pianoforte. I hope you like music?"

"I do indeed, Your Grace." He sat next to Olivia on the settee and took her hand in his, in awe of the odd feeling of completion in his heart.

In the knowledge that his life would be made whole with Olivia at his side, he wondered at the miracle of love. He never knew such joy existed. Was he only half a person until this day?

Chapter Twenty

Sebastian met with his instructors on the Friday before the final weeks of training. This was the academy's first graduating class and there were no hard and fast rules.

The spymaster presided at the head of the large rectangular table in the meeting room. Hugh Denville, calisthenics instructor, was on his right, Andre Fourier, fencing master, sat next to him, boxing master Evelyn Hawes next, followed by Sensei Yukio Nori, martial arts expert. Mrs. Hunnicut sat opposite Sebastian at the other end of the table. Next to her sat Tom Deff, stable master, Ned Mason, swimming instructor, and Harry Green, archery and rifle instructor. Aaron Foster, codes and ciphers wizard, sat next on Sebastian's immediate left. In all, nine men and one woman had assembled to decide the fate of the first six trainees.

"We'll take John Carter first. How say you?" Sebastian nodded to Denville to begin.

"Pass. He'll make the home office a good spy, sir. An arrogant beginning, to be sure, but his boxing match with Riggs set him straight, I believe."

"Good form as a fencer, sir. Pass," said Fourier.

"Carter deserved the whipping Riggs gave him in the boxing ring, but he had the good grace to apologize. I'd have to give him a pass," said Hawes.

Sensei Nori had not yet learned to master his "R"s, nor was he ever likely to learn to use the letter "L" in the English tongue. What was odd was the fact that, to his ear alone, he spoke intelligible English. "Cahta mastah mashiah ahts," he said. "Pahss."

"If Carter were assigned a domestic spying post, he'd be haughty enough to pass himself off as an excellent butler in a large estate," said Mrs. Hunnicut dryly. This brought a chuckle to the table. "Pass."

"He's a bruising rider, spymaster. Pass," said Tom Deff.

"Strong swimmer, as well. Pass," added Ned Mason.

"Pass. An excellent eye for archery and rifle," said Harry Green.

"Pass. Carter did well on my codes and ciphers examination," added Aaron Foster.

"Carter, then, is our first successful graduate," Sebastian said. "Who's next?"

"Olivia Fairchild," said Denville, consulting his list.

Sebastian steeled himself, but showed no sign of anxiety for the success of the woman he loved. "How say you, Denville?"

"Fairchild reached fifty push-ups this morning, sir. Pass."

To Sebastian's surprise, the others applauded her achievement.

"My star pupil, sir. Pass," said Fourier beaming.

"In spite of the fact that she nearly killed me?" Sebastian asked, a playful smile on his lips.

"Your own fault, *mon ami*. Have you not forgiven her?"

"Long since. You are correct, Fourier, my own fault. And I have most certainly forgiven her." *In fact, I mean to marry her.*

"Pass. Excellent swimmer." Ned Mason blushed, the

memory of her first swim class reddening his face from his forehead to his neckline.

The glowing reports and a "pass" on Olivia continued until Sebastian reached Mrs. Hunnicut.

"Fail," she said.

The word stunned the room into silence.

"Explain yourself, ma'am."

"Of course, sir. Let me first assure you all that I am most fond of Fairchild and I mean her no malice. But she has a serious flaw, one which I fear could cost Fairchild her life in a clandestine operation. I've seen this trait in her more than once, you see. She is unable to follow directions. Further, she manages to subvert them to suit herself. It may be subtle at times, to be sure, but it is there nevertheless."

"I see your point, ma'am, and I would have to agree," said Denville. "I recall to mind that, when she thought the spymaster was dead, she ran away."

"She disobeyed when she stole off to attend her sister's betrothal," offered Tom Deff.

"My heart stopped when she joined the lads for a swim session and stripped bare," said Ned Mason. No one dared laugh at this, yet a few lips twitched.

Foster looked thoughtful. "It would be a pity to fail the first woman spy in our academy. Especially since she is such an outstanding trainee. There must be some test we can devise for her. An additional task, perhaps. I'd hate to have to turn her out altogether, for she has a fine mind. It would be a great loss, in my view. She's received many other glowing reports this morning. If she passes a final test, I would be happy to recommend she be assigned to the codes and ciphers department in the home office. There she would be safely out of harm's way," pleaded Foster, a rare hint of passion in his voice.

Sebastian looked down at his papers for a moment. When he looked up, his eyes went directly to Mrs. Hunnicut. "If we were to agree to Foster's suggestion for an additional task to prove herself, ma'am, what would you suggest?"

The silence in the room held for what seemed like ages, but in fact was only a few moments.

After giving it some thought, Mrs. Hunnicut said, "Fairchild detests scrubbing the kitchen galley on her hands and knees. An odious task for anyone, I must own. We could request it of her once again and if she refuses, she fails, but if she agrees, she passes."

A murmur of approval swept round the table at this.

"Fine idea, ma'am."

"It's for her own good."

"It isn't personal, after all."

"It may well toughen her."

"Put it to a vote."

"All those in favor?" Sebastian asked, trying to keep his knees from giving way, for he knew she would blame him and he dreaded it. Every hand went up, which made it unnecessary to ask if any were opposed.

The official letters of decision were delivered to the trainees at breakfast the next morning. There were whoops of joy from those who passed. Carter, Perkins, Robert Reed and his brother William had passed without condition, but Rufus was ordered to restudy the codes and ciphers manual and take the test again in the morning. And Fairchild was ordered to report to the scullery after breakfast.

Jenny helped her into the scullery maid's costume and handed her the scrub brush and the pail. "I've found a pair o' gloves, miss. 'Twill keep your hands from gittin' all rough and raw like they did the last time."

"Thank you, Jenny," Olivia said. "You're a dear. Now leave me to my task." She took the pail out to the pump and filled it. Back in the kitchen, she hung it on its hook in the fireplace and waited for it to heat up. When the water was warm enough to dissolve the harsh soap made with lye, but not too hot to burn her hands, she carried the heavy pail to the back stairway, got on her knees and began to scrub the black and white tiles.

After each small section, she wiped the suds with her rinsing cloth, rose to wring it out and fell to her knees to begin another part, careful to scrub it spotless. The water had no chance to evaporate, for she added tears of humiliation.

The hallway that led to the kitchen galley took her the better part of two hours, she was that careful in her work. Her back aching, she was ready to begin scrubbing the kitchen galley. She rose to change the water at the well.

She was not surprised to see the spymaster waiting at the pump for her. Her tongue was coated with acid when she addressed him. "Have you come here to witness my humiliation or to gloat? Which is it, sir?"

"This was not my doing, my dearest love."

She put her hands on her hips and growled like a rabid dog. "Oh no? Too bad, sir. I was about to thank you for arranging such a delightful task as a token of your affection for me. Well, then. Here's a present for you, *my dearest love!*" She emptied the pail of blackened water onto him, soaking his buckskins as well as his boots.

He jumped back, but not in time. "Take care, or . . ."

"Or I shan't complete your spy program and graduate with my class?" she asked. "Tsk, tsk. And I purchased a brand new gown for the occasion. Too bad." She put the pail under the pump and put her hand on the handle.

"Allow me," Sebastian said, his eyes pleading for forgiveness.

"Oh no, sir. I shan't allow you to deprive me of my favorite spy task. Not on your life! I take pride in my work, but of course, you may not have noticed."

"I didn't order this task for you. You must believe me when I tell you it was beyond my control, Olivia."

"It is always beyond your control, isn't it? I fully understand your dilemma, sir. Why should the spymaster take the blame when he can foist it onto his subordinates? I'm sure it pleases you to know that when my father discovers that you have failed me, he will be most gratified." She tried to push past him, but he held the kitchen door for her and followed her inside.

She struggled to lift the pail to its hook in the fireplace, shoving him aside with her hip when he attempted to take it from her. "I don't need your help, sir. Not at all. Never again, in fact." She fought back the tears that threatened to betray her.

"You think I've failed you once again, I see. But it isn't so. I cannot tell you how sorry . . ."

"Then don't even try. You're in my way, sir. Be so kind as to leave so I can accomplish this task. Or must you persist in staying to gloat?"

"No, my love. You will graduate with your class when you complete this final task. It isn't personal, you know."

"Oh, isn't it? I can't recall any of my colleagues being asked to scrub floors! Oh well, perhaps I am mistaken. Women do a much better job at floor scrubbing, don't they?"

"I can't bear to see you so unhappy, my darling. After you graduate and we marry, you'll forget all about this." He waited for a response, but when she refused to answer him, he turned to the kitchen door to let himself out into the yard.

"Meooow!" cried her kitten when Sebastian stepped on his tail.

Olivia dropped her scrub brush and rushed to pick up the injured animal. "It isn't enough to humiliate me, is it? You had to add insult to injury and step on Sebastian, too!"

"Sebastian?" His lips quirked, but before he could protest again, Olivia tucked the mewling kitten in her blouse, sat back on her knees, picked up the filthy brush from the floor and flung it at him with all her might, hitting him squarely in the chest.

"I beg your pardon. Do forgive me, sir. Brush must have been too sudsy. Slipped right out of my hands."

Chapter Twenty-One

London—Tuesday, The Seventeenth of September

Fairchild House was open for the season once again. The family returned from Brighton earlier than was their custom, for the purpose of witnessing Olivia's graduation from the academy.

While the duchess busied herself making plans for a betrothal ball for Olivia and Sebastian, the duke spent his time closeted with his man of business. The younger girls continued their lessons in the schoolroom with Mrs. Trumball. Georgiana studied French, a language she was adept at, Mary practiced the pianoforte, and Jane, who had shown no aptitude in any of her studies, managed to get into everyone else's hair.

Wilson Academy—The betrothal notice had already appeared in all the London papers, much to Olivia's chagrin, for she was determined to cry off. But her parents did not know that yet, for she hadn't found the time to tell them. She decided she would do so after graduation.

She was a study in misery, but she kept it to herself. Sebastian was not the man for her. That was clear when, in spite of all his promises, he broke another and had her scrub floors, betraying her for the last time, she decided. It galled her, too, that he found it convenient to blame others for his action time and again. What kind of man can call himself honorable if he can't—or won't—take the blame for his actions, official or not?

Was there a man who would go to the ends of the earth for her as she would for him? If she couldn't have such a paragon for a husband, she would have no one at all. The thought depressed her, for her arms still ached to hold Sebastian. How is it, she wondered, that she could love him in spite of his lack of spine? She felt so bruised. Would the pain ever go away? Or would she always suffer thus? Not knowing the answer to that question tortured her.

As if she were sleepwalking, Olivia fulfilled her final duties during this last week at Wilson Academy mechanically. She followed orders to the letter, not daring to question any one of them. She responded with civility when spoken to, but offered only the briefest of answers. She laughed at the antics of her fellow trainees, yet her passion was no longer engaged, neither for spying nor for camaraderie and certainly not for love.

"You asked to see me, sir?" she asked when Sebastian sent for her.

He looked drawn, as if he hadn't slept well. "Sit down, Olivia."

"I would prefer it if you would address me as Fairchild, just as you do the other trainees, sir." She sat on the edge of the chair opposite his desk, her hands folded in her lap, her face devoid of expression.

"I'm not ready to give up on our love so easily. Why won't you listen to reason?"

"We have a difference of opinion, sir. What you call reason, I call betrayal. I poured my heart out to you when you offered for me. Defend me, I pleaded. Stand up for me. Take my side. It's clear that you are incapable of doing any of these things, sir, which clearly indicates we are not suited. Why belabor the point?"

"Why? Because I love you, you little fool!" He pounded his desk. "Be reasonable, Livy. I cannot control the world for you, even though I wish it were so! I didn't suggest the additional task. It came from one of the other instructors. Face facts, my love. You don't take orders well. At our staff meeting, this point was brought up. Why, you may well ask, is it so crucial to obey orders without question? Because when a spy disregards orders, she not only puts her life in danger, but very likely the lives of others. I had no choice but to agree, especially when the vote was unanimous."

"Unanimous? No one defended me, then? Not even you?"

Sebastian searched her eyes, his face set in stone. "Can you not see that the fault lies within you? The odious task you were assigned was not meant to humiliate you. It was designed to teach you the importance of obeying orders. Did you learn nothing from the assignment, then? Be careful how you answer, Fairchild. Your career hangs in the balance."

"You would sack me, even at this late date? Yes. I suppose you would. It's what you've always wanted, isn't it?"

"Don't taunt me, my love. It won't work. I don't propose to suffer having your death on my hands when the home office assigns you to a dangerous mission and you sabotage the order to suit your whim. If you persist in thinking this is betrayal on my part, then so be it. I'd rather have you remain alive and furious with me, than die because you're so damned contrary."

Olivia lowered her eyes and examined her hands for what seemed like an eternity to Sebastian.

"Well, Fairchild? Can you learn to obey orders without question? It's up to you whether you go or you stay to graduate."

She looked up at him, her eyes blurred with tears. "I want to learn to obey orders, sir. Teach me how."

"Right, then. We begin at once. Are you ready?"

"Yes, sir," she said in a bleak tone, sounding as if she were on her way to the gallows.

He broke into a wide grin and said, "Then put your anger aside and come into my arms. Kiss me you foolish darling."

London—At dusk, Chris and Helena sat hand in hand in his garden. Few words were needed to describe their anguish, for he was to leave on special assignment in the morning.

"Can you not reveal where you've been posted, my darling?"

"You know I can't, Helena, but I promise to write often. I'll send it in the diplomatic pouch along with my dispatches to the home office. The messenger will take your letters to me and forward them in the same way."

She took a deep breath and said, "It's a dangerous assignment, isn't it?"

Chris took her in his arms and kissed her. "Need you ask? You are to become the wife of a spy and as such, you must learn to bear up."

Her eyes clouded. "I cannot 'bear up' as you so blithely put it, if it means I'm going to lose you."

"Don't let me see your tears, my angel. I want a sweeter parting tucked into my memory. One that will go a much longer way to ease my loneliness."

"Take me with you, then. That would be even sweeter."

"You know I can't. I promised your father . . ."

"Devil take my father!" Helena said with unaccustomed bitterness. She began to sob in earnest.

Chris held her close and let her weep, but his heart was

torn. At last he said, "A fine farewell this is, my love! Should you fall to pieces at every parting, we shall soon grow to detest one another. You for my leaving and me for your weeping." He took out his cloth and wiped her tears away. "Leave off, do!"

She pushed his hand away and rose to pace in front of him.

Where was his gentle Helena? he wondered. He couldn't fail to note the rage in her eyes. "Don't let us part this way, my love. We haven't much time left to us."

She stopped pacing in front of him and pulled him to his feet. " Take me to your bed."

"What?"

"Take me to your bed and make love to me. Now."

"Helena! You are being unreasonable."

"Am I? I think not. I will at least have the memory of your passion to keep me warm until you return."

Chris tried to hug her, but she held him off. "I mean it, Chris." She folded her arms and tapped her foot. "Well?"

"Don't you think I want to make love to you, dear heart? Bloody hell! The thought of you in my bed keeps me awake till all hours."

"Then throw caution to the winds and do it. We're betrothed, for heaven's sake! What harm if we both want this?"

"I won't father a bastard! That's where the harm lies!"

"Perhaps," she challenged, "you don't love me enough."

Exasperated as her words hit their mark, he grabbed her and crushed her to him, bruising her mouth with his. "Love you enough? Love you enough, you little tease? You must be barmy." He grabbed her hand and pulled her without mercy toward the terrace doors. "Dignity be damned. You've torn mine to shreds, you wretch."

"Chris, stop! You're hurting me!"

He paused at the door, but did not let go of her hand. "I

thought you were a willing partner in our illicit pleasure. Or have you changed your mind?"

"I've never seen this . . . this side of you. This wild side."

His smile was bestial. "Indeed! Do you see what lengths you have driven me to, my bewitching Greek goddess?" He lifted her in his arms and mounted the stairs to his chamber.

"Put me down this instant."

"I won't."

"I've changed my mind."

"Too late." He turned the knob with one hand, entered the room and kicked the door shut with his boot.

"I cannot believe you have a mind to . . . to rape me."

"Can't you? Just you wait and see to what lengths you have driven me." He dumped her on his bed and began to tear off his neckcloth.

She turned her face away to hide the gleam of triumph in her eyes, then feigned a sob, the grin well hidden from her beloved. In a trembling voice, she said, "You are beyond redemption, you brute." Helena covered her eyes with the back of one hand.

"Do with me what you will, you monster."

Chapter Twenty-Two

Graduation Day—Saturday, The Twenty-eighth of September

The ceremony was held on the ground floor auditorium of the home office, now bursting with proud relatives. The first graduating class sat upon the dais on the left side of the speaker's podium while the instructors sat on the right, directly behind the spymaster, sat the home secretary Viscount Henry Sidmouth, and a gentleman whose chest was bedecked with ribbons, marking him as a diplomat from a foreign country.

The audience hushed when the spymaster rose to the podium. "Good morning, ladies and gentlemen. I am Sir Sebastian Brooks, spymaster. You are all here today to witness the first graduating class to complete England's new intelligence training program. These dedicated students—five brave men and one heroic woman—have acquitted themselves in outstanding fashion and, I have no doubt, will make a major contribution to the safe keeping of our country. To present the awards, I give you Viscount Sidmouth, England's home secretary."

Polite applause followed Sidmouth to the podium. For dramatic effect, he stopped to survey his audience, for he was an accomplished speaker and knew how to electrify his listeners.

"History is being made here today, ladies and gentlemen. Not only do we honor five courageous young men who have dedicated their lives to the service of their country, but we also honor one brave young woman, the only one to graduate in the first graduating class." He nodded to Olivia and waited for the applause to end. "I have the pleasure to present certificates of completion to our graduates this morning." He nodded to the spymaster.

Sebastian began by calling each trainee to the podium. One by one they stepped up to receive a certificate and a handshake from the spymaster as well as from the home secretary. At the end of this brief service, Sidmouth held up his hand for quiet.

"We have another guest this morning," he said. "Count Ivor Wengor, special attaché to Prince Joachim of Zarkovia. The count has returned to England to present three medals of honor. The first is to Sir Sebastian Brooks for foiling the plot to assassinate His Majesty, Prince Joachim." Applause continued while Count Wengor placed the gold medal attached to a ribbon around Sebastian's neck.

"Unfortunately, in the course of doing his duty, the spymaster was captured by four assassins bent on destroying good relations between England and Zarkovia. Two of the spymaster's trainees rescued him and disarmed the villains. They are Mr. Rufus Riggs and Lady Olivia Fairchild. Will you step forward, please?"

When the two received their medals, Count Wengor bent to kiss Olivia's hand for which he received enthusiastic applause. But Sidmouth was not finished. He waved the palms of his hands up and down until everyone was seated once again, Count Wengor still standing by his side.

"Prince Joachim of Zarkovia wishes to bestow yet

another gift upon these three brave protectors of the Prince of Zarkovia."

The diplomat retrieved three long scrolls of parchment tied with red ribbon from an aide, who then withdrew. As Sidmouth called each one's name, Count Wengor bowed and handed them a scroll.

"Zarkovia has granted you honorary citizenship for life. We must applaud not only these three new dual citizens, but also all the other graduates." When the applause died down, Sidmouth added, "Our ceremony has come to an end. Please join us for a celebratory feast in the garden."

Each family gathered around their graduate and congratulated them as they partook of a lavish buffet. The twins, who came from a large family, basked in the boisterous affection of country folk, making them the loudest contingent.

The Duke of Heatham hugged his daughter to him. "Well, Livy. In spite of the fact that you disobeyed me, let me be the first to admit that I am exceedingly proud of you. Not only did your dream come true, but you have proved to be a heroine. Well done."

Olivia hugged him. "Thank you, Father. Your hard-won approval means a lot to me."

"What's next for you, my dear?" asked her mother.

"On Monday, all of the graduates are to meet here in the home office for our assignments. I'll know then what's in store for me."

Her mother beamed. "Then we have our girl to ourselves for the entire weekend, don't we?"

Olivia's eyes filled with tears. "May we go home now? I want that above all things."

"Tears, child? And on the day of your triumph?" her father asked, puzzlement wrinkling his brow.

"They're tears of happiness, Father. I've come home at last."

"Ah, here is your suitor. Well done, Brooks, for both the ceremony and for your heroic deed."

"Thank you, Your Grace." Sebastian turned to Olivia and took her hands in his. "Congratulations to you as well, my love."

"Thank you, sir." She changed the subject. "This is my brother Edward, sir. He is down from Oxford for my graduation. I don't believe you two have met."

"Yes we have, my dear. He was at Heatham the night we announced our betrothal."

Edward bounced forward and offered his hand. "Of course we have. Again, I wish you both happiness."

"Since I have no family of my own, I look forward to having you as a brother. Do you hunt?"

Jane sidled over next to Sebastian. "My brother doesn't care for hunting, sir, but you should see him handle a curricle! No one can beat him in a race."

"That so?" Sebastian chucked her under her chin. "And how are you today, my young beauty?"

"I'm not a beauty, sir," she answered blushing from ear to ear. Yet the look on her face said otherwise.

Sebastian laughed. "If I say you are beautiful, young lady, you must accept my word, for I fancy myself an expert in such matters."

Olivia stiffened, but she did not allow her feelings to surface as the family gathered round her and continued their banter. It was her father who asked the anticipated question. The one she most dreaded.

The duke took both Sebastian's hand and his daughter's hand in each one of his and said, "Well, you two. Graduation, although a grand affair, is over with. It's time for an even grander one. When shall we celebrate your betrothal?"

"We haven't had the time to discuss it, Your Grace."

"Join us for dinner tomorrow, then, when we shall fix the date."

Sebastian raised an eyebrow to Olivia, but her eyes refused to meet his. "If my betrothed permits?"

She smiled and bowed to him, but her resentment caused her stomach to lurch. *He thinks the kiss he ordered me to give him makes up for all the misery he never fails to put in my way. What an act he's putting on for my family. They can't hear the false notes he sings, but I can and it sickens me. I won't tolerate his two-faced ways for the rest of my life. What scheme is he up to now? No matter. I know what I must do. Only one way out of this farce for me.*

Olivia passed her hand over her brow and said to him, "Will you excuse me till tomorrow, sir? I want to go home now, for I have a headache. Will you offer my apologies to my colleagues and to all the instructors?"

"Of course, my dear."

The duchess, alarmed by the threat of illness to her daughter, at once turned to her son. "Order our carriages, Edward."

"Yes, Mother." Olivia's brother sped out of the garden just as Viscount Sidmouth came upon the family.

"Congratulations, Fairchild." He tweaked her chin, oblivious to the pain in her eyes. When he turned to her father, he said, "Well, Duke? I hope, old friend, you have forgiven me for disobeying you and training your daughter to be a spy. I always knew I was right to accept her into the program in spite of your misgivings. And see how she has proved me correct. Indeed, she has exceeded my expecta—"

At this, Olivia burst into tears and ran out of the garden, astonishing all the guests into silence. Her sister Helena was hard on her heels, followed by Georgiana and Mary. But Jane, unwilling to miss a word that might tweak her love of intrigue, remained with her mother.

"You must excuse us all, sir," interrupted the duchess.

"My daughter is so overwrought by the day's events, she suffers a headache. We're going to take her home now."

"By all means, ma'am," Sidmouth answered. His eyes narrowed as he watched the family turn away to follow their parents out.

"That's odd, Brooks. What ails your trainee? She looked fine to me. Do you know what to make of it?"

Sebastian's brows met in a frown. "I've no doubt it's as she says, sir. She suffers a headache."

The home secretary viewed her departure in terms of what it would mean to him. "Women are often prone to tears and to headaches, I suppose. I wonder. Would these feminine emotions interfere with her work for us?"

"I don't believe so, sir. She has already proven herself to be a consummate professional. More than once."

"Then I charge you to see to it that her emotions are kept in proper check. Can't have a weeper in our midst, can we?"

"No, sir."

"I'm off, then. You may stay as long as you like and celebrate with your people, but I have an appointment with the Regent. I am to present the Zarkovian envoy to His Majesty."

Sebastian's eyes followed his superior and Count Wengor until they were out of sight, but still he did not move. Without revealing his unease, his thoughts were focused on Olivia and her mystifying behavior. Today ought to have been one of the happiest days of her life. Why hadn't she taken pleasure in her graduation? Why hadn't she taken pleasure when she won the special award for her bravery in saving his life? And most important, why hadn't she been overjoyed with her father's hard-won approval of her quest to be a spy?

She had not even allowed her eyes to meet his, though he had tried for the connection—usually a subtle exchange of understanding between lovers. She ran from him as if

he were the devil himself. Did his love for her not count
for anything? His heart was heavy with the burden of her
bewildering emotions. He wondered whether he would
ever learn to understand her. What possessed her to burst
into tears?

Chapter Twenty-Three

Fairchild House—Sunday, The Twenty-ninth of September

Olivia sat in the window seat overlooking the garden, an unopened book in her lap, though it was well past three in the afternoon. After chapel and the usual family repast, she'd begged off and had gone up to her chamber to rest. When the door to her chamber was opened by her sister Helena, she turned.

"Livy? He's here. Dunston's put him in the morning room. He wants to see you."

No need to ask her sister who "he" was. Olivia had expected Sebastian to call, especially after his dramatic performance at graduation yesterday. She wondered what he thought he could accomplish after their last blistering bout of words. Perhaps he was waiting for her to cry off. Was he not man enough to make the announcement? Well, so be it. *She* would perform that office. She wasn't ashamed to admit to her family that she'd made a mistake. The truth was that she and the spymaster would not suit. She'd been through worse trials than this these past twelve weeks. At least, there hadn't been a betrothal ball. No invitations had been posted yet, which made things simpler. Less painful.

Less painful? Then why did she feel herself to be twisted in knots? Why did she feel so listless inside? Why could she not sleep at night? Why did food and drink taste like bitter herbs and wine gone sour?

"What are you doing, Helena?"

"Since you have no abigail to help you dress, I'm choosing an appropriate gown for you to wear when you see Sebastian."

"Can't you just tell him to go away? Tell him I don't want to see him."

"No, dearest. If you mean to cry off, you'll have to do it yourself." Helena put the gown on the bed and fell to her knees before her sister. She took both her hands. "Look me in the eye, Livy. Can you honestly tell me you don't love him?"

Olivia fought back tears. "I love him so much, I feel as if every angry hornet in the nest has stung me. But I can't tie myself to a man who betrays me time and time again. I can't spend the rest of my life in regret at having married such a traitor. You of all people well know I've managed to reach my goal in spite of his opposition. If I'm to marry, I want a helpmate to love, don't you see? Someone who encourages my dreams because of his love for me. That man downstairs? All he wants from me is to be ready to greet him at the door and fly away to his bed."

Helena giggled. "Livy! You're making me blush!"

"Am I? You're such a cool one, Helena. Do you wish me to believe that you and Chris haven't . . . you know."

Helena rose and squeezed into the window seat next to her sister. In a mock serious tone, she said, "You have no idea how hard I had to work to force Chris into bed with me. Harder still was to persuade him it was his idea. But it was all for nothing, my girl. Do you know what that scoundrel did? At the last minute he changed his mind, declaring he had no intention of 'dishonoring' the woman he loved. Can you believe it?"

The sisters went off into a peal of laughter that brought tears to their eyes.

"What is all this? I had not expected to find my two oldest daughters turned into schoolroom gigglers. Especially when there's an impatient suitor waiting to see one of you," said the duchess as she entered the chamber. Her lively eyes belied her stern tone of voice. In truth, she was delighted to see Olivia laughing again. With a mother's intuition, she'd known her daughter was in pain without quite knowing the reason why or how to ease it.

"Let us help you dress, Livy. Your young man has been waiting almost an hour."

"All right, Mother. But it won't hurt him to wait, believe me. He's far too used to being obeyed at the drop of a hat. A habit I doubt he would be able to rid himself of."

Her mother laughed. "A bit of advice, dear. When he changes a habit you consider odious, be sure to make him think it was his own idea."

Her mood was lightened by her mother and her sister's absurd banter while they helped her dress. She was able to greet Sebastian with a lighter heart, if not a friendlier manner. She swept into the morning room and offered her hand. "How are you, Sebastian?"

His eyes lit up at the warmth in her voice. He took her hand and bent to kiss it, but she pulled it away when Dunston shut the door behind him. "No need to pretend any longer. Dunston is out of earshot." She walked to the terrace doors, threw them open and beckoned to him. "Care to join me for a stroll in the garden? We shall have more privacy there."

He recognized the danger in her voice, yet he felt helpless to fight it. "As you wish, my dear." He offered his arm, relieved that she took it and they proceeded down the path toward the arbor.

"This is the rose garden. My mother's favorite. And on the left is the annual garden, much prized by my father," she said as if taking a stranger on tour.

He stopped and turned her to him. "And you, my love? What do you prize most?"

Without skipping a beat, she tilted her head and said, "Loyalty. Loyalty above all. That, too, may be found in a garden. If one nurtures the plants properly, from seed to maturity, they reward us with their scent and their beauty." She smiled, but the look on her face told him another tale.

"I can learn, you know. If only you will agree to be my instructor, my love."

"I have given you everything that is within my power to give, Sebastian. My love. My loyalty. My virginity. Yet you've failed me time and again. The one gift I prize most, sir, is loyalty. How many more lessons shall you need? And how long must it take before you learn what to you must seem such an alien trait?"

Sebastian brushed her brow with his fingertip. "A lifetime? Say you forgive me, my dearest heart, and I will spend the rest of my life . . ."

She flicked his hand away as if it were a bothersome insect and walked on. "Such a familiar tune, but off key, let me assure you. You're in danger of becoming a dead bore, you know."

"Tell me how to make it right for you, Olivia. I've never been in love before. I don't know how."

She wheeled around to face him, but kept him at arm's length. The look on her face was strained. "Shall I draw you a map? Would that help you find your way? I think not. I have a strong suspicion that it just isn't in you to return love with loyalty." Her voice rose higher. "I *killed* to save your life, you wretch!"

"Don't you think I know that? You killed to save me without giving a thought to your own safety. Go ahead and tongue-lash away, my love. I deserve it."

"What good would that do? You are too set in your ways to change."

"Don't give up on me, I beg of you. By all means draw me a map if you think it would help me to find the way to your heart again. How can I persuade you to change your mind? I cannot eat. I cannot sleep. I love you. I cannot think of anything but how much I want to take you in my arms."

"Taking me in your arms is just lust, Sebastian. Not love." She turned and walked away.

But he followed her every step and let go a shaky laugh. "Lust? Guilty as charged. I won't deny that I lust after you, but any country lass can satisfy a man's lust. It happens that I haven't fallen in love with a country lass. It's love of you that's driving me to Bedlam. I never dreamed love could be so full of pain. Can we not start over, my darling?"

They had reached the latticed arbor where two seats faced one another. Olivia sat on one seat and indicated the opposite one with a nod of her head. Sebastian flipped the tails of his coat and took it, stretching one knee out and resting his elbow on the other. He looked directly into Olivia's eyes and said, "Well? Do we remain betrothed or do we not?"

"I wish it were so, but I fear not. I cannot abide the thought of a lifetime of misery and disappointment."

"Is your love so lost to me, my dearest heart, that you cannot even speak my name? Is it so painful on your lips?"

"Sebastian."

The sound gladdened him. "My fate is in your hands, my darling. I know it's a lot to ask of you, but can you forgive me?"

She fell silent for a time. At last, she said softly, "I, too, have spent many sleepless nights. I, too, cannot eat. I, too, am tortured by this dilemma."

Sebastian rose and pulled her to her feet. "It appears we're both finding the road to love full of uncharted danger. Perhaps that's as it is meant to be." He held her gently to him, but did not try to kiss her. "Can you see your way clear to loving me even a little? That would be enough for a start."

She buried her head in his coat and whispered, "It hurts, Sebastian. I can't bear the pain. It hurts too much."

"Oh my poor dear darling. *Life* hurts. Don't you know that? Perhaps we have to learn that lesson together. Shall we give it another try?"

Before she could answer, a child's high-pitched voice interrupted. Jane put her hands on her wide hips and grinned at them. "There you are, you two lovebirds! You're late. The whole family is waiting for you in the drawing room."

"You've found us out, my pretty damsel," said Sebastian. "You are by far, the most beautiful imp in all of England. You do know that, don't you?"

The child blushed, but she was pleased all the same. "You're teasing me again, sir. I have crooked teeth and I'm too fat to be beautiful."

"Not at all. Your teeth have character and you have a pleasing shape. If Rubens were alive, he'd beg you to be his model."

"Who's he?"

"A famous artist who loved to paint beautiful women like you."

"How silly you are, brother-in-law." She giggled nevertheless. "Everyone says I'm too fat because I eat so many scones."

He glared at her with mock severity. "Who tells such lies about you, my love? Show the lying dastard to me and I shall smite him with my sword in a single thrust." He scooped her up in his arms and nuzzled her neck, tickling her into more giggles.

When he put her down, he added, "Can you give your sister and me just a few more moments? Go back and inform the family we'll be along presently."

"Take your time, Sebastian. I'll just tell them I haven't been able to find you."

"You're the best friend a man could have, Jane dearest. If I hadn't already offered for your sister, I'd wait for you to grow old enough to receive my attentions."

The child's red cheeks grew redder. She grinned at him, waved, and skipped off.

Olivia looked at him in astonishment. "Sebastian! How did you ever tame that unruly brat?"

"None of you seem to understand that a little flattery goes a long way with Jane. I meant what I said. She's pretty in spite of all that baby fat. She'll surprise you all one day." He hesitated.

"What is it?"

"Your parents expressed a wish to arrange our betrothal ball."

"I'm not ready, Sebastian. Can we ask them to postpone the decision for a week? I'll agree to a date then, for I'll know where the home office has assigned me."

Sebastian's heart thudded, for he already knew where she had been assigned.

Chapter Twenty-Four

London—Monday, The Seventh of October

When the Fairchild carriage drew up to the home office, Olivia tapped her foot as she waited for the footman to let down the steps. She made every effort to control her impatience, yet it wasn't easy for her. Once inside the building, she reported to the waiting room on the second floor as instructed.

There she found the Reed twins and Carter. The electricity of tension rippled through them all as they waited to hear where they had been assigned.

"Where are Riggs and Perkins?" Olivia asked.

"Perkins has yet to arrive and Riggs is in the home secretary's office receiving his assignment," answered Carter.

An out-of-breath Perkins arrived. "Well, friends. Are we all on tenterhooks?"

"Undoubtedly," answered Olivia. "Have you been running, dear boy? How are you, Perkins?"

"You may all wish me happiness. I am betrothed to my dear Amelia."

"What's she want with a rascal like you?" teased Billy Reed.

"Ten to one she'll cry off when she learns you've been assigned to some wilderness like America," tweaked Bobby Reed. "Place your bets, please."

"I wish you every happiness, Perkins," Olivia said warmly, holding out her hand to grasp his.

"As well I, Perkins, you lucky dog. I saw the lovely Amelia at graduation. As pretty a woman as I ever laid eyes on." Carter pumped his hand up and down.

"Leave off, Carter. Let us have our turn at that scoundrel," protested Bobby.

"You're a sly one, Perkins. You never told us you had a sweetheart," teased Billy.

The door to the home secretary's office opened to reveal Riggs, a grin stretched wide as the English Channel on his face. The other trainees surrounded him at once.

"I'm for Belgium," he whispered. "Top secret. Belgium! Imagine! I'm assigned to the new ambassador there." He sat down, clearly overcome by his good fortune.

"Robert Reed and William Reed," a clerk announced upon entering the room. "Follow me, please."

"I know they don't want to be separated," said Olivia. "I hope they get their wish."

The twins returned in less than ten minutes. "France," said Billy.

"Both of us," echoed his brother Bobby.

In short order, Perkins learned he was assigned to Scotland, and Carter to Spain. Whoops of joy and shouts of congratulations filled the room.

Olivia was the last to enter Viscount Sidmouth's office.

"We'll wait here to learn where you've been assigned, Fairchild," said Riggs.

"Right and tight. All for one and one for all, I say," echoed Perkins.

"I wish you the best of luck, Fairchild," said Carter.

The twins merely kissed her, one on each cheek. But before

he backed away, Billy whispered in her ear. "Odds be damned, me beauty. In me heart you'll always be my odds-on favorite."

She thought being last might not bode well for her, but she turned the knob and entered with a smile on her face. Sidmouth was seated at his desk while Sebastian chose to remain at the window, his arms folded, leaning on the sill.

"Come in, my dear," said the home secretary in a hearty voice. "And how does your father?"

"He's well, sir," she answered, wondering why he asked since he'd seen her father at graduation not two days earlier.

"Sit, Fairchild," said Sebastian, a grim look on his face. His eyes pointed to the chair opposite Sidmouth.

"The spymaster and I have decided that you have earned a well-deserved rest. We are offering all of you six weeks of holiday before you begin your work as intelligence agents," said the home secretary as if conferring the crown jewels upon her and the other men.

Something was wrong. Olivia sensed it in Sebastian's rigid stance and in the viscount's false heartiness. What? She folded her hands in her lap and sat back, deciding it was wiser to say nothing for the moment.

"You have been recommended for your new post—a most prestigious one, let me assure you—by none other than Sir Aaron Foster, the most outstanding professional decoder in the country. At his recommendation, you are to work in the home office in the codes and ciphers department, a great honor."

A violent storm unleashed itself in her soul. One that turned her world upside down.

Unwilling to betray her emotions, Olivia rose from her chair with dignity. She said in a sober voice, "Thank you for this opportunity, home secretary. I thank you as well, spymaster, for all your support. Good day to you both."

In the waiting room, she faced the other trainees and announced, "Right here. Codes and ciphers."

"Bloody hell! That's no better than a mere clerk's position. Why did they bother to train you for intelligence work? You don't deserve such shabby treatment, Fairchild. What bad luck!" said Riggs with indignation.

Carter added in a consoling voice, "Buck up, lass. Better to swallow this and show them what you're made of, my dear. Maybe then you'll be assigned to a decent foreign post, for we all know that's what you wanted."

"Maybe we ought to protest as a group. Fairchild deserves a better appointment. She's as good as all of us. Better, in fact," said Perkins, his cheeks blotched with anger.

"The odds are against you, lass," said Billy, sadness in his tone.

"Truth be told, Fairchild. Do you think your father had a hand in this?" asked his brother Bobby.

Olivia shrugged. She looked from one to the other, as she fought back tears. "You're all such dears. It was an honor to know you and I shall always treasure our time together. Don't forget me." Before they could react, she wheeled around and ran from the room.

In her carriage, she vowed to find a way out in spite of this new humiliation. When the footman let down the steps, she descended as though she were a queen. The first to greet her was the butler.

"Where is my father, Dunston?"

"His Grace is in his study, milady. Shall I . . ."

"Don't bother. I know the way."

She entered the room without stopping to knock. "Father?"

His Grace looked up, not at all pleased with the dark look on his daughter's face. Wisely, he chose not to scold her for entering without first knocking. "What is it, Livy?"

"I want you to be the first to know that I am not going to

wed Sir Sebastian Brooks after all and I shall so inform him at once."

"You're crying off? May I ask why?"

"You may ask Sir Sebastian Brooks why, sir. Perhaps he'll tell you, for he well knows the reason, but I shall not lower my dignity to tell you. As a matter of fact, I suspect you know the reason already. You and Sebastian and the home secretary must have had quite a jolly laugh when you decided to pull the rug out from under me." She wheeled around and opened the door, her gown swirling as if to echo the righteous indignation she felt. Nor was she at all surprised by the butler, who jumped back when she exited the room.

"Instead of eavesdropping at every opportunity, my good man, do something useful and send my mother to my chamber at once." She swept past the astonished Dunston, picked up her skirts and took the stairs two at a time, as though she were still in training at the academy. She slammed the door to her chamber and went at once to her desk where she reached for a quill and note paper and began to write.

"I heard you bang your door, Livy. Something wrong?" asked Helena whose chamber was next to hers.

She put the quill down and turned to her sister. "I'm writing to break my betrothal to Sebastian."

"Are you mad? What's gotten into you? Just yesterday you told me you loved him."

"It's over and done with. I don't want to talk about it any more. Time for me to move on. I have a long holiday before I begin my new position and I plan to spend it at Bodmin Castle. You may travel with me if you wish. I'd be glad to have your company, but only if you promise not to harass me. If you'd rather not join me, I'd just as soon go alone."

"Don't be daft. You know perfectly well I'll go with you. When do we leave?"

"Tomorrow, unless that's too soon for you to be ready."

"Tomorrow is fine. Have you informed our parents?"

"I've sent for Mother. She can tell Father, for he and I are no longer on speaking terms."

When the duchess entered the room, she felt the tension at once. "What's wrong, Livy? You look as pale as a ghost."

She hugged her Mother and kissed both her cheeks. "Nothing I can't cure, Mother. In fact, I am about to set my world right. I've already told His Grace that I am no longer betrothed to Sebastian." A hint of bitterness crept into her voice.

"May I ask why, dearest?"

"We don't suit. I am writing to him to inform him of my decision."

Her mother was nothing if not a shrewd judge on the subject of her children. "What happened this morning at the home office? And why has it upset you so, Livy?"

"I ought to have been prepared for this new slap in the face, Mother, but I wasn't. At the end of twelve weeks of rigorous training—twelve weeks in which I destroyed all of my once lovely fingernails, in which I had to cut off my beautiful long curls, in which my hands have been made calloused from scrubbing the bloody kitchen galley, in which my bottom still shows bruises from being thrown from a horse, in which I nearly lost my eyesight—I'm back where I began. I regret to inform you that, while all the other trainees were assigned to exotic foreign posts, I have been relegated to the office of codes and ciphers in the home office. A lofty position only slightly above the lowly file clerk I once was."

The room went silent as Olivia turned back to her desk to finish her note to Sebastian. At a nod from her mother, Helena tiptoed out. Olivia heard the door shut, but paid it no mind. She finished the brief letter, folded it, wrote its destination on the envelope, poured hot wax on it and sealed it with her impression. When an under maid answered her ring, she handed the letter to her.

"Tell Dunston to have this letter delivered to Sir Sebastian Brooks at the home office at once."

"Yes, milady." The young girl curtseyed and bowed out of the room. Only then did Olivia turn to her mother. She folded her hands on her lap.

"Done, Mother. With your permission, I leave for Bodmin Castle. Helena has agreed to accompany me there if you will allow it."

"Of course, I'll allow it. Does that mean you are not going to accept the assignment at the home office?"

Olivia's lips drew thin. "Not at all. I have been granted a long holiday before I begin, but I most certainly will report to duty." Her mother looked puzzled. "My work begins the middle of November. In the meantime, I need to be far away from London. You do understand that, don't you?"

The duchess opened her arms to her daughter. "Of course I understand. Come here, my dear."

Olivia took a seat on the settee next to her and rested her head on her mother's shoulders. A peaceful silence reigned for a brief time as they sat side by side, hands entwined. "I confess I didn't see this blow coming, Mother. I should have been prepared. A woman doesn't stand a tinker's chance in a man's world, does she? All the other trainees are off to foreign posts while I molder in the London office. I won't lie to you. The appointment was a slap in the face. It stunned me.

"What's worse, when Sidmouth delivered the news to me, Sebastian was in the home secretary's office and he didn't say a word in my defense. He hurt me, Mother. If he drew a knife through my heart, he couldn't have hurt me more. I'll never forgive him for refusing to stand up for me. Never."

"How awful that must have made you feel."

"I was mortified. Especially when the man who professes his love for me just stands there in silence while the noose

around my neck tightens. I can never trust a man like that."
The tears began to roll down her cheeks.

Without a word, the duchess held her daughter and let her
tears wash away her pain. It was a long time before Olivia
found some semblance of peace in her troubled soul and
was able to stop crying.

"It will help me to have Helena with me at Bodmin."

Her mother wiped away the last of her tears. "Of course,
dear. Bodmin Castle hasn't been used by the family in years,
but I'll send enough servants along to make you comfortable. I believe we have a man of business in Cornwall. I'll
write to tell him to see to whatever repairs may be necessary.
When shall you leave?"

"The sooner the better. Tomorrow morning, if that's all
right with you?"

"I think it's a wise decision. You shall take the brougham, Helena's abigail Amy, one of the other under maids as
an abigail for you, Casper as driver, and two footmen. It's a
long journey to Cornwall, Livy. You'll have to stop overnight
on the way. I'll ask your father to recommend decent inns."

"You may ask him, but I don't want to see him before I
leave."

Her mother looked into her eyes. "You think your father
had a hand in this odious assignment in the home office?"

"Yes. Let's not discuss this tiresome affair any more. I
can't bear it."

"He's still your father, Livy. He loves you very much."

"I haven't forgotten that, Mother. But you must allow me
the time to heal our rift."

Her mother heaved a deep sigh. "As you wish, dear."

"As for my abigail, there is a young lady at the academy I
would prefer to hire. She's an Irish lass named Jenny
O'Toole. She's a scullery maid there, but she has considerable
talent as a hairdresser and wants very much to become a lady's

maid. Though she lacks polish, I'd be delighted to have her. With your permission, I shall write to Mrs. Hunnicut at once. If she agrees, and I have no doubt she will, Jenny can travel by mail coach and join me at Bodmin as soon as she is able."

Chapter Twenty-Five

Bodmin Castle, Cornwall—Sunday, The Thirteenth of October

Heavy rain blurred the carriage window, its gray gloom matching Olivia's mood when she and Helena reached Bodmin Castle. The rutted roads made the ride uncomfortable, but she took no notice. When Helena's abigail Amy attempted to complain, her mistress silenced her with a forbidding look. They passed through the first toll-gate and sought refuge for the night at a respectable inn where they were greeted royally by a landlord well acquainted with the duke.

Helena took charge, for Olivia carried too heavy a burden in her heart to utter more than a few syllables at a time. In short order, arrangements were made with the ostler for their horses, their carriage, and a second carriage carrying their clothing as well as two more under maids. Casper and the two footmen were housed in rooms over the stable, while Amy saw to the needs of her mistress as well as to the needs of Lady Olivia.

"The innkeeper has arranged dinner, Livy. Would you like to rest until then?"

Olivia looked up at Helena from her seat in the private

parlor where she had taken refuge. "No, dear. I'm not at all weary. You go ahead and lie down for a bit. I'll just sit here, if you don't mind."

"I do mind, you ninny. You're breaking my heart. What can I do to shake you out of your doldrums?"

"Forgive me, Helena. I didn't mean to burden you with my sorrows. Perhaps I will lie down until dinnertime." She rose and linked arms with her sister. "Give me time to heal, dearest. Bodmin Castle may be the answer, I hope. We'll ride every morning when the weather permits, take long walks across the moors the way we used to when we were children, and visit old friends."

"I'll own that it may help to heal your sore heart, but only if you allow it to do so, Livy. It won't happen by itself, you know. You must help it along."

She sighed. "I wish I knew how. When I find a way, I promise you I'll try, dearest."

The inn was comfortable, but the sisters left early the next morning, for they had a long journey ahead of them. Bodmin Castle was nearly sixty miles from London.

London—"You have a visitor, Your Grace." Dunston handed him the visitor's card.

When the duke read the name on the card, he said in a sharp tone, "What do you mean by keeping him waiting, you fool? Send him in at once." Duly chastised, Dunston opened the door wider.

"Sebastian, my good fellow. Come in, come in," said the duke, rising to greet him. He shook his hand, led him to a comfortable fireplace chair and sat opposite him.

"Brandy, Dunston. At once."

"It is already here, Your Grace." Dunston sniffed, insulted by the intimation that he did not know what was expected of him. A footman placed the tray of brandy and two snifters on a table at the duke's side.

"I don't wish to be disturbed. Do I make myself clear?"

The butler deigned to answer with only a nod and bowed out, allowing himself the satisfaction of shutting the door with a small, yet defiant, bang.

"Rascal keeps his ear glued to the door. Listens to every word. I'd sack him if I could, but he's been with us since we married and the duchess won't hear of it."

The duke poured the brandy and handed one snifter to Sebastian. "Truth is, I welcome your company lad, for you find me quite alone. My wife and my daughters are away. How are you faring, son?"

"Not at all well, Your Grace. I miss your daughter. I write to her every day, but she hasn't answered any of my letters."

"My Livy's a stubborn puss, lad. She's furious with me as well, I don't mind telling you. Wouldn't even talk to me before she left. She thinks I had a hand in her unhappy assignment, but you know I did not."

Sebastian attempted a smile, but there was no joy in it. "The home secretary refused to listen to my plea, Your Grace. I argued in favor of assigning her a vacant post in the ambassador's office in Italy. I'm sure she would have been pleased with that, but he chose his own path." Sebastian did not add the words, "as usual," though they lay on his tongue.

The duke sipped his brandy. "You are his spymaster, are you not? Why didn't he take your recommendation?"

"May I be frank?" The duke nodded in assent. "Viscount Sidmouth has had a long career in government service. He is arrogant. Thinks he is a law unto himself. My suspicion is that he meant this assignment to please you, Your Grace. He knows you to be an influential member of Parliament. And as such, you may one day be in a position to help him achieve passage of some bill, or perhaps assist him when he requests an increase in funds for the home office. In either case, the home secretary would then take pains to remind you that you owe him a favor."

The duke nodded in agreement. "You have that right, I believe. Sidmouth might have been a better prime minister if he had paid more attention to the country and less to his damnable manipulations. What's he want from me now?"

"I haven't the faintest idea, Your Grace. The home secretary keeps his own counsel. Perhaps he wants nothing more than your good will at the moment. But be on your guard, my lord duke. He's sure to call in the favor at some future date, I promise you."

The duke frowned. "Well, he shan't curry any favor with me that I don't want to give, I can tell you."

"I don't doubt that, Your Grace."

The duke lapsed into silence for a moment. At last he said, "Let me ask you something. Why do you chafe under his service if you're so unhappy?"

Sebastian grinned. "You are most perceptive, Your Grace. I thought it was right for me. When the war was over, I sold out to take the post after the home secretary sold me on it. He promised me a free hand in developing this unique spy training program. *Carte blanche,* so to speak. I'll own that designing the space, finding outstanding instructors and creating a rigorous curriculum was a challenge I found hard to resist. It seemed the perfect antidote to a battle-weary soldier."

"What changed your mind?"

Sebastian hesitated.

"You may speak freely, son. You have my word that I shall hold what you tell me in the strictest confidence."

"Thank you, Your Grace. To be frank, the viscount does not keep his word. He meddles and I find that intolerable. After I had designed the property, employed the instructors, created the program and selected the trainees—with the exception of your daughter—I became nothing more than a clerk writing reports for a man who interfered whenever he had a notion."

The duke eyed Sebastian. "I take it my daughter's selection did not have your approval?"

"No, Your Grace. I met her briefly for the first time at the Hobbleton Ball last June, before I knew she had been selected by the viscount. At the time, I didn't believe any woman could withstand the rigors of the program."

"Have you changed your mind?"

"She changed it for me, sir. Your daughter is brave and brilliant and . . . wonderful." A wave of pain spread across his face.

"I'd advise you to wipe that black look from your face, my boy. And leave off that Your Grace business. Call me duke or sir. In time, I trust you will call me father-in-law, for I'm that fond of you. I have not given up hope that you and my daughter will patch things up and get on with your life together, for I suspect that my Livy is still very much in love with you."

Sebastian's smile replaced a bit of the blackness in his heart. "Is she? Then you've given me hope to cling to, sir. I wish I may know the way to win your daughter back, but I do not. She thinks I betrayed her, but it was no such thing. I fought for her hard, but I lost. Sidmouth's as stubborn as a mule. Once he takes a position, right or wrong, he never backs down."

The Duke of Heatham knew well that he had more power if it came to a test of wills. A few chosen words in the right ears would bring Sidmouth up sharp. Nothing could be easier to arrange than a set-down to trim the home secretary's wings.

Aloud, he said, "Let us put talk of that pompous ass aside for the moment, son. Let us instead put our heads together and discover how best to bring about a reconciliation between you and my daughter. Isn't that what we both want?"

Sebastian's eyes filled with a glimmer of hope. "Devoutly, sir. Share your thoughts with me. I'm prepared to do anything you recommend. I'll even resign my post if that would help me win her back."

"No need to do anything as rash as all that." The duke sipped his brandy, lost in thought. "Suppose you were to take a leave—a long holiday, perhaps. Could you arrange that?"

"It won't be at all difficult, sir."

"My daughter has gone to one of my estates. She's at Bodmin Castle in Cornwall with her sister Helena. My wife and my other three daughters are on their way there as we speak. And I plan to join them when I finish my business in London. Why not spend some time in the neighborhood?"

"Gladly. I'll apply for leave at once. But what if she still refuses to see me?"

"Allow me to let you in on a little secret, son. Young people are often loathe to take advice from their elders, but perhaps this bit of wisdom may do you some good. It has sustained a happy married life for me for twenty-five years."

"What is it, sir?"

"When the weather is stormy, marital discord works havoc, if you take my meaning."

"I do, sir, but please. Don't keep me in suspense. What have you done to overcome the discord? What is this powerful secret?"

The duke raised his snifter as if in a toast and said, "We married men learn it is always wisest to have the last word in a marital dispute. To end it, we say the two magic words our wives love to hear—'Yes, dear.'"

"Yes, dear? I don't understand, sir."

A sly grin accompanied the duke's chuckle. "Successful

married chaps who apologize, right or wrong, are then free to do precisely as they please."

Bodmin Castle—The arrival of her mother and her younger sisters lifted Olivia's spirits. The duchess brought letters for Helena, who retired to her room to read them, for they were all from Chris. But when she handed Olivia her letters, she glanced at the handwriting and threw them into the fireplace without bothering to read them.

Despite that display of scorn, the family's presence proved a welcome distraction for her and they settled into a comfortable routine which Olivia found soothing. There were morning rides, afternoon walks and in the evening after an early dinner, her mother plied her needlepoint while Olivia and her sisters played piquet. They were entertained by Mary, whose talent at the pianoforte soothed Olivia's sore heart.

The only jarring note in this pleasant reunion was Jane, who persisted in her endless tattling—about the house servants, about the stable boys and about the kitchen maids. In a short space of time, Jane had managed to crawl under everyone's skin, to the point where complaints to Her Grace became a daily occurrence. The unpleasant situation came to a head when the housekeeper, Mrs. Shaw, begged the duchess to find occupations for Jane other than spying on the staff and reporting their shortcomings.

Her Grace turned to Olivia to resolve this domestic crisis, and she undertook the task of persuading Jane to leave off plaguing the staff. "Mind you, Jane. It's not the thing at all to spy on the servants," she began. "They won't like you very much and it will not help you win their friendship. You don't want that, do you?"

A tear rolled down the child's chubby cheek. " There's

nobody for me to play with and not much to do around here," she said fretfully. She reached for another scone, her fourth.

Olivia refrained from curtailing the child's robust appetite. Cure one fault at a time, she thought. Surely Jane would outgrow her penchant for overeating as she grew older.

She wiped the extra cream off the corner of her sister's lips and said, "Let's put our heads together, darling, and find some new ways to entertain you. What is the thing you think you would most like to do?"

Jane tore her eyes from the sweets tray. "Well," she said, pondering the question with care. "Maybe if I could learn how to ride a horse . . ."

Chapter Twenty-Six

Bodmin, Cornwall—Friday, The Eïghteenth of October

Sebastian engaged two chambers and a private parlor at the Pig and Whistle Inn in Bodmin, a short ride from the duke's castle. He paid the landlord a month in advance, informing him that he didn't know how long he'd be staying, at the same time extracting his promise that he would not let the rooms to anyone else for the following month.

Sebastian had always turned to his friend Darlington in times of trouble, but Chris was no longer in England. Instead, he appealed to his aide Hugh Denville, the only other man ever admitted into his confidence, to accompany him to Bodmin.

The young man, a Dover lad, having never been to Cornwall, seized the opportunity to travel with his mentor. For his part, Sebastian was grateful for the distraction Hugh's company provided.

When they reached the inn that afternoon, Denville ordered dinner to be served at seven o'clock, unpacked Sebastian's clothing, arranged for a bath for the spymaster and prepared a change of clothing for him before attending to his own needs. Preparations well in hand, the two men strolled outside to stretch their legs, necessary after the long, tedious journey from London.

"I imagine I ought to call at Bodmin Castle in the morning, Hugh."

"Think a minute, sir. What if Fairchild refuses to see you there, the way she refused to see you in London?"

Sebastian's eyes radiated intense sadness. "I won't give up, Hugh. If I have to, I'll call every day until she relents and grants me an audience."

Hugh stopped walking. He placed a restraining hand on his mentor's shoulder. "I have a suggestion, if you'd care to listen."

"She won't talk to you either, I'm sure. She knows how close we are."

"Don't try to outguess me, my friend. First hear me out."

"What, then?"

"Allow me to ride out to Bodmin Castle early tomorrow. Alone. I'm willing to bet Fairchild rides. I'll chat up the stable boys. Grease their grubby fists. I've never met a stable hand willing to turn down a few extra bob. Let me try to discover when she rides, if her direction is always the same and whether she rides alone or with someone else."

"I need to see her alone, Hugh. To explain . . ."

"Not a good idea, sir. Better for you if there's someone with her. She won't be uncivil in front of a footman or a companion. She'll have to talk to you. And for heaven's sake, don't try to explain anything. Just be pleasant."

Sebastian barked a laugh. "Are you suggesting I have a tendency to be unpleasant?"

"You want the truth?"

"Nothing less."

Denville took the plunge, along with a deep breath. "If you must know, you've become so accustomed to giving orders, you sometimes forget there are those of us who dislike snapping to attention when you do, especially when we were already prepared to carry out that very order without your heavy-handedness. You're not in the army any longer, sir."

Sebastian raised an eyebrow. "Doesn't go over too well, does it? Does Fairchild feel the same way, do you suppose?"

"She's no fool, sir. I'm sure she does."

"I wonder. Fairchild thinks I betrayed her. How am I to convince her it was no such thing?"

Denville threw up his hands. "Bloody hell, sir! Now you're behaving like a fool. Any lovesick schoolboy knows that he must do his damnedest to convince the lass that he loves her. Don't beg Fairchild for her forgiveness, for if you do, she'll despise you all the more and you'll lose her for good."

"Since when have you become so full of worldly wisdom? Have you ever been in love?"

His aide grinned. "I was in love once, but I lost the lady precisely because I begged. That was a long time ago."

Sebastian paced up and down in his sitting room the next morning, waiting for Hugh to return from Bodmin Castle. He drank his coffee, but spurned much of the breakfast, having little appetite for food. He could not tear his mind away from Olivia, vowing to do better the next time. If there was a next time.

She wanted loyalty? He'd give her that. She wanted trust? He'd give her that, too. She wanted devotion? She already had that if she but knew of his sleepless nights and haunted days. He had to find a way to convince her he was worthy of her love. But how? What miracle could he perform to make her believe in him?

If he failed, he would resign his post. Travel to foreign climes. He'd never return to his beloved England again, not as long as he lived. Never had he felt such a weight. It was like a stone in his being, sinking his spirits.

The door opened at last, putting an end to his despondency. "Well, Hugh?"

"We'll have to hire the fastest horses we can find, sir. Every morning at seven, Fairchild rides across the moors like the wind. She's never alone, I'm told. One of her sisters or a groom rides with her, but she won't be hard to find, for she wears her training uniform and rides astride her stallion the way she did at Wilson Academy."

Sebastian's eyes came alive. "Well done, Hugh. Bloody well done!" He rang for a waiter. "Take these cold dishes away and bring us a fresh hot breakfast. Suddenly, I'm as hungry as a lion."

Hugh turned to Sebastian and grinned. "Take care how you spend your blunt, sir. When I tell you how much this information cost, I don't want you to lose your appetite once more."

"Who cares? Have you her route as well?"

"Of course. Let's shop for an appropriate horse for you."

"We'll make that two horses. I want you with me."

"As you wish, sir. After we buy them, we'll travel the route ourselves to become familiar with it."

"Perfect!"

Sebastian and Hugh had little trouble finding two lively chestnuts to purchase. The landlord's brother-in-law, it turned out, had a stable nearby.

"You shouldn't have shown such eagerness to buy. The stableman took note of it at once. Paid too much, you did," grumbled Hugh. "At this rate, you may not be able to afford Lady Olivia."

Sebastian chuckled. "It will be worth every farthing I own, if I could win my lady back."

"Every quid, more like," Denville teased. He tapped his

heels to his stallion and led him down the road toward the moors. They rode out of town in silence, conversation proving difficult since the wind swallowed their words. Sebastian followed his aide on the narrow path until they reached the moors. Hugh quickened his pace, Sebastian hard on his heels.

They were about to turn back when three figures appeared as specks on the landscape, two riding astride and one riding sidesaddle. Sebastian's heartbeat thundered in anticipation. The specks grew larger as they rode nearer. Sebastian spied the drab gray training clothes and the flying golden curls first. And his heart stopped. Olivia. He spurred his horse in an attempt to pass Denville, but his aide put a hand up to restrain him.

"Hold off, sir. See their direction first. The man's a groom, but who's the lass with her?"

"One of her sisters, most likely. She has a slew of them."

"It's a good idea to curb your impatience a bit longer. They're slowing down. If they dismount, we'll ride up and greet them pleasant-like."

A look of admiration spread Sebastian's smile from ear to ear. "Good strategy, Hugh. Clear-headed thinking. Where did you learn such clever tactics?"

Denville put forward a sly grin. "Let's just say I had the best of teachers during the Waterloo campaign."

Sebastian chortled. "You'll make a fine diplomat, my friend. This reminds me. Our strategy is that we're two friends on holiday. Get used to calling me Sebastian all the time, will you? Look! They're dismounting just as you predicted."

"Good sign. We'll ride up slow-like. Don't want to frighten them into bolting, do we? Wait till we're close enough before you greet them. And keep a bloody smile on your face, if you want to convince the lady you've mended your ways. Keep your hands off her as well."

"You're a hard taskmaster. Come along with me, Hugh."

"Coward," Hugh said, but the grin on his face signaled approval.

When they were close enough, the two dismounted near the astonished groom, whose horse held a small basket attached to his saddle. Without a word, Hugh handed their reins to the lad. A gold coin fell into the groom's hand at the same time, and he made no protest.

"Be brave," Hugh whispered, as he nudged Sebastian toward the women. Unaware that they were being followed, as they had their backs to the men.

"Why, it's Lady Olivia and Lady Georgiana," said Sebastian in a pleasant tone. "What a surprise to find you here. I believe you know Mr. Denville, Lady Olivia. May I introduce you to him as well, Lady Georgiana? Hugh is one of our instructors at the training academy as well as being my close friend."

Georgiana smiled and offered her hand to Hugh. "How do you do, Mr. Denville? We have met after all. At my sister's graduation ceremony, I believe."

"So we did, ma'am." He raised her hand to his lips.

"We were about to explore the ruins just the other side of this outcropping. You may join us if you like," said sixteen-year-old Georgiana, her eyes sparkling, for it was the first time a gentleman had kissed her hand. She chose to ignore her sister's reproving glance.

"We'd be delighted to join you. Let me help you over this mound, ma'am," Sebastian said to Olivia, attempting to take her arm.

"I can bloody well help myself," she muttered, brushing his hand away.

Sebastian followed her, embarrassed at the rebuff. A bleak look stole across his face.

"Buck up, sir," whispered Hugh. He turned to Georgiana and offered his hand.

"Thank you," she said, delighted.

Olivia walked toward the ancient ruin, fully aware that Sebastian followed. *Like a bloody sheep being led to slaughter.* She whirled without warning and said, "Is there something you wish to say to me, sir?"

Sebastian paused, nearly tripping, for his hands were clasped behind his back. He had all he could do to keep from frowning at her strident tone. "Nothing in particular, Olivia." He looked beyond her at the ruins with apparent interest. "How old are these, do you think?"

"I haven't the faintest idea." *What's he up to now?*

"Sixteenth century, I'd guess. See here?" He climbed into the well and pointed to what was left of a rectangular surface. "This was some sort of fireplace for cooking. Built just this way back then."

"How is it you know so much about the sixteenth century?"

"I studied the architecture of that period with the local vicar, a scholar of some note. My father had great respect for his knowledge and engaged him to tutor me."

She struggled to hold onto her anger toward him, but her curiosity was aroused. "Where did you grow up?"

"A small village near Bath." To keep from putting his arms around her, he kept his hands clasped behind his back. He gripped them so tight, his knuckles turned white.

A few feet away, yet out of earshot, Georgiana and Denville were engaged in what appeared to be a lively conversation. "I wonder what those two can possibly find to talk about. They have so little in common," Olivia said.

Sebastian was relieved to hear her speak with a bit less tension. "You'd be surprised. Hugh can be witty. He's also intelligent, a fact that you may not have noticed when you were a trainee. At Wilson Academy when he's working, he's all business."

"So we learned."

"I'll let you in on a little secret. Hugh never talks back to anyone." He paused. "Anyone but me, that is."

She laughed, a natural laugh full of surprise, which to his mind loosened her rigidity another notch.

"We trainees never noticed his wit, because he was always a straight arrow." She hesitated, then added, "Let me ask you something, sir. How is it you two are here and not at Wilson Academy planning for the next class of trainees?"

"We're on holiday."

"Why Bodmin? It's quite far from Havelshire."

"Hugh had a desire to visit. He's never been to Cornwall."

"Liar!" Her laugh infected him and together they made enough noise to gain the notice of Georgiana and Denville.

"What's so funny, you two?"

"An inside joke, Georgie. Hard to explain. Shall we invite these brash interlopers to share our picnic?"

"Good idea." Georgiana put two fingers in her mouth and whistled for their groom.

"Extraordinary," said Hugh in admiration. "Who taught you to whistle like that?"

"My brother Edward, but only after I threatened to drown him in our lake."

The groom trotted up and produced a blanket which he spread on what passed as a patch of grass within the rocky terrain. He put the basket in the middle and looked at Olivia.

"Thank you, Wells. We'll unpack the food ourselves." She dismissed him with a nod and he disappeared back over the outcropping.

Georgiana fell to her knees opposite Olivia and proceeded to help her sister lay out the contents of the picnic basket.

"We'd hate to take the food out of the mouths of you and your sister, ma'am. If we're imposing upon you, we'll withdraw and leave you to enjoy your picnic," said Hugh.

"Don't be silly, sir. There's enough for all of us. Besides, cook's famous for her fried chicken. Bodmin men have been known to battle over it at church socials. Sit. Both of you," commanded Olivia.

"It would please me so, if you would call me Hugh. And it would bring my colleague down off his high horse if you would lower yourself enough to call him Sebastian. Lord knows I've heard him called worse."

The sisters chuckled. "All right. Hugh and Sebastian it is. Help yourselves."

Unable to concede that she was enjoying the picnic, Olivia managed to fool herself into thinking she was being companionable for Georgiana's sake. It surprised her that Hugh engaged in such a pleasant conversation, never once mentioning Wilson Academy. Instead he told humorous tales of the lighter side of army life which made the sisters laugh.

She couldn't help but notice how Sebastian's eyes crinkled at the corners just before he threw back his head and laughed at some familiar jest. And though he avoided looking directly at her, his eyes were alive in a way she had never noticed before.

When she first saw him, her impulse was to throw rocks at him. She wanted to shout at him. She wanted to turn her back on him and ignore him. It was a wonder to her that she did none of those things. Perhaps, she thought, this was the better way. Her anger toward him lingered. It was tearing her apart. Better to regain some inner peace and get on with her life.

When she returned to London to begin her work in the home office, she wasn't likely to see much of him. Time would pass and heal her wounded heart, and when they did meet in the course of their work, there would no longer be any strain. Less pain. Much better this way.

"I wonder if Cook would consider an offer of marriage from me," said Hugh, his eyes twinkling. "I would eat like a king for the rest of my life if she said yes."

"You've never met Cook, then," Georgiana said when she stopped giggling. "She must weigh twenty stone. Besides, she's much too old for a young buck like you."

"Why, Georgiana! You think me a young buck, eh? That's the nicest thing anyone's ever called me." They continued to banter while the men packed up the basket, lighter for the absence of food and drink.

Hugh offered Georgiana one arm while his other carried the basket back to their horses.

"Will you take my arm, Olivia?" Sebastian crooked his elbow.

She rested her hand on his forearm and allowed him to lead the way. The motion took away the cheerfulness from her heart. In its place, clouds and cold settled in. How odd. Only a moment ago, all was sunny and warm.

The noise woke the sleeping groom, who jumped to attention and began to untie the horses. Hugh helped Georgiana into the saddle while Sebastian offered his clasped hands to boost Olivia's foot up.

"What fun we had this afternoon," said Georgiana. "How long are you two planning to stay in Bodmin?"

"We've let rooms in Bodmin for a month, but we may stay longer," answered Hugh.

"Then you must join our family for dinner one evening. Where are you staying?"

"We're at the Pig and Whistle Inn," said Sebastian. His eyes found Olivia's. "We'd be delighted, but only if you wish it," he added in a low voice.

"I'll ask my mother to extend the invitation. Good-bye."
She turned her horse away. "I'll race you back to the stables,
Georgie."

Sebastian shaded his eyes to the fading sun and watched her
ride off until she disappeared from his sight.

Chapter Twenty-Seven

Bodmin Castle—Monday, The Twenty-first of October

The chance meeting with Sebastian and Denville threw Olivia off balance. The result was that she tossed and turned most of the night, finally dropping off into an exhausted sleep just before dawn. Two hours later, someone was shaking her. It took her a few moments to wake, thinking the shaking was part of her dream rather than reality.

"You awake, Livy?" asked Jane.

She sat up and rubbed her eyes. "I am now, poppet. What time is it?" She stretched, willing herself awake for her young sister, at the same time yearning to crawl back under the covers again. "What is it?"

"It's almost nine. I thought of something."

Olivia hid her puzzlement, for she had no idea what Jane was talking about. She sat up and asked, "What is it you've thought of so early in the morning, Jane?" She patted a place next to her and Jane scrambled up onto the bed.

"I like horses. I used to be afraid of them, you know, but I'm not anymore. I would very much like to learn to ride one, as I mentioned earlier." In that plump little face her huge eyes took on a solemn look.

"Clever girl! Give me a few moments to wash and dress, and we'll go to the stables together. Have you had your breakfast?"

"A long time ago, Livy."

"Ring for Jenny for me, will you? I'll have my chocolate while she helps me dress." She took Jane's face in her hands and added, "And ask her to see if she can find one teeny little scone for my sweet little sister."

Jane rang the bell and when Jenny responded, she gave her Olivia's order, then turned to watch her sister wash. "I heard Mother tell Dunston we're to have guests for dinner tonight."

"Really? How nice." Jane had been eavesdropping again. Olivia tried not to frown. Instead she went to her closet and chose a simple blue morning dress. At the knock, she said, "Get the door Jane dear. It must be Jenny with my breakfast."

"Morning, milady. Morning, Jane." Jenny put the tray down. "Turn around, milady. I'll do up your buttons."

By the time Olivia sat down to her chocolate, Jane had swallowed her scone. "Who are our guests tonight, dear? Do you know?" she asked.

"I happened to overhear Mother tell Dunston it's Sir Sebastian Brooks and Mr. Denville. I wasn't eavesdropping, Livy. Really I wasn't. I was just standing near."

Olivia's heart went out to the child. She was so much in need of attention. She didn't know how poor Jane, the youngest of them all, had gotten so lost within such a large family. "I'm sure you didn't mean to eavesdrop, poppet. Even though it may seem like that to some people. Never mind. Come along with me." She took her hand and led her out of the room. "You're about to have a new adventure."

Sean O'Bryan, the young stable master, was more than happy to oblige when Olivia told him what was needed.

"Faith, Miss Jane. I have just the filly for ye. Come along and have a look at her." He led them inside to a stall at the end of the long line of stalls.

"This here's the pony I have in mind, Miss Jane. Do ye think she'll do fer ye?"

Jane's eyes lit up at the sight of a sturdy, white pony, dappled with gray spots. "Can I pet her? What's her name?"

Sean held his chin in his hand. "Funny thing. I haven't had time to name her yet. Would you like the honor? Here." He reached into his pocket. "Give her a lump o' this sugar and rub her nose so she gets to know ye."

The horse whinnied when Jane offered the treat and rubbed her nose. "She likes me, Livy," the child said in surprise.

"Of course she does, poppet. What shall you call her?"

"I know! Sugar, because she likes sweets, just like me."

It's a perfect match, Olivia thought, checking her grin. "Would you like to ride her, Jane?"

"I don't know." She looked up at the stable man. "I've never been on a horse before, sir."

Sean stroked his chin and examined Jane as though she were another filly. "I'd be happy to teach you, Miss Jane. But you need proper riding gear. You can't ride without a decent pair of riding boots and a riding dress meant for sidesaddle."

"Where can we purchase these for her, sir?" asked Olivia.

"They's a fine riding shop in Bodmin, milady. Right next to the Pig and Whistle Inn."

"Can Sugar pull us in an open carriage?"

"No, milady. Best I hitch the horses as knows how. Casper can drive you."

"Thank you, Sean. We'll be ready in half an hour. Come, Jane. We need to tell Mother first."

Olivia and Jane found their mother and their other sisters in the morning room. Her Grace agreed, asking if Olivia's other sisters might like to join them. Country living was far too tranquil for the lively Fairchild women, much used to the bustle of London and its myriad attractions. Thus the outing meant just for Jane threatened to turn into a pleasant jaunt for all of them, by now thoroughly bored and desirous of a change of scene.

"Do you mind if your sisters join you, Jane?" asked Her Grace.

"I don't want to spoil your fun, Jane, but I've outgrown my riding boots," said Mary.

"And my riding skirt has a terrible tear that even Amy can't mend," added Helena.

Olivia grasped Jane's hand and turned to her sisters. "This was meant to be Jane's special day with me." She lifted her sister's chin and looked into her eyes. "It's up to you, poppet. Shall we give these other sassy sisters permission to join us?"

Jane was flattered when she found herself the center of attention within the sea of her sisters. As they pleaded their cause, she looked from one to the other, her eyes appraising them. "All right, you lot can come, but I get to choose my riding clothes first."

In the rush of preparedness, Olivia found time to warn each of her sisters not to scold and to be attentive to Jane. Her Grace followed her daughters out to where the family coach was waiting. "Kiss your mother good-bye, poppet, then lead the way," said Olivia.

"Don't be too long. We have guests for dinner, Livy."

As Olivia had hoped, Jane was having a grand time as the center of attention within the circle of her sisters. When Olivia whispered something in the riding shop proprietor's ear when they entered, Mr. Smith gave a slight nod, took Jane by the hand and fitted her for riding boots himself. Her sisters fussed over the styles, arguing on the child's behalf as to which style was most appealing.

The owner's wife, an accomplished dressmaker, devoted her full attention to Jane as if she were a grand duchess instead of a young child. As she took her measurements, she said, "I know just the right color for your riding costume, milady. Can you believe it? It was delivered to me for another customer, but you may have it if you like it. I'll just tell my customer she'll have to wait for another shipment since I had to use it for a grand lady."

"That royal blue color for your skirt and jacket is a clever choice, Jane. It matches your eyes, too. With a frilly white blouse, you'll look charming."

"Would you like me to trim your riding suit and your bonnet with some black braid, milady?" asked the dressmaker.

"Could you trim it with white and gray braid instead? My pony Sugar is white with gray spots."

"Jane! You have a pony of your own? I don't believe it!" said Georgiana in mock horror.

Jane rose to the occasion and, behaving more like an adult than the child she was, said with dignity, "Oh yes I do. And I'm going to learn how to ride her, too! Just as soon as my new boots and my riding clothing are finished."

The proprietors of Smith Emporium had not had such a profitable day in years. By the time all the Fairchild sisters completed their purchases, and arrangements were made for delivery to Bodmin Castle, they were in high good humor.

Olivia said, "We have just enough time for lemonade and poppy seed cakes next door at the Pig and Whistle. Casper has engaged a private parlor for us, but I promised Mother we'd be home early, so we'll have to be quick about it."

"Don't make such a fuss with my hair for tonight, Jenny."

"But I thought you said Sir Sebastian Brooks and Mr. Denville were invited to dinner."

"I did, but there's no need to dress as though we're at a

ball in London. A simple style, please. And put that green silk gown away. I'll wear the cream muslin instead."

"Yes, milady," Jenny said, suppressing a frown over Olivia's prim choice. But she well knew it would be useless to argue.

Satisfied at last, Olivia stepped out of her chamber in time to greet Helena and Georgiana, both dressed more lavishly, though in simple country fashion. Helena wore pale blue silk and Georgiana had on a gown of lavender. They entered the drawing room together, to find that Sebastian and Hugh, dressed in formal black, were already there.

Her Grace smiled at her daughters. She turned to her guests and said, "Here are my eldest daughters. I believe you know Sir Sebastian Brooks and Mr. Denville, my dears?"

"Yes, Mother," said Olivia. "How are you, sir?" She offered her hand and Sebastian raised it to his lips.

"I'm well, ma'am. You and your sisters were in Bodmin this afternoon, were you not? Denville and I caught sight of the lot of you when we returned from our afternoon ride."

"Yes. We escorted our youngest sister Jane, who was fitted for her first riding costume, quite an occasion for her. We were all there to cheer her along. She's only eight years old, you know."

"How old is Mary?" asked Denville.

"Mary is fourteen. She's an accomplished pianist, but you can decide for yourself. She'll play for us after dinner." Olivia wondered why her mouth felt so dry.

"I look forward to hearing her then."

"Dinner is served, Your Grace," announced the butler.

Sebastian sprang forward and offered his arm to the matriarch. "Allow me, Your Grace."

"May I?" asked Denville of Georgiana, who had already fallen a little bit in love with the gallant soldier.

"Delighted," she said and rested her hand on his arm.

"Deelighted!" mocked Helena in a whisper as she linked

her arm through Olivia's and they made their way into the dining room. "She'll make that poor man melt like butter before the evening is out."

Olivia stifled a laugh. "Poor Denville. I feel sorry for him. I do hope he doesn't make the mistake of falling in love with her. He can't know it, but for Georgie, flirting is just practice for her debut next year."

Her Grace sat at the head of the table, Denville on her right, Olivia seated next to him. Opposite, Sebastian sat next to his hostess, followed by Helena and Georgiana.

"How long do you plan to stay in Bodmin?"

"A month or perhaps two, Your Grace. We're on holiday."

"A charming time of year to visit North Cornwall. The fall foliage is at its best, for the leaves always turn color first this far north."

"A month or two? What wonderful news. Then you shall both be here for the Fall Assembly in Bodmin. It's this Saturday evening at seven, in Congress Hall. The country dances are great fun. Do say you'll join us," said Georgiana.

Sebastian scratched his head. "We're both a bit rusty, Lady Georgiana."

"They're not hard. Won't you say you'll join us?"

"We'll be there, ma'am," said Denville, a wide grin on his face.

Sebastian turned to Helena. "Have you heard from your betrothed, ma'am?"

"Kind of you to ask," she said. "Darlington's letters reach me through official dispatches, but I have no idea where he is."

"You aren't meant to, ma'am," he said gently.

"Yes, I know that. But it doesn't make our separation any easier to bear."

"Separations never are. Take heart, dear lady. He'll return to you soon."

Her Grace tapped her crystal wine goblet and rose from

her seat. "We shall leave you to your brandy, gentlemen. Join us in the drawing room when you are ready." She nodded to her daughters.

Mary and Jane, having eaten earlier with their governess in the nursery, were already in the drawing room when their mother and sisters entered. Olivia settled next to her mother, who occupied herself with her needlepoint as usual. It didn't take Sebastian and Hugh long to join the ladies.

"Mary is going to play for you, gentlemen. You may decide for yourselves whether she has talent. Please take your seats."

Mary seated herself at the pianoforte while Georgiana stood ready to turn the pages for her.

"Will you allow me to turn in your place?" Hugh asked Georgiana. "My mother used to play and I always turned the pages for her. Do take a seat and enjoy the music."

"Thank you, sir. How gallant," she said in a low voice meant for his ears alone.

Sebastian found Jane sitting on a settee by herself. "May I join you, milady?"

The child blushed twelve different shades of red. "Yes, sir."

He took his seat and leaned over to whisper in her ear. "May I say that you are the prettiest sister here tonight?"

Her eyes lit up as though they were Christmas candles and she sat up straighter. "No I'm not. Georgie's the prettiest."

He chucked her chin and smiled. "You are the prettiest. Never argue with a gentleman when he pays you a compliment, milady."

Olivia's suspicions were aroused once more. He'd ignored her before dinner. He ignored her during dinner. And he was ignoring her now. Then why was he here? She tried to listen to Mary play lively country tunes, but her heart was confused and her mind wandered elsewhere.

At the end of the set, everyone applauded, a signal for servants to enter with the tea tray. " Thank you, Mary. After your tea, you and Jane may say goodnight to our guests. It's time for you to retire."

When Sebastian offered Jane the plate of sweets, she declined them, much to Olivia's shock. Was she cured? Perhaps, but she didn't think so. When Mrs. Trumball appeared to lead them to bed, Jane and Mary kissed their mother goodnight and curtseyed to the gentlemen.

"Mary has a remarkable talent, Your Grace," said Sebastian when they were gone. "And Jane shall grow to be a great beauty." He rose and added, "Come, Hugh. We'll take our leave as well. Thank you for a lovely dinner and an equally lovely evening, Your Grace."

"So early?" asked Georgiana, clearly disappointed.

"We're planning to visit The Lost Gardens of Heligan tomorrow," said Hugh. "Have you seen them?"

"Many times," answered Helena. "But there is always more to see. It's vast."

"Would you and your sisters care to join us on our expedition? I, for one, would consider it a pleasure to escort you."

"Oh, Mother. May we have your permission? It would be so much fun. We could make it a picnic. I'm sure Cook wouldn't mind," said Georgiana, her enthusiasm bubbling over.

Her Grace looked questioningly at Olivia.

"I have no objection, Mother," she said. "It would be a treat for Mary and Jane as well. They've never been."

"Well, if the rest of you are agreeable, I suppose there's no harm in it. Join us at nine tomorrow morning for breakfast, gentlemen. You may leave soon after."

"Thank you, Your Grace." Sebastian took her hand and raised it to his lips.

"I'll see you out," said Olivia.

She waited at the steps while their horses were brought up. Hugh walked down as if searching for them, but really to give them a moment to themselves.

"What are you up to, Sebastian?"

"I love you, Olivia. I cannot stop loving you, my darling. Let me give you fair warning right now. I mean to do everything in my power to win you back. I won't give up." His hands were clenched at his sides, though he itched to use them to crush her in his arms and kiss her.

"Your horses are here. Goodnight," she said in a strained voice and walked back inside. She went directly to her mother's chamber and knocked on the door.

"Come in, Livy. I was expecting you."

Olivia laughed. "Are you clairvoyant, Mother? How did you know it would be me?" Her mother was seated at her desk, finishing a letter. She sealed it with wax and rang for a servant.

"Ask the butler to have this delivered to Sir Henry Tremayne at Heligan."

When the servant was gone, she turned back to Olivia. "I watched your face all evening, my dear. If nothing else, the strain tells its own tale. You're still in love with Sebastian." Her mother stated it as a fact, not a question.

"How is it possible to love a man and find him unbearable to live with, Mother?"

"What's on your mind, Livy?"

"Sebastian cannot be trusted, Mother. If I were fool enough to wed him, I'd face a lifetime of grief. Unless, of course, I murdered him in the first year of our marriage, which may be a strong possibility. You cannot imagine how horrible he was to me during training."

Olivia used her fingers to tick off his offenses. "One. He told me the day I arrived he didn't want me in his academy. Two. He did everything in his power to sabotage me so that I would fail." Olivia stopped, her breath coming hard, as though she'd done fifty push-ups. "Three. He challenged me to a duel. And I won."

"Oh, my," said Her Grace. "You certainly taught him a lesson then, didn't you?"

"Not quite, Mother. I nearly killed him. In fact, when I thought I had actually murdered him, I ran away."

"You ran away more than once, didn't you?"

This brought Olivia up short. "I had to come to Chris and Helena's betrothal ball, didn't I? But the spymaster couldn't understand that, could he? Instead, he went out of his way to humiliate me on the dance floor. In front of everyone."

Her mother shook her head in sympathy.

"And then he denied me the opportunity he gave all the other trainees, to protect the prince of Zarkovia. I went anyway and saved his life, but did he care? Did he? Did he?"

"Lower your voice, Livy. The servants . . ."

"But the worst of it was when he betrayed me. After all my training, he allowed Viscount Sidmouth to assign me to a mere clerk's post. I might just as well not have been trained at all. Of what use was it if he was determined to bury me in an office?"

"Do you love him, dear?"

Her mother's question startled her. "Do I love him? I can't sleep for wondering. The food I swallow tastes like sawdust for wondering. In my head I argue with him all day long for wondering. How can I trust a man who betrays me time and again, Mother? A man who is domineering? A man who sees all women as fit only to scrub floors? I hate him Mother. I hate him."

"If that were true, my darling daughter, you wouldn't be here trying to convince me. You do love Sebastian, don't you?"

Olivia fell on her knees and buried her head in her mother's lap. "If this is love, Mother, why does it feel so painful? Why does it hurt so much?"

"Love *is* painful, but not always, Livy. Shall I tell you a secret? Your father can be a difficult man. He's opinionated.

He's obstinate. He's overbearing. He's domineering. He rarely admits he's wrong. Yet I love him with all my heart. Yes. Even when we disagree, and that's more often than any of you know, my dear, for we hide our disputes from our children, I love him."

Olivia looked up in time to see a stab of grief furrow her mother's brow. "What is it, Mother?" she asked in alarm.

Chapter Twenty-Eight

Thursday, The Twenty-fourth of October

"I've never told this tale to anyone, my dear," said the duchess. "Perhaps it's time I did. It may help for you to know it now. Come sit beside me, Livy."

She had never seen that look on her mother's face before. There was steel in it, but there was also pain. She rose up and drew a chair opposite her mother. "What tale is it you wish to tell me, Mother?"

Her mother drew in a breath and said, "When Mary was two years old, your father shocked me enough to want to take my children and leave him forever. No, Livy. Don't take my hands in sympathy. It makes the telling harder."

"What had Father done to distress you so?"

"He fell in love with another woman."

"Oh, Mother! How that must have hurt."

The duchess nodded. "Hurt? I was devastated. I bore him an heir. I presented him with four beautiful daughters. I shared his bed. I listened to his sorrows and shared his joys. What more must a wife do?" Her words were tinged with bitterness.

"Who was she, Mother?"

"She was a beautiful eighteen-year-old. Your father was nearing fifty by then. Anxious to make her mark on the stage, she saw him as the key to her success. When the affair came to my attention, your father had established her in a London town house while I remained at Heatham raising our children."

"Good God! How you must have suffered. How long did the affair last?"

"Two years. When I determined to leave him, he begged me to stay and promised he would end it. Little did I know the chit had already become a stage presence. She no longer needed his support and was glad to give him up. She kept the London town house and all the jewels, of course."

"And you forgave him?"

Her mother's smile held irony. "No, my dear. Not right away. I'm afraid I was vindictive. To repay his villainy, I determined to make him suffer, something I have been ashamed of, from that day to this, for it denies my true character. I agreed to let him come back into our family for the sake of our children, but I did not allow him back into my bed for three more years."

Olivia was stunned, for she had always supposed there was nothing but love and contentment between her parents. At the recollection of her own dilemma, a crack of laughter escaped her lips. "You forgave him in the end, didn't you?"

"Yes, I forgave him dear. Jane was the result of our reconciliation."

"You are so brave, Mother, to have borne such a humiliating trial. I wish I could be like you, but I'm not sure I can."

"Is Sebastian past forgiveness, my child?"

A high phaeton with the Heatham coat of arms emblazoned on both doors, carried Olivia and Jane, seated opposite Georgiana and Helena to the Heligan Gardens. Mary begged off the excursion, preferring to stay home with Her Grace, though her sisters knew her passion for music was what kept her from all other pursuits. Their driver Casper was perched outside on the high seat in front while two footmen stood behind. Four matched bays led the coach, while Sebastian and Hugh rode astride their horses, one on either side of the vehicle.

The mood was festive as the sisters bantered. Though Olivia did not feel much like participating, she joined in out of loyalty to Jane. She could not rid her mind of her father's betrayal. She now understood his indifference toward his youngest daughter Jane. Clearly, the child was a painful reminder of his fall from grace.

"Do you not think Mr. Denville handsome?" asked Georgiana.

"Sebastian's much more so," declared Jane with authority. Her unwavering loyalty to the man who thought her beautiful enough to marry would not be shaken.

Helena laughed. "Leave off, you two. It's not proper to judge gentlemen by their appearance. And you beware, Georgie. Don't let your feelings for Mr. Denville run away with you. You have your debut to look forward to next year."

"I agree. A mere flirtation is one thing, but you are only sixteen. Do not imagine yourself in love with Denville," warned Olivia.

Georgiana blushed. "Oh, I don't, believe me. But you'll have to admit, his manners are engaging, not to mention his wit. He's such fun to be with."

"Those things are true," replied Olivia. "But I don't want you to attach more importance to these traits than are necessary. They are merely the attributes of a well-brought-up gentleman."

When Casper drew the carriage to a stop in front of Heligan House, Sir Henry Tremayne greeted them. They had been invited by the old gentleman to see the gardens after he had received a polite note from Her Grace.

The Heligan estate was one of the largest in Cornwall, rivaling only Bodmin Castle in size. Built in 1603 by the first Tremayne, Sir William, it boasted one thousand acres. Its charm lay in its gardens, for the Tremaynes were devoted botanists from first to last.

"Thank you for inviting us on such short notice, Sir Henry," said Olivia, who was first to alight.

Sir Henry looked beyond her into the carriage. "But where is my old friend the duchess? I had so looked forward to renewing my acquaintance with her today."

"Mother wasn't well enough to undertake the journey. She sends you her good wishes and her most sincere regrets."

The gentleman was clearly disappointed. "Do send her my wishes for a speedy recovery. Come in then, dear friends. My butler will show you the way to the guest chambers where you may refresh yourselves. Luncheon awaits you on the terrace."

Olivia shook his hand and said, "Allow me to introduce our escorts, sir. This is Sir Sebastian Brooks and his traveling companion, Mr. Hugh Denville."

Tremayne's eyes lit up, for he had lived a solitary life since the death of his wife. He shook hands with them, gave orders to see to their horses, and said, "Would you care to join me for some Madeira before lunch, gentlemen?"

When the Fairchild sisters joined them on the terrace, they found the three gentlemen behaving as though they had known one another for ages. Luncheon became a cheerful affair on such a beautiful day, the sight of the famous Heligan Gardens in view.

After lunch, Sir Henry excused himself, promising to join

them for tea before they left for the day. The old gentleman was in the habit of resting after lunch.

Sebastian maneuvered to accompany Olivia and Jane, who took possession of his arms in their walk through the gardens. At the same time, Denville escorted Georgiana and Helena.

"Sir Henry is a good man. A bit lonely since his wife died, he informed us," said Sebastian.

"He's a dedicated botanist, you know. His gardens are well known throughout England."

Sebastian smiled. "Yes. He admitted it was his passion over our Madeira before lunch."

They came upon a folly built in the fashion of a Greek temple. "A good Grecian replica," said Sebastian examining it with the eye of a connoisseur.

"Have you been to Greece?"

"Yes," he said. " Travel on the Continent was a gift from my father when I finished my studies at Oxford."

"My brother Edward wants to travel," said Jane.

"Yes. His Grace and I talked about it at our . . . when I had dinner with your family in London."

Jane looked up at her escort, her blue eyes twinkling. "At your betrothal dinner, you mean. Are you and Livy still planning to marry?"

"Jane!" exploded Olivia. "That's a most impolite question."

Sebastian looked into the child's eyes, which were swimming with tears at her sister's rebuke. He patted Jane's hand and smiled, but his words were meant for her sister. "It's a reasonable question, Jane. I've been wondering the very same thing. Suppose we ask your sister for her answer?" He handed the child his handkerchief.

"That isn't fair, Sebastian," Olivia muttered.

"Ah, but all's fair in love and war. I meant it when I warned you I wouldn't give up, Olivia."

Jane listened to the exchange with great interest, her head bobbing back and forth from one adult to the other.

"Why don't you give him another chance, Livy?"

Sebastian shouted out a laugh. "My dearest darling friend Jane. If your sister persists in refusing to give me another chance, I shall crawl into a hole in the wall and stay there until you come of age. If you'll have me, I'll have you for my wife instead." He turned to Olivia and added, "There's no profit for either of us in looking back, is there? Won't you allow me to resume courting you, my love?"

"I'll think about it. Come, Jane. It's time we found the others and started for home." She took the child's hand and fairly flew down the path. Away from Sebastian.

Sir Henry and their tea awaited them on the terrace when they returned. It took some time for the family to get underway, but at last they were riding toward home, much to Olivia's relief.

She was in such turmoil over Sebastian's request, she paid little heed to her sisters' chatter, preferring to stare out the window instead. Drat the man! She could be happy wallowing in misery if only he would go away and leave her be.

The group reached home in little less than an hour, to be greeted by the welcome news that His Grace had arrived from London. He was waiting to greet his children in the drawing room. Her sisters ran up the steps, eager to see their father, but Olivia lingered behind.

"I want a word with you, Sebastian. Will you join me in the library?"

Having heard the danger in Olivia's voice, Hugh took Sebastian's reins and busied himself with the horses.

She entered first, but when Sebastian attempted to shut the door, she said, "No. Leave the door open, please. What I have to say to you won't take long."

"What is it, my darling?" he asked.

"I'm not your darling and I don't appreciate your tactics. You overstepped the bounds when you attempted to use my little sister to gain an advantage over me. Let me assure you that it won't work."

"What, pray tell, must I do, since you won't give me so much as the time of day?"

"It's four o'clock."

"Don't be silly. Just tell me how I may repair the damage between us."

"The truth?"

"When did you ever give me anything but the truth, my darling? May I shut the door, while you proceed to rip up at me once again? I don't fancy ugly glares from the servants afterwards."

She was about to refuse this request, but remembered in time how large the ears of her household were. "All right. Shut the door, but don't come any nearer. Stay where you are." She walked to the windows and leaned on the sill, her hands folded across her chest.

He shut the door behind him and said, "Well?"

"I don't think you can change your ways."

He took a small step forward. "Is it the gallows for me before trial? At the very least, you must first enumerate my sins."

"Don't come any closer. For one, you are arrogant."

"Not toward you. What else?" He took another step.

"You are prejudiced against women."

"That was before I met you. It's true no longer. Go on." His foot inched forward.

"You are egotistical and vain."

"Once you're mine, my love, it will be unnecessary for me to display such vulgarities." He took a larger step forward, but she took no notice for her tears began to blur her vision.

"Why should I wed an odious man who is overbearing,

dictatorial, opinionated, wholly impossible? A man who ignores my wishes? A man who thwarts me at every turn?"

He reached the window and used both thumbs to wipe her tears away. "Is it because you love me just a little, perhaps? Is it because you cannot live without me? Is it because you know you cannot bear to think of a life without me at your side?"

"Why, you arrogant . . . you'll never change. You wouldn't know how," she challenged.

"Can you change your ways, my darling? I don't think so. Lucky for me that I love you just the way you are. A sparrow is always a sparrow. A fish remains a fish all its life. Don't you know we are destined for one another?"

"B . . . but we argue all the time. That cannot be a design for happiness, can it?"

He feathered his lips across her brow to smooth the lines. "I cannot promise you we won't ever lock horns once we're married. In fact, I'm reasonably sure we'll battle from sunup to sundown, but I can promise that our life together shall never be dull. I promise you this as well. You shall be my equal in all things."

He drew her to him and pressed her head to his chest. "I know now that you're made for adventure, my love. Well, so be it. I promise you that this time I'll rise to the occasion."

"Will you, indeed? Then you've piqued my curiosity, Sebastian. After thwarting me at every turn during my training, I find it hard to believe. Can it be true? How do you plan to accomplish such a miraculous turnabout?"

He detected the smallest of cracks in her armor. He shouted a laugh, an exultant burst of triumph. "I give you fair warning, my love. When you marry me, be prepared to ride side by side for the rest of your life. If I race like the wind, you shall race like the wind. Indeed, I don't doubt that it will be a bumpy ride for both of us. Come what may, I'm ready for whatever life has in store for us." He drew her close and felt a shiver run through her. It enflamed his boldness.

"If I choose to climb the Matterhorn, you shall climb beside me, no matter the danger. And if I choose to swim the Hellespont, so shall you. I give you fair warning, Fairchild. I shall yield no advantage. If you thrust, I shall parry. If you run away, I shall find you. If you lock your door, I shall break it down." His lips found hers and he plundered them, assaulting her as if in battle.

At last, he broke away and held her at arm's length. His lips quivered when he noted that her eyes were closed. "Well, my love? Shall you make me whole again? Are you ready to risk resuming our battered betrothal?"

She snaked her hands around his waist. "Kiss me again, Sebastian." Her voice held an ethereal quality.

"No."

Olivia's eyes flew open. "No?"

"Not before I have your answer, my foolish darling."

"Yes, dear," she replied with rare humility.

His kiss felt like a feather on her lips. "No more than one, you lusty little beast. We have just enough time to prepare for dinner and make our announcement to your family. Our *last* announcement. I must hurry back to the inn with Hugh to dress."

"Livy's coming," reported Jane to the family and their guests.

Olivia entered the drawing room and stopped suddenly, her eyes sweeping across the room at the unexpected additions to the family. "What are you doing here, Edward?" she asked her brother.

"Halloo, big sister," he said and gripped her into a bear hug. "Father ordered me to come, Livy."

"Uncle Charles?" she said, addressing her father's brother.

"Your father summoned me as well," grinned the vicar. "How are you, my child?"

"Bewildered, to say the least."

Sebastian stepped forward and took her hand. "Actually, it was all my doing." He turned to her father. "Thank you for your, er—cooperation, Your Grace."

"What on earth are you talking about?" she demanded.

"I asked your father to gather the family for a reason, my love." He dropped to one knee. "Will you marry me?"

She blushed to the roots of her hair and pulled him to his feet. "We're already betrothed."

"Sorry. I omitted an important word. Will you marry me tomorrow?"

"Tomorrow? As soon as that?" Her eyes flew around the room and took in the smiling faces of her family. They came to rest on her uncle. "Is that why you're here, Uncle Charles?"

"Why else, my child?" The duke's younger brother grinned as he took her hands in his. "What shall your answer be, Livy?"

"Yes. What shall your answer be, my love?" echoed Sebastian.

Olivia's sober eyes searched Sebastian's merry ones. "My answer? My answer is yes."

"Dinner is served, my lords and ladies," interrupted the butler, unaware that he had interrupted an historic family moment.

Dinner was an engaging affair for the entire Fairchild family. At the end of the lavish meal, Her Grace rose and said, "Come, my dears. We shall leave the gentlemen to their brandy." She turned to her husband and added, "Don't take too long, my lord."

"Yes, dear," he answered, a sparkle in his eyes.

When the women settled in the drawing room, Olivia said, "What shall I wear for my wedding tomorrow, Mother?"

"I was hoping you'd ask, Livy. I married your father in our chapel right here at Bodmin Castle. Did you know that? My wedding gown is packed away in the attic." She giggled like a young girl. "With a minimum of adjustment, I'm sure it can be made to fit, for I was a sprite of a thing then."

Olivia hugged her mother. "I would be honored to wear it, Mother."

"It's already in your chamber, dear. You can try it on before you retire."

"May I play the wedding march for you, Livy? I know it well," said Mary.

"Oh, Mary! I would like that above all." Olivia turned to Jane.

"And shall you be my flower girl, poppet? That would make me very happy."

Jane looked ready to burst with joy. "Oh yes. That would be so fine!"

"Did you procure the special license for me, sir?" asked Sebastian as the men savored their brandy in the dining room. He poured his future father-in-law more brandy.

"Of course, my boy. But I do think it better if you omitted mentioning it to your bride. You don't want to give my daughter reason to rail at you for being so sure of yourself, do you?"

Sebastian laughed. "I daresay it won't make a bit of difference this time." His eyes widened with mischief. "She actually said, 'yes, dear,' when I proposed this time."

"She won't blame you, Tony," said the duke's brother. "Livy is likely to think I procured the special license for her."

"No doubt you're right, Charles," His Grace responded. "Drink up, gentlemen. It's time we joined the ladies."

Chapter Twenty-Nine

Bodmin Castle—Saturday, The Twenty-sixth of October

Olivia woke from a peaceful night's sleep, her first in weeks.

When Jenny drew back the drapes, she said, "It's a beautiful day for a weddin', milady. Amy and I stayed up late to fix the hem of your gown. We took in the tucks as well."

Olivia stretched like a cat and yawned. "You're wonderful, Jenny. Thank you and thank Amy for me."

"'Twasn't much, milady. We were glad to do it for you. Shall I bring you your chocolate? While you drink it, I'll prepare your bath."

"All right, dear." Olivia put her feet in her slippers and went to her window. Indeed, it was a beautiful day. No cloud marred the brilliant blue sky. She turned as Jenny answered a knock on the door.

"Morning, Mrs. Bride," said Helena. "May your sisters join you?"

"Of course, you ninnies." Her sisters, disheveled from sleep, padded in wearing their slippers and robes. Olivia turned to Jenny and said, "Bring us all some chocolate, dear."

"And some scones if you please," added Jane, which remark caused her sisters to laugh.

Jenny curtseyed. "Yes, your la'ships."

When she shut the door, Olivia said, "Jenny and Amy were up half the night fixing mother's gown for me."

"Can we sit on the floor in a circle and tell tales one last time?" Jane asked.

"What a good idea, poppet, but it should never be for the last time, should it? Why don't we promise to do it every time one of us marries?"

"That would start a tradition in our family, wouldn't it? I'd like that above everything," said Jane.

"But not above scones, eh?" teased Georgiana.

"I only want one," answered Jane, pouting.

Olivia defended her. "It's my wedding day. Have as many as you like, poppet."

"Let's start the circle," said Georgiana. She sat on the floor and crossed her legs.

"It ought to be a secret tradition. Sisters only."

"Why, Jane!" the duchess interrupted, having heard this last statement as she entered the chamber. "I don't mind its being a secret tradition, but would you omit your own mother?"

Jane blushed. "Oh no, Mother. But wouldn't you rather be seated in a chair?"

Her Grace laughed and sat on the floor next to Jane. "Not until I'm in my dotage, you impudent puss!" One by one, her loving eyes examined her beautiful daughters. "Well? Will someone tell me what we do in our circle?"

"We tell stories, Mother. Why don't you begin?"

"All right. I'll tell you all about the day Livy was born. I woke that morning with a feeling in my bones that this was the day I would be birthing for the very first time. But I didn't let on to your father. He was far too scatterbrained, for it was also his first birthing, you see. He would have driven me to distraction by asking after my health every few seconds. I'll skip over the details of birthing. You'll have your chance to discover it on your own one day. Suffice it to say it isn't at all as horrid as some women make it out to be. What's more, the prize is well worth it."

The duchess gazed at Olivia with warmth. "When the nurse first put you into my arms, Livy, I fell in love for the second time in my life. You were the most exquisite little bit of a thing I had ever seen. Why, when no one was looking, I counted your tiny fingers and toes just to make sure you had them all."

Her daughters laughed at this.

"Go on, Mother," urged Jane. "Tell us more."

"Well, my dears. I was afraid your father would be disappointed, for he so wanted an heir, but that notion flew right out of his thoughts as soon as he set eyes on his firstborn. He astounded me by sending the servants out of the room, picking his treasure up carefully, and dancing around the room with her. Imagine, Livy! Your father actually sang you a lullaby on that day, of all things."

"Father did that? I thought him too dignified," said Georgiana.

The duchess laughed. "You know only one side of him then. The man behind all the puffed-up air that goes with being a duke can be playful, and has a wicked sense of humor. Time and again he surprises me with it in the privacy of our chambers." Her daughters laughed, though none of them could envision their staid father being playful.

At the end of two hours of storytelling and giggling, the duchess glanced at the clock on Olivia's mantel. "Oh dear, children. Livy's wedding is less than two hours away. We must all get ready. Hurry back to your chambers at once."

* * *

Olivia lay in her tub savoring its warmth, while Jenny washed her hair. Two thoughts played in her head, both a soothing melody. The first sang of her family's love, and the second sang of the love she felt for Sebastian.

She only half listened to Jenny's chatter as the young girl combed the tangles out of her wet hair. She wrapped each section with strips of cloth meant to enhance the curls when they dried. Jenny refused to allow her to examine herself in the mirror until after she had helped her dress and was finished administering the final touches to her hair. When she led her mistress to the mirror, she said, a note of triumph in her voice, "You may look now, yer la'ship."

Olivia's eyes widened in wonder at what she saw. Her mother's form-fitting gown was a long-sleeved ivory Belgian lace affair, studded with crystals. It fell to the floor to her toes, but the back was longer, its train flowing behind.

"Oh, Jenny. Thank you!"

Her abigail wiped away a tear. "Sit down, your la'ship, and let me attach the veil."

The small family chapel was filled not only with the immediate family, but also with guests. Sir Henry Tremayne had ridden over from Heligan to attend, bringing with him the squire, the town magistrate and their wives. Tradition dictated that the Fairchild farm tenants and all the servants witness the wedding as well, for most of them had known Olivia since she was an infant.

When everyone was seated, Mary began to play a selection she had written especially for her sister's wedding. Jane was first to walk down the aisle, strewing white rose petals on the red carpet. When she reached the front of the chapel, she took her seat between Georgiana and her brother Edward.

Next, Helena, the bridesmaid, walked down the aisle.

Her arm rested on Hugh Denville, the groom's attendant. Hugh escorted Helena to one side and took his place next to Sebastian.

Mary waited for the double doors to the chapel to be opened by two footmen in livery before she began the wedding march, a signal for the bride's entrance. Olivia appeared, one hand resting on her father's forearm, the other holding a bouquet of fragrant white roses. These and all the other flowers in the chapel were a gift from Sir Henry, cut fresh that morning from the Heligan Gardens.

Sebastian was stunned, in awe at the sight of his bride. Is this the woman who was to be his wife? he wondered. It was as if a halo surrounded her. Her exquisite gown clung to her as though it were a second skin. Her hair was held in place by a crown of tiny white rosebuds, from which hung a short veil.

Sebastian met his bride and offered his arm. When they turned to face the vicar, Mary stopped playing. Her uncle began to intone the wedding service in a deep, theatrical voice. Olivia tried to attend to every word, yet her mind kept wandering off. *I never thought to marry. Am I doing the right thing?* The doubt startled her, but when she heard her uncle ask if she would take Sebastian to be her lawful wedded husband, she answered in a strong voice, "I will," and all doubt disappeared.

Sebastian repeated his vows, slipped the ring Hugh handed him on his bride's finger, lifted her veil and kissed her. When he raised his head, he looked into her eyes and bent to whisper in her ear, "Remember! With my body I thee worship." Olivia swallowed a giggle to avoid shocking their guests.

The sun warmed the festivities as guests feasted on the wedding breakfast which took place outdoors on the large terrace. An orchestra played waltzes and lively country sets, enhancing the celebration. Olivia had retired to her chamber to change into a less formal gown for the dancing.

"Happy, Livy?" her father asked as he waltzed with his daughter.

"Ask me again in ten years, Father." She touched his face with one hand, a smile on her lips and added with a roguish grin, "Your secret in this whole affair is well known to me, you know. Did you think to hoodwink me into marriage? What a devious scoundrel you are. Mother says you can display a wicked sense of humor, but not in front of the rest of the world, eh?"

"Your mother's been spreading tales, has she? She shall suffer severely when I call her to account for revealing our most intimate secrets." His eyes told a different tale as he bantered with his daughter.

"Make my mother suffer? You'll do no such thing, you odious man!" Her words became serious when the music ended. "I see now what you and mother have established for all your children. It's a life of mutual love, full of understanding, isn't it? I will strive for the same, I promise you."

The duke's eyes watered as he gazed into her eyes. He reached for his handkerchief, wiped the tears and blew his nose. "Go away, you disobedient chit! I give you leave to torture your husband as much as you have managed to torture me!"

"Excuse me, father-in-law. I do believe this is my dance. May I snatch her from your clutches?" The duke stepped back and bowed while Sebastian circled Olivia's waist and held her hand high. When the musicians struck up a lively country tune, he whirled his wife around at such a pace, she felt dizzy.

"Stop, you beast! I shall faint if you don't."

"What's that you say? My wife a fainter? I don't believe it," he teased. "All right, then. Let's have a glass of champagne." He took two glasses from a footman's tray.

"No champagne for me. Bring me lemonade instead." The footman bowed at the order and hurried off.

"I want to remember this day for the rest of my life, my darling husband. And not in a haze of spirits."

"All right. Are you interested in hearing the plans I've made for the rest of today? And tomorrow? And the day after that?"

The footman returned with her lemonade and she took a sip. "Of course. What are they?"

"Tremayne has offered us his guest house for our honeymoon. I sent Hugh to visit it for us. He believes it to be perfect. It's at the edge of a small pond and it's quite secluded. Your cook has prepared a mountain of fried chicken and other delectables for us to take with us."

"How are we to get there, darling?"

"Hugh hired a curricle and two fine horses. I'll drive us there whenever you're ready."

She put her hands on her hips and raised an eyebrow. "*You* will not drive us anywhere, dear husband! I'll have you know *I'm* one of the finest whipsters in all of England. *I'll* drive us there."

"Why, you little shrew! I say it's my hired curricle and I say *I* shall drive it!"

"Then you'll bloody well go on our honeymoon by yourself! Enjoy your stay." She turned to walk away, but he grabbed her and pulled her to him.

"Sebastian!" she said, scandalized. "Not in front of my family and all of our guests. What can you be thinking?"

"I'm thinking it's time I taught you to obey me, you wretch. Now, don't argue. Jenny's already packed your things and everything we need is tied on back." He picked her up in his arms, but she struggled.

"Put me down!"

"Not on your life, my darling. Will you be so kind as to close your mouth and shut your eyes? It's too much to ask of a man to smother you with kisses in order to shut you up and carry you at the same time. You wouldn't want me to drop you on your adorable derriere, would you?"

"Oh, all right. But I promise you this. It's the last order of yours that I'm ever going to obey."

With her eyes shut, she wasn't able to see her family and all their wedding guests rushing from the terrace to the front steps. Two footmen held the heavy front doors open for him. "Are you planning to carry me to Heligan? Put me down." She attempted to wriggle out of his arms.

"Stop struggling or I'll . . ."

"Or you'll what?" she said, in saucy defiance.

"Or I really will drop you on your rear end. Right in front of your parents and all of our guests." He loosened his grip and set her down. "Better take a look around you, my love. See what you're up against?"

Olivia swiveled her head left and right and turned ashen. "You beast! You don't play fair!"

"I don't, do I? How clever of you to notice. Now smile to the nice people and wave while I lead you down the steps and place you in our curricle. On the passenger side, of course."

How could she not smile, she thought, biting back a sassy retort. A wicked scheme intruded and made her eyes gleam with mischief.

"Good-bye all. Thank you for coming to our wedding. Isn't my new husband wonderful? He's agreed to allow me to show you all how well I drive." She slithered away and climbed into the curricle. On the driver's side. "Coming, darling?"

"Yes, dear," he said through his teeth. His stormy eyes emerged from under furrowed brows, a threatening glare meant only for her.

She held the reins and said in a loud voice, "Wave good-bye to our guests, darling."

When he turned to wave, he was still standing. At this point she cracked the whip and he nearly lost his balance when the spry young horses took off.

Sebastian resisted the urge to laugh. He kept his silence until they were well out of sight. "Where are you taking me for our honeymoon, dear wife?" he asked, folding his arms and enjoying the scenery.

"I'm waiting for you to give me our direction, my darling husband."

He shook his head. "Not me. With your excellent training as a spy, I'm sure you are clever enough to discover our destination all by your sweet little self."

She drew in the reins and stopped the horses. "I've made my point, my love. If I promise to behave and relinquish the reins to you, will you be so kind as to lead us to our honeymoon nest?" She leaned over and kissed him, her hands busy with the buttons of his trousers.

"What are you doing, wife?"

"It's legal now, isn't it?" She slid her hand inside his pants, but he stopped her and heaved a sigh. He pulled the reins for the horses to stop, grabbed her and crushed her mouth to his. When he came up for air, he said, "You win, but only because I'm as hard as a rock. After I ravish you, I'll decide what punishment to mete out to my disobedient wife."

She batted her eyelashes at him and said, all meekness, "Yes, dear." And tossed the reins to him.

"That's better!" He cracked the whip and urged the horses on to their destination. When at last he drew up to a small cottage, a grizzled farmer stood outside the picket fence.

"This is Mr. Diggers, dear. He's caretaker here. Lives down the road. He'll see to anything we need." Sebastian stepped down and offered Olivia his hand. Which she

promptly ignored. She hopped off without his help while
the caretaker untied the basket Cook had prepared, as well
as two portmanteaus. He carried them inside, but when
Olivia tried to follow him, Sebastian stayed her hand, forcing her to wait with him at the gate.

"Will you be needin' anythin' else today, yer lord and la'-
ship?"

"Thank you, but no. Just stable the horses and take care
of them for us until we send for them."

Mr. Diggers climbed into the curricle, nodded and drove off.

Olivia laughed. "Mr. Diggers is a man of few words. Typical of all the Cornish," she said as she opened the gate.

Without a word, Sebastian swept his bride up in his arms
and walked toward the door.

"What are you doing, Galahad?"

"I'm carrying my bride across the threshold. Our very
first threshold."

"Mmmm. How manly." She nuzzled his ear.

He didn't put her down until he reached the bedchamber
in the back of the cottage. There he dumped her unceremo-
niously on the bed.

"Beast!" she said with a gurgle of laughter.

"Stay where you are, my love. I want to show you something." He took a few steps to the drapery opposite the bed
and pushed them aside to reveal French doors. When he threw
these open, she saw an enchanting pond just a few steps
beyond the tiny terrace.

"Oh, Sebastian! It's breathtaking." She began to rise, but
he put a hand up.

"Take your clothes off, wife. Slowly, if you please."

"But I want to see . . ."

"Later. Do as I say." He began to remove his coat, the
look of lust in his eyes making them glow.

Olivia tilted her head and mimicked in a cockney accent,

"Fancy a bit of a tup, guv?" She slipped her gown off her shoulders, one side at a time. "Only a ha'penny for easy and quick, but if'n you mean to be rough and take long, it'll cost you a shilling."

"How much for violent plunder?"

"I hold myself dear, sir. Cost you ten pounds for a decent plunder."

"Done. Cheap at twice the price, I might add. Take off your gown. Slowly."

"I can't undo the buttons meself. They're in the back."

"Remove your slippers and your stockings first. Then I'll help you." He sat and pulled off first his boots, then his stockings. His shirt came next. And finally his trousers. He came toward her and ordered, "Turn your back to me."

When she did as he asked, he unbuttoned her gown one button at a time, pausing only to kiss each bare spot underneath. He inhaled roses, the scent that drove him wild. "No chemise, my love?"

"No. It would have spoiled the line of my morning gown. Can you unbutton me just a bit faster?"

"Not on your life. This is proving to be far too much fun." When he reached her waist, he pushed her gown down and held both breasts while he kissed her, his lips traveling down her spine to the last button. He let go of her breasts and continued to unbutton her. "There," he said with a hoarse voice, and discarded the gown on the floor. "Lie down and let me feast my eyes on my bride."

She did as he asked, longing to run her fingers down his chest, now slick with sweat. She shivered, but not from cold. His lips found one breast, then the other, sending heat through her in wild waves. One hand spread her legs apart. His fingers played while he raised himself high enough to kiss her, his tongue exploring her mouth.

"Don't stop, my love," she panted when he pulled his lips away and slid down her body.

"I won't," he murmured, and buried his face between her legs, his tongue laving her until she gasped for breath. She arched her back, while his hands lifted her buttocks. He could feel the heat of her coursing through him like a raging river, making him harder still.

"Sebastian," she screamed, her body shuddering under the battering of his tongue. She clutched his hair and moaned as wave after wave of pleasure assaulted her.

Her screams drove him wild as he removed the hands that clutched his hair so painfully. Breathing hard, he fell on his back by her side and tried to calm himself.

"Why do you stop, my love?"

He turned toward her, a slight smile on his lips. "Let me rest a bit. I'd rather not embarrass myself."

"May I touch you there?"

"No. Not if you wish me to consummate our union as man and wife. Lie still for a moment." He could feel her eyes upon him. "You're making love to me with your eyes, aren't you?"

"I can't help it. I want to explore every bit of you. Every ripple. Every ridge. Every crevice. Your body is magnificent, my love." She leaned over him and inhaled deeply.

"Stop it. You're driving me mad, you little tease." He rolled on top of her, pushing her legs apart as he did. His engorged penis found her entrance, but he held back. "Slow is better, my love."

Olivia let him inch into her, biting her lip to keep from breathing too hard. She reached up and wiped the sweat from his brow. "I love you, Sebastian. I always will. For the rest of our lives."

His pace quickened and she arched to meet his thrusts. He went deeper. Harder. Faster. Until he exploded inside her, his thrusts taking her with him to another world. It brought her to life like a blinding light in a tunnel. She felt glory in the throbbing of her inner muscles, as they grasped and released him over and over again.

He tried to roll away, but she held him close. "No, don't move yet."

"I'll crush you, my sweet." He rose up on his palms.

"You're not such a heavy burden. And I'm not such a delicate flower."

He laughed. "You want the truth? In the throes of passion I may have forgotten your name."

"Then let me introduce you, sir. My name is Mrs. Brooks, wife of England's premier spymaster."

He shook his head and turned serious. "You're only half correct, ma'am." He rolled on his back and lifted her with him until she rested on top of him.

"Which half?"

"If I heard the vicar correctly, there can be no doubt in my mind that you are Mrs. Brooks, milady. But you are no longer the wife of the spymaster."

She sat bolt upright. "What are you talking about? Have you resigned your post? Why would you do such a thing?"

"Actually, I was asked to resign by the home secretary." He raised an eyebrow as if appraising her. "Have I mentioned that you have beautiful breasts, Mrs. Brooks?"

"Forget my breasts."

"Forget them? Never!"

"What are you going to do when I begin my work in the home office? I must report there in twelve days."

"I don't really know. Perhaps by then I'll have received news of my new assignment."

"Your . . . what?"

"My new assignment." His hands played with her nipples.

"Stop that. You're joking, aren't you?"

"I was never more serious in my life. If you don't believe me, ask Hugh. He's the new spymaster. He's leaving tomorrow to return to Wilson Academy because he must get ready for the new class of trainees. They begin the first of November."

"Will they send you off to foreign parts, do you think?"

He shrugged. "I haven't the faintest idea. Now be a good soldier and stop asking questions. We're on our honeymoon, remember?" He nodded toward the open terrace doors. "The sun is setting on the pond, but it's still warm outside. What would you say, wife, to a swim?"

"Lovely idea, husband. I'll get my bathing costume."

"Don't be daft. I meant just as we are."

She laughed, a magnificent sound that quivered in his ears, very like church bells pealing.

Chapter Thirty

Bodmin Castle—Friday, The First of November

When the newlyweds returned to the duke's castle, they were greeted in the morning room by the duchess. The duke, his brother and his son Edward having had business in London, returned the previous day.

"How are you, Your Grace?" Sebastian bent to kiss her hand.

She smiled at her new son-in-law. "Let's settle upon a less formal address first, Sebastian. You may call me ma'am in place of mother-in-law if you prefer, but do leave off calling me 'Your Grace.'"

"With pleasure, ma'am."

Upon entering the morning room, Helena said, "I hope you two lovebirds had a wonderful honeymoon. Hello, brother-in-law." She bent to plant a kiss on his cheek.

"Stay away from him, Helena. He's all mine," said Olivia in mock anger. She hugged her sister.

The duchess observed the foolery among her eldest children with fondness. "You two may stay here as long as you like, but it's time for me to take the rest of my family back to Heatham where we remain until the season in London begins."

"Of course, Mother." Helena turned to Sebastian and Olivia. "I've already begun making arrangements. Shall you two be staying on?"

Olivia looked at her husband, a question in her eyes.

"No, ma'am. We leave for London. I have a town house there my bride has never seen. I'd like us to settle in before we begin our work for the home office."

"Sebastian! I didn't know you had quarters in London."

He grinned at her. "You never asked, my love. Where did you think I stayed whenever I was in London?"

Georgiana entered the morning room, a wistful expression on her face. For in spite of her sister Livy's warning to beware imagining an attachment toward Hugh Denville, she fancied herself romantically bound to that gentleman. In point of fact, the love-struck sixteen-year-old had been moping around like an abandoned wife ever since her imagined lover left Bodmin. Had Denville known of this fanciful *tendre*, he would have been astonished, for during his stay, he was nothing if not correct in his behavior toward the young woman.

The duchess knew from Georgiana's air of sobriety as well as from her frequent sighs that she suffered a bad case of calf love. Was she not herself sixteen once? Even so, she wished that the duke had not gone back to London so soon after Livy's wedding. His firmness of purpose was something she needed now.

"Why so down in the mouth, Georgie?" asked an unsuspecting Sebastian.

Olivia came to her rescue. "Never mind that, dear. Georgie just can't wait for her debut. Isn't that right, little sister?"

"Oh, yes. My debut," she answered tragically.

Helena and Olivia burst out laughing.

"Oh, you two! You don't understand anything about . . . anything!" She ran out of the room, which only made her sisters laugh harder.

"Don't tease her so, you two. Give her time to get over it," said the duchess.

"Get over what?" asked Sebastian. "Is Georgiana ill?"

Olivia took his hand and led him off to their chamber. "Never mind, darling. It's a woman thing. You wouldn't understand."

The family began to pack in readiness for their respective journeys. Olivia and Sebastian to London and the duchess, Helena, Georgiana, Mary and Jane to Heatham. Olivia and Sebastian chose to accompany the family to Brighton and stay until they were assured that the family was comfortably settled. Then they would return to London to begin their assignments.

In the midst of all the arrangements, Amy Wells, Helena's abigail, interrupted her mistress. "May I have a word, milady?"

"Of course, Amy." She glanced at the young woman's face. "You've been crying. What's wrong, dear?"

"Me da passed, milady. I've just had this here letter." She held it up as if to corroborate her tale. "I've got to leave your employ. Me ma can't run our inn without me help, you see."

"Oh, Amy. I'm so sorry to lose you, but I do understand. You must do your duty to your mother. She needs you now. If your circumstances should ever change, dear, you shall always have a place with our family."

"Thank you kindly, milady." Amy sniffed.

"Where is your home, Amy?"

"Less than a day's ride, milady. Me family lives near Land's End in South Cornwall. I'll take the mail coach today at four, if y'can have someone drive me to town. The coach leaves from the Pig and Whistle in Bodmin."

"Of course, love. Pack your things and I'll arrange it."
Helena hurried to her mother's chamber and told her the news.

"Poor child. Have Casper drive her to Bodmin as soon as
she is ready." The duchess went to her desk and removed a
twenty pound note. "It's little enough, but give her this as a
parting gift and offer our condolences to her family."

"Thank you, Mother." Helena withdrew, her heart gladdened by her mother's kind gesture.

When the packing was done, the family departed, leaving
a skeleton staff to drape the furniture with Holland covers,
draw the drapes shut, and do whatever else was required, for
Bodmin Castle would not likely be used until the next family
wedding.

London—Monday, The Eleventh of November—Sebastian
accompanied Olivia to the home office building on the appointed day, he to discover his new assignment and she to
begin her work in the codes and ciphers division. The offices
were housed in a separate wing of the building, far removed
from the clerical section, a fact which gave her some satisfaction, however grim.

When she reported to her division, she was escorted into
her new supervisor's office. "Mr. Gaines? I'm Fairchild, your
new decoder."

"Welcome. Your excellent reputation precedes you.
Aaron Foster has nothing but the highest praise for your
work." He came around his desk and held a chair for her.

"Thank you, sir. Forgive me if I ask an impertinent question. What do all the decoders call one another during the
workday?"

Gaines looked puzzled. "We address one another by our
surnames. Why do you ask?"

"Could you and all my colleagues see your way clear to

affording me the same courtesy? It would please me very much if I were addressed only as Fairchild."

He grinned, not in the least offended. "I understand that you are a newlywed."

"Yes, I am. What has that got to do with anything?"

"Would you not prefer that we address you as 'Brooks'?"

She laughed in appreciation of his sly wit. "Why not? But be patient with me. I'm such a newlywed, I may forget to answer to my new name."

Her morning flew by, what with being introduced to her colleagues—four in number—examining her new office— it had a window!—and attending a meeting in the board-room that lasted through lunch, served right where they sat so as not to interrupt the flow of their thoughts. Decoders were single-minded. They did not like to have their puzzle-solving habits interfered with.

When Olivia returned to her office after the meeting was adjourned, she was surprised to find that her first day at work was almost over. "Come in," she said, in answer to the knock on her door.

A slight young man with dark hair and large brown eyes peered in and said, "Afternoon, ma'am. I've been assigned to you. My name is Quill."

She laughed. "You don't mean like the pen?"

"Exactly like the pen, ma'am. Do you mind?" His pleading eyes spoke volumes.

There was no doubt in her mind that the young man had had to endure much bad humor for being named so. "How old are you?"

"Twenty, ma'am."

"If you're good at what you do, we'll deal famously, Quill." The clock on the wall over the door chimed five times.

"Go home, Quill. I shall see you in the morning."

"Good night, ma'am."

Olivia sat in her carriage, willing it to fly home with greater speed, but the London traffic refused to cooperate. She was anxious to greet her husband. What was his assignment? she wondered. Would it take him far from her? And if it did could she bear the separation?

She sat back and stared out the window. All in all, her first day had been filled with surprises. Good ones. She liked Gaines, her supervisor, and she found no fault with any of her new colleagues. No one patronized her or treated her with deference due to her title, false or sincere. Yes, she would manage tolerably well in codes and ciphers. Especially if she could come home to Sebastian every night of the week.

Olivia flew up the steps of Sebastian's town house on Half Moon Street. She smiled at Sebastian's butler, who was about to offer his felicitations for the tenth time. "Not now, Spurgis. Where is my husband?"

"I believe he is in his chamber, milady."

Squelching the urge to giggle for forgetting that it was her town house, too, and Spurgis was her butler as well. She lifted her skirt and took the steps two at a time.

She opened the door to their bedchamber and called out, "Sebastian? I'm home, darling." When there was no answer, she searched for him in their small dressing room and in the adjoining sitting room, but he was nowhere on the second floor.

She rang for Jenny, and when she appeared at her door, she asked, "Where is my husband?"

"He an't come home that I know about, your la'ship. Your bath will be up in a moment. Let me help you get ready for dinner, milady."

"Is there no letter for me?"

"No, milady."

Jenny chatted away about nothing very important, but

while Olivia appeared to be listening, her mind was gripped with fear. All curiosity about his assignment vanished and in its place was fear for his safety.

Why was there no letter informing her that he would be late for dinner? Had an accident befallen him? She pictured him lying trampled under the wheels of a carriage. He loved to walk. Perhaps he'd decided to stroll home and footpads murdered him. She suppressed the urge to dress and scour the streets of London for her love, berating herself for entertaining such foolish horrors.

She allowed Jenny to put the finishing touches to her hair, got up and went down to the drawing room. She rang for the butler. "Will it put Cook out of temper if I ask her to wait dinner for Sir Sebastian?"

"I'll ask her straightaway, milady," answered Spurgis. He returned with the news that she would keep dinner warm, offering the information that the cook hoped there would then be no loss of quality in the food. "May I bring you refreshment, milady?"

"Lemonade, please."

By then it was seven o'clock. She picked up a novel she had begun to read, but she could not seem to attend to the words. The clock struck eight, and Sebastian did not appear. Her fears grew out of all proportion. What if the Russians had sent assassins to murder him?

By ten o'clock, she was ready to summon the Bow Street Runners to search for him, but she scotched the idea.

She nodded off in her easy chair by the fire only to wake with a start when the clock struck midnight. On the table by her side sat a tray of food. Her dinner, she supposed, but she had no appetite. She rang.

"Yes, your la'ship?" He glanced at the untouched tray. "You haven't eaten, milady." There was pity for his mistress in Sturgis' eyes.

"I'm not hungry. Take the tray back to the kitchen, Sturgis. And go to bed. Tell the rest of the staff to do so as well. The porter can let Sir Sebastian in when he returns. I shall wait for him upstairs in my chamber."

Olivia mounted the stairs, dragging her feet as though they were weighted down with lead. She shut the door and leaned on it, taking deep breaths to calm her nerves. Searching for a bit of inner peace, she began to hum a chant, something Sensei Nori had taught her to use in times of stress. Still chanting softly, she lay down on their bed, grasping Sebastian's pillow to her breast, a poor substitute for the man she loved.

When the effectiveness of the chants wore off, she cried into Sebastian's pillow until she fell into an uneasy sleep.

At half past one in the morning, Sebastian shook his wife and said softly, "Livy? Forgive me for being so late, my darling." He kissed her cheek and stroked her hair.

Without a word, she threw her arms around his neck and began to sob.

"Shhh, my love. I'm here. No need to cry." He gave a quiet laugh and added, "Let go of me, wench. You're strangling me."

"I thought you were murdered by footpads or Russian assassins and you were moldering in some dark alleyway," she said, as tragically as an actress on stage.

His eyes danced with amusement. "And make you a widow so soon after our wedding? Oh no, my love. I won't allow you to cry off so easily." Before she had time to answer, he brushed her lips with his, one hand holding her head and the other caressing her breast.

She pulled away and searched his eyes, a question in hers. "It's almost two in the morning, Sebastian. Where the devil have you been all this time?"

"Mmmm. The smell of roses lingers still. You take them with you wherever you go, don't you, my love?"

She scrambled off the bed and began to pace up and down, her arms crossed. In a dangerous voice he knew only too well, she asked, "Don't you dare lie to me, Sebastian. Where have you been?"

Sebastian laughed at her. He lay back and clasped his hands behind his head. "Rest easy, my love. You're the only lightskirt in my life. It's almost morning. We have too little time left for a tumble, let alone for the violent plunder I have in mind."

"Not until you tell me where you've been." Her eyes narrowed. "I'm serious, Sebastian."

"Can't you see by the cut of my trousers how much I lust for you? Oh well. If you must know, you stubborn puss, I was with Sidmouth."

"Sidmouth? I don't believe it. He's too old to keep his eyes open past ten."

"You're wrong, pet. He's riddled with steel when he fights for what he wants."

Curiosity softened her words. "Did it have something to do with your assignment?"

"It had everything to do with it."

"Care to share it with me?"

"You won't like it." He turned his head away to hide a grin.

"Better an odious assignment than you lying dead somewhere in a back alley in London. Out with it. Where have you been assigned?"

Sebastian feigned sobriety. "It will take me far from here, I can tell you."

Her heart sank. "How far? And for how long?"

"Can't say. Depends on the success of the mission."

"All right. Give me the details."

"First stop is Malta. Their government fears French domination. They've asked us to protect them as well as their trade routes from the French. It may take me even farther afield."

She lost her temper. "For heaven's sake, Sebastian. Don't torture me by dragging this out. Get on with it."

He placed one hand over hers. "Egypt. But I can say no more."

His revelation stunned her, but she recovered her wits, though tears began to roll down her cheeks. She sat at the foot of their bed and wondered why her dolt of a husband hadn't the good grace to reach for her and console her.

"Oh, my dearest, dearest darling wife. I never dreamed I would see you so unhappy."

She sobbed, "What if you don't come back to me? What shall I do without you?"

There was such desolation in her voice, he could hardly bear it. This time she didn't pull away when he reached for her and held her, kissing away her tears with much tenderness.

"I need you so. Make love to me, my darling," she whispered.

Her despair made him feel like a wretch, yet he made gentle love to her, though she begged for plunder. "Not tonight, my love," he murmured. "Tonight I want to gentle you."

It was sweet, but unsatisfying. It was soft, but disappointing. It was kind, but indecisive. It was not what she wanted and so she told him. "What's wrong with you tonight, Sebastian? Where's your fire? I have need of flame and you give me ash. Why?"

Without a word, he rose to retrieve something from his dresser. He handed it to her in silence.

"What's this?"

"It's a letter for you from the home secretary. You'd best read it, my love."

Her face held an avalanche of questions, but she did as he asked. She broke the wafer and spread the letter on the bed. The words were few, but their meaning was clear. Two emotions swept through her like a whirlwind. The first was elation and the second was fury. She scrambled to her knees and began pounding her husband on the chest hard enough to cause him pain, yet he did nothing to stop her.

"Why couldn't you just tell me I've been reassigned, you beast!"

Epilogue

Egypt, The Arabian Desert—April Fool's Day, 1817

That fateful night back in November, when Olivia had read the letter from Viscount Sidmouth, she felt as if Sebastian had taken her heart and made it his own. It wasn't so much the coveted prize he had won for her. It was the fact that he'd fought the home secretary long and hard, knowing that he risked his own career. But he had prevailed after all. Her Sebastian had won her the right to be a spy. He could not have given her a more wondrous gift.

Never again would she have reason to doubt his love for her. Never again would she have reason to mistrust him. Never again would she have reason to doubt his devotion, for he had done this magnificent thing. The one thing she yearned for most. He had made her dream come true. He had placed her deepest longings well before his own. How odd, she thought, struck by the strangeness of her thoughts. To fight for one's right to die for another isn't love at all, but mere heroism. But to fight for another's right to *be!* Sebastian had come to understand what *being* meant to her. Ah, that indeed is love in its most selfless guise.

For them, there would be no fancy balls or routs or

musicales, but that was just fine. Instead they would travel the world. Instead they would win the respect of the intelligence network in England for the quality of their work. That would be more than enough for a lifetime.

They were in the Arabian Desert, where jagged plateaus led down to the sea and up to volcanic mountains. The arid land held a few small villages, all struggling to survive. It lay between the Mediterranean Sea, the Gulf of Aqaba and the Gulf of Suez, the latter being of strategic interest to England. The Egyptians had excavated a canal across the Isthmus as early as the thirteenth century BC. Neglected since the eighth century AD, it fell into disrepair. The French vied with the English for the right to cut a new canal—and to control it. It would shorten the journey for merchant ships plying their trade between Europe, Asia and Africa.

Olivia and Sebastian lay side by side in the sand. They wore Arabian djellabahs that covered them from head to toe. Kefayas wrapped around their heads protected them from the sun, the wind and the sand. Their eyes were trained on binoculars through which they spied a caravan of camels carrying large bundles, moving along single file. Were they nomads or were they rebels carrying guns and ammunition meant to aid the enemy? It was hard to tell at this distance.

Olivia spit the sand from her mouth and said, "Sebastian?"

He put his lips to her ear and whispered. "Shhh. Sound carries in the desert. What is it, my love?"

In answer, she rolled on her back and reached for his hand. Eager to repay his precious gift with one of her own, she covered his hand and pressed it gently on her stomach.

With a bewildered expression, he mouthed one word: *What?*

It took only a moment for his hand to experience a remarkable sensation. A slight quiver made it tingle. Knowledge dawned when he began to feel a delicate ballet under his palm, very like a tiny fish swimming across a gentle pond. He drew in his breath. It took him less than a moment to realize that the sensation he was privileged to feel was the feathery movement of his son—or daughter—who would one day soon emerge from the womb to meet its parents.

"Oh my God!" he said aloud, heedless of the echo of his words reverberating across the desert. His fingers tugged his wife's kefaya only low enough to kiss her lips without allowing so much as a kernel of sand to vandalize her cherished mouth.

He said softly, a sly smile on his face, "I wonder, my darling helpmate. Does this put an end to your career as a spy?"

A wicked twinkle did a jig in her eyes. She crossed her fingers to deny the lie she was about to utter to the man she loved.

"Yes, dear."

AUTHOR'S NOTE

When I read Jane Austen and Georgette Heyer, they make me feel as though I am living in the world of the Regency era (1811–1820) in England. Many readers must feel as I do, for there are enough historical romances and scholarly books written about this colorful period to fill a library and the list keeps growing.

This novel includes a key character of the times, "The Right Honorable" Henry Addington (1757–1844) 1st Viscount Sidmouth* who became prime minister of England (1801–1804) after William Pitt the Younger resigned. He botched things with the Treaty of Amiens, causing a lull in the war with France. Sidmouth was succeeded by the same prime minister he replaced three years earlier.

As secretary of the home office charged with the safety of the country (1812–1822), Sidmouth used his power to crush the opposition. He suspended habeas corpus (1817) and helped pass repressive legislation. In spite of this abuse of power, Sidmouth managed to remain active in government until his death.

The Lost (in 1914) Gardens of Heligan* also appears in this work. The gardens were developed by the owners, the Tremayne family, famous botanists and horticulturists. They are located near Mevagissy in North Cornwall. Featured in a TV series in 1970, the gardens are open to visitors year round.

Historical fiction is meant to reflect the times in which an author sets the characters. It enriches our lives. I hope you share this view with me. Happy reading!

—Pearl Wolf

*In addition to historical works, the Internet was my research tool.

Please turn the page for an exciting sneak peek of
Pearl Wolf's next historical romance,
TOO HOT FOR A RAKE,
coming in 2010!

London, April Fools' Day, 1818

Lady Helena Fairchild shivered in anticipation as she stole across the lawn. The night was misted in fog. Only the dim glow of the street lamps pierced the gloom. She paused under the familiar oak tree and stopped to listen. When she heard no sounds from within, she gathered her silk gown, tucked it into her pantalets, turned and climbed the tree.

With customary ease, she slithered along a sturdy branch that led to the balcony. Her hands and feet found purchase on the ornate grillwork and she let go of the tree limb. It snapped back with such a loud crack, she froze, waited a heart stopping moment, and then eased herself over the balustrade. The door was ajar. She stepped into Darlington's chamber and waited for her eyes to adjust to the dark.

She followed the sound of gentle snores coming from the bed a few steps away. The bed curtains weren't drawn, for the night was warm, one of those rare April nights that made the air feel as if it were already the middle of May. Her fingers trembled as she loosened the ribbons of her bodice. She pushed both sleeves off her shoulders and shifted her gown to undo the back buttons until it slipped from her hips and fell to the floor. She removed her chemise and her pantalets. A shock of cold air brushed her nude body. A small, irregular mountain of discarded clothing, rested on the Aubusson rug.

There was no turning back now. She lifted the quilt and climbed into his bed. A small smile curved her lips when she noted that he favored the right side of the bed when he slept. That was a good sign, for she favored the left.

Though the erratic pounding of her heart seemed too loud to her ears, Chris didn't stir. She touched him. His arm was strong and warm and firm. How muscular he had become since she'd seen him last. Was it only a year? His brawny body filled her with wonder. He turned again, pulling the quilt with him. It slid to the floor on his side of the bed. Her eyes widened in astonishment, for he wore nothing. *Where was his nightshirt?*

She hesitated, trapped between panic and curiosity. Curiosity won. She dared to stroke his back with a feathery touch. Her hand trailed down to his buttocks and came to rest on one dimpled cheek. He sighed. She pulled her hand away, caught between fear of waking him and hope. She waited a few seconds and touched again, astonished at her own boldness.

She hadn't anticipated the spark of electricity that tore through her. When a beam of moonlight fell across him, she raised herself on one elbow and rested her chin on her hand to examine his body. She could not believe her good fortune. Once scrawny, the boy she'd fallen in love with when she was still in the schoolroom had grown into a powerfully built man.

Darlington turned and flung an arm across her chest, sending her flat on her back. His hand came to rest on one breast, which caused her nipples to pucker. When the rhythm of his breathing gentled and her heart ceased its knocking, she lifted his wrist and placed his arm by his side. The moon skittered behind a cloud, plunging the room into darkness.

Helena dared to spread her fingers through the crisp hairs on his chest, trailing down to the indentation in his navel. She steeled herself to explore further. Her hand traveled down to the mound of hair below his waist. He sighed in his sleep and threw one leg over her thighs, pinning her to the bed. She touched something soft and allowed herself a tiny smile. When his manhood began to engorge, she jerked away, but his hand shot out and kept hers where it was. If he woke now, surely he would willingly seduce . . .

A blinding light transformed the chamber into bright daylight when the door to the hallway flew open. Chris would have to marry her now. She had but a moment's regret that they hadn't had time to complete their love making.

"What's wrong, Waverley? I heard noise. Are you awake?"

Chris? But who's this in his bed? Helena burrowed her head under the pillow.

A voice fogged in sleep, said, "That you Darlington?"

Chris banged the door shut behind him and set the candelabra down. "Have you lost your senses, Waverley? How dare you seduce one of my maids? I never dreamed a guest in my home would behave in such a fashion."

Desmond sat up and rubbed the sleep from his eyes. "Maid? What maid?"

"Get out of bed, lass, and return to your room at once."

She whimpered at the anger in his voice.

"Oh, for heaven's sake, don't cry. Do as I say. I promise not to sack you."

Christopher Darlington wore his dressing gown, having had no time for proper attire in the middle of the night. His blond hair was uncombed and lay limp, a few strands pasted to his forehead. Myopic gray eyes squinted at the bed's inhabitants.

Helena drew in her breath, lifted one corner of the pillow and said meekly, "I'm not a maid, Chris. It's me."

His hand shook as he fumbled in his pocket for his spectacles. When he jammed them on his nose, he found his voice and said, "Helena? What are you doing here? Cover yourself, for heaven's sake!"

Darlington's guest felt as if he were a spectator watching a melodrama whose leading lady had the body and the face of an angel. When she spoke, her eyes shone like two obsidians and her hair bounced in a crown of burnished curls.

"Um. I can explain." Her head swiveled as she searched for the quilt, but it wasn't there.

Waverley reached for the fallen cover and threw it over them both. His eyes met hers with a questioning intensity that made her turn red. "I await your, er . . . explanation with interest, ma'am."

Helena sat up and clutched the quilt to her bosom. Distracted by the sight of his wavy black hair and startling blue eyes, she managed to glare at him. "I thought that *he* was *you*, Chris. What's this . . . rake doing in your bed?"

Waverley managed to turn his laugh into a cough.

Chris ignored her question. "Collect your clothing and get dressed at once, Helena."

She swung her legs off the bed and attempted to yank the cover with her, but Waverley held his end in a firm grip. "Oh no you don't. Not before my host hands me my dressing gown."

Darlington glanced around him, found Waverley's robe on the back of a chair and launched it toward the bed as if it were the main sail of a ship.

Without warning, Waverley let go of the quilt and Helena fell off the bed, quilt and all.

"Cur," she grumbled as she wrapped the quilt around her. "Turn your head!" She held the cover with one hand, gathered her clothing with the other and side-stepped across the room toward the dressing screen.

When she emerged a few moments later, she turned her head from Chris to Waverley and back to Chris. She jutted her chin out. "How is it that this *rake* is occupying your chamber?"

"You chose the wrong chamber," growled Darlington. "This is the guest chamber. The Marquis of Waverley is my guest."

Oh dear! Was I in bed with a marquis? Her heart sank at the mortification.

"You owe me an apology, Darlington," Waverley drawled, examining his fingernails. "The young lady is not a maid who woke me from a deep sleep." He turned to Helena and added, "You needn't blush, ma'am. I merely supposed I was in the midst of a delightful dream." He stretched, yawned and ran his fingers through his hair.

"A nightmare, more like!" she said bitterly.

His eyes danced with amusement. "Allow me to assure you, ma' am, that nothing drastic occurred. You were not violated, ma'am. Not by me, in any event."

Nothing drastic occurred? What of your engorgement? What of the heat that seared my loins? You call that nothing?

"Why is the marquis here, Chris?"

Waverley took a step toward her, picked up her hand and kissed it. "Darlington was kind enough to invite me, ma'am."

"Don't touch me." She drew her hand away.

Darlington stepped between them. "How did you get in here, Helena?"

She glanced at the open door to the balcony.

"You climbed the oak tree? You're not a child anymore. You might have fallen and broken your neck this time."

"Would you care to make the introduction, Darlington?"

"Sorry. This is Lady Fairchild, my betro . . . my next door neighbor."

"Lady Fairchild." Waverley made an exaggerated leg.

Helena cast her eyes down. "How do you do, Lord Waverley," she murmured, appalled at what she'd done to this man, at the embarrassing places her hands had explored, at how readily he had responded. At how much she took pleasure in it.

"It isn't polite to stare," said Waverley, his eyes filled with amusement.

"My apologies, sir. For . . . for calling you a rake."

"Accepted, ma'am."

Chris interrupted. "I'm waiting for an explanation, Helena."

"Nothing happened, Darlington," repeated the marquis.

"He's right, Chris. I haven't been compromised."

"I beg to differ. The mere act of being in bed with a naked man is enough to be deemed a compromise."

"Is it indeed?" she challenged. "The fault is yours then, for having driven me to this desperate act." She paused, her breath coming in anguished bursts. "We need to talk, Chris. In private."

"Lord Waverley will excuse us, I'm sure."

Waverley held the door open for them. "Pleasure to meet you, ma'am."

Before Helena could make some biting retort, Darlington grabbed her by the elbow and attempted to push her toward the door, but she refused to budge.

"No, Chris. The servants . . ."

"They've all gone to bed. We'll finish this in the library."

They spoke not a word as he led her downstairs, but once inside, Helena broke the silence. "Tonight was nothing more than a horrid mistake. I wanted to welcome you on the night of your return home, Chris. Besides, what difference can it possibly make? Are we not to be married soon?"

Chris paced back and forth, hands clasped behind him. "Do you know what you've done? You don't even know who the marquis is, do you?"

"If he's a peer, he's a gentleman. He won't breathe a word of this."

"Oh, won't he? Waverley's bounced around Europe for years. Do you know what they call him there? No. How could you?"

Helena recoiled at his fury. "You needn't shout at me. Well? What do they call him?"

"I found him in Paris at Madame Z's salon. When I asked for Lord Waverley, she laughed and said, *'Ah, oui. Le roue 'Anglais'.* I had to wait for him to finish his assignation before I could inform him that his father died and he was the new Marquis of Waverley, summoned home by order of the Regent."

"He's known as the English rake in Europe? I've never heard of him. Perhaps his reputation isn't known here."

"If it isn't, it will be. Rumors travel like waves across the channel. If it becomes known that you have been in bed with him, your reputation is ruined."

"Then we ought to marry at once. Make it right. You know I love you, Chris."

"Marry you? No. We're finished."

"Finished? Am I to understand that you no longer wish to marry me?"

Chris forced a laugh. "How can I marry a woman who disgusts me? You destroyed all hope for our happiness when I saw you naked in bed with Waverley. You knew I hoped to become an ambassador for England one day. Your brash conduct has shown me that you can never be a proper wife for a diplomat."

Had he battered her with a cudgel, he could not have wounded her more. She turned ashen and said, "What a pretty speech. How noble of you to think of England first, before the woman who has loved you all these years."

He ignored her words and said, "In spite of what you may think of me, I'm a man of honor. I'll call on your father in the morning to inform him of my decision. I don't intend to tell him *why*. Perhaps that will salvage your reputation. The duke is free to announce that it was you who cried off. That way, you may still marry."

"No, Chris. I shan't ever marry. I won't put myself through the pain of loving and losing again, I promise you that."